The Altrurian Romances are a peculiarly American expression of the impulse that lay behind Bacon's *New Atlantis* and More's *Utopia*: the urge to reveal the shortcomings of a real society by contrasting it implicitly and explicitly with an ideal one. The present volume brings together for the first time Howells' major writings in this vein and thus offers a fascinating recapitulation of Howells' social thought as it evolved over a period of twenty years. In *A Traveller from Altruria* (1892–93) Aristides Homos, an emissary of the Altrurian Commonwealth (where altruism is the basis of society), comes to New Hampshire, and in the course of a visit with Mr. Twelvemough, a conventional popular novelist, critically explores American values and conditions. The criticism is carried outside of New Hampshire in a series of eleven "Letters of an Altrurian Traveller" (1893–94). The first five take meets representative Americans of all classes, visits New England, New York, and Chicago, and discovers that social equality is a myth, political democracy is giving way to a savage plutocracy, and that "the vast majority of Americans still regard the idea of human brotherhood with distrust and dislike." Howells' "fables" are both a deft and stinging satire and a rich source of realistic detail about American life at the turn of the century. (*Volume 20 of A Selected Edition of W. D. Howells*)

CLARA and RUDOLF KIRK, Visiting Professors of English at the University of Illinois, Chicago Circle, are the authors of several biographical and critical studies of Howells. SCOTT BENNETT is Assistant Professor of English at the University of Illinois in Champaign-Urbana and a member of the Editorial Board of *A Selected Edition of W. D. Howells*.

A SELECTED EDITION OF W. D. HOWELLS

Volume 20

The Altrurian Romances

W. D. HOWELLS

The Altrurian Romances

Introduction and Notes to the Text
by Clara and Rudolf Kirk

Text Established by Scott Bennett

EDWIN H. CADY, GENERAL EDITOR
RONALD GOTTESMAN, TEXTUAL EDITOR
DAVID J. NORDLOH, ASSOCIATE TEXTUAL EDITOR

INDIANA UNIVERSITY PRESS

Bloomington and London

1968

Acknowledgments

For indispensable support in money and morale the editors of this volume and the Howells Edition Center gladly express their gratitude to Barnaby C. Keeney and the National Endowment for the Humanities; to William M. Gibson and the Center for Editions of American Authors, Modern Language Association of America; to Elvis J. Stahr, President, and Joseph L. Sutton, Dean of Faculties, Indiana University; to Herman B Wells and the Indiana University Foundation; and to William White Howells and the Heirs of W. D. Howells.

Special thanks are also due Jane C. Scarola, Ann Hofstra, and Thomas Wortham, who contributed substantially to the completion of the volume.

We are also indebted to:

George Arms, University of New Mexico
Carol Bennett, Urbana, Illinois
William H. Bond, Houghton Library, Harvard University
Cecil Byrd, Indiana University Library
William Cagle, Indiana University Library
Robert O. Dougan, Henry E. Huntington Library
John Noyes Mead Howells, Kittery Point, Maine
Carolyn Jakeman, Houghton Library, Harvard University
Mrs. Margaret Johnson, Urbana, Illinois
James B. Meriwether, University of South Carolina
Mrs. June Moll, University of Texas Library
Louis C. Moloney, Southwest Texas State Library
Organized Research, Southwest Texas State College
Anthony Shipps, Indiana University Library
Mrs. Neda Westlake, Van Pelt Library, University of Pennsylvania

Contents

Illustration: ink sketch of Howells by Valerian Gribayédoff,
    from a photograph, published in "The Making of
    an Illustrated Magazine," *Cosmopolitan*, XIV (Janu-
    ary 1893), 264.   *facing page xxxiv*

Introduction

WHEN Howells began to edit the Library Edition of his works in 1909, he decided to publish in one volume his two Altrurian Romances, *A Traveler from Altruria* (1894) and *Through the Eye of the Needle* (1907). In 1911, only six of the more than thirty volumes projected by Harper and Brothers appeared, and the Altrurian Romances were not among them. No more volumes in this much advertised, *de luxe* edition were ever published. In bringing together these two "fables," as Howells called them, the author's wish is finally fulfilled.

Howells expressed this wish in a "Bibliographical" preface to the proposed volume, which remained unpublished for many years after his death.[1] There he observed that the two Altrurian Romances were "of one blood," though so divided by the lapse of time that "they might seem mother and daughter rather than sisters" (p. 3). He might have said that *A Traveler from Altruria* was the grandmother of *Through the Eye of the Needle*, for the actual daughter of the first Altrurian Romance was "Letters of an Altrurian Traveller." These "Letters" appeared in eleven installments in the *Cosmopolitan Magazine* (November 1893 through September 1894) and followed "A Traveller from Altruria," published in the same magazine (November 1892 through October 1893). "A Traveller from Altruria" was brought out in book form by Harper and Brothers in May 1894, under the same title. "Letters of an Altrurian Traveller," however, was never republished by Harper as a book. The last six "Letters," with many omissions, interpolations, and alterations, became the twenty-seven chapters of Part I of *Through the Eye of the Needle* when, in 1907, Howells was ready to publish in book

---

1. The preface was first printed in George Arms, "Howells's Unpublished Prefaces," *NEQ*, XVII (1944), 580–591.

form a second Altrurian Romance. *A Traveler from Altruria,* the "Letters," and *Through the Eye of the Needle,* then, may be said to be "of one blood," though their relationship is more complex than Howells suggested.

EVOLUTION OF THE ROMANCES

In the "Bibliographical" preface, Howells supplied certain details about the composition of his Romances. He set forth his "abiding conviction" that "the economic solution of the 'riddle of the painful earth' is to be by emulation and not by competition." "The first fable was printed in *The Cosmopolitan Magazine,*" wrote Howells in retrospect, "as a sort of sociological serial" (p. 3). But the page-proof of "Bibliographical" makes it clear that this dream, however much it was concerned with economic and social problems, seemed to him in 1909 more akin to fiction. Across the proof Howells wrote, "Group II vol XII"; and it was explicitly his intention to have the Library Edition issued in two parts, "such volumes as are not fiction" in a first group "and afterwards the novels as the second part."[2]

In the present volume, "Bibliographical" is followed by "A Traveller from Altruria," the first of the Altrurian Romances. Then come the first five of the "Letters of an Altrurian Traveller." The first two of these five "Letters" were never reprinted by Howells. The next three (with a portion of "Letter" IX) were transformed into essays, "Glimpses of Central Park" and "New York Streets," and included in *Impressions and Experiences* (1896). Since they were there so altered as to change their nature, they do not appear in this volume except in their original form.

The last six of the *Cosmopolitan* "Letters" (except for the first portion of "Letter" IX) became Part I of *Through the Eye of the Needle,* which with Part II completes the main text of the present volume. Howells' remark to his brother in 1907, "I am writing a

---

2. See Robert W. Walts, "William Dean Howells and His 'Library Edition'," *PBSA,* LII (1958), 287. The quotation is part of a letter from Frederick A. Duneka to Howells, 16 February 1904.

sequel to the Altrurian business which you stereotyped for me twelve years ago under the title *The Eye of the Needle*,"[3] indicates that something like the final title had been in his mind since 1895. The title expressed the theme of the "Romance" developed in the last six "Letters"; the first five "Letters," as we have seen, Howells either left in the columns of the *Cosmopolitan*, or converted into essays for *Impressions and Experiences*.

The fact that "Letter" IX was divided between *Through the Eye of the Needle* and the essay "New York Streets" provides an opportunity to learn how Howells divided the material in this letter between romance and essay. In the portion of "Letter" IX used in *Through the Eye of the Needle*, Mr. Twelvemough, the successful writer of popular fiction, meets the Altrurian at a New York dinner party, and in the course of the evening the question of whether fiction should deal with "anything but loves of young people" comes up for discussion. One guest remarks on the "comfort" she found in Mr. Twelvemough's books, and another adds that "people liked them because they felt sure when they took up one of his novels they had not got hold of a tract on political economy in disguise." The artist present expresses the thought that "there are certain phases of political economy, dramatic moments, human moments, which might be very fitly treated in art. For instance," he adds, "who would object to Mr. Twelvemough's describing an eviction from an East side tenement-house on a cold winter night, with the mother and her children huddled about the fire the father had kindled with pieces of the household furniture?" (pp. 330–331). The exclamation of horror from one of the guests perhaps convinces Mr. Twelvemough, who remains silent, that details of this sort do not belong in a romance. In any case, Howells did incorporate such a scene as his artist describes in the essay "An East-Side Ramble" (first printed in *Impressions and Experiences*). Paragraphs from the first portion of "Letter" IX, which sounded more like a "tract on political economy in disguise" than did the second half, were

---

3. See Mildred Howells, *Life in Letters of William Dean Howells* (Garden City, N.Y., 1928), II, 235; hereafter cited as *Life in Letters*.

introduced into "New York Streets" and excluded from *Through
the Eye of the Needle*. The second half of "Letter" IX offered no
such scenes and could safely be incorporated into a Romance,
though they too carried a "disguised" social message.

Part II of *Through the Eye of the Needle*, completed in less than
a month, brought to a conclusion the Romance left unresolved in
1895.[4] It purports to be written by "a woman's hand," and is,
therefore, "not to be credited with the firm and unerring touch
of a man's" (p. 273). Like Part I, it is made up of letters, this time
written from Altruria, and by Eveleth Strange, who, after first
breaking her engagement, left her fortune in New York and
married the Altrurian. Howells had always "distinctly wished"
to visit his Utopia, he remarked in "Bibliographical." "How do
you think *A Visit to Altruria* would take?" he had written on
8 March 1895 to the editor of the Boston *Herald*, indicating that
he had thought, after completing "Letters of an Altrurian
Traveller," of accompanying Aristides Homos to Altruria.[5]

THE CONCEPT OF ALTRURIA

Howells was already thinking about the remote land of
Altruria before he left "The Editor's Study." In his farewell essay
(*Harper's Monthly*, LXXXIV, March 1892, 640–643), he informed his readers that, having tidied up his office in Franklin
Square and packed away his "moral bric-à-brac," he glanced
up at a strange map still suspended from the wall. "What is this
hanging here?" he asked himself. "A map of Altruria? It is an
outlandish region inhabited by people of heart, a sort of economic

---

4. Howells says in "Bibliographical" that he wrote the second part in "less than
a month" (p. 4). He was perhaps referring to the writing of the first draft. He seems,
however, to have spent considerably more time on the revision, for on 16 January
1907 he complained to Frederick A. Duneka that he had received "only the printed
sheets of The Eye of the Needle." He asked for the introduction and the "beginning
of the second part, which I am now going on with." Again on 5 March he wrote
Duneka that he had "finished 'Through the Eye of the Needle' . . . and now there
remain only a few bits to be written into the narrative, here and there, so that by
next Monday I hope to give you the copy of the whole second part" (MSS at the
American Antiquarian Society).

5. MS at the Huntington Library, San Marino, California. Used by permission.

Pays du Tendre. It ought not to be tolerated; and yet I traversed part of it in my *Little Journey in the World,* and the inhabitants, though not much better than early Christian socialists, seem to mean well. Leave the map for a while!"[6] To understand how this map happened to be in the Study—and why Howells left it there—one must look back several years to his first use of the term "Altruria."

Howells' mistrust of unregulated competition, which in the post-Civil War period he saw as an index of the change of this country from a rural to an industrial society, found expression in the word "altruism." Auguste Comte had first used the term in its current meaning in his *System of Positive Polity* (1851–1854), but Howells himself coined the name "Altruria" to designate an imaginary island in the Aegean Sea where altruism was translated into social manners and customs as well as into law and government. Characteristically, Howells seized upon a popular concept, attached it to a word just then entering the popular imagination, and gave it fresh meaning.[7]

In "The Editor's Study" of December 1890 (*Harper's Monthly,* LXXX, 152–156), Howells informed his readers that he had just wiped the dust and frost off the Study window, and observed that "a momentous change" had come over the world, "tacit, but no less millenial." It was obvious to him, he wrote, that the old order had been succeeded by the new, and "that the former imperfect republic of the United States of America had given place to the ideal commonwealth, the Synthetized Sympathies of Altruria." This commonwealth, Howells continued, was in turn a province in the larger Federation of the World, "represented by a delegation eager to sacrifice their selfish interests in the Parliament of Man."

Howells' use of the phrase, "the Synthetized Sympathies of Altruria," recalls a letter of 14 September 1888, written by

---

6. Howells borrowed the title from Charles Dudley Warner's novel, *A Little Journey in the World* (1889).

7. See Louis J. Budd, "Altruism Arrives in America," *American Quarterly,* VIII (1956), 40–52.

Henry Mills Alden, editor of *Harper's Monthly*, to Howells, in which Alden quotes J. W. Harper as writing him:

"I'm quite sure that we could enlist Howells's sympathy, his altruism—in other words, his warm democratic heart in the preparation of a *feuilleton* for the *Weekly* which would be a powerful presentation of the life of our great metropolis, social, educational, economical, political—as shown in our schools, colleges, charitable organisations, reformatory institutions, prisons, courts of law, occupations & amusements—our streets & parks & factories & clubs—the rich & the poor, the idler & the worker, the silly men & bad men & frivolous women—the elevated railroads, the monopolies, the nuisances—& Hunter's Point.[8]

"Possibly lessons might be drawn from these observations, showing the real assimilation of interests in these diverse classes & occupations of the community, with suggestions for the improvement of society, with the conclusion that one man is as good as another & 'a good deal better, too.' But I should not make this the avowed object of the series—for the avowal would deter readers. When the 'sights of New York' have been dramatically shown from week to week, the reader will 'catch on,' & be prepared for the writer's conclusions, which, indeed, he will anticipate. The *synthetic* plan is the sympathetic plan. When the teacher has dazzled his class with the results of a brilliant experiment, curiosity is stimulated, & his admiring youngsters are prepared for the reason of the thing & eager to know the principle of it.

"Such a series by Howells would command the interest of all classes, afford food for reflection & conversation in society, & would be largely quoted."[9]

---

8. Hunter's Point—so called in the 1890's—was a station on the Long Island Railroad in an industrial area of Queens, just over the line from Brooklyn and across from Manhattan. See King's *Handbook of New York City* (Boston, [1893]), p. 135 and maps.

9. MS at Harvard, as are all letters cited hereafter, unless otherwise noted. Permission to quote unpublished passages from the letters written by Howells has been granted by William White Howells for the Heirs of the Howells Estate. Permission to quote from the unpublished letters owned by Harvard has been granted by William H. Bond, Librarian, for the Howells Committee of the Houghton Library. Republication of this material also requires these permissions.

We have no such sketches written at the time; Harper's letter, however, may have influenced Howells in writing *A Hazard of New Fortunes*. The first chapters of this novel appeared in *Harper's Weekly* (23 March 1889, pp. 217, 222–223), and they depict several aspects of the "life of our great metropolis" as the Marches search for living quarters. Into this ramified study of social conflict, Howells poured all the thoughts on "how a man shall save his soul," suggested to him by the reading of Tolstoy and others and emphasized anew by the personal tragedy of his daughter's death in the same year. Howells' paragraphs on Tolstoy's book, *What to Do ?* in "The Editor's Study" (*Harper's Monthly*, LXXVIII, 1888, 159) are in a sense a statement of the theme of *A Hazard of New Fortunes*. "The whole of his testimony," wrote Howells of Tolstoy, "is against the system by which a few men win wealth and miserably waste it in idleness and luxury, and the vast mass of men are overworked and underfed." Tolstoy raised the question of "how a man shall save his soul" while seeking "the phantom of personal happiness" and ignoring "the fact that there is and can be no happiness but in the sacrifice of self for others. . . . Christ and the life of Christ is at this moment inspiring the literature of the world as never before." These thoughts, soon to be expressed in his Altrurian writings, were shared by many men and women of the time who felt with Howells that a momentous change was about to take place in the world.

When Howells moved to Boston, where he remained from December 1889 to December 1891, he was naturally drawn into association with a group of Christian Socialists who were, like himself, dissatisfied with conventional religion as well as with the platforms of both political parties. Edward Bellamy was launching his Nationalist Clubs; Edward Everett Hale was arranging meetings of a Tolstoy group; Hamlin Garland was attempting to win support for the new drama of social protest; and Phillips Brooks was backing a young Episcopal minister, W. D. P. Bliss, who had established a mission in Boston called "The Church of the Carpenter." Howells was welcomed by these men—most of them old friends and associates—because the thoughts on society expressed in his novels, from *A Minister's Charge* to *A Hazard of New Fortunes*, were considered germane to the general movement. Bliss, for example, in his Christian Socialist magazine, *The Dawn*, listed Howells' *Annie Kilburn* among "The Few Best Books on Socialism," summarizing it by the phrase, "What Social Christianity comes to in New England."[10]

Though Howells joined no group, he attended meetings of both Christian Socialists and Nationalists and listened with interest to the discussions presaging a "new order." Born and reared in the tradition of liberalism, he was aware that in the growing tension between capital and labor the old political loyalties were no longer valid. Republicans and Democrats alike had grown so selfish that, as he wrote his father in April 1890, "By and by labor will be so pinched that the politicians will have to put a socialistic plank into a platform, and then the party that stands on it will win" (*Life in Letters*, II, 3).

Several months later, after a defeat of the Republican ticket in Ohio, Howells again wrote his father: "You mustn't be too much cast down by the elections. I look forward to the decay of both the old parties, and the growth of a new one that will mean true equality and real freedom, and not the images we have been mocked with hitherto." Howells was referring to the People's Party, then being discussed by the Christian Socialists, when he wrote in this letter that his "faith in the grand and absolute change" about to come over the country was so strong that he could not grieve over the defeat or the success of either the Republican or the Democratic Party. Howells ended his letter with the hope "that a party 'of the people, for the people' will rise up in their place, and make this a country where no man who will work need want."[11] The People's Party became, in 1892, the Populist Party, absorbing many of the Christian Socialists

---

10. See Clara and Rudolf Kirk, "Howells and the Church of the Carpenter," *NEQ*, XXXII (1959), 185–206.

11. *Life in Letters*, II, 8–9; in 1892 the Populist Party polled more than a million votes.

with whom Howells had associated during his two years in Boston. The ideas he had discussed with them, which were reflected in his letter to his father, were soon expressed in his Altrurian Romances.

"A TRAVELLER" AND THE *COSMOPOLITAN*

During the summer of 1891, a small pamphlet by John Brisben Walker, entitled "The Church and Poverty," came into Howells' hands.[12] Since the writer voiced so many of Howells' own views concerning the need for "brotherliness between the rich and the poor," Howells immediately wrote him a letter of appreciation. Howells' note led to a meeting and a suggestion from Walker that Howells write a series of "sociological essays" for the *Cosmopolitan*. Howells, at that time, did not wish once again to commit himself to the routine of the monthly essay, and so did not accept the proposal.

When, however, on 4 December 1891 Walker made him an offer that was more tempting, both from a practical and an idealistic point of view, Howells reconsidered. Not only was he offered more money,[13] but also he was promised freedom to express his views. An immensely successful business man, Walker had bought the *Cosmopolitan* in 1889 with the intention of making it a popular platform for the reform movements of the day. He too had been moved by Bliss's call to action in *The Dawn*, "a journal of revolution toward practical Christianity," and he looked upon Howells as the very man to cast into literary form the ideas they shared. His invitation to Howells to devote his entire time to the *Cosmopolitan*, and Howells' acceptance of the

---

12. See Charles E. L. Wingate, "Boston Letter," *Critic*, XVII (16 January 1892), 41. In his pamphlet, Walker used the Biblical phrase "the eye of the needle" to describe the rich man's dilemma. In an essay entitled "Are the Americans Bible Readers?" Howells mentions the rich man and a needle's eye; see *Literature*, n.s. I (1899), 585–586. Though a Roman Catholic, Walker had attended several services of the Church of the Carpenter.

13. Walker offered Howells approximately $15,000 a year; see "The Napoleon of the Magazines," New York *Herald*, 3 September 1893, p. 13.

offer, were not surprising to those who were aware of their common interest in Christian Socialism.

Howells wrote to Charles Eliot Norton on 12 December 1891, under the letterhead of "The Cosmopolitan Magazine, Editorial Department," to explain his recent move. In becoming co-editor of the magazine, he said, "I am to be associated with the owner, Mr. John Brisben Walker, a man of generous ideals, who will leave me absolute control in literature, and whom I think with in many other matters" (*Life in Letters*, II, 19). Norton replied promptly, warning Howells that he would have "hard work to lift 'The Cosmopolitan' out of the atmosphere in which it has flourished,—an atmosphere in which there has been a large mingling of the nitrous oxide gas of second-rate vulgarity." Howells assured Norton in his reply that he had no intention of lowering his ideals and that he could not realize those of any other man. "That is my greatest safeguard," he wrote, "but the way seems open to do good, and I am hopeful."[14]

A Boston newspaper reporter asked Howells whether, in joining the staff of the *Cosmopolitan*, he was searching for a special audience for the ideas he wished now to express. Howells replied: "No, there is no special audience that I try to address. I endeavor to do my best with my nose to the desk. The simple matter is, here is an idea involving a certain question, and the problem is to get it artistically out."[15] The "certain question" Howells had in mind was the implication of socialism—which he preferred to call "altruism"—for "plutocratic" America. Walker placed under the masthead of the *Cosmopolitan*, beginning with the issue of January 1892, the familiar slogan, "From every man according to his ability: to everyone according to his need." Howells' Altrurian essays were his answer to the problem of how to give literary expression to these socialistic concepts.

Though Howells found himself unable to work with "the Napoleon of the Magazines," as Walker was called, and after a

14. Norton to WDH, 19 December 1891; WDH to Norton, 29 December 1891.
15. See Spencer H. Coon, "Mr. Howells Talks," Boston *Advertiser*, 26 December 1891, p. 3.

few months withdrew from the editorship of the *Cosmopolitan*, the two men continued an association. At the close of June 1892, for example, Walker and Howells exchanged letters on the strike against the Carnegie Iron and Steel Company at Homestead, Pennsylvania. Walker wrote to Howells, then summering in New Hampshire, that he intended to contribute to the September issue of the *Cosmopolitan* an article to be called "The 'Homestead' Object Lesson." In the same letter he expressed his approval of the name Howells had proposed for his series "A Traveller from Altruria," for Walker wished to encourage Howells "to work upon the problems which concern humanity." Though Howells had not accepted Walker's original invitation to contribute sociological essays to the *Cosmopolitan*, he now saw an opportunity to write "a sort of sociological serial" in the form of a "fable" (p. 3), in which he might suggest the possibility of a "practical altruism" as a "national polity" (p. 93). Why, indeed, should the Altrurian system be considered "so very un-American" (p. 93), and why should this idea not be woven into a loosely constructed story, suggesting the direction in which American democracy should develop?

RECEPTION OF THE ALTRURIAN LETTERS

The following autumn Howells' readers found in the Altrurian series a fictionalized expression of these views. They already knew the most popular novelist of the period to be an open defender of civil rights, for his famous letter addressed to the New York *Tribune* (6 November 1887, p. 5) pleading for a new trial for the Chicago Anarchists had been widely publicized. Now these social ideas found expression in his Altrurian fable.

During the publication of this serial, Howells told an interviewer, he received "more letters about it than about any other story he had written in many and many a year—'letters from all over the country and from all kinds of people.' "[16]

---

16. Marrion Wilcox, "Works of William Dean Howells," *Harper's Weekly*, 4 July 1896, p. 656.

Though Howells was, indeed, accepted in the 1890's as a writer whose views of society were worth consideration, the seriousness of his attack in the *Cosmopolitan* came as something of a surprise. Edward Bellamy hailed the first installment of "A Traveller from Altruria" in a three-column review in his Nationalist magazine, the *New Nation* (26 November 1892) as an exposé of "our caste distinctions based on wealth and consequent occupation." Later, in a briefer comment in the *New Nation* (14 October 1893), Bellamy connected Howells with "the present trend of thought in this country," marked by "the hope of a near and radical social transformation." Bellamy, who had known Howells during his two years in Boston, expressed gratified surprise that "the leading novelist of the time should have turned aside from the conventional types of polite fiction to give his country-men this drastic arraignment of the way we live now, and this glowing exposition of a nobler, higher, better life which beckons us on."

But Howells' long line of social novels, from *The Minister's Charge* to *A Hazard of New Fortunes*, could hardly have been imagined by a "writer of the conventional types of polite fiction." The society novelist, moreover, was satirized in "A Traveller from Altruria" in the person of Mr. Twelvemough, the agitated host of Mr. Aristides Homos. The Altrurian was the spokesman for Howells' most cherished social beliefs; Homos' views were clearly socialistic in tenor and were recognized as such by Howells' readers. They sprang, however, from the classical-Christian tradition of the Declaration of Independence and the Constitution, in which Howells had been born and reared in the days before the Civil War, and to which he hoped the country would return. In "A Traveller from Altruria" the urgency of his ideas broke through the form of the novel.

The reviewer for the *Critic*, however, found the ideas of Plato, Bacon, Thomas More, William Morris, and Bellamy, which were "all jumbled and shaken up together in Mr. Howells's book," distinctly disagreeable, for to him the idea of socialism was distasteful. Is it worthwhile, the reviewer wondered, to consider seriously the gospel Mr. Howells preaches? It is one of democracy in terms of equality—and that means socialism, which is a dream "and not even a beautiful dream."[17]

Howells' way of dealing with the Altrurian's question as to the real cause of the workingman's discontent in America might well have justified the reviewer's belief that the gospel Howells preached in "A Traveller from Altruria" was socialism. To Aristides Homos' inquiry, Mr. Twelvemough had replied myopically: "What is the cause of the workingman's discontent? It is very simple: the walking-delegate" (p. 43). The Altrurian's question had troubled Howells sufficiently to move him to look for himself at this new character on the labor scene. On his return to New York late in 1891, Howells sought out Abraham Cahan, editor of the *Arbeiter Zeitung*, a leading Yiddish newspaper. Cahan had thought of Howells—all of whose novels he claimed to have read—as a realist of such honesty that he might almost be counted among the socialists. "Mr. Howells is not a socialist," Cahan admitted, "and yet, unconsciously, free from the pressure of partisan passion, merely at the bidding of his realistic instinct, he accentuates in his works . . . and brings into high relief a fact in American life which lays bare the fictitiousness of American equality." So impressed was Cahan by the socialistic tone of Howells' Altrurian series, then beginning to appear in the *Cosmopolitan*, that he had several columns of "A Traveller from Altruria" translated into Yiddish for his newspaper.[18]

The five-day visit Howells paid to Chicago in September 1893 to view the World's Columbian Exposition convinced him that his socialistic dream could also be beautiful, as the next series, "Letters of an Altrurian Traveller," indicated. The first of the "Letters" was, in fact, an essay on socialism. The second was an illustration of the beautiful civilization that might be constructed on cooperative rather than competitive principles;

---

17. *Critic*, XXIV (1894), 434.
18. See Clara and Rudolf Kirk, "Abraham Cahan and William Dean Howells, the Story of a Friendship," *American Jewish Historical Quarterly*, LII (1962), 27–57.

it was devoted to the Altrurian's contemplation of "the World's Fair City," as Howells called the group of classical buildings constructed on new land dredged up from the bottom of Lake Michigan. The very architecture bespoke in terms of beauty understandable to the simplest citizen a rational solution to social problems. The Fair, to Howells and to Homos, was "pure Altruria," for here was a non-competitive world of classic beauty, enjoyed by rich and poor alike. These first two "Letters" of the series were never reprinted in Howells' lifetime, perhaps because they reflected too obviously the views of the editors of the *Cosmopolitan* to satisfy the House of Harper.

THE "LETTERS" AND THE HOUSE OF HARPER

The remaining nine "Letters" of the second Altrurian series were concerned with Aristides Homos' attempt for the second time to sustain "the shock of American conditions" in the great metropolis. His return to New York, described in the third letter, was like coming back to Babylon after a visit to the New Jerusalem, as Homos lamented to his friend in Altruria.

Before this second series was half completed, Harper and Brothers brought out in book form the first series, *A Traveler from Altruria*, with such revisions as seemed to Howells, perhaps with the advice of his editor, desirable. Though the book plates for the first series of Altrurian essays were used at once, plates for the second were laid aside, awaiting a conclusion, as Howells explained in "Bibliographical."

The history of Howells' relationship to the House of Harper during the 1890's, however, throws further light on the question as to why the whole series of "Letters" never became a book. Though Howells states in "Bibliographical" that he was not satisfied with what seemed to him the "logical" ending of the second series, to Harper perhaps a more important reason for not risking another volume was that the first had touched on too sensitive an issue. Few reviews appeared, and most of those that did implied that Howells was now socialistically inclined.[19] As Howells wrote to Sylvester Baxter on 23 March 1893, "I am glad you like the Altrurian. There is very little return from it in print, but I hope it is making at least a silent impression. Of course it is a prickly subject for the ordinary magazine noticer to touch."[20]

In September 1894, immediately after the last of the Altrurian "Letters" had appeared in the *Cosmopolitan*, both the New York *Daily Herald* (23 September) and the *Daily Tribune* (30 September) published articles in their Sunday editions pointing out that Altrurian thought was really socialistic. The title of the article in the *Herald* was "Poets Become Socialists Too," and the subtitle read "Howells Champions Socialism." Howells was in fact considered by the unidentified author of the article as "the foremost champion of socialism among literary men of the present time." He continued: "The novelist's entrance into the field of economics, holding a lance for unpopular doctrine, has been the cause of much surprise and mystification to his friends and admirers." Readers of *A Hazard of New Fortunes*, *Silas Lapham*, and *The World of Chance*, however, realize "that the novelist has long been a serious student of such questions." The critic for the *Daily Tribune* neatly summed up his view of *A Traveler from Altruria* in the caption of his article, "Socialism Idealized." These, and other notices of a similar tenor, possibly contributed to the Harper decision not to bring out as a book the "Letters of an Altrurian Traveller."

All references to Aristides Homos were removed when "Letters" III, IV, and V were altered for *Impressions and Experiences* in 1896, and the author himself, as a thoughtful citizen of New York, was made to voice the softened comment of the Altrurian.

---

19. *A Traveler from Altruria* was reviewed in the following: *Athenaeum*, No. 3480 (7 July 1894), p. 29; *Atlantic Monthly*, LXXIV (1894), 701–704; *Critic*, n.s. XXI (1894), 434; *Dial*, XVII (1894), 154; *Epitome and Events* (Los Angeles), I (1894), 4; *Harper's Bazar*, XXVII (1894), 475; *Harper's Monthly*, LXXXIX (1894), 648; *Nation*, LIX (1894), 107; New York *Daily Herald*, 23 September 1894, Sixth Section, p. 14; New York *Daily Tribune*, 30 September 1894, p. 14.

20. MS at the Huntington Library. Used by permission.

One example among many which might be cited is his change in "Letter" V of the phrase "labor due to all from all" to the less provocative words "productive labor" when he rewrote the passage for Harper and wished to tone down the socialistic implications. More important is the omission of the opening pages of "Letter" III, in which Howells had emphasized "the brute ugliness" of New York, and of the paragraph of "Letter" IV describing the filth and litter of the city streets in winter. "I am rather quiescent in my social thinking just now," he admitted to Baxter on 27 July 1896, though only the year before he had written to the same friend, "Perhaps you saw my essay on Equality in the November *Century*. The C. is to print Fraternity. Liberty will be in the next Forum."[21] Howells was perhaps not so much "quiescent" in his social thinking at that time as he was cautious in his relationship to his publishers.

To many readers, however, Howells had come to seem an outspoken social critic. In an article signed "G" in the *American Fabian* and quoted at length in the *Literary Digest*, one writer announced that Howells "has made his art the instrument of a great purpose." This purpose is especially to be noted in his Altrurian Romances; "his 'A Traveller from Altruria,' the most definite and comprehensive expression of his social ideals, and his 'Letters of an Altrurian Traveller,' describing from the viewpoint of a Socialist the characteristics of the plutocratic city of New York, have set many thousands of minds forward on the right path."[22] Did Harper and Brothers approve of this new departure? We know, at least, that they did not publish the "Letters" as a book after the series had come to a conclusion in the *Cosmopolitan*.

For Howells' own rather ambiguous account of his relations

---

21. MSS at the Huntington Library. Used by permission. The second letter is dated 18 November 1895; Howells was referring to his essays "Equality as the Basis of Good Society," *Century*, LI (1895), 63–67; "Who Are Our Brethren?" *Century*, LI (1896), 932–936; and "The Nature of Liberty," *Forum*, XX (1895), 401–409.

22. "Mr. Howells' Socialism," *American Fabian*, IV (1898), 1–2; *Literary Digest*, XVI (1898), 340–341. William M. Gibson and George Arms suggest the writer was W. J. Ghent; see *A Bibliography of William Dean Howells* (New York, 1948), p. 127.

with Harper and Brothers one may turn to his essay "Mr. Howells's Paper," written at the request of J. Henry Harper in 1912. In his "Paper," Howells looked back on events that had happened between 1886, when he joined the Harper staff, and 1900, when the firm found itself near bankruptcy. He remembered lunching with J. W. Harper and talking "our affairs over in detail." Mr. Harper, Howells wrote, "skilfully led up to what a man might or might not say in the Harper periodicals." Howells had been warned by George William Curtis, his predecessor in the "Easy Chair," that the House "rang a little bell" at the approach of the Editor of the "Chair" to a forbidden subject.[23] Curtis had indeed resigned his position on *Harper's Weekly* in 1882 because, as he wrote later, "My article . . . despite my request, was perverted and made to misrepresent my views." The House of Harper disavowed the "mistake" and Curtis resumed his position as editor—but he did not forget the experience.[24] Howells himself had been urged by Alden to transform the hero of *The Minister's Charge* into a somewhat more heroic character. This he refused to do, but the following year (1888), Howells did at Alden's request re-write a too realistic love scene in *April Hopes*.[25]

Howells had learned, however, from his earlier experience in the "Study" that editorial pressure was seldom exerted. He recalled with appreciation that during the six years of his first contract with the firm, he had been treated with a tolerance which he said had put him on his "conscience." He was, nevertheless, always listening for "the tinkle of the little bell" from the office of J. W. Harper admonishing him to remember that he was writing for readers of refined and cultivated tastes and conserva-

---

23. *The House of Harper*, ed. J. Henry Harper (New York, 1912), p. 321.

24. Edward Cary, *George William Curtis* (Boston, 1894), pp. 274–275. See also Gordon Milne, *George William Curtis and the Genteel Tradition* (Bloomington, Indiana, 1956), p. 167.

25. Howells wrote about *The Minister's Charge* to James R. Osgood on 12 May 1884 and asked him to transmit the message to Alden; *Life in Letters*, I, 361–362. The *April Hopes* episode was amusingly presented by Alden in "The Editor's Study," *Harper's Monthly*, CII (1900), 159–160.

tive political views.[26] The bell never rang, but Howells was aware that at any moment it might be sounded, especially after the appearance of such comment as that of Bellamy and those soon to come out in leading New York papers, naming Howells among the socialists.

Howells' unfailing "good-manners" successfully veiled in his "Paper" any clear statement concerning the editorial control exerted by Harper and Brothers in managing their vast publishing interests. In 1919, however, when he was asked by the magazine to write a memorial essay in honor of Henry Mills Alden, Howells wrote that "The publishers constantly advised with [Alden] and he with them, and he was of such rare make that he could see the reason of their opinions, which were rather theirs than his. Their mutual relation was a mechanism, which was finally without a jar. . . . The ideal [of the magazine] remained the publishers', with their instinct for a popularity, and its realization was the editor's, with his taste, his knowledge, his acquaintance with literature, and his unselfish intelligence."[27]

THROUGH THE EYE OF THE NEEDLE

Between the appearance of *Impressions and Experiences* in 1896 and *Through the Eye of the Needle* in 1907, Howells made no literary use of his Altrurian material. When he turned to it again, as a man of seventy, Harper and Brothers was under new management. In his Harper "Paper," Howells tells of reading in the New York *Tribune*, in 1899, after a sleepless night on a Pullman, of the failure of the House of Harper. Hastening down to Franklin Square, he soon learned that the firm had been forced into

---

26. Everett Carter believes that Howells did, in fact, feel the pressure of censorship by the House of Harper in spite of this disavowal. See *Howells and the Age of Realism* (Philadelphia, 1950), pp. 184–185. When a memorial service for the Chicago Anarchists was held in Boston (11 November 1888) a letter of sympathy from Howells, who was not present, was read aloud. Alden promptly wrote to Howells, requesting permission to state the "facts" in *Harper's Weekly* (24 November 1888, p. 887), lest the position of the Harper firm be misunderstood. See also Clara M. Kirk, *W. D. Howells, Traveler from Altruria* (New Brunswick, N.J., 1962), pp. 21–22.

27. "Editor's Easy Chair: In Memoriam," *Harper's Monthly*, CXL (1919), 133–134.

receivership and that J. P. Morgan was prepared to help in the "reorganization." When the confusion of the bankruptcy proceedings had cleared somewhat and Howells had conferred with the new head, Colonel George Harvey, he could write with relief to his sister, "I am very happy . . . in a new relation I have formed with Harpers which I will simply say includes taking all I write at a fixed price, and making me literary adviser of the house" (*Life in Letters*, II, 137).

Having kept clear of a salaried position on the staff of the Harper periodicals for almost a decade (though he continued to contribute to them regularly), Howells now welcomed the chance to take over the "Editor's Easy Chair" which had fallen vacant at the death of George William Curtis and had remained empty for the intervening eight years. "In reviving the 'Easy Chair', " wrote Henry Mills Alden at the head of Howells' first contribution (*Harper's Monthly*, CII, December 1900, 153–158), "it is our good fortune that we are able to commit the new department to the man who, of all living writers, is the fit master to conduct it on the old and familiar lines that ensured its prosperity in the thoughts and affections of readers." In this Christmas issue, Alden also observed in his comments in "The Editor's Study," the "Easy Chair" has "justly emphasized the altruistic suggestions of the holy season." Howells continued to write his monthly column for the "Easy Chair" until his death in 1920, but though he expressed freely his views on war, woman suffrage, women's hats, tipping, current art exhibitions—in fact, on any subject that interested him—the old vehemence had left him. As Alden remarked, "the unwritten law of this Magazine, in every part of it, [is] to avoid the discussion of what are known as 'burning questions,' and of themes that divide sects in religion, parties in politics, and classes in society." He immediately insisted, however, that no periodical valued individuality more and that its readers could expect Howells' "heart as well as his thought" to be revealed in his essays.[28] That Howells found little

---

28. "The Editor's Study," *Harper's Monthly*, CII (1900), 160–161.

difficulty in reconciling the law of the magazine and the impulses of his heart is indicated by the imaginary dialogue in the same issue of *Harper's* which he held with the resurrected Easy Chair, left in the corner by his predecessor. To the Chair's "what is now 'the conversation of the town'?" the "unreal Editor" replied, "Well, you know, that is an embarrassing topic, for the Easy Chair is supposed to have no politics, and 'the conversation of the town' is so largely political, just now" (p. 156). Moreover, Howells was more interested in his novels than in his essays for the "Easy Chair" (or "Uneasy Chair" as he called it). "It might have been wiser for me to keep out of that place," he wrote to Thomas Bailey Aldrich soon after he had returned to the Harper office, "but at 63 one likes a fixed income, even when the unfixed is not bad. Essaying has been the enemy of the novelist that was in me. One cannot do both kinds without hurt to both" (*Life in Letters*, II, 138).

In 1907 Howells attempted once more to reconcile the essayist with the novelist by writing Part II of *Through the Eye of the Needle* and thus completing the unfinished Romance. "There is now a revival of interest in such speculations," he wrote his brother, "and the publishers think the book, with an interesting sequel, giving an account of life in Altruria, will succeed. I hope so. But my books, none of them, go far, you know" (*Life in Letters*, II, 235). Howells remembered that more than a decade earlier Harper had not published *The Eye of the Needle*—as he had then named it—either because of his own inability to find a satisfactory ending or because of the publisher's hesitation to venture on a second Altrurian Romance.

The ironic "Introduction" that Howells wrote in 1907 for his second Altrurian Romance is perhaps of as much interest as the "interesting sequel." Here Howells himself seemed to rub his eyes at the vast changes that he perceived had come over the country since the visit of the Altrurian to the Fair in 1893. He concluded that he could make Part I palatable to readers of 1907 only by adopting a lightly satiric attitude towards his Altrurian; in doing so, Howells not infrequently hid a more bit-ing satire. "He is entangled in his social sophistries regarding all the competitive civilizations," wrote Howells, introducing the Altrurian to another generation; "he cannot apparently do full justice to the superior heroism of charity and self-sacrifice practised in countries where people live *upon* each other as the Americans do, instead of *for* each other as the Altrurians do" (p. 267).

The Traveler, Howells pointed out, visited this country when it was at the beginning of an economic depression, extending from 1894 to 1898, which was relieved only by the Spanish-American War. With the resulting accumulation of money, the conditions of the laboring man have been so improved, he dryly observed, that he is now united with the capitalist "in bonds of the closest affection." Were the Altrurian Emissary to return to New York, "he might not now so totally condemn" this "heaping-up of riches." The "unrestricted activity" of commerce and industry had produced civic-minded millionaires who have so raised the level of our civilization that "even our business-men cannot wholly escape culture." Granted that war is evil—even a small war—our conflict with Spain had ushered in a Golden Age (or "Age on a Gold Basis") which Americans had been enjoying so long that they were sure it would not be followed by a period of adversity. Howells apologized to the reader for failing to reach "a more absolute conclusion" in his study of the Altrurian civilization, so "fundamentally alien" to our own. Attractive as that strange land might be to "an enthusiastic nature" such as that of the American wife of Aristides, certain "misgivings" intruded upon the mind of the elderly author of the Altrurian Romances when, after a lapse of many years, he attempted to bring the thoughts of two decades into a coherent whole.

In a letter to Charles Eliot Norton written on 15 April 1907, Howells called *Through the Eye of the Needle* "my own dream of a Utopia." When he actually accompanied Homos to Altruria, he found that the ideas of the inhabitants on money, work, family life, and religion were closely related to those of the Christian Socialists; that the Regionic capital looked remarkably like the "White City" of the Chicago Exposition of 1893; and that the contents of a typical Altrurian periodical were reminiscent of those proposed by Howells for the *Cosmopolitan* many years ago. Norton had never been fully in sympathy with Howells' social ideas, and Howells hardly expected him to care about this latest expression of them, "unless for its confessions of imperfections even in Utopia." He added, somewhat sadly, "All other dreamers of such dreams have had nothing but pleasure in them; I have had touches of nightmare" (*Life in Letters*, II, 242).

Writing Part II of *The Needle* in 1907 did not resolve to Howells' satisfaction his doubts concerning an ideal civilization. Altruria itself, when visited with the wife of Aristides Homos, seemed less alluring than the distant view of that utopian land given by the Altrurian on his visit to America. Moreover, the route to Altruria had become less clear to Howells after the lapse of years. When Howells wrote the "Letters of an Altrurian Traveller" in 1894, Altruria seemed to have moved from the Aegean and to occupy the place on the map where Australia and New Zealand are found. As Homos explained to his American friends, those lands "are more like Altruria than any other countries in the plutocratic world," and hence seem to be on the very spot where Altruria lies. When Howells touched up the "Letters" to form Part I of *Through the Eye of the Needle*, he omitted this specific reference to the location of Altruria, and retained only his hostess' remark that she had often studied the map of that part of the world after she had talked with the Altrurian, but she had never been able to find Altruria—"it was no use."

Although *Through the Eye of the Needle* was praised in this country and in England for the author's "inimitable way of putting things," few critics expressed unmixed enthusiasm for Howells' "almost faultless little pieces of irony," and the reviewer for the *Athenaeum* flatly remarked, "Unhappily, these sociological criticisms are not conveyed in an interesting form of fiction." The front-page review in the New York *Times*, on the other hand, began with, "We can never have anything but welcome for our genial friend Mr. Homos of Altruria." One may read *Through the Eye of the Needle* "simply as a romance," he warned the reader, "or one may read it, as we are sure Mr. Howells would like to have it read, as a serious study of sociology." Though he tells us of "our sins and shortcomings," Howells has a "large tolerance which disarms resentment."[29]

In the "Easy Chair" of September 1918 (*Harper's Monthly*, CXXXVII, 589–592), Howells attempted to support the part of the United States in World War I by commenting on "the long war between Altruria and the autocracy of Egoria." But his faith in his Altrurians was now less firm. Shaken by the new problems faced by the country, Howells invoked the Altrurian's attitude towards taxation, conscription, charity, and the function of law. Hating war though he did, he considered that even in Altruria war with less civilized neighbors could not always be avoided. His justification of military conscription and the income tax was given in terms of his old belief in "equality." This interesting— and certainly unromantic—essay marks the last appearance of the Altrurians. The dream, however, of a better social order lingered on.

Curiously enough, in the last "Easy Chair" Howells was to write for *Harper's* (CXL, April 1920, 710–712), he referred again to "travelers" from a more perfect world—Mars, in this case— who landed by mistake in New York. Howells interviewed the friendly pair, who expressed "an intense and penetrating democracy" and gave him their views on war, money, religion, drama, the vote, and taxes. He told the couple that he was glad they had come to visit New York; they replied that they had intended to land in New Zealand, because it was "So much more socialized than any other terrestrial country. More in sympathy with our own planet, which is entirely socialized." What could

---

29. *Through the Eye of the Needle* was reviewed in the following: *Athenaeum*, I (1907), 786; *Independent*, LXII (1907), 1207; *Literary Digest*, XXXIV (1907), 885–886; London *Times*, 24 May 1907, p. 165; *Nation*, LXXXIV (1907), 434–435; *North American Review*, CLXXXVI (1907), 127–130; *Outlook*, LXXXVI (1907), 339; *Putnam's Monthly*, II (1907), 619; *Spectator*, XCVIII (1907), 836; New York *Times*, 20 April 1907, p. 255; 11 May 1907, p. 297; 15 June 1907, p. 581.

the authorities do with the Martians, since it hardly seemed possible to return them to Mars? After due consideration, "as the next best thing they were sent to Russia upon the theory that they were Bolshevists." At the close of his life, Howells continued to visit in his imagination the distant land which, in his prime, he had thought of as a blueprint for America.

C. K.

R. K.

WILLIAM DEAN HOWELLS

"*A Traveller from Altruria*"

The Altrurian Romances

BIBLIOGRAPHICAL

THE TWO ROMANCES grouped here are books of one blood, but in birth so far divided from each other by time that they might seem mother and daughter rather than sisters. Yet they are of the same generation and born of the same abiding conviction: the conviction that the economic solution of the "riddle of the painful earth" is to be by emulation and not by competition.

A Traveller from Altruria was written, with intervals of summer hotel sojourn, in the large apartment-house in West Fifty-ninth Street, where I lived, off and on, with my family for some fifteen years. Off and on, I say, for twice we left it and twice we came back to it after a stay elsewhere of a year or so. Our inconstant allegiance became the amusement of that amusing friend of the family, J. L. F., who said, He would not mind our moving so much, if we didn't always move into the same place.

He might have made a kindred joke about the recurrent continuity of motive in these romances, for it remained unchanged through every change of time and place; however often I left it, just as often I came back to it. The first fable was printed in *The Cosmopolitan Magazine* as a sort of sociological serial, and the first half of the second followed in the next year, say the year 1894. The first was republished in book form on its conclusion in the magazine, but the first part of the second was withheld after stereotyping for nearly fifteen years, waiting the author's hope, or his despair, of getting something more final, or something more cheerful than the ending which the story seemed logically to have assigned itself. He had always distinctly wished, if he

3

had only vaguely meant, to visit his Utopia with one of his characters, and report of its happy conditions. He had constantly believed in these, and in their practicability everywhere, and at last, suddenly, almost unexpectedly, the heroine invited him to accompany her to Altruria, where she was going to repent of her rejection of the Altrurian hero. He accepted promptly, eagerly, it might be said, and he rendered his report of the visit at once. This second part of the second romance is not very long, but it seemed to him something of a feat to write it in less than a month. To be sure, something like it had been long in his mind, and he had only to set down his swiftly following fancies in their succession. In his study, or his vision of idealities, which in some similitude must one day be the actualities of the world, he indulged an active conscience in its anxieties so far as to admit the possibility of imperfection even in the ideal commonwealth of Altruria; or in other terms, he suffered his dream of it to experience slight touches of nightmare. After all, he was dealing with human nature, and though human nature, which the individualists declare cannot be changed, has been constantly changed for the better, he found that it had not been entirely perfected even in Altruria. This consummation is reserved for the human nature of the American republic, upon which the author of these books confidently relies for the verification of his brightest hopes.

The second half of the second romance herein offered the reader was written in an apartment hotel rather well up on the West Side, like those in which the author was wont to tarry while preparing himself for his returns to West Fifty-ninth Street. It was very presently added to the first half, written so long before, and it was published with it in 1907, a month or two after it was imagined.

W. D. H.

A TRAVELLER FROM ALTRURIA

I CONFESS that with all my curiosity to meet an Altrurian, I was in no hospitable mood towards the traveller when he finally presented himself, pursuant to the letter of advice sent me by the friend who introduced him. It would be easy enough to take care of him in the hotel; I had merely to engage a room for him, and have the clerk tell him his money was not good if he tried to pay for anything. But I had swung fairly into my story; its people were about me all the time; I dwelt amidst its events and places, and I did not see how I could welcome my guest among them, or abandon them for him. Still, when he actually arrived, and I took his hand as he stepped from the train, I found it less difficult to say that I was glad to see him than I expected. In fact, I was glad, for I could not look upon his face without feeling a glow of kindness for him. I had not the least trouble in identifying him, he was so unlike all the Americans who dismounted from the train with him, and who all looked hot, worried and anxious. He was a man no longer young, but in what we call the heyday of life, when our own people are so absorbed in making provision for the future that they may be said not to live in the present at all. This Altrurian's whole countenance, and especially his quiet, gentle eyes, expressed a vast contemporaneity, with bounds of leisure removed to the end of time; or, at least, this was the effect of something in them which I am obliged to report in rather fantastic terms. He was above the middle height and he carried himself vigorously. His face was sunburnt, or sea-burnt, where it was not bearded; and although I knew from my friend's letter that he was a man of learning and distinction in his own country, I should never have supposed him a person of scholarly life, he was so far from sicklied over with anything like the pale cast of thought. When he took the hand I offered him in my half-hearted welcome he gave it a grasp that decided me to confine our daily greetings to something much less muscular.

"Let me have your bag," I said, as we do when we meet people at the train, and he instantly bestowed a rather heavy valise upon me, with a smile in his benignant eyes, as if it had been the greatest favor. "Have you got any checks?" I asked.

"Yes," he said, in very good English, but with an accent new to me: "I bought two." He gave them to me and I passed them to our hotel porter, who was waiting there with the baggage cart. Then I proposed that we should walk across the meadow to the house, which is a quarter of a mile or so from the station. We started, but he stopped suddenly and looked back over his shoulder. "Oh, you needn't be troubled about your trunks," I said. "The porter will get them to the house all right. They'll be in your room by the time we get there."

"But he's putting them into the wagon himself," said the Altrurian.

"Yes; he always does that. He's a strong young fellow. He'll manage it. You needn't—" I could not finish saying he need not mind the porter; he was rushing back to the station, and I had the mortification of seeing him take an end of each trunk and help the porter toss it into the wagon; some lighter pieces he put in himself, and he did not stop till all the baggage the train had left was disposed of.

I stood holding his valise, unable to put it down in my embarrassment at this eccentric performance, which had been evident not to me alone, but to all the people who arrived by the train, and all their friends who came from the hotel to meet them. A number of these passed me on the tally-ho coach; and a lady, who had got her husband with her for over Sunday, and was in very good spirits, called gayly down to me: "Your friend seems fond of exercise!"

"Yes," I answered dryly; the sparkling repartee which ought to have come to my help failed to show up. But it was impossible to be vexed with the Altrurian when he returned to me, unruffled by his bout with the baggage, and serenely smiling.

"Do you know," he said, "I fancied that good fellow was ashamed of my helping him. I hope it didn't seem a reflection upon him in any way before your people? I ought to have thought of that."

"I guess we can make it right with him. I dare say he felt more surprised than disgraced. But we must make haste a little now; your train was half an hour late, and we shall not stand so good a chance for supper if we are not there pretty promptly."

"No?" said the Altrurian. "Why?"

"Well," I said, with evasive lightness, "first come, first served, you know. That's human nature."

"Is it?" he returned, and he looked at me as one does who suspects another of joking.

"Well, isn't it?" I retorted; but I hurried to add: "Besides, I want to have time after supper to show you a bit of our landscape. I think you'll enjoy it." I knew he had arrived in Boston that morning by steamer, and I now thought it high time to ask him: "Well, what do you think of America, anyway?" I ought really to have asked him this the moment he stepped from the train.

"Oh," he said, "I'm intensely interested," and I perceived that he spoke with a certain reservation. "As the most advanced country of its time, I've always been very curious to see it."

The last sentence raised my dashed spirits again, and I said confidently: "You must find our system of baggage checks delightful." I said this because it is one of the first things we brag of to foreigners, and I had the habit of it. "By the way," I ventured to add, "I suppose you meant to say you *brought* two checks when I asked you for them at the train just now? But you really said you *bought* them."

"Yes," the Altrurian replied, "I gave half a dollar apiece for them at the station in Boston. I saw other people doing it," he explained, noting my surprise. "Isn't it the custom?"

"I'm happy to say it isn't yet, on most of our roads. They were tipping the baggage man, to make sure that he checked their baggage in time, and put it on the train. I had to do that myself when I came up; otherwise it might have got along here some-time next day. But the system is perfect."

"The poor man looked quite worn out," said the Altrurian, "and I am glad I gave him something. He seemed to have several hundred pieces of baggage to look after, and he wasn't embarrassed like your porter by my helping him put my trunks into the car. May I confess that the meanness of the station, its insufficient facilities, its shabby waiting rooms, and its whole crowded and confused appearance gave me rather a bad im-pression?"

"I know," I had to own, "it's shameful; but you wouldn't have found another station in the city so bad."

"Ah, then," said the Altrurian, "I suppose this particular road is too poor to employ more baggage men, or build new sta-tions; they seemed rather shabby all the way up."

"Well, no," I was obliged to confess, "it's one of the richest roads in the country. The stock stands at about 180. But I'm really afraid we shall be late to supper, if we don't get on," I broke off; though I was not altogether sorry to arrive after the porter had disposed of the baggage. I dreaded another display of active sympathy on the part of my strange companion; I have often felt sorry myself for the porters of hotels, but I have never thought of offering to help them handle the heavy trunks that they manage.

The Altrurian was delighted with the hotel; and in fact it did look extremely pretty, with its branching piazzas full of well-dressed people, and its green lawns where the children were playing. I led the way to the room which I had taken for him next my own; it was simply furnished, but it was sweet with matting, fresh linen and pure white-washed walls. I flung open the window blinds and let him get a glimpse of the mountains purpling under the sunset, the lake beneath, and the deeply foliaged shores.

"Glorious! Glorious!" he sighed.

"Yes," I modestly assented. "We think that's rather fine." He stood tranced before the window, and I thought I had better say, "Well, now I can't give you much time to get the dust of travel off; the dining room doors close at eight, and we must hurry down."

"I'll be with you in a moment," he said, pulling off his coat.

I waited impatiently at the foot of the stairs, avoiding the question I met on the lips and in the eyes of my acquaintance. The fame of my friend's behavior at the station must have spread through the whole place; and everybody wished to know who he was. I answered simply he was a traveller from Altruria; and in some cases I went farther and explained that the Altrurians were peculiar.

In much less time than it seemed my friend found me; and then I had a little compensation for my suffering in his behalf. I could see that, whatever people said of him, they felt the same mysterious liking at sight of him that I had felt. He had made a little change in his dress, and I perceived that the women thought him not only good-looking, but well-dressed. They followed him with their eyes as we went into the dining room, and I was rather proud of being with him, as if I somehow shared the credit of his clothes and good looks. The Altrurian himself seemed most struck with the head waiter, who showed us to our places, and while we were waiting for our supper I found a chance to explain that he was a divinity student from one of the fresh-water colleges, and was serving here during his summer vacation. This seemed to interest my friend so much that I went on to tell him that many of the waitresses, whom he saw standing there subject to the order of the guests, were country school mistresses in the winter.

"Ah, that is as it should be," he said; "that is the kind of thing I expected to meet with in America."

"Yes," I responded, in my flattered national vanity, "if America means anything at all it means the honor of work and the recognition of personal worth everywhere. I hope you are going to make a long stay with us. We like to have travellers visit us who can interpret the spirit of our institutions as well as read their letter. As a rule, Europeans never quite get our point of view. Now a great many of these waitresses are ladies, in the true sense of the word, self-respectful, intelligent, refined, and fit to grace——"

I was interrupted by the noise my friend made in suddenly pushing back his chair and getting to his feet. "What's the matter?" I asked. "You're not ill, I hope?"

But he did not hear me. He had run half down the dining hall toward the slender young girl who was bringing us our supper. I had ordered rather generously, for my friend had owned to a good appetite, and I was hungry myself with waiting for him, so that the tray the girl carried was piled up with heavy dishes. To my dismay I saw, rather than heard at that distance, the Altrurian enter into a polite controversy with her, and then, as if overcoming all her scruples by sheer strength of will, possess himself of the tray and make off with it toward our table. The poor child followed him, blushing to her hair; the head waiter stood looking helplessly on; the guests, who at that late hour were fortunately few, were simply aghast at the scandal; the Altrurian alone seemed to think his conduct the most natural thing in the world. He put the tray on the side table near us, and in spite of our waitress's protests insisted upon arranging the little bird-bath dishes before our plates. Then at last he sat down, and the girl, flushed and tremulous, left the room, as I could not help suspecting, to have a good cry in the kitchen. She did not come back, and the head waiter, who was perhaps afraid to send another in her place, looked after our few wants himself. He kept a sharp eye on my friend, as if he were not quite sure he was safe, but the Altrurian resumed the conversation with all that lightness of spirits which I noticed in him after he helped the porter with the baggage. I did not think it the moment to take him to task for what he had just done; I was not even sure that it was the part of a host to do so at all, and between the one doubt and the other I left the burden of the talk to him.

"What a charming young creature!" he began. "I never saw anything prettier than the way she had of refusing my help, absolutely without coquetry or affectation of any kind. She is, as you said, a perfect lady, and she graces her work, as I am sure she would grace any exigency of life. She quite realizes my ideal of an American girl, and I see now what the spirit of your country must be from such an expression of it." I wished to tell him that while a country school teacher who waits at table in a summer hotel is very much to be respected in her sphere, she is not regarded with that high honor which some other women command among us; but I did not find this very easy, after what I had said of our esteem for labor; and while I was thinking how I could hedge, my friend went on. "I liked England greatly, and I liked the English, but I could not like the theory of their civilization, or the aristocratic structure of their society. It seemed to me iniquitous, for we believe that inequality and iniquity are the same in the last analysis."

At this I found myself able to say: "Yes, there is something terrible, something shocking, in the frank brutality with which Englishmen affirm the essential inequality of men. The affirmation of the essential equality of men was the first point of departure with us, when we separated from them."

"I know," said the Altrurian. "How grandly it is expressed in your glorious Declaration."

"Ah, you have read our Declaration of Independence then?"

"Every Altrurian has read that," answered my friend.

"Well," I went on smoothly, and I hoped to render what I was going to say the means of enlightening him without offence concerning the little mistake he had just made with the waitress; "of course we don't take that in its closest literality."

"I don't understand you," he said.

"Why, you know it was rather the political than the social traditions of England that we broke with, in the revolution."

"How is that?" he returned. "Didn't you break with monarchy and nobility and ranks and classes?"

"Yes, we broke with all those things."

"But I found them a part of the social as well as the political structure in England. You have no kings or nobles here. Have you any ranks or classes?"

"Well, not exactly, in the English sense. Our ranks and classes, such as we have, are what I may call voluntary."

"Oh, I understand. I suppose that from time to time certain ones among you feel the need of serving, and ask leave of the commonwealth to subordinate themselves to the rest of the state, and perform all the lowlier offices in it. Such persons must be held in peculiar honor. Is it something like that?"

"Well, no, I can't say it's quite like that. In fact, I think I'd better let you trust to your own observation of our life."

"But I'm sure," said the Altrurian, with a simplicity so fine that it was a long time before I could believe it quite real, "that I shall approach it so much more intelligently with a little instruction from you. You say that your social divisions are voluntary. But do I understand that those who serve among you do not wish to do so?"

"Well, I don't suppose they would serve if they could help it," I replied.

"Surely," said the Altrurian with a look of horror, "you don't mean that they are slaves!"

"Oh, no! Oh, no!" I said; "the War put an end to that. We are all free, now, black and white."

"But if they do not wish to serve, and are not held in peculiar honor for serving——"

"I see that my word 'voluntary' has misled you," I put in. "It isn't the word exactly. The divisions among us are rather a process of natural selection. You will see, as you get better acquainted with the workings of our institutions, that there are no arbitrary distinctions here, but the fitness of the work for the man and the man for the work determines the social rank that each one holds."

"Ah, that is fine!" cried the Altrurian with a glow of enthusiasm. "Then I suppose that these intelligent young people who teach school in winter and serve at table in the summer are in a sort of provisional state, waiting for the process of natural selection to determine whether they shall finally be teachers or waiters."

"Yes, it might be stated in some such terms," I assented, though I was not altogether easy in my mind. It seemed to me that I was not quite candid with this most candid spirit. I added, "You know we are a sort of fatalists here in America. We are great believers in the doctrine that it will all come out right in the end."

"Ah, I don't wonder at that," said the Altrurian, "if the process of natural selection works so perfectly among you as you say. But I am afraid I don't understand this matter of your domestic service yet. I believe you said that all honest work is honored in America. Then no social slight attaches to service, I suppose?"

"Well, I can't say that, exactly. The fact is, a certain social slight does attach to service, and that is one reason why I don't quite like to have students wait at table. It won't be pleasant for them to remember it in after life, and it won't be pleasant for their children to remember it."

"Then the slight would descend?"

"I think it would. One wouldn't like to think one's father or mother had been at service."

The Altrurian said nothing for a moment. Then he remarked, "So it seems that while all honest work is honored among you, there are some kinds of honest work that are not honored so much as others."

"Yes."

"Why?"

"Because some occupations are more degrading than others."

"But why?" he persisted, as I thought a little unreasonably.

"Really," I said, "I think I must leave you to imagine."

"I am afraid I can't," he said sadly. "Then, if domestic service is degrading in your eyes, and people are not willingly servants among you, may I ask why any are servants?"

"It is a question of bread and butter. They are obliged to be."

"That is, they are forced to do work that is hateful and disgraceful to them because they cannot live without?"

"Excuse me," I said, not at all liking this sort of pursuit, and feeling it fair to turn even upon a guest who kept it up. "Isn't it so with you in Altruria?"

"It was so once," he admitted, "but not now. In fact, it is like a waking dream to find oneself in the presence of conditions here that we outlived so long ago."

There was an unconscious superiority in this speech that nettled me, and stung me to retort: "We do not expect to outlive them. We regard them as final, and as indestructibly based in human nature itself."

"Ah," said the Altrurian with a delicate and caressing courtesy, "have I said something offensive?"

"Not at all," I hastened to answer. "It is not surprising that you do not get our point of view exactly. You will, by and by, and then, I think, you will see that it is the true one. We have found that the logic of our convictions could not be applied to the problem of domestic service. It is everywhere a very curious and perplexing problem. The simple old solution of the problem was to own your servants; but we found that this was not consistent with the spirit of our free institutions. As soon as it was abandoned the anomaly began. We had outlived the primitive period when the housekeeper worked with her domestics and they were her help, and were called so; and we had begun to have servants to do all the household work, and to call them so. This state of things never seemed right to some of our purest and best people. They fancied, as you seem to have done, that to compel people through their necessities to do your hateful drudgery, and to wound and shame them with a name which every American instinctively resents, was neither republican nor Christian. Some of our thinkers tried to mend matters by making their domestics a part of their families; and in the life of Emerson you'll find an amusing account of his attempt to have his servant eat at the same table with himself and his wife. It wouldn't work. He and his wife could stand it, but the servant couldn't."

I paused, for this was where the laugh ought to have come in. The Altrurian did not laugh, he merely asked: "Why?"

"Well, because the servant knew, if they didn't, that they were a whole world apart in their traditions, and were no more fit to associate than New Englanders and New Zealanders. In the mere matter of education——"

"But I thought you said that these young girls who wait at table here were teachers."

"Oh, I beg your pardon; I ought to have explained. By this time it had become impossible, as it now is, to get American girls to take service except on some such unusual terms as we have in a summer hotel; and the domestics were already ignorant foreigners, fit for nothing else. In such a place as this it isn't so bad. It is more as if the girls worked in a shop or a factory. They command their own time, in a measure; their hours are tolerably fixed, and they have each other's society. In a private family they would be subject to order at all times, and they would have no social life. They would be in the family, but not of it. American girls understand this, and so they won't go out to service in the usual way. Even in a summer hotel the relation has its odious aspects. The system of giving fees seems to me degrading to those who have to take them. To offer a student or a teacher a dollar for personal service—it isn't right, or I can't make it so. In fact, the whole thing is rather anomalous with us. The best that you can say of it is that it works, and we don't know what else to do."

"But I don't see yet," said the Altrurian, "just why domestic service is degrading in a country where all kinds of work are honored."

"Well, my dear fellow, I have done my best to explain. As I intimated before, we distinguish; and in the different kinds of labor we distinguish against domestic service. I dare say it is partly because of the loss of independence which it involves. People naturally despise a dependent."

"Why?" asked the Altrurian, with that innocence of his which I was beginning to find rather trying.

"Why?" I retorted. "Because it implies weakness."

"And is weakness considered despicable among you?" he pursued.

"In every community it is despised practically, if not theoretically," I tried to explain. "The great thing that America has done is to offer the race an opportunity: the opportunity for any man to rise above the rest, and to take the highest place, if he is able." I had always been proud of this fact, and I thought I had put it very well, but the Altrurian did not seem much impressed by it.

He said: "I do not see how it differs from any country of the past in that. But perhaps you mean that to rise carries with it an obligation to those below. 'If any is first among you, let him be your servant.' Is it something like that?"

"Well, it is not quite like that," I answered, remembering how very little our self-made men as a class had done for others. "Everyone is expected to look out for himself here. I fancy that there would be very little rising if men were expected to rise for the sake of others, in America. How is it with you in Altruria?" I demanded, hoping to get out of a certain discomfort I felt, in that way. "Do your risen men generally devote themselves to the good of the community after they get to the top?"

"There is no rising among us," he said, with what seemed a perception of the harsh spirit of my question; and he paused a moment before he asked in his turn, "How do men rise among you?"

"That would be rather a long story," I replied. "But putting it in the rough, I should say that they rose by their talents, their shrewdness, their ability to seize an advantage and turn it to their own account."

"And is that considered noble?"

"It is considered smart. It is considered at the worst far better than a dead level of equality. Are all men equal in Altruria? Are they all alike gifted or beautiful, or short or tall?"

"No, they are only equal in duties and in rights. But, as you said just now, that is a very long story. Are they equal in nothing here?"

"They are equal in opportunities."

"Ah!" breathed the Altrurian, "I am glad to hear that."

I began to feel a little uneasy, and I was not quite sure that this last assertion of mine would hold water. Everybody but ourselves had now left the dining room, and I saw the head waiter eying us impatiently. I pushed back my chair and said, "I'm sorry to seem to hurry you, but I should like to show you a very pretty sunset effect we have here before it is too dark. When we get back, I want to introduce you to a few of my friends. Of course, I needn't tell you that there is a good deal of curiosity about you, especially among the ladies."

"Yes, I found that the case in England, largely. It was the women who cared most to meet me. I understand that in America society is managed even more by women than it is in England."

"It's entirely in their hands," I said, with the satisfaction we all feel in the fact. "We have no other leisure class. The richest men among us are generally hard workers; devotion to business is the rule; but as soon as a man reaches the point where he can afford to pay for domestic service, his wife and daughters expect to be released from it to the cultivation of their minds and the enjoyment of social pleasures. It's quite right. That is what makes them so delightful to foreigners. You must have heard their praises chanted in England. The English find our men rather stupid, I believe; but they think our women are charming."

"Yes, I was told that the wives of their nobility were sometimes Americans," said the Altrurian. "The English think that you regard such marriages as a great honor, and that they are very gratifying to your national pride."

"Well, I suppose that is so in a measure," I confessed. "I imagine that it will not be long before the English aristocracy derives as largely from American millionaires as from kings' mistresses. Not," I added virtuously, "that we approve of aristocracy."

"No, I understand that," said the Altrurian. "I shall hope to get your point of view in this matter more distinctly by and by. As yet, I'm a little vague about it."

"I think I can gradually make it clear to you," I returned.

II

WE LEFT the hotel, and I began to walk my friend across the meadow toward the lake. I wished him to see the reflection of the afterglow in its still waters, with the noble lines of the mountain range that glassed itself there; the effect is one of the greatest charms of that lovely region, the sojourn of the sweetest summer in the world, and I am always impatient to show it to strangers.

We climbed the meadow wall and passed through a stretch of woods, to a path leading down to the shore, and as we loitered along in the tender gloom of the forest, the music of the hermit-thrushes rang all round us, like crystal bells, like silver flutes, like the drip of fountains, like the choiring of still-eyed cherubim. We stopped from time to time and listened, while the shy birds sang unseen in their covert of shadows; but we did not speak till we emerged from the trees and suddenly stood upon the naked knoll overlooking the lake.

Then I explained, "The woods used to come down to the shore here, and we had their mystery and music to the water's edge; but last winter the owner cut the timber off. It looks rather ragged now." I had to recognize the fact, for I saw the Altrurian staring about him over the clearing, in a kind of horror. It was a squalid ruin, a graceless desolation, which not even the pitying twilight could soften. The stumps showed their hideous mutilation everywhere; the brush had been burned, and the fires had scorched and blackened the lean soil of the hill slope, and blasted it with sterility. A few weak saplings, withered by the flames, drooped and straggled about; it would be a century before the forces of nature could repair the waste.

"You say the owner did this," said the Altrurian. "Who is the owner?"

"Well, it does seem too bad," I answered evasively. "There has been a good deal of feeling about it. The neighbors tried to buy him off before he began the destruction, for they knew the value of the woods as an attraction to summer-boarders; the city cottagers, of course, wanted to save them, and together they offered for the land pretty nearly as much as the timber was worth. But he had got it into his head that the land here by the lake would sell for building lots if it was cleared, and he could make money on that as well as on the trees; and so they had to go. Of course, one might say that he was deficient in public spirit, but I don't blame him, altogether."

"No," the Altrurian assented, somewhat to my surprise, I confess.

I resumed, "There was no one else to look after his interests, and it was not only his right but his duty to get the most he could for himself and his own, according to his best light. That is what I tell people when they fall foul of him for his want of public spirit."

"The trouble seems to be, then, in the system that obliges each man to be the guardian of his own interests. Is that what you blame?"

"No, I consider it a very perfect system. It is based upon individuality, and we believe that individuality is the principle that differences civilized men from savages, from the lower animals, and makes us a nation instead of a tribe or a herd. There isn't one of us, no matter how much he censured this man's want of public spirit, but would resent the slightest interference with his property rights. The woods were his; he had the right to do what he pleased with his own."

"Do I understand you that, in America, a man may do what is wrong with his own?"

"He may do anything with his own."

"To the injury of others?"

"Well, not in person or property. But he may hurt them in taste and sentiment as much as he likes. Can't a man do what he pleases with his own in Altruria?"

"No, he can only do right with his own."

"And if he tries to do wrong, or what the community thinks is wrong?"

"Then the community takes his own from him." Before I could think of anything to say to this he went on: "But I wish you would explain to me why it was left to this man's neighbors to try and get him to sell his portion of the landscape?"

"Why, bless my soul!" I exclaimed, "who else was there? You wouldn't have expected to take up a collection among the summer boarders?"

"That wouldn't have been so unreasonable; but I didn't mean that. Was there no provision for such an exigency in your laws? Wasn't the state empowered to buy him off at the full value of his timber and his land?"

"Certainly not," I replied. "That would be rank paternalism."

It began to get dark, and I suggested that we had better be going back to the hotel. The talk seemed already to have taken us away from all pleasure in the prospect; I said, as we found our way through the rich, balsam-scented twilight of the woods, where one joy-haunted thrush was still singing, "You know that in America the law is careful not to meddle with a man's private affairs, and we don't attempt to legislate personal virtue."

"But marriage," he said; "surely you have the institution of marriage?"

I was really annoyed at this. I returned sarcastically: "Yes, I am glad to say that there we can meet your expectation; we have marriage, not only consecrated by the church, but established and defended by the state. What has that to do with the question?"

"And you consider marriage," he pursued, "the citadel of morality, the fountain of all that is pure and good in your private life, the source of home and the image of heaven?"

"There are some marriages," I said with a touch of our national humor, "that do not quite fill the bill, but that is certainly our ideal of marriage."

"Then why do you say that you have not legislated personal virtue in America?" he asked. "You have laws, I believe, against theft and murder and slander and incest and perjury and drunkenness?"

"Why, certainly."

"Then it appears to me that you have legislated honesty, regard for human life, regard for character, abhorrence of unnatural vice, good faith and sobriety. I was told on the train coming up, by a gentleman who was shocked at the sight of a man beating his horse, that you even had laws against cruelty to animals."

"Yes, and I am happy to say that they are enforced to such a degree that a man cannot kill a cat cruelly without being punished for it." The Altrurian did not follow up his advantage, and I resolved not to be outdone in magnanimity. "Come, I will own that you have the best of me on those points. I must say you've trapped me very neatly, too; I can enjoy a thing of that kind when it's well done, and I frankly knock under. But I had in mind something altogether different when I spoke. I was thinking of those idealists who want to bind us hand and foot, and render us the slaves of a state where the most intimate relations of life shall be penetrated by legislation, and the very hearthstone shall be a tablet of laws."

"Isn't marriage a rather intimate relation of life?" asked the Altrurian. "And I understood that gentleman on the train to say that you had laws against cruelty to children and societies established to see them enforced. You don't consider such laws an invasion of the home, do you, or a violation of its immunities? I imagine," he went on, "that the difference between your civilization and ours is only one of degree, after all, and that America and Altruria are really one at heart."

I thought his compliment a bit hyperbolical, but I saw that it was honestly meant, and as we Americans are first of all patriots, and vain for our country before we are vain for ourselves, I was not proof against the flattery it conveyed to me civically if not personally.

We were now drawing near the hotel, and I felt a certain glow of pleasure in its gay effect, on the pretty knoll where it stood. In its artless and accidental architecture it was not unlike one of our immense coastwise steamboats. The twilight had thickened to dusk, and the edifice was brilliantly lighted with electrics, story above story, which streamed into the gloom around like the lights of saloon and stateroom. The corner of wood making into the meadow hid the station; there was no other building in sight; the hotel seemed riding at anchor on the swell of a placid sea. I was going to call the Altrurian's attention to this fanciful resemblance when I remembered that he had not been in our country long enough to have seen a Fall River boat, and I made toward the house without wasting the comparison upon him. But I treasured it up in my own mind, intending some day to make a literary use of it.

The guests were sitting in friendly groups about the piazzas or in rows against the walls, the ladies with their gossip and the gentlemen with their cigars. The night had fallen cool after a hot day, and they all had the effect of having cast off care with the burden of the week that was past and to be steeping themselves in the innocent and simple enjoyment of the hour. They were mostly middle-aged married folk, but some were old enough to have sons and daughters among the young people who went and came in a long, wandering promenade of the piazzas, or wove themselves through the waltz past the open windows of the great parlor; the music seemed one with the light that streamed far out on the lawn flanking the piazzas. Everyone was well dressed and comfortable and at peace, and I felt that our hotel was in some sort a microcosm of the republic.

We involuntarily paused, and I heard the Altrurian murmur, "Charming, charming! This is really delightful!"

"Yes, isn't it?" I returned, with a glow of pride. "Our hotel here is a type of the summer hotel everywhere; it's characteristic in not having anything characteristic about it; and I rather like the notion of the people in it being so much like the people in all the others that you would feel yourself at home wherever you met such a company in such a house. All over the country, north and south, wherever you find a group of hills or a pleasant bit of water or a stretch of coast, you'll find some such refuge as this for our weary toilers. We began to discover some time ago that it would not do to cut open the goose that laid our golden eggs, even if it looked like an eagle, and kept on perching on our banners just as if nothing had happened. We discovered that, if we continued to kill ourselves with hard work, there would be no Americans pretty soon."

The Altrurian laughed. "How delightfully you put it! How quaint! How picturesque! Excuse me, but I can't help expressing my pleasure in it. Our own humor is so very different."

"Ah?" I said; "what is your humor like?"

"I could hardly tell you, I'm afraid; I've never been much of a humorist myself."

Again a cold doubt of something ironical in the man went through me, but I had no means of verifying it, and so I simply remained silent, waiting for him to prompt me if he wished to know anything further about our national transformation from bees perpetually busy into butterflies occasionally idle. "And when you had made that discovery?" he suggested.

"Why, we're nothing if not practical, you know, and as soon as we made that discovery we stopped killing ourselves and invented the summer resort. There are very few of our business or professional men, now, who don't take their four or five weeks' vacation. Their wives go off early in the summer, and if they go to some resort within three or four hours of the city, the men leave town Saturday afternoon and run out, or come up, and spend Sunday with their families. For thirty-eight hours or so, a hotel like this is a nest of happy homes."

"That is admirable," said the Altrurian. "You are truly a practical people. The ladies come early in the summer, you say?"

"Yes, sometimes in the beginning of June."

"What do they come for?" asked the Altrurian.

"What for? Why, for rest!" I retorted with some little temper.

"But I thought you told me awhile ago that as soon as a husband could afford it he relieved his wife and daughters from all household work."

"So he does."

"Then what do the ladies wish to rest from?"

"From care. It is not work alone that kills. They are not

relieved from household care even when they are relieved from household work. There is nothing so killing as household care. Besides, the sex seems to be born tired. To be sure, there are some observers of our life who contend that with the advance of athletics among our ladies, with boating and bathing, and lawn-tennis and mountain climbing and freedom from care, and these long summers of repose, our women are likely to become as superior to the men physically as they now are intellectually. It is all right. We should like to see it happen. It would be part of the national joke."

"Oh, have you a national joke?" asked the Altrurian. "But, of course! You have so much humor. I wish you could give me some notion of it."

"Well, it is rather damaging to any joke to explain it," I replied, "and your only hope of getting at ours is to live into it. One feature of it is the confusion of foreigners at the sight of our men's willingness to subordinate themselves to our women."

"Oh, I don't find that very bewildering," said the Altrurian. "It seems to me a generous and manly trait of the American character. I'm proud to say that it is one of the points at which your civilization and our own touch. There can be no doubt that the influence of women in your public affairs must be of the greatest advantage to you; it has been so with us."

I turned and stared at him, but he remained insensible to my astonishment, perhaps because it was now too dark for him to see it. "Our women have no influence in public affairs," I said quietly, after a moment.

"They haven't? Is it possible? But didn't I understand you to imply just now that your women were better educated than your men?"

"Well, I suppose that, taking all sorts and conditions among us, the women are as a rule better schooled, if not better educated."

"Then, apart from the schooling, they are not more cultivated?"

"In a sense you might say they were. They certainly go in for a lot of things: art and music, and Browning and the drama, and foreign travel and psychology, and political economy and heaven knows what all. They have more leisure for it; they have all the leisure there is, in fact; our young men have to go into business. I suppose you may say our women are more cultivated than our men; yes, I think there's no questioning that. They are the great readers among us. We poor devils of authors would be badly off if it were not for our women. In fact, no author could make a reputation among us without them. American literature exists because American women appreciate it and love it."

"But surely your men read books?"

"Some of them; not many, comparatively. You will often hear a complacent ass of a husband and father say to an author: 'My wife and daughters know your books, but I can't find time for anything but the papers nowadays. I skim them over at breakfast, or when I'm going in to business on the train.' He isn't the least ashamed to say that he reads nothing but the news-papers."

"Then you think that it would be better for him to read books?"

"Well, in the presence of four or five thousand journalists with drawn scalping knives I should not like to say so. Besides, modesty forbids."

"No, but really," the Altrurian persisted, "you think that the literature of a book is more carefully pondered than the literature of a daily newspaper?"

"I suppose even the four or five thousand journalists with drawn scalping knives would hardly deny that."

"And it stands to reason, doesn't it, that the habitual reader of carefully pondered literature ought to be more thoughtful than the readers of literature which is not carefully pondered, and which they merely skim over on their way to business?"

"I believe we began by assuming the superior culture of our women, didn't we? You'll hardly find an American that isn't proud of it."

"Then," said the Altrurian, "if your women are generally

better schooled than your men, and more cultivated and more
thoughtful, and are relieved of household work in such great
measure, and even of domestic cares, why have they no part in
your public affairs?"

I laughed, for I thought I had my friend at last. "For the best
of all possible reasons: they don't want it."

"Ah, that's no reason," he returned. "Why don't they want it?"

"Really," I said, out of all patience, "I think I must let you
ask the ladies themselves," and I turned and moved again
toward the hotel, but the Altrurian gently detained me.

"Excuse me," he began.

"No, no," I said:

> " 'The feast is set, the guests are met,
>   Mayst hear the merry din.'

Come in and see the young people dance!"

"Wait," he entreated, "tell me a little more about the old
people first. This digression about the ladies has been very
interesting, but I thought you were going to speak of the men
here. Who are they, or rather, what are they?"

"Why, as I said before, they are all business men and professional men; people who spend their lives in studies and counting
rooms and offices, and have come up here for a few weeks or a
few days of well-earned repose. They are of all kinds of occupations: they are lawyers and doctors and clergymen and
merchants and brokers and bankers. There's hardly any calling
you won't find represented among them. As I was thinking just
now, our hotel is a sort of microcosm of the American republic."

"I am most fortunate in finding you here, where I can avail
myself of your intelligence in making my observations of your
life under such advantageous circumstances. It seems to me that
with your help I might penetrate the fact of American life, possess myself of the mystery of your national joke, without stirring
beyond the piazza of your hospitable hotel," said my friend. I
doubted it, but one does not lightly put aside a compliment like
that to one's intelligence, and I said I should be very happy to

be of use to him. He thanked me, and said, "Then, to begin with, I understand that these gentlemen are here because they are all overworked."

"Of course. You can have no conception of how hard our business men and our professional men work. I suppose there is nothing like it anywhere else in the world. But, as I said before, we are beginning to find that we cannot burn the candle at both ends and have it last long. So we put one end out for a little while every summer. Still, there are frightful wrecks of men strewn all along the course of our prosperity, wrecks of mind and body. Our insane asylums are full of madmen who have broken under the tremendous strain, and every country in Europe abounds in our dyspeptics." I was rather proud of this terrible fact; there is no doubt but we Americans are proud of over-working ourselves; heaven knows why!

The Altrurian murmured, "Awful! Shocking!" but I thought somehow he had not really followed me very attentively in my celebration of our national violation of the laws of life and its consequences. "I am glad," he went on, "that your business men and professional men are beginning to realize the folly and wickedness of overwork. Shall I find some of your other weary workers here, too?"

"What other weary workers?" I asked in turn, for I imagined I had gone over pretty much the whole list.

"Why," said the Altrurian, "your mechanics and day laborers, your iron moulders and glass blowers, your miners and farmers, your printers and mill operatives, your trainmen and quarry hands. Or do they prefer to go to resorts of their own?"

III

IT WAS NOT easy to make sure of such innocence as prompted this inquiry of my Altrurian friend. The doubt whether he could really be in earnest was something that I had already felt; and it was destined to beset me, as it did now, again and again. My first thought was that of course he was trying a bit of cheap irony on me, a mixture of the feeble sarcasm and false sentiment that makes us smile when we find it in the philippics of the industrial agitators. For a moment I did not know but I had fallen victim to a walking-delegate on his vacation, who was employing his summer leisure in going about the country in the guise of a traveller from Altruria, and foisting himself upon people who would have had nothing to do with him in his real character. But in another moment I perceived that this was impossible. I could not suppose that the friend who had introduced him to me would be capable of seconding so poor a joke, and besides I could not imagine why a walking-delegate should wish to address his clumsy satire to me particularly. For the present, at least, there was nothing for it but to deal with this inquiry as if it were made in good faith, and in the pursuit of useful information. It struck me as grotesque; but it would not have been decent to treat it as if it were so. I was obliged to regard it seriously, and so I decided to shirk it.

"Well," I said, "that opens up rather a large field, which lies somewhat outside of the province of my own activities. You know, I am a writer of romantic fiction, and my time is so fully occupied in manipulating the destinies of the good old-fashioned hero and heroine, and trying always to make them end in a happy marriage, that I have hardly had a chance to look much into the lives of agriculturists or artisans; and to tell you the truth I don't know what they do with their leisure. I'm pretty certain, though, you won't meet any of them in this hotel; they couldn't afford it, and I fancy they would find themselves out of their element among our guests. We respect them thoroughly; every American does; and we know that the prosperity of the country rests with them; we have a theory that they are politically sovereign, but we see very little of them, and we don't associate with them. In fact, our cultivated people have so little interest in them socially that they don't like to meet them, even in fiction; they prefer refined and polished ladies and gentlemen, whom they can have some sympathy with; and I always go to the upper classes for my types. It won't do to suppose, though, that we are indifferent to the working-classes in their place. Their condition is being studied a good deal just now, and there are several persons here who will be able to satisfy your curiosity on the points you have made, I think. I will introduce you to them."

The Altrurian did not try to detain me this time. He said he should be very glad indeed to meet my friends, and I led the way toward a little group at the corner of the piazza. They were men whom I particularly liked, for one reason or another; they were intelligent and open-minded, and they were thoroughly American. One was a banker; another was a minister; there was a lawyer, and there was a doctor; there was a professor of political economy in one of our colleges; and there was a retired manufacturer—I do not know what he used to manufacture: cotton or iron, or something like that. They all rose politely as I came up with my Altrurian, and I fancied in them a sensation of expectancy created by the rumor of his eccentric behavior which must have spread through the hotel. But they controlled this if they had it, and I could see, as the light fell upon his face from a spray of electrics on the nearest pillar, that sort of liking kindle in theirs which I had felt myself at first sight of him.

I said, "Gentlemen, I wish to introduce my friend, Mr. Homos," and then I presented them severally to him by name. We all sat down, and I explained: "Mr. Homos is from Altruria. He is visiting our country for the first time, and is greatly interested in the working of our institutions. He has been asking me some rather hard questions about certain phases of our civilization; and the fact is that I have launched him upon you because I don't feel quite able to cope with him."

They all laughed civilly at this sally of mine, but the professor asked, with a sarcasm that I thought I hardly merited, "What point in our polity can be obscure to the author of 'Glove and Gauntlet' and 'Airs and Graces'?"

They all laughed again, not so civilly, I felt, and then the banker asked my friend, "Is it long since you left Altruria?"

"It seems a great while ago," the Altrurian answered, "but it is really only a few weeks."

"You came by way of England, I suppose?"

"Yes; there is no direct line to America," said the Altrurian.

"That seems rather odd," I ventured, with some patriotic grudge.

"Oh, the English have direct lines everywhere," the banker instructed me.

"The tariff has killed our shipbuilding," said the professor. No one took up this firebrand, and the professor added, "Your name is Greek, isn't it, Mr. Homos?"

"Yes; we are of one of the early Hellenic families," said the Altrurian.

"And do you think," asked the lawyer, who, like most lawyers, was a lover of romance, and was well read in legendary lore especially, "that there is any reason for supposing that Altruria is identical with the fabled Atlantis?"

"No, I can't say that I do. We have no traditions of a submergence of the continent, and there are only the usual evidences of a glacial epoch which you find everywhere to support such a theory. Besides, our civilization is strictly Christian, and dates back to no earlier period than that of the first Christian commune after Christ. It is a matter of history with us that one of these communists, when they were dispersed, brought the gospel to our continent; he was cast away on our eastern coast on his way to Britain."

"Yes, we know that," the minister intervened; "but it is perfectly astonishing that an island so large as Altruria should have been lost to the knowledge of the rest of the world ever since the beginning of our era. You would hardly think that there was a space of the ocean's surface a mile square which had not been traversed by a thousand keels since Columbus sailed westward."

"No, you wouldn't. And I wish," the doctor suggested in his turn, "that Mr. Homos would tell us something about his country, instead of asking us about ours."

"Yes," I coincided, "I'm sure we should all find it a good deal easier. At least I should; but I brought our friend up in the hope that the professor would like nothing better than to train a battery of hard facts upon a defenceless stranger." Since the professor had given me that little stab, I was rather anxious to see how he would handle the desire for information in the Altrurian which I had found so prickly.

This turned the laugh on the professor, and he pretended to be as curious about Altruria as the rest, and said he would rather hear of it. But the Altrurian said: "I hope you will excuse me. Sometime I shall be glad to talk of Altruria as long as you like; or if you will come to us, I shall be still happier to show you many things that I couldn't make you understand at a distance. But I am in America to learn, not to teach, and I hope you will have patience with my ignorance. I begin to be afraid that it is so great as to seem a little incredible. I have fancied in my friend here," he went on, with a smile toward me, "a suspicion that I was not entirely single in some of the inquiries I have made, but that I had some ulterior motive, some wish to censure or satirize."

"Oh, not at all!" I protested, for it was not polite to admit a conjecture so accurate. "We are so well satisfied with our condition that we have nothing but pity for the darkened mind of the foreigner, though we believe in it fully: we are used to the English tourist."

My friends laughed, and the Altrurian continued: "I am very glad to hear it, for I feel myself at a peculiar disadvantage among you. I am not only a foreigner, but I am so alien to you in all the traditions and habitudes that I find it very difficult to get upon common ground with you. Of course I know theoretically what you are, but to realize it practically is another thing. I had read so much about America and understood so little that I could not rest without coming to see for myself. Some of the apparent contradictions were so colossal"—

"We have everything on a large scale here," said the banker, breaking off the ash of his cigar with the end of his little-finger, "and we rather pride ourselves on the size of our inconsistencies even. I know something of the state of things in Altruria, and, to be frank with you, I will say that it seems to me preposterous. I should say it was impossible, if it were not an accomplished fact; but I always feel bound to recognize the thing done. You have hitched your wagon to a star and you have made the star go; there is never any trouble with wagons, but stars are not easily broken to harness, and you have managed to get yours well in hand. As I said, I don't believe in you, but I respect you."

I thought this charming, myself—perhaps because it stated my own mind about Altruria so exactly and in terms so just and generous.

"Pretty good," said the doctor, in a murmur of satisfaction, at my ear, "for a bloated bond-holder."

"Yes," I whispered back, "I wish I had said it. What an American way of putting it! Emerson would have liked it himself. After all, *he* was our prophet."

"He must have thought so from the way we kept stoning him," said the doctor, with a soft laugh.

"Which of our contradictions," asked the banker, in the same tone of gentle bonhomie, "has given you and our friend pause, just now?"

The Altrurian answered after a moment: "I am not sure that it is a contradiction, for as yet I have not ascertained the facts I was seeking. Our friend was telling me of the great change that had taken place in regard to work, and the increased leisure that your professional people are now allowing themselves; and I was asking him where your workingmen spent their leisure."

He went over the list of those he had specified, and I hung my head in shame and pity; it really had such an effect of mawkish sentimentality. But my friends received it in the best possible way. They did not laugh; they heard him out, and then they quietly deferred to the banker, who made answer for us all:

"Well, I can be almost as brief as the historian of Iceland in his chapter on snakes: those people have no leisure to spend."

"Except when they go out on a strike," said the manufacturer, with a certain grim humor of his own; I never heard anything more dramatic than the account he once gave of the way he broke up a labor-union. "I have seen a good many of them at leisure then."

"Yes," the doctor chimed in, "and in my younger days, when I necessarily had a good deal of charity-practice, I used to find them at leisure when they were 'laid off.' It always struck me as such a pretty euphemism. It seemed to minify the harm of the thing so. It seemed to take all the hunger and cold and sickness out of the fact. To be simply 'laid off' was so different from losing your work and having to face beggary or starvation!"

"Those people," said the professor, "never put anything by. They are wasteful and improvident, almost to a man; and they learn nothing by experience, though they know as well as we do that it is simply a question of demand and supply, and that the day of overproduction is sure to come, when their work must stop unless the men that give them work are willing to lose money."

"And I've seen them lose it, sometimes, rather than shut down," the manufacturer remarked; "lose it hand over hand, to keep the men at work; and then as soon as the tide turned the men would strike for higher wages. You have no idea of the ingratitude of those people." He said this towards the minister, as if he did not wish to be thought hard—and in fact he was a very kindly man.

"Yes," replied the minister, "that is one of the most sinister features of the situation. They seem really to regard their employers as their enemies. I don't know how it will end."

"I know how it would end if I had my way," said the professor. "There wouldn't be any labor-unions, and there wouldn't be any strikes."

"That is all very well," said the lawyer, from that judicial mind which I always liked in him, "as far as the strikes are concerned, but I don't understand that the abolition of the unions would affect the impersonal process of laying-off. The law of demand and supply I respect as much as any one—it's something like the constitution; but all the same I should object extremely to have my income stopped by it every now and then.

I'm probably not so wasteful as a workingman generally is; still I haven't laid by enough to make it a matter of indifference to me whether my income went on or not. Perhaps the professor has." The professor did not say, and we all took leave to laugh. The lawyer concluded, "I don't see how those fellows stand it."

"They don't, all of them," said the doctor. "Or their wives and children don't. Some of them die."

"I wonder," the lawyer pursued, "what has become of the good old American fact that there is always work for those who are willing to work? I notice that wherever 5000 men strike in the forenoon, there are 5000 men to take their places in the after-noon—and not men who are turning their hands to something new, but men who are used to doing the very thing the strikers have done."

"That is one of the things that teach the futility of strikes," the professor made haste to interpose, as if he had not quite liked to appear averse to the interests of the workingman; no one likes to do that. "If there were anything at all to be hoped from them it would be another matter."

"Yes, but that isn't the point, quite," said the lawyer.

"By the way, what is the point?" I asked, with my humorous lightness.

"Why, I supposed," said the banker, "it was the question how the working-classes amused their elegant leisure. But it seems to be almost anything else."

We all applauded the neat touch, but the Altrurian eagerly entreated: "No, no! never mind that, now. That is a matter of comparatively little interest. I would so much rather know some-thing about the status of the workingman among you."

"Do you mean his political status? It's that of every other citizen."

"I don't mean that. I suppose that in America you have learned, as we have in Altruria, that equal political rights are only means to an end, and as an end have no value or reality. I meant the economic status of the workingman, and his social status."

I do not know why we were so long girding up our loins to meet this simple question. I myself could not have hopefully undertaken to answer it; but the others were each in their way men of affairs, and practically acquainted with the facts, except perhaps the professor; but he had devoted a great deal of thought to them, and ought to have been qualified to make some sort of response. But even he was silent; and I had a vague feeling that they were all somehow reluctant to formulate their knowledge, as if it were uncomfortable or discreditable. The banker continued to smoke quietly on for a moment; then he suddenly threw his cigar away.

"I like to free my mind of cant," he said, with a short laugh, "when I can afford it, and I propose to cast all sorts of American cant out of it, in answering your question. The economic status of the workingman among us is essentially the same as that of the workingman all over the civilized world. You will find plenty of people here, especially about election time, to tell you differently, but they will not be telling you the truth, though a great many of them think they are. In fact, I suppose most Americans honestly believe because we have a republican form of government, and manhood-suffrage, and so on, that our economic conditions are peculiar, and that our workingman has a status higher and better than that of the workingman anywhere else. But he has nothing of the kind. His circumstances are better, and provisionally his wages are higher, but it is only a question of years or decades when his circumstances will be the same and his wages the same as the European workingman's. There is nothing in our conditions to prevent this."

"Yes, I understood from our friend here," said the Altrurian, nodding toward me, "that you had broken only with the political tradition of Europe, in your revolution; and he has explained to me that you do not hold all kinds of labor in equal esteem; but"—

"What kind of labor did he say we did hold in esteem?" asked the banker.

"Why, I understood him to say that if America meant anything at all it meant the honor of work, but that you distinguished and did not honor some kinds of work so much as others: for instance, domestic service, or personal attendance of any kind."

The banker laughed again. "Oh, he drew the line there, did he? Well, we all have to draw the line somewhere. Our friend is a novelist, and I will tell you in strict confidence that the line he has drawn is imaginary. We don't honor any kind of work any more than any other people. If a fellow gets up, the papers make a great ado over his having been a wood-chopper, or a bobbin-boy, or something of that kind, but I doubt if the fellow himself likes it; he doesn't if he's got any sense. The rest of us feel that it's infra dig., and hope nobody will find out that we ever worked with our hands for a living. I'll go farther," said the banker, with the effect of whistling prudence down the wind, "and I will challenge any of you to gainsay me from his own experience or observation. How does esteem usually express itself? When we wish to honor a man, what do we do?"

"Ask him to dinner," said the lawyer.

"Exactly. We offer him some sort of social recognition. Well, as soon as a fellow gets up, if he gets up high enough, we offer him some sort of social recognition; in fact, all sorts; but upon condition that he has left off working with his hands for a living. We forgive all you please to his past on account of the present. But there isn't a workingman, I venture to say, in any city, or town, or even large village, in the whole length and breadth of the United States who has any social recognition, if he is still working at his trade. I don't mean, merely, that he is excluded from rich and fashionable society, but from the society of the average educated and cultivated people. I'm not saying he is fit for it; but I don't care how intelligent and agreeable he might be—and some of them are astonishingly intelligent, and so agreeable in their tone of mind and their original way of looking at things that I like nothing better than to talk with them—all of our invisible fences are up against him."

The minister said: "I wonder if that sort of exclusiveness is quite natural? Children seem to feel no sort of social difference among themselves."

"We can hardly go to children for a type of social order," the professor suggested.

"True," the minister meekly admitted. "But somehow there is a protest in us somewhere against these arbitrary distinctions; something that questions whether they are altogether right. We know that they must be, and always have been, and always will be, and yet—well, I will confess it—I never feel at peace when I face them."

"Oh," said the banker, "if you come to the question of right and wrong, that is another matter. I don't say it's right. I'm not discussing that question; though I'm certainly not proposing to level the fences; I should be the last to take my own down. I say simply that you are no more likely to meet a workingman in American society than you are to meet a colored man. Now you can judge," he ended, turning directly to the Altrurian, "how much we honor labor. And I hope I have indirectly satisfied your curiosity as to the social status of the workingman among us."

We were all silent. Perhaps the others were occupied like myself in trying to recall some instance of a workingman whom they had met in society, and perhaps we said nothing because we all failed.

The Altrurian spoke at last.

"You have been so very full and explicit that I feel as if it were almost unseemly to press any further inquiry; but I should very much like to know how your workingmen bear this social exclusion."

"I'm sure I can't say," returned the banker. "A man does not care much to get into society until he has something to eat, and how to get that is always the first question with the workingman."

"But you wouldn't like it yourself?"

"No, certainly, I shouldn't like it myself. I shouldn't complain of not being asked to people's houses, and the workingmen don't; you can't do that; but I should feel it an incalculable loss. We may laugh at the emptiness of society, or pretend to be sick of it, but there is no doubt that society is the flower of civilization, and to be shut out from it is to be denied the best privilege of a civilized man. There are society-women—we have all met them —whose graciousness and refinement of presence are something of incomparable value; it is more than a liberal education to have been admitted to it, but it is as inaccessible to the working-man as—what shall I say? The thing is too grotesquely impossible for any sort of comparison. Merely to conceive of its possibility is something that passes a joke; it is a kind of offence."

Again we were silent.

"I don't know," the banker continued, "how the notion of our social equality originated, but I think it has been fostered mainly by the expectation of foreigners, who argued it from our political equality. As a matter of fact, it never existed, except in our poorest and most primitive communities, in the pioneer days of the West, and among the gold-hunters of California. It was not dreamt of in our colonial society, either in Virginia, or Pennsylvania, or New York, or Massachusetts; and the fathers of the republic, who were mostly slaveholders, were practically as stiffnecked aristocrats as any people of their day. We have not a political aristocracy, that is all; but there is as absolute a division between the orders of men, and as little love, in this country as in any country on the globe. The severance of the man who works for his living with his hands from the man who does not work for his living with his hands is so complete, and apparently so final, that nobody even imagines anything else, not even in fiction. Or, how is that?" he asked, turning to me. "Do you fellows still put the intelligent, high-spirited, handsome young artisan who wins the millionaire's daughter into your books? I used sometimes to find him there."

"You might still find him in the fiction of the weekly story-papers; but," I was obliged to own, "he would not go down with my readers. Even in the story-paper fiction he would leave off working as soon as he married the millionaire's daughter, and go to Europe, or he would stay here and become a social leader, but he would not receive workingmen in his gilded halls."

The others rewarded my humor with a smile, but the banker

said: "Then I wonder you were not ashamed of filling our friend up with that stuff about our honoring some kinds of labor. It is true that we don't go about openly and explicitly despising any kind of honest toil—people don't do that anywhere now; but we contemn it in terms quite as unmistakable. The workingman acquiesces as completely as anybody else. He does not remain a workingman a moment longer than he can help; and after he gets up, if he is weak enough to be proud of having been one it is because he feels that his low origin is a proof of his prowess in rising to the top against unusual odds. I don't suppose there is a man in the whole civilized world—outside of Altruria, of course —who is proud of working at a trade, except the shoemaker Tolstoi, and he is a count, and he does not make very good shoes."

We all laughed again; those shoes of Count Tolstoi's are always such an infallible joke. The Altrurian, however, was cocked and primed with another question; he instantly exploded it. "But are all the workingmen in America eager to rise above their condition? Is there none willing to remain among the mass because the rest could not rise with him, and from the hope of yet bringing labor to honor?"

The banker answered: "I never heard of any. No, the American ideal is not to change the conditions for all, but for each to rise above the rest if he can."

"Do you think it is really so bad as that?" asked the minister timidly.

The banker answered: "Bad? Do you call that bad? I thought it was very good. But good or bad, I don't think you'll find it deniable, if you look into the facts. There may be workingmen willing to remain so for other workingmen's sake, but I have never met any—perhaps because the workingman never goes into society."

The unfailing question of the Altrurian broke the silence which ensued: "Are there many of your workingmen who are intelligent and agreeable—of the type you mentioned a moment since?"

"Perhaps," said the banker, "I had better refer you to one of our friends here, who has had a great deal more to do with them than I have. He is a manufacturer and he has had to do with all kinds of work-people."

"Yes, for my sins," the manufacturer assented; and he added, "They are often confoundedly intelligent, though I haven't often found them very agreeable, either in their tone of mind or their original way of looking at things."

The banker amiably acknowledged his thrust, and the Altrurian asked, "Ah, they are opposed to your own?"

"Well, we have the same trouble here that you must have heard of in England. As you know now that the conditions are the same here, you won't be surprised at the fact."

"But the conditions," the Altrurian pursued; "do you expect them always to continue the same?"

"Well, I don't know," said the manufacturer. "We can't expect them to change of themselves, and I shouldn't know how to change them. It was expected that the rise of the trusts and the syndicates would break the unions, but somehow they haven't. The situation remains the same. The unions are not cutting one another's throats, now, any more than we are. The war is on a larger scale—that's all."

"Then let me see," said the Altrurian, "whether I clearly understand the situation, as regards the workingman in America. He is dependent upon the employer for his chance to earn a living, and he is never sure of this. He may be thrown out of work by his employer's disfavor or disaster, and his willingness to work goes for nothing; there is no public provision of work for him; there is nothing to keep him from want, nor the prospect of anything."

"We are all in the same boat," said the professor.

"But some of us have provisioned ourselves rather better and can generally weather it through till we are picked up," the lawyer put in.

"I am always saying the workingman is improvident," returned the professor.

"There are the charities," the minister suggested.

"But his economical status," the Altrurian pursued, "is in a state of perpetual uncertainty, and to save himself in some measure he has organized, and so has constituted himself a danger to the public peace?"

"A very great danger," said the professor.

"I guess we can manage him," the manufacturer remarked.

"And socially he is non-existent?"

The Altrurian turned with this question to the banker, who said, "He is certainly not in society."

"Then," said my guest, "if the workingmen's wages are provisionally so much better here than in Europe, why should they be discontented? What is the real cause of their discontent?"

I have always been suspicious, in the company of practical men, of an atmosphere of condescension to men of my calling, if nothing worse. I fancy they commonly regard artists of all kinds as a sort of harmless eccentrics, and that literary people they look upon as something droll, as weak and soft, as not quite right. I believed that this particular group, indeed, was rather abler to conceive of me as a rational person than most others, but I knew that if even they had expected me to be as reasonable as themselves they would not have been greatly disappointed if I were not; and it seemed to me that I had put myself wrong with them in imparting to the Altrurian that romantic impression that we hold labor in honor here. I had really thought so, but I could not say so now, and I wished to retrieve myself somehow. I wished to show that I was a practical man, too, and so I made answer: "What is the cause of the workingman's discontent? It is very simple: the walking-delegate."

IV

I suppose I could not have fairly claimed any great originality for my notion that the walking-delegate was the cause of the labor troubles: he is regularly assigned as the reason of a strike in the newspapers, and is reprobated for his evil agency by the editors, who do not fail to read the workingmen many solemn lessons, and fervently warn them against him, as soon as the strike begins to go wrong—as it nearly always does. I understand from them that the walking-delegate is an irresponsible tyrant, who emerges from the mystery that habitually hides him and from time to time orders a strike in mere rancor of spirit and plenitude of power, and then leaves the workingmen and their families to suffer the consequences, while he goes off somewhere and rolls in the lap of luxury, careless of the misery he has created. Between his debauches of vicious idleness and his accesses of baleful activity he is employed in poisoning the mind of the workingman against his real interests and real friends. This is perfectly easy, because the American workingman, though singularly shrewd and sensible in other respects, is the victim of an unaccountable obliquity of vision which keeps him from seeing his real interests and real friends—or at least from knowing them when he sees them.

There could be no doubt, I thought, in the mind of any reasonable person that the walking-delegate was the source of the discontent among our proletariat, and I alleged him with a confidence which met the approval of the professor, apparently, for he nodded, as if to say that I had hit the nail on the head this time; and the minister seemed to be freshly impressed with a notion that could not be new to him. The lawyer and the doctor were silent, as if waiting for the banker to speak again; but he was silent, too. The manufacturer, to my chagrin, broke into a laugh. "I'm afraid," he said, with a sardonic levity which surprised me, "you'll have to go a good deal deeper than the walking-delegate. He's a symptom; he isn't the disease. The thing keeps on and on, and it seems to be always about wages; but it isn't about wages at the bottom. Some of those fellows know it and some of them don't, but the real discontent is with the whole system, with the nature of things. I had a curious revelation on that point the last time I tried to deal with my men as a union. They were always bothering me about this and about that, and there was no end to the bickering. I yielded point after point, but it didn't make any difference. It seemed as if the more I gave

the more they asked. At last I made up my mind to try to get at
the real inwardness of the matter, and I didn't wait for their
committee to come to me—I sent for their leading man, and said
I wanted to have it out with him. He wasn't a bad fellow, and
when I got at him, man to man that way, I found he had sense,
and he had ideas—it's no use pretending those fellows are fools;
he had thought about his side of the question, any way. I said:
'Now what does it all mean? Do you want the earth, or don't you?
When is it going to end?' I offered him something to take, but
he said he didn't drink, and we compromised on cigars. 'Now
when is it going to end?' said I, and I pressed it home, and
wouldn't let him fight off from the point. 'Do you mean when it
is all going to end?' said he. 'Yes,' said I, 'all. I'm sick of it. If
there's any way out I'd like to know it.' 'Well,' said he, 'I'll tell
you, if you want to know. It's all going to end when you get the
same amount of money for the same amount of work as we do.'"

We all laughed uproariously. The thing was deliciously
comical; and nothing, I thought, attested the Altrurian's want
of humor like his failure to appreciate this joke. He did not even
smile in asking, "And what did you say?"

"Well," returned the manufacturer, with cosy enjoyment, "I
asked him if the men would take the concern and run it themselves." We laughed again; this seemed even better than the
other joke. "But he said 'No;' they would not like to do that.
And then I asked him just what they would like, if they could
have their own way, and he said they would like to have me run
the business, and all share alike. I asked him what was the sense
of that, and why if I could do something that all of them put
together couldn't do I shouldn't be paid more than all of them
put together; and he said that if a man did his best he ought to
be paid as much as the best man. I asked him if that was the
principle their union was founded on, and he said 'Yes,' that
the very meaning of their union was the protection of the weak
by the strong, and the equalization of earnings among all who
do their best."

We waited for the manufacturer to go on, but he made a

dramatic pause at this point, as if to let it sink into our minds; and he did not speak until the Altrurian prompted him with the question, "And what did you finally do?"

"I saw there was only one way out for me, and I told the fellow I did not think I could do business on that principle. We parted friends, but the next Saturday I locked them out, and smashed their union. They came back, most of them—they had to—but I've treated with them ever since 'as individuals'."

"And they're much better off in your hands than they were in the union," said the professor.

"I don't know about that," said the manufacturer, "but I'm sure I am."

We laughed with him, all but the minister, whose mind seemed to have caught upon some other point, and who sat absently by.

"And is it your opinion, from what you know of the working-men generally, that they all have this twist in their heads?" the professor asked.

"They have, until they begin to rise. Then they get rid of it mighty soon. Let a man save something—enough to get a house of his own, and take a boarder or two, and perhaps have a little money at interest—and he sees the matter in another light."

"Do you think he sees it more clearly?" asked the minister.

"He sees it differently."

"What do you think?" the minister pursued, turning to the lawyer. "You are used to dealing with questions of justice"—

"Rather more with questions of law, I'm afraid," the other returned pleasantly, putting his feet together before him and looking down at them, in a way he had. "But still, I have a great interest in questions of justice, and I confess that I find a certain wild equity in this principle, which I see nobody could do business on. It strikes me as idyllic—it's a touch of real poetry in the rough-and-tumble prose of our economic life."

He referred this to me as something I might appreciate in my quality of literary man, and I responded in my quality of practical man, "There's certainly more rhyme than reason in it."

He turned again to the minister:

"I suppose the ideal of the Christian state is the family?"

"I hope so," said the minister, with the gratitude that I have seen people of his cloth show when men of the world conceded premises which the world usually contests; it has seemed to me pathetic.

"And if that is the case, why the logic of the postulate is that the prosperity of the weakest is the sacred charge and highest happiness of all the stronger. But the law has not recognized any such principle, in economics at least, and if the labor unions are based upon it they are outlaw, so far as any hope of enforcing it is concerned; and it is bad for men to feel themselves outlaw. How is it," the lawyer continued, turning to the Altrurian, "in your country? We can see no issue here, if the first principle of organized labor antagonizes the first principle of business."

"But I don't understand precisely yet what the first principle of business is," returned my guest.

"Ah, that raises another interesting question," said the lawyer. "Of course every business man solves the problem practically according to his temperament and education, and I suppose that on first thoughts every business man would answer you accordingly. But perhaps the personal equation is something you wish to eliminate from the definition."

"Yes, of course."

"Still, I would rather not venture upon it first," said the lawyer. "Professor, what should you say was the first principle of business?"

"Buying in the cheapest market and selling in the dearest," the professor promptly answered.

"We will pass the parson and the doctor and the novelist as witnesses of no value. They can't possibly have any cognizance of the first principle of business; their affair is to look after the souls and bodies and fancies of other people. But what should you say it was?" he asked the banker.

"I should say it was an enlightened conception of one's own interests."

"And you?"

The manufacturer had no hesitation in answering: "The good of Number One first, last and all the time. There may be a difference of opinion about the best way to get at it; the long way may be the better, or the short way; the direct way or the oblique way, or the purely selfish way, or the partly selfish way; but if you ever lose sight of that end you might as well shut up shop. That seems to be the first law of nature, as well as the first law of business."

"Ah, we musn't go to nature for our morality," the minister protested.

"We were not talking of morality," said the manufacturer; "we were talking of business."

This brought the laugh on the minister, but the lawyer cut it short: "Well, then, I don't really see why the trades-unions are not as business-like as the syndicates in their dealings with all those outside of themselves. Within themselves they practice an altruism of the highest order, but it is a tribal altruism; it is like that which prompts a Sioux to share his last mouthful with a starving Sioux, and to take the scalp of a starving Apache. How is it with your trades-unions in Altruria?" he asked my friend.

"We have no trades-unions in Altruria," he began.

"Happy Altruria!" cried the professor.

"We had them formerly," the Altrurian went on, "as you have them now. They claimed, as I suppose yours do, that they were forced into existence by the necessities of the case; that without union the workingman was unable to meet the capitalist on anything like equal terms, or to withstand his encroachments and oppressions. But to maintain themselves they had to extinguish industrial liberty among the workingmen themselves, and they had to practice great cruelties against those who refused to join them or who rebelled against them."

"They simply destroy them here," said the professor.

"Well," said the lawyer, from his judicial mind, "the great syndicates have no scruples in destroying a capitalist who won't come into them, or who tries to go out. They don't club him or stone him, but they undersell him and freeze him out; they don't break his head, but they bankrupt him. The principle is the same."

"Don't interrupt Mr. Homos," the banker entreated; "I am very curious to know just how they got rid of labor unions in Altruria."

"We had syndicates, too, and finally we had the reductio ad absurdum—we had a federation of labor unions and a federation of syndicates, that divided the nation into two camps. The situation was not only impossible, but it was insupportably ridiculous."

I ventured to say, "It hasn't become quite so much of a joke with us yet."

"Isn't it in a fair way to become so?" asked the doctor; and he turned to the lawyer: "What should you say was the logic of events among us for the last ten or twenty years?"

"There's nothing so capricious as the logic of events. It's like a woman's reasoning—you can't tell what it's aimed at, or where it's going to fetch up; all that you can do is to keep out of the way if possible. We may come to some such condition of things as they have in Altruria, where the faith of the whole nation is pledged to secure every citizen in the pursuit of happiness; or we may revert to some former condition, and the master may again own the man; or we may hitch and joggle along indefinitely, as we are doing now."

"But come now," said the banker, while he laid a caressing touch on the Altrurian's shoulder, "you don't mean to say honestly that everybody works with his hands in Altruria?"

"Yes, certainly. We are mindful, as a whole people, of the divine law, 'In the sweat of thy brow shalt thou eat bread.'"

"But the capitalists? I'm anxious about Number One, you see."

"We have none."

"I forgot, of course. But the lawyers, the doctors, the parsons, the novelists?"

"They all do their share of hand-work."

The lawyer said: "That seems to dispose of the question of the workingman in society. But how about your minds? When do you cultivate your minds? When do the ladies of Altruria cultivate their minds, if they have to do their own work, as I suppose they do? Or is it only the men who work if they happen to be the husbands and fathers of the upper classes?"

The Altrurian seemed to be sensible of the kindly skepticism which persisted in our reception of his statements, after all we had read of Altruria. He smiled indulgently, and said: "You musn't imagine that work in Altruria is the same as it is here. As we all work, the amount that each one need do is very little, a few hours each day at the most, so that every man and woman has abundant leisure and perfect spirits for the higher pleasures which the education of their whole youth has fitted them to enjoy. If you can understand a state of things where the sciences and arts and letters are cultivated for their own sake, and not as a means of livelihood"—

"No," said the lawyer, smiling, "I'm afraid we can't conceive of that. We consider the pinch of poverty the highest incentive that a man can have. If our gifted friend here," he said, indicating me, "were not kept like a toad under the harrow, with his nose on the grindstone, and the poorhouse staring him in the face"—

"For heaven's sake," I cried out, "don't mix your metaphors so, anyway!"

"If it were not for that and all the other hardships that literary men undergo—

'Toil, envy, want, the patron and the jail'—

his novels probably wouldn't be worth reading."

"Ah!" said the Altrurian, as if he did not quite follow this joking—and to tell the truth, I never find the personal thing in very good taste. "You will understand, then, how extremely difficult it is for me to imagine a condition of things like yours— although I have it under my very eyes—where the money consideration is the first consideration."

"Oh, excuse me!" urged the minister, "I don't think that's quite the case."

"I beg your pardon," said the Altrurian, sweetly; "you can see how easily I go astray."

"Why, I don't know," the banker interposed, "that you are so far out in what you say. If you had said that money was always the first motive, I should have been inclined to dispute you, too; but when you say that money is the first consideration, I think you are quite right. Unless a man secures his financial basis for his work, he can't do his work. It's nonsense to pretend otherwise. So the money consideration is the first consideration. People here have to live by their work, and to live they must have money. Of course, we all recognize a difference in the qualities, as well as in the kinds, of work. The work of the laborer may be roughly defined as the necessity of his life; the work of the business man as the means, and the work of the artist and scientist as the end. We might refine upon these definitions and make them closer, but they will serve for illustration as they are. I don't think there can be any question as to which is the highest kind of work; some truths are self-evident. He is a fortunate man whose work is an end, and every business man sees this, and owns it to himself at least when he meets some man of an æsthetic or scientific occupation. He knows that this luckier fellow has a joy in his work, which he can never feel in business; that his success in it can never be embittered by the thought that it is the failure of another; that if he does it well, it is pure good; that there cannot be any competition in it—there can be only a noble emulation, as far as the work itself is concerned. He can always look up to his work, for it is something above him; and a business man often has to look down upon his business, for it is often beneath him, unless he is a pretty low fellow."

I listened to all this in surprise; I knew that the banker was a cultivated man, a man of university training, and that he was a reader and a thinker; but he had always kept a certain reserve in his talk, which he now seemed to have thrown aside for the sake of the Altrurian, or because the subject had a charm that lured him out of himself. "Well, now," he continued, "the question is of the money consideration, which is the first consideration with us all: does it, or doesn't it degrade the work, which is the life, of those among us whose work is the highest? I understand that this is the misgiving which troubles you in view of our conditions?"

The Altrurian assented, and I thought it a proof of the banker's innate delicacy that he did not refer the matter, so far as it concerned the æsthetic life and work, to me; I was afraid he was going to do so. But he courteously proposed to keep the question impersonal, and he went on to consider it himself. "Well, I don't suppose any one can satisfy you fully. But I should say that it put such men under a double strain, and perhaps that is the reason why so many of them break down in a calling that is certainly far less exhausting than business. On one side, the artist is kept to the level of the workingman, of the animal, of the creature whose sole affair is to get something to eat and somewhere to sleep. This is through his necessity. On the other side, he is exalted to the height of beings who have no concern but with the excellence of their work, which they were born and divinely authorized to do. This is through his purpose. Between the two, I should say that he got mixed, and that his work shows it."

None of the others said anything, and since I had not been personally appealed to, I felt the freer to speak. "If you will suppose me to be speaking from observation rather than experience," I began.

"By all means," said the banker, "go on," and the rest made haste in various forms to yield me the word.

"I should say that such a man certainly got mixed, but that his work kept itself pure from the money consideration, as it were, in spite of him. A painter, or actor, or even a novelist, is glad to get all he can for his work, and, such is our fallen nature, he does get all he knows how to get; but when he has once fairly passed into his work, he loses himself in it. He does not think whether it will pay or not, whether it will be popular or not, but whether he can make it good or not."

"Well, that is conceivable," said the banker. "But wouldn't he rather do something he would get less for, if he could afford it, than the thing he knows he will get more for? Doesn't the money consideration influence his choice of subject?"

"Oddly enough, I don't believe it does," I answered, after a moment's reflection. "A man makes his choice once for all when he embraces the æsthetic life, or rather it is made for him; no other life seems possible. I know there is a general belief that an artist does the kind of thing he has made go because it pays; but this only shows the prevalence of business ideals. If he did not love to do the thing he does he could not do it well, no matter how richly it paid."

"I am glad to hear it," said the banker, and he added to the Altrurian: "So you see we are not so bad as one would think. We are illogically better, in fact."

"Yes," the other assented. "I knew something of your literature as well as your conditions before I left home, and I perceived that by some anomaly, the one was not tainted by the other. It is a miraculous proof of the divine mission of the poet."

"And the popular novelist," the lawyer whispered in my ear, but loud enough for the rest to hear, and they all testified their amusement at my cost.

The Altrurian, with his weak sense of humor, passed the joke. "It shows no signs of corruption from greed, but I can't help thinking that fine as it is, it might have been much finer if the authors who produced it had been absolutely freed to their work, and had never felt the spur of need."

"Are they absolutely freed to it in Altruria?" asked the professor. "I understood you that everybody had to work for his living in Altruria."

"That is a mistake. Nobody works for his living in Altruria; he works for others' living."

"Ah, that is precisely what our workingmen object to doing here!" said the manufacturer. "In that last interview of mine with the walking-delegate he had the impudence to ask me why my men should work for my living as well as their own."

"He couldn't imagine that you were giving them the work to do—the very means of life," said the professor.

"Oh, no, that's the last thing those fellows want to think of."

"Perhaps," the Altrurian suggested, "they might not have found it such a hardship to work for your living if their own had been assured, as it is with us. If you will excuse my saying it, we should think it monstrous in Altruria for any man to have another's means of life in his power; and in our condition it is hardly imaginable. Do you really have it in your power to take away a man's opportunity to earn a living?"

The manufacturer laughed uneasily. "It is in my power to take away his life; but I don't habitually shoot my fellowmen, and I never dismissed a man yet without good reason."

"Oh, I beg your pardon," said the Altrurian. "I didn't dream of accusing you of such inhumanity. But you see our whole system is so very different that, as I said, it is hard for me to conceive of yours, and I am very curious to understand its workings. If you shot your fellowman, as you say, the law would punish you; but if for some reason that you decided to be good you took away his means of living, and he actually starved to death"—

"Then the law would have nothing to do with it," the professor replied for the manufacturer, who did not seem ready to answer. "But that is not the way things fall out. The man would be supported in idleness, probably, till he got another job, by his union, which would take the matter up."

"But I thought that our friend did not employ union labor," returned the Altrurian.

I found all this very uncomfortable, and tried to turn the talk back to a point that I felt curious about. "But in Altruria, if the literary class is not exempt from the rule of manual labor where do they find time and strength to write?"

"Why, you must realize that our manual labor is never engrossing or exhausting. It is no more than is necessary to keep the body in health. I do not see how you remain well here, you people of sedentary occupations."

"Oh, we all take some sort of exercise. We walk several hours a day, or we row, or we ride a bicycle, or a horse, or we fence."

"But to us," returned the Altrurian, with a growing frankness, which nothing but the sweetness of his manner would have excused, "exercise for exercise would appear stupid. The barren expenditure of force that began and ended in itself, and produced nothing, we should—if you will excuse my saying so—look upon as childish, if not insane or immoral."

V

AT THIS MOMENT, the lady who had hailed me so gaily from the top of the coach while I stood waiting for the Altrurian to help the porter with the baggage, just after the arrival of the train, came up with her husband to our little group and said to me: "I want to introduce my husband to you. He adores your books." She went on much longer to this effect, while the other men grinned round and her husband tried to look as if it were all true, and her eyes wandered to the Alturian, who listened gravely. I knew perfectly well that she was using her husband's zeal for my fiction to make me present my friend; but I did not mind that, and I introduced him to both of them. She took possession of him at once and began walking him off down the piazza, while her husband remained with me and the members of our late conference drifted apart. I was not sorry to have it broken up for the present; it seemed to me that it had lasted quite long enough, and I lighted a cigar with the husband, and we strolled together in the direction his wife had taken.

He began, apparently in compliment to literature in my person, "Yes, I like to have a book where I can get at it when we're not going out to the theatre, and I want to quiet my mind down after business. I don't care much what the book is; my wife reads to me till I drop off, and then she finishes the book herself and tells me the rest of the story. You see, business takes it out of you so! Well, I let my wife do most of the reading, anyway. She knows pretty much everything that's going in that line. We haven't got any children, and it occupies her mind. She's up to all sorts of things—she's artistic, and she's musical, and she's dramatic, and she's literary. Well, I like to have her. Women are funny, anyway."

He was a good-looking, good-natured, average American of

the money-making type; I believe he was some sort of a broker, but I do not quite know what his business was. As we walked up and down the piazza, keeping a discreet little distance from the corner where his wife had run off to with her capture, he said he wished he could get more time with her in the summer—but he supposed I knew what business was. He was glad she could have the rest, anyway; she needed it.

"By the way," he asked, "who is this friend of yours? The women are all crazy about him, and it's been an even thing between my wife and Miss Groundsel which would fetch him first. But I'll bet on my wife every time, when it comes to a thing like that. He's a good-looking fellow—some kind of foreigner, I believe; pretty eccentric, too, I guess. Where is Altruria, anyway?"

I told him, and he said: "Oh, yes. Well, if we are going to restrict immigration, I suppose we sha'n't see many more Altrurians, and we'd better make the most of this one. Heigh?"

I do not know why this innocent pleasantry piqued me to say: "If I understand the Altrurians, my dear fellow, nothing could induce them to emigrate to America. As far as I can make out, they would regard it very much as we should regard settling among the Esquimaux."

"Is that so?" asked my new acquaintance, with perfect good temper. "Why?"

"Really, I can't say, and I don't know that I've explicit authority for my statement."

"They are worse than the English used to be," he went on. "I didn't know that there were any foreigners who looked at us in that light now. I thought the War settled all that."

I sighed. "There are a good many things that the War didn't settle so definitely as we've been used to thinking, I'm afraid. But for that matter, I fancy an Altrurian would regard the English as a little lower in the scale of savagery than ourselves even."

"Is that so? Well, that's pretty good on the English, anyway," said my companion, and he laughed with an easy satisfaction that I envied him.

"My dear!" his wife called to him from where she was sitting with the Altrurian, "I wish you would go for my shawl. I begin to feel the air a little."

"I'll go if you'll tell me where," he said, and he confided to me, "Never knows where her shawl is, one-quarter of the time."

"Well, I think I left it in the office somewhere. You might ask at the desk; or, perhaps it's in the rack by the dining-room door —or maybe up in our room."

"I thought so," said her husband, with another glance at me, as if it were the greatest fun in the world, and he started amiably off.

I went and took a chair by the lady and the Altrurian, and she began at once: "Oh, I'm so glad you've come! I have been trying to enlighten Mr. Homos about some of the little social peculiarities among us, that he finds so hard to understand. He was just now," the lady continued, "wanting to know why all the natives out here were not invited to go in and join our young people in the dance, and I've been trying to tell him that we consider it a great favor to let them come and take up so much of the piazza and look in at the windows."

She gave a little laugh of superiority, and twitched her pretty head in the direction of the young country girls and country fellows who were thronging the place that night in rather unusual numbers. They were well enough looking, and as it was Saturday night they were in their best. I suppose their dress could have been criticised; the young fellows were clothed by the ready-made clothing store, and the young girls after their own devices from the fashion-papers; but their general effect was good and their behavior was irreproachable; they were very quiet—if anything, too quiet. They took up a part of the piazza that was yielded them by common usage, and sat watching the hop inside, not so much enviously, I thought, as wistfully; and for the first time it struck me as odd that they should have no part in the gayety. I had often seen them there before, but I had never thought it strange they should be shut out. It had always seemed quite normal, but now, suddenly, for one baleful moment, it seemed abnormal. I suppose it was the talk we had been having about the workingmen in society which caused me to see the thing as the Altrurian must have seen it; but I was, nevertheless, vexed with him for having asked such a question, after he had been so fully instructed upon the point. It was malicious of him, or it was stupid. I hardened my heart and answered: "You might have told him, for one thing, that they were not dancing because they had not paid the piper."

"Then the money consideration enters even into your social pleasures?" asked the Altrurian.

"Very much. Doesn't it with you?"

He evaded this question, as he evaded all straightforward questions concerning his country: "We have no money consideration, you know. But do I understand that all your social entertainments are paid for by the guests?"

"Oh, no, not so bad as that, quite. There are a great many that the host pays for. Even here, in a hotel, the host furnishes the music and the room free to the guests of the house."

"And none are admitted from the outside?"

"Oh, yes, people are welcome from all the other hotels and boarding-houses and the private cottages. The young men are especially welcome; there are not enough young men in the hotel to go round, you see." In fact, we could see that some of the pretty girls within were dancing with other girls; half-grown boys were dangling from the waists of tall young ladies and waltzing on tiptoe.

"Isn't that rather droll?" asked the Altrurian.

"It's grotesque!" I said, and I felt ashamed of it. "But what are you to do? The young men are hard at work in the cities, as many as can get work there, and the rest are out West, growing up with the country. There are twenty young girls for every young man at all the summer-resorts in the East."

"But what would happen if these young farmers—I suppose they are farmers—were invited in to take part in the dance?" asked my friend.

"But that is impossible."

"Why?"

"Really, Mrs. Makely, I think I shall have to give him back to you!" I said.

The lady laughed. "I am not sure that I want him back."

"Oh, yes," the Altrurian entreated, with unwonted perception of the humor. "I know that I must be very trying with my questions; but do not abandon me to the solitude of my own conjectures. They are dreadful!"

"Well, I won't," said the lady, with another laugh. "And I will try to tell you what would happen if those farmers or farm hands, or whatever they are, were asked in. The mammas would be very indignant, and the young ladies would be scared, and nobody would know what to do, and the dance would stop."

"Then the young ladies prefer to dance with one another and with little boys"—

"No, they prefer to dance with young men of their own station; they would rather not dance at all than dance with people beneath them. I don't say anything against these natives here; they are very civil and decent. But they have not the same social traditions as the young ladies; they would be out of place with them, and they would feel it."

"Yes, I can see that they are not fit to associate with them," said the Altrurian, with a gleam of common sense that surprised me, "and that as long as your present conditions endure, they never can be. You must excuse the confusion which the difference between your political ideals and your economic ideals constantly creates in me. I always think of you politically first, and realize you as a perfect democracy; then come these other facts, in which I cannot perceive that you differ from the aristocratic countries of Europe in theory or practice. It is very puzzling. Am I right in supposing that the effect of your economy is to establish insuperable inequalities among you, and to forbid the hope of the brotherhood which your polity proclaims?"

Mrs. Makely looked at me, as if she were helpless to grapple with his meaning, and for fear of worse, I thought best to evade it. I said, "I don't believe that anybody is troubled by those distinctions. We are used to them, and everybody acquiesces in them, which is a proof that they are a very good thing."

Mrs. Makely now came to my support. "The Americans are very high-spirited, in every class, and I don't believe one of those nice farm boys would like being asked in any better than the young ladies. You can't imagine how proud some of them are."

"So that they suffer from being excluded as inferiors?"

"Oh, I assure you they don't feel themselves inferior! They consider themselves as good as anybody. There are some very interesting characters among them. Now, there is a young girl sitting at the first window, with her profile outlined by the light, whom I feel it an honor to speak to. That's her brother, standing there with her—that tall, gaunt young man with a Roman face; it's such a common type here in the mountains. Their father was a soldier, and he distinguished himself so in one of the last battles that he was promoted. He was badly wounded, but he never took a pension; he just came back to his farm and worked on till he died. Now the son has the farm, and he and his sister live there with their mother. The daughter takes in sewing, and in that way they manage to make both ends meet. The girl is really a first-rate sempstress, and *so* cheap! I give her a good deal of my work in the summer, and we are quite friends. She's very fond of reading; the mother is an invalid, but she reads aloud while the daughter sews, and you've no idea how many books they get through. When she comes for sewing, I like to talk with her about them; I always have her sit down; it's hard to realize that she isn't a lady. I'm a good deal criticised, I know, and I suppose I do spoil her a little; it puts notions into such people's heads, if you meet them in that way; they're pretty free and independent as it is. But when I'm with Lizzie I forget that there is any difference between us; I can't help loving the child. You must take Mr. Homos to see them, Mr. Twelvemough. They've got the father's sword hung up over the head of the mother's bed; it's very touching. But the poor little place *is* so bare!"

Mrs. Makely sighed, and there fell a little pause, which she broke with a question she had the effect of having kept back.

"There is one thing I should like to ask you, too, Mr. Homos. Is it true that everybody in Altruria does some kind of manual labor?"

"Why, certainly," he answered, quite as if he had been an American.

"Ladies, too? Or perhaps you have none!"

I thought this rather offensive, but I could not see that the Altrurian had taken it ill. "Perhaps we had better try to understand each other clearly before I answer that question. You have no titles of nobility as they have in England"—

"No, indeed! I hope we have outgrown those superstitions," said Mrs. Makely, with a republican fervor that did my heart good. "It is a word that we apply first of all to the moral qualities of a person."

"But you said just now that you sometimes forgot that your sempstress was not a lady. Just what did you mean by that?"

Mrs. Makely hesitated. "I meant—I suppose I meant—that she had not the surroundings of a lady; the social traditions."

"Then it has something to do with social as well as moral qualities—with ranks and classes?"

"Classes, yes; but as you know, we have no ranks in America." The Altrurian took off his hat and rubbed an imaginable perspiration from his forehead. He sighed deeply. "It is all very difficult."

"Yes," Mrs. Makely assented, "I suppose it is. All foreigners find it so. In fact it is something that you have to live into the notion of; it can't be explained."

"Well, then, my dear madam, will you tell me without further question, what you understand by a lady, and let me live into the notion of it at my leisure?"

"I will do my best," said Mrs. Makely. "But it would be so much easier to tell you *who* was or who was not a lady! However, your acquaintance is so limited yet, that I must try to do something in the abstract and impersonal for you. In the first place, a lady must be above the sordid anxieties in every way. She need not be very rich, but she must have enough, so that she need not be harrassed about making both ends meet, when she ought to be devoting herself to her social duties. The time is past with us when a lady could look after the dinner, and perhaps cook part of it herself, and then rush in to receive her guests, and do the amenities. She must have a certain kind of house, so that her entourage won't seem cramped and mean, and she must have nice frocks, of course, and plenty of them. She needn't be of the smart set; that isn't at all necessary; but she can't afford to be out of the fashion. Of course she must have a certain training. She must have cultivated tastes; she must know about art, and literature, and music, and all those kind of things, and though it isn't necessary to go in for anything in particular, it won't hurt her to have a fad or two. The nicest kind of fad is charity; and people go in for that a great deal. I think sometimes they use it to work up with, and there are some who use religion in the same way; I think it's horrid; but it's perfectly safe; you can't accuse them of doing it. I'm happy to say, though, that mere church association doesn't count socially so much as it used to. Charity is a great deal more insidious. But you see how hard it is to define a lady. So much has to be left to the nerves, in all these things! And then it's changing all the time; Europe's coming in, and the old American ideals are passing away. Things that people did ten years ago would be impossible now, or at least ridiculous. You wouldn't be considered vulgar, quite, but you would certainly be considered a back number, and that's almost as bad. Really," said Mrs. Makely, "I don't believe I can tell you what a lady is."

We all laughed together at her frank confession. The Altrurian asked, "But do I understand that one of her conditions is that she shall have nothing whatever to do?"

"Nothing to *do!*" cried Mrs. Makely. "A lady is busy from morning till night! She always goes to bed perfectly worn out!"

"But with what?" asked the Altrurian.

"With making herself agreeable and her house attractive, with going to lunches, and teas, and dinners, and concerts, and theatres, and art exhibitions, and charity meetings, and receptions, and with writing a thousand and one notes about them, and accepting and declining, and giving lunches and dinners, and making calls and receiving them, and I don't know what all. It's the most hideous slavery!" Her voice rose into something like a shriek; one could see that her nerves were going at the mere thought of it all. "You don't have a moment to yourself; your life isn't your own!"

"But the lady isn't allowed to do any useful kind of work?"

"*Work!* Don't you call all that work, and *useful?* I'm sure I envy the cook in my kitchen at times; I envy the woman that scrubs my floors. Stop! Don't ask why I don't go into my kitchen, or get down on my knees with the mop! It isn't possible! You simply can't! Perhaps you could if you were very grande dame, but if you're anywhere near the line of necessity, or ever have been, you can't. Besides, if we did do our own household work, as I understand your Altrurian ladies do, what would become of the servant class? We should be taking away their living, and that would be wicked."

"It would certainly be wrong to take away the living of a fellow-creature," the Altrurian gravely admitted, "and I see the obstacle in your way."

"It's a mountain," said the lady, with exhaustion in her voice, but a returning amiability; his forbearance must have placated her.

"May I ask what the use of your society life is?" he ventured, after a moment.

"Use? Why should it have any? It kills time."

"Then you are shut up to a hideous slavery without use, except to kill time, and you cannot escape from it without taking away the living of those dependent on you?"

"Yes," I put in, "and that is a difficulty that meets us at every turn. It is something that Matthew Arnold urged with great effect in his paper on that crank of a Tolstoi. He asked what would become of the people who need the work, if we served and waited on ourselves, as Tolstoi preached. The question is unanswerable."

"That is true; in your conditions, it is unanswerable," said the Altrurian.

"I think," said Mrs. Makely, "that under the circumstances we do pretty well."

"Oh, I don't presume to censure you. And if you believe that your conditions are the best"—

"We believe them the best in the best of all possible worlds," I said, devoutly; and it struck me that if ever we came to have a national church, some such affirmation as that concerning our economical conditions ought to be in the confession of faith.

The Altrurian's mind had not followed mine so far. "And your young girls?" he asked of Mrs. Makely, "how is their time occupied?"

"You mean after they come out in society?"

"I suppose so."

She seemed to reflect. "I don't know that it is very differently occupied. Of course, they have their own amusements; they have their dances, and little clubs, and their sewing societies. I suppose that even an Altrurian would applaud their sewing for the poor?" Mrs. Makely asked rather satirically.

"Yes," he answered; and then he asked, "Isn't it taking work away from some needy sempstress, though? But I suppose you excuse it to the thoughtlessness of youth."

Mrs. Makely did not say, and he went on:

"What I find it so hard to understand is how you ladies can endure a life of mere nervous exertion, such as you have been describing to me. I don't see how you keep well."

"We *don't* keep well," said Mrs. Makely, with the greatest amusement. "I don't suppose that when you get above the working classes, till you reach the very rich, you would find a perfectly well woman in America."

"Isn't that rather extreme?" I ventured to ask.

"No," said Mrs. Makely, "it's shamefully moderate," and she seemed to delight in having made out such a bad case for her sex. You can't stop a woman of that kind when she gets started; I had better left it alone.

"But," said the Altrurian, "if you are forbidden by motives of humanity from doing any sort of manual labor, which you must leave to those who live by it, I suppose you take some sort of exercise?"

"Well," said Mrs. Makely, shaking her head gaily, "we prefer to take medicine."

"You must approve of that," I said to the Altrurian, "as you consider exercise for its own sake insane or immoral. But, Mrs. Makely," I entreated, "you're giving me away at a tremendous rate. I have just been telling Mr. Homos that you ladies go in for athletics so much, now, in your summer outings, that there is danger of your becoming physically as well as intellectually superior to us poor fellows. Don't take that consolation from me!"

"I won't, altogether," she said. "I couldn't have the heart to, after the pretty way you've put it. I don't call it very athletic, sitting round on hotel piazzas all summer long, as nineteen-twentieths of us do. But I don't deny that there is a Remnant, as Matthew Arnold calls them, who do go in for tennis, and boating, and bathing, and tramping and climbing." She paused, and then she concluded gleefully. "And you ought to see what wrecks they get home in the fall!"

The joke was on me; I could not help laughing, though I felt rather sheepish before the Altrurian. Fortunately, he did not pursue the inquiry; his curiosity had been given a slant aside from it.

"But your ladies," he asked, "they have the summer for rest, however they use it. Do they generally leave town? I understood Mr. Twelvemough to say so," he added with a deferential glance at me.

"Yes, you may say it is the universal custom in the class that can afford it," said Mrs. Makely. She proceeded as if she felt a tacit censure in his question. "It wouldn't be the least use for us to stay and fry through our summers in the city, simply because our fathers and brothers had to. Besides, we are worn out at the end of the season, and they want us to come away as much as we want to come."

"Ah, I have always heard that the Americans are beautiful in their attitude towards women."

"They are perfect dears," said Mrs. Makely, "and here comes one of the best of them."

At that moment her husband came up and laid her shawl across her shoulders. "Whose character is that you're blasting?" he asked, jocosely.

"Where in the world did you find it?" she asked, meaning the shawl.

"It was where you left it: on the sofa, in the side parlor. I had to take my life in my hand, when I crossed among all those waltzers in there. There must have been as many as three couples on the floor. Poor girls! I pity them, off at these places. The fellows in town have a good deal better time. They've got their clubs, and they've got the theatre, and when the weather gets too much for them, they can run off down to the shore for the night. The places anywhere within an hour's ride are full of fellows. The girls don't have to dance with one another there, or with little boys. Of course, that's all right, if they like it better." He laughed at his wife, and winked at me, and smoked swiftly, in emphasis of his irony.

"Then the young gentlemen whom the young ladies here usually meet in society, are all at work in the cities?" the Altrurian asked him, rather needlessly, as I had already said so.

"Yes, those who are not out West, growing up with the country, except, of course, the fellows who have inherited a fortune. They're mostly off on yachts."

"But why do your young men go West to grow up with the country?" pursued my friend.

"Because the East is *grown* up. They have got to hustle, and the West is the place to hustle. To make money," added Makely, in response to a puzzled glance of the Altrurian.

"Sometimes," said his wife, "I almost hate the name of money."

"Well, so long as you don't hate the thing, Peggy!"

"Oh, we must have it, I suppose," she sighed. "They used to

say about the girls who grew into old maids just after the Rebellion that they had lost their chance in the war for the union. I think quite as many lose their chance now in the war for the dollar."

"Mars hath slain his thousands, but Mammon hath slain his tens of thousands," I suggested lightly; we all like to recognize the facts, so long as we are not expected to do anything about them; then, we deny them.

"Yes, quite as bad as that," said Mrs. Makely.

"Well, my dear, you are expensive, you know," said her husband, "and if we want to have you, why we've got to hustle, first."

"Oh, I don't blame you, you poor things! There's nothing to be done about it; it's just got to go on and on; I don't see how it's ever to end."

The Altrurian had been following us with that air of polite mystification which I had begun to dread in him. "Then, in your good society you postpone, and even forego, the happiness of life in the struggle to be rich?"

"Well, you see," said Makely, "a fellow don't like to ask a girl to share a home that isn't as nice as the home she has left."

"Sometimes," his wife put in, rather sadly, "I think that it's all a mistake, and that we'd be willing to share the privations of the man we loved."

"Well," said Makely, with a laugh, "we wouldn't like to risk it."

I laughed with him, but his wife did not, and in the silence that ensued there was nothing to prevent the Altrurian from coming in with another of his questions. "How far does this state of things extend downward? Does it include the working-classes, too?"

"Oh, no!" we all answered together, and Mrs. Makely said: "With your Altrurian ideas I suppose you would naturally sympathize a great deal more with the lower classes, and think they had to endure all the hardships in our system; but if you could realize how the struggle goes on in the best society, and how we all have to fight for what we get, or don't get, you would be disposed to pity our upper classes, too."

"I am sure I should," said the Altrurian.

Makely remarked, "I used to hear my father say that slavery was harder on the whites than it was on the blacks, and that he wanted it done away with for the sake of the masters."

Makely rather faltered in conclusion, as if he were not quite satisfied with his remark, and I distinctly felt a want of proportion in it; but I did not wish to say anything. His wife had no reluctance.

"Well, there's no comparison between the two things, but the struggle certainly doesn't affect the working classes as it does us. They go on marrying and giving in marriage in the old way. They have nothing to lose, and so they can afford it."

"Blessed am dem what don't expect nuffin! Oh, I tell you it's a workingman's country," said Makely, through his cigar smoke. "You ought to see them in town, these summer nights, in the parks and squares and cheap theatres. Their girls are not off for their health, anywhere, and their fellows are not off growing up with the country. Their day's work is over and they're going in for a good time. And, then, walk through the streets where they live, and see them out on the stoops with their wives and children! I tell you, it's enough to make a fellow wish he was poor himself."

"Yes," said Mrs. Makely, "it's astonishing how strong and well those women keep, with their great families and their hard work. Sometimes I really envy them."

"Do you suppose," said the Altrurian, "that they are aware of the sacrifices which the ladies of the upper classes make in leaving all the work to them, and suffering from the nervous debility which seems to be the outcome of your society life?"

"They have not the remotest idea of it! They have no conception of what a society woman goes through with. They think we do nothing. They envy us, too, and sometimes they're so ungrateful and indifferent, if you try to help them, or get on terms with them, that I believe they hate us."

"But that comes from ignorance?"

"Yes, though I don't know that they are really any more ignorant of us than we are of them. It's the other half on both sides."

"Isn't that a pity, rather?"

"Of course it's a pity, but what can you do? You can't know what people are like unless you live like them, and then the question is whether the game is worth the candle. I should like to know how you manage in Altruria."

"Why, we have solved the problem in the only way, as you say, that it can be solved. We all live alike."

"Isn't that a little, just a very trifling little bit monotonous?" Mrs. Makely asked, with a smile. "But there is everything, of course, in being used to it. To an unregenerate spirit—like mine, for example—it seems intolerable."

"But why? When you were younger, before you were married, you all lived at home together.—Or, perhaps, you were an only child?"

"Oh, no, indeed! There were ten of us."

"Then you all lived alike, and shared equally?"

"Yes, but we were a family."

"We do not conceive of the human race except as a family."

"Now, excuse me, Mr. Homos, that is all nonsense. You cannot have the family feeling without love, and it is impossible to love other people. That talk about the neighbor, and all that, is all well enough"—She stopped herself, as if she dimly remembered Who began that talk, and then went on: "Of course, I accept it as a matter of faith, and the spirit of it, nobody denies that; but what I mean is, that you must have frightful quarrels all the time." She tried to look as if this were where she really meant to bring up, and he took her on the ground she had chosen.

"Yes, we have quarrels. Hadn't you at home?"

"We fought like little cats and dogs, at times."

Makely and I burst into a laugh at her magnanimous frankness. The Altrurian remained serious. "But because you lived alike, you knew each other; and so you easily made up your quarrels. It is quite as simple with us, in our life as a human family."

This notion of a human family seemed to amuse Mrs. Makely more and more; she laughed and laughed again. "You must excuse me!" she panted, at last. "But I cannot imagine it! No, it is too ludicrous! Just fancy the jars of an ordinary family multiplied by the population of a whole continent! Why, you must be in a perpetual squabble! You can't have any peace of your lives! It's worse, far worse, than our way!"

"But, madam," he began, "you are supposing our family to be made up of people with all the antagonistic interests of your civilization; as a matter of fact"—

"No, no! *I know human nature*, Mr. Homos!" She suddenly jumped up and gave him her hand. "Good night!" she said, sweetly, and as she drifted off on her husband's arm, she looked back at us and nodded in gay triumph.

The Altrurian turned upon me with unabated interest. "And have you no provision in your system for finally making the lower classes understand the sufferings and sacrifices of the upper classes in their behalf? Do you expect to do nothing to bring them together in mutual kindness?"

"Well, not this evening," I said, throwing the end of my cigar away. "I'm going to bed, aren't you?"

"Not yet."

"Well, good night. Are you sure you can find your room?"

"Oh, yes. Good night."

VI

I LEFT my guest abruptly, with a feeling of vexation not very easily definable. His repetition of questions about questions which society has so often answered, and always in the same way, was not so bad in him as it would have been in a person of our civilization; he represented a wholly different state of things, the inversion of our own, and much could be forgiven him for that reason, just as in Russia much could be forgiven to an American, if he formulated his curiosity concerning imperialism from a purely republican experience. I knew that in Altruria, for instance, the possession of great gifts, of any kind of superiority, involved the sense of obligation to others, and the wish to identify one's self with the great mass of men, rather than the ambition to distinguish one's self from them; and that the Altrurians honored their gifted men in the measure they did this. A man reared in such a civilization must naturally find it difficult to get our point of view; with social inclusion as the ideal, he could with difficulty conceive of our ideal of social exclusion; but I think we had all been very patient with him; we should have made short work with an American who had approached us with the same inquiries. Even from a foreigner, the citizen of a republic founded on the notion, elsewhere exploded ever since Cain, that one is his brother's keeper, the things he asked seemed inoffensive only because they were puerile; but they certainly were puerile. I felt that it ought to have been self-evident to him that when a commonwealth of 60,000,000 Americans based itself upon the great principle of self-seeking, self-seeking was the best thing, and whatever hardship it seemed to work, it must carry with it unseen blessings in ten-fold measure. If a few hundred thousand favored Americans enjoyed the privilege of socially contemning all the rest, it was as clearly right and just that they should do so, as that 4000 American millionaires should be richer than all the other Americans put together. Such a status, growing out of our political equality and our material prosperity must evince a divine purpose to any-one intimate with the designs of providence, and it seemed a kind of impiety to doubt its perfection. I excused the misgivings which I could not help seeing in the Altrurian to his alien traditions, and I was aware that my friends had done so, too. But if I could judge from myself he must have left them all sensible of their effort; and this was not pleasant. I could not blink the fact that although I had openly disagreed with him on every point of ethics and economics, I was still responsible for him as a guest. It was as if an English gentleman had introduced a blatant American democrat into tory society; or, rather, as if a southerner of the olden time had harbored a northern abolitionist, and permitted him to inquire into the workings of slavery among his neighbors. People would tolerate him as my guest for a time, but there must be an end of their patience with the tacit enmity of his sentiments, and the explicit vulgarity of his ideals, and when the end came, I must be attainted with him.

I did not like the notion of this, and I meant to escape it if I could. I confess that I would have willingly disowned him, as I had already disavowed his opinions, but there was no way of doing it short of telling him to go away, and I was not ready to do that. Something in the man, I do not know what, mysteriously appealed to me. He was not contemptibly puerile without being lovably childlike, and I could only make up my mind to be more and more frank with him, and to try and shield him, as well as myself, from the effects I dreaded.

I fell asleep planning an excursion further into the mountains, which should take up the rest of the week that I expected him to stay with me, and would keep him from following up his studies of American life where they would be so injurious to both of us as they must in our hotel. A knock at my door roused me, and I sent a drowsy "Come in!" towards it from the bed-clothes without looking that way.

"Good morning!" came back in the rich, gentle voice of the Altrurian. I lifted my head with a jerk from the pillow, and saw him standing against the closed door, with my shoes in his hand. "Oh, I am sorry I waked you! I thought"—

"Not at all, not at all!" I said. "It's quite time, I dare say. But you oughtn't to have taken the trouble to bring my shoes in!"

"I wasn't altogether disinterested in it," he returned. "I wished you to compliment me on them. Don't you think they are pretty well done, for an amateur?" He came toward my bed, and turned them about in his hands, so that they would catch the light, and smiled down upon me.

"I don't understand," I began.

"Why," he said, "I blacked them, you know."

"You blacked them!"

"Yes," he returned, easily. "I thought I would go into the baggage-room, after we parted last night, to look for a piece of mine that had not been taken to my room, and I found the porter there, with his wrist bound up. He said he had strained it in handling a lady's Saratoga—he said a Saratoga was a large trunk—and I begged him to let me relieve him at the boots he was blacking. He refused, at first, but I insisted upon trying my hand at a pair, and then he let me go on with the men's boots; he said he could varnish the ladies' without hurting his wrist. It needed less skill than I supposed, and after I had done a few pairs he said I could black boots as well as he."

"Did anybody see you?" I gasped, and I felt a cold perspiration break out on me.

"No, we had the whole midnight hour to ourselves. The porter's work with the baggage was all over, and there was nothing to interrupt the delightful chat we fell into. He is a very intelligent man, and he told me all about that custom of feeing which you deprecate. He says that the servants hate it as much as the guests; they have to take the tips, now, because the landlords figure on them in the wages, and they cannot live without them. He is a fine, manly fellow, and"—

"Mr. Homos," I broke in, with the strength I found in his assurance that no one had seen him helping the porter black boots, "I want to speak very seriously with you, and I hope you will not be hurt if I speak very plainly about a matter in which I have your good solely at heart." This was not quite true, and I winced inwardly a little when he thanked me with that confounded sincerity of his, which was so much like irony; but I went on: "It is my duty to you, as my guest, to tell you that this thing of doing for others is not such a simple matter here, as your peculiar training leads you to think. You have been deceived by a superficial likeness; but, really, I do not understand how you could have read all you have done about us, and not realized before coming here that America and Altruria are absolutely distinct and diverse in their actuating principles. They are both republics, I know; but America is a republic where every man is for himself, and you cannot help others as you do at home; it is dangerous—it is ridiculous. You must keep this fact in mind, or you will fall into errors that will be very embarrassing to you in your stay among us, and," I was forced to add, "to all your friends. Now, I certainly hoped, after what I had said to you, and what my friends had explained of our civilization, that you would not have done a thing of this kind. I will see the porter, as soon as I am up, and ask him not to mention the matter to anyone, but I confess I don't like to take an apologetic tone with him; your conditions are so alien to ours that they will seem incredible to him, and he will think I am stuffing him."

"I don't believe he will think that," said the Altrurian, "and I hope you won't find the case so bad as it seems to you. I am extremely sorry to have done wrong"—

"Oh, the thing wasn't wrong in itself. It was only wrong under the circumstances. Abstractly, it is quite right to help a fellow-being who needs help; no one denies that, even in a country where every one is for himself."

"I am so glad to hear it," said the Altrurian. "Then, at least, I have not gone radically astray; and I do not think you need take the trouble to explain the Altrurian ideas to the porter. I have done that already, and they seemed quite conceivable to him; he said that poor folks had to act upon them, even here, more or less, and that if they did not act upon them, there would be no chance for them at all. He says they have to help each other, very much as we do at home, and that it is only the rich folks among you who are independent. I really don't think you need speak to him at all, unless you wish; and I was very careful to guard my offer of help at the point where I understood from you and your friends that it might do harm. I asked him if there was not someone who would help him out with his bootblacking for money, because in that case I should be glad to pay him; but he said there was no one about who would take the job; that he had to agree to black the boots, or else he would not have got the place of porter, but that all the rest of the help would consider it a disgrace, and would not help him for love or money. So it seemed quite safe to offer him my services."

I felt that the matter was almost hopeless, but I asked, "And what he said, didn't that suggest anything else to you?"

"How, anything else?" asked the Altrurian, in his turn.

"Didn't it occur to you that if none of his fellow servants were willing to help him black boots, and if he did it only because he was obliged to, it was hardly the sort of work for you?"

"Why, no," said the Altrurian, with absolute simplicity. He must have perceived the despair I fell into at this answer, for he asked, "Why should I have minded doing for others what I should have been willing to do for myself?"

"There are a great many things we are willing to do for ourselves that we are not willing to do for others. But even on that principle, which I think false and illogical, you could not be justified. A gentleman is not willing to black *his own* boots. It is offensive to his feelings, to his self-respect; it is something he will not do if he can get anybody else to do it for him."

"Then, in America," said the Altrurian, "it is not offensive to the feelings of a gentleman to let another do for him what he would not do for himself?"

"Certainly not."

"Ah," he returned, "then we understand something altogether different by the word gentleman in Altruria. I see, now, how I have committed a mistake. I shall be more careful hereafter."

I thought I had better leave the subject, and, "By the way," I said, "how would you like to take a little tramp with me today, farther up into the mountains?"

"I should be delighted," said the Altrurian, so gratefully, that I was ashamed to think why I was proposing the pleasure to him.

"Well, then, I shall be ready to start as soon as we have had breakfast. I will join you down stairs in half an hour."

He left me at this hint, though really I was half afraid he might stay and offer to lend me a hand at my toilet, in the expression of his national character. I found him with Mrs. Makely, when I went down, and she began, with a parenthetical tribute to the beauty of the mountains in the morning light, "Don't be surprised to see me up at this unnatural hour. I don't know whether it was the excitement of our talk last night, or what it was, but my sulfonal wouldn't act, though I took fifteen grains, and I was up with the lark, or should have been, if there had been any lark outside of literature to be up with. However, this air is so glorious that I don't mind losing a night's sleep, now and then. I believe that with a little practice one could get along without any sleep at all, here; at least *I* could. I'm sorry to say, poor Mr. Makely *can't*, apparently. He's making up for his share of my vigils, and I'm going to breakfast without him. Do you know, I've done a very bold thing: I've got the head waiter to give you places at our table; I know you'll hate it, Mr. Twelvemough, because you naturally want to keep Mr. Homos to yourself, and I don't blame you at all; but I'm simply not going to *let* you, and that's all there is about it."

The pleasure I felt at this announcement was not unmixed, but I tried to keep Mrs. Makely from thinking so, and I was immensely relieved when she found a chance to say to me in a low voice, "I know just how you're feeling, Mr. Twelvemough, and I'm going to help you keep him from doing anything ridiculous, if I can. I *like* him, and I think it's a perfect shame to have people laughing at him. I know we can manage him between us."

We so far failed, however, that the Altrurian shook hands with the head waiter, when he pressed open the wire netting door to let us into the dining-room, and made a bow to our waitress of the sort one makes to a lady. But we thought it best to ignore these little errors of his, and reserve our moral strength for anything more spectacular. Fortunately we got through our breakfast with nothing worse than his jumping up, and stooping to hand the waitress a spoon she let fall; but this could easily pass for some attention to Mrs. Makely at a little distance. There were not many people down to breakfast, yet; but I could see that there was a good deal of subdued sensation among the waitresses, standing with folded arms behind their tables, and that the head waiter's handsome face was red with anxiety.

Mrs. Makely asked if we were going to church. She said she was driving that way and would be glad to drop us. "I'm not going myself," she explained, "because I couldn't make anything of the sermon, with my head in the state it is, and I'm going to compromise on a good action. I want to carry some books and papers over to Mrs. Camp. Don't you think that will be quite as acceptable, Mr. Homos?"

"I should venture to hope it," he said, with a tolerant seriousness not altogether out of keeping with her lightness.

"Who is Mrs. Camp?" I asked, not caring to commit myself on the question.

"Lizzie's mother. You know I told you about them last night. I think she must have got through the books I lent her, and I know Lizzie didn't like to ask me for more, because she saw me talking with you and didn't want to interrupt us. Such a nice girl! I think the Sunday papers must have come, and I'll take them over, too; Mrs. Camp is always so glad to get them, and she is so delightful when she gets going about public events. But perhaps you don't approve of Sunday papers, Mr. Homos."

"I'm sure I don't know, madam. I haven't seen them yet. You know this is the first Sunday I've been in America."

"Well, I'm sorry to say you won't see the old Puritan Sabbath," said Mrs. Makely, with an abrupt deflection from the question of the Sunday papers. "Though you ought to, up in these hills. The only thing left of it is rye-and-Indian bread, and these baked beans and fish-balls."

"But they are very good?"

"Yes, I dare say they are not the worst of it."

She was a woman who tended to levity, and I was a little afraid she might be going to say something irreverent, but if she were, she was forestalled by the Altrurian asking, "Would it be very indiscreet, madam, if I were to ask you some time to introduce me to that family?"

"The Camps?" she returned. "Not at all. I should be perfectly delighted." The thought seemed to strike her, and she asked, "Why not go with me this morning, unless you are inflexibly bent on going to church, you and Mr. Twelvemough?"

The Altrurian glanced at me, and I said I should be only too glad, if I could carry some books, so that I could compromise on a good action, too. "Take one of your own," she instantly suggested.

"Do you think they wouldn't be too severe upon it?" I asked.

"Well, Mrs. Camp might," Mrs. Makely consented, with a smile. "She goes in for rather serious fiction; but I think Lizzie would enjoy a good, old-fashioned love-story, where everybody got married, as they do in your charming books."

I winced a little, for everyone likes to be regarded seriously, and I did not enjoy being remanded to the young-girl public; but I put a bold face on it, and said, "My good action shall be done in behalf of Miss Lizzie."

Half an hour later, Mrs. Makely having left word with the clerk where we were gone, so that her husband need not be alarmed when he got up, we were striking into the hills on a two-seated buckboard, with one of the best teams of our hotel, and one of the most taciturn drivers. Mrs. Makely had the Altrurian get into the back seat with her, and, after some attempts to make talk with the driver, I leaned over and joined in their talk. The Altrurian was greatly interested, not so much in the landscape— though he owned its beauty, when we cried out over it from point to point—but in the human incidents and features. He noticed the cattle in the fields, and the horses we met on the road, and the taste and comfort of the buildings, the variety of the crops, and the promise of the harvest. I was glad of the respite his questions gave me from the study of the intimate character of our civilization, for they were directed now at these more material facts, and I willingly joined Mrs. Makely in answering them. We explained that the finest teams we met were from the different hotels or boarding-houses, or at least from the farms where the people took city people to board; and that certain shabby equipages belonged to the natives who lived solely by cultivating the soil. There was not very much of the soil cultivated, for the chief crop was hay, with here and there a patch of potatoes or beans, and a few acres in sweet-corn. The houses of the natives, when they were for their use only, were no better than their turnouts; it was where the city boarder had found shelter that they were modern and pleasant. Now and then we came to a deserted homestead, and I tried to make the Altrurian understand how farming in New England had yielded to the competition of the immense agricultural operations of the west. "You know," I said, "that agriculture is really an operation out there, as much as coal-mining is in Pennsylvania, or finance in Wall street; you have no idea of the vastness of the scale." Perhaps I swelled a little with pride in my celebration of the national prosperity, as it flowed from our western farms of five, and ten, and twenty thousand acres; I could not very well help putting on the pedal in these passages. Mrs. Makely listened almost as eagerly as the Altrurian, for, as a cultivated American woman, she was necessarily quite ignorant of her own country, geographically, politically and historically. "The only people left in the hill country of New England," I concluded, "are those who are too old or too lazy to get away. Any young man of energy would be ashamed to stay, unless he wanted to keep a boarding-house or live on the city vacationists in summer. If he doesn't, he goes west and takes up some of the new land, and comes back in middle-life, and buys a deserted farm to spend his summers on."

"Dear me!" said the Altrurian, "Is it so simple as that? Then we can hardly wonder at their owners leaving these wornout farms; though I suppose it must be with the pang of exile, sometimes."

"Oh, I fancy there isn't much sentiment involved," I answered, lightly.

"Whoa!" said Mrs. Makely, speaking to the horses, before she spoke to the driver, as some women will. He pulled them up, and looked round at her.

"Isn't that Reuben Camp, *now*, over there by that house?" she asked, as if we had been talking of him; that is another way some women have.

"Yes, ma'am," said the driver.

"Oh, well, then!" and "Reuben!" she called to the young man, who was prowling about the dooryard of a sad-colored old farmhouse, and peering into a window here and there. "Come here a moment—won't you, please?"

He lifted his head and looked round, and when he had located the appeal made to him, he came down the walk to the gate and leaned over it, waiting for further instructions. I saw that it was the young man whom we had noticed with the girl Mrs. Makely called Lizzie, on the hotel piazza, the night before.

"Do you know whether I should find Lizzie at home, this morning?"

"Yes, she's there with mother," said the young fellow, with neither liking nor disliking in his tone.

"Oh, I'm so glad!" said the lady. "I didn't know but she might be at church. What in the world has happened here? Is there anything unusual going on inside?"

"No, I was just looking to see if it was all right. The folks wanted I should come round."

"Why, where are they?"

"Oh, they're gone."

"Gone?"

"Yes; gone west. They've left the old place, because they couldn't make a living here, any longer."

"Why, this is quite a case in point," I said. "Now, Mr. Homos, here is a chance to inform yourself at first hand about a very interesting fact of our civilization;" and I added, in a low voice, to Mrs. Makely, "Won't you introduce us?"

"Oh, yes! Mr. Camp, this is Mr. Twelvemough, the author— you know his books, of course; and Mr. Homos, a gentleman from Altruria."

The young fellow opened the gate he leaned on, and came out to us. He took no notice of me, but he seized the Altrurian's hand

and wrung it. "I've heard of *you*," he said. "Mrs. Makely, were you going to our place?"

"Why, yes."

"So do, then! Mother would give almost anything to see Mr. Homos. We've heard of Altruria, over our way," he added, to our friend. "Mother's been reading up all she can about it. She'll want to talk with you, and she won't give the rest of us much of a chance, I guess."

"Oh, I shall be glad to see her," said the Altrurian, "and to tell her everything I can. But won't you explain to me first something about your deserted farms here? It's quite a new thing to me."

"It isn't a new thing to us," said the young fellow, with a short laugh. "And there isn't much to explain about it. You'll see them all through New England. When a man finds he can't get his funeral expenses out of the land, he don't feel like staying to be buried in it, and he pulls up and goes."

"But people used to get their living expenses here," I suggested. "Why can't they now?"

"Well, they didn't use to have western prices to fight with; and then the land wasn't wornout so, and the taxes were not so heavy. How would you like to pay twenty to thirty dollars on the thousand, and assessed up to the last notch, in the city?"

"Why, what in the world makes your taxes so heavy?"

"Schools and roads. We've got to have schools, and you city folks want good roads when you come here in the summer, don't you? Then the season is short, and sometimes we can't make a crop. The frost catches the corn in the field, and you have your trouble for your pains. Potatoes are the only thing we can count on, except grass, and when everybody raises potatoes, you know where the price goes."

"Oh, but now, Mr. Camp," said Mrs. Makely, leaning over towards him, and speaking in a cosey and coaxing tone, as if he must not really keep the truth from an old friend like her, "isn't it a good deal because the farmers' daughters want pianos, and the farmers' sons want buggies? I heard Professor Lumen saying, the other day, that if the farmers were willing to work, as they used to work, they could still get a good living off their farms, and that they gave up their places because they were too lazy, in many cases, to farm them properly."

"He'd better not let *me* hear him saying that," said the young fellow, while a hot flush passed over his face. He added, bitterly, "If he wants to see how easy it is to make a living up here, he can take this place and try, for a year or two; he can get it cheap. But I guess he wouldn't want it the year round; he'd only want it a few months in the summer, when he could enjoy the sightliness of it, and see me working over there on my farm, while he smoked on his front porch." He turned round and looked at the old house, in silence a moment. Then, as he went on, his voice lost its angry ring. "The folks here bought this place from the Indians, and they'd been here more than two hundred years. Do you think they left it because they were too lazy to run it, or couldn't get pianos and buggies out of it, or were such fools as not to know whether they were well off? It was their *home*; they were born, and lived and died here. There is the family burying ground, over there."

Neither Mrs. Makely nor myself was ready with a reply, and we left the word with the Altrurian, who suggested, "Still, I suppose they will be more prosperous in the west, on the new land they take up?"

The young fellow leaned his arms on the wheel by which he stood. "What do you mean by taking up new land?"

"Why, out of the public domain"—

"There *ain't* any public domain that's worth having. All the good land is in the hands of railroads, and farm syndicates, and speculators; and if you want a farm in the west you've got to buy it; the east is the only place where folks give them away, because they ain't worth keeping. If you haven't got the ready money, you can buy one on credit, and pay ten, twenty and thirty per cent. interest, and live in a dug-out on the plains—till your mortgage matures." The young man took his arms from the wheel and moved a few steps backwards, as he added, "I'll see you over at the house later."

The driver touched his horses, and we started briskly off again. But I confess I had quite enough of his pessimism, and as we drove away I leaned back toward the Altrurian, and said, "Now, it is all perfect nonsense to pretend that things are at that pass with us. There are more millionaires in America, probably, than there are in all the other civilized countries of the globe, and it is not possible that the farming population should be in such a hopeless condition. All wealth comes out of the earth, and you may be sure they get their full share of it."

"I am glad to hear you say so," said the Altrurian. "What is the meaning of this new party in the west that seems to have held a convention lately? I read something of it in the train yesterday."

"Oh, that is a lot of crazy Hayseeds, who don't want to pay back the money they have borrowed, or who find themselves unable to meet their interest. It will soon blow over. We are always having these political flurries. A good crop will make it all right with them."

"But is it true that they have to pay such rates of interest as our young friend mentioned?"

"Well," I said, seeing the thing in the humorous light, which softens for us Americans so many of the hardships of others, "I suppose that man likes to squeeze his brother man, when he gets him in his grip. That's human nature, you know."

"Is it?" asked the Altrurian.

It seemed to me that he had asked something like that before when I alleged human nature in defence of some piece of everyday selfishness. But I thought best not to notice it, and I went on: "The land is so rich out there that a farm will often pay for itself with a single crop."

"Is it possible?" cried the Altrurian. "Then I suppose it seldom really happens that a mortgage is foreclosed, in the way our young friend insinuated."

"Well, I can't say that exactly," and having admitted so much, I did not feel bound to impart a fact that popped perversely into my mind. I was once talking with a western money-lender, a very good sort of fellow, frank and open as the day; I asked him whether the farmers generally paid off their mortgages, and he answered me that if the mortgage was to the value of a fourth of the land, the farmer might pay it off, but if it were to a half, or a third even, he never paid it, but slaved on and died in his debts. "You may be sure, however," I concluded, "that our young friend takes a jaundiced view of the situation."

"Now, really," said Mrs. Makely, "I must insist upon dropping this everlasting talk about money. I think it is perfectly disgusting, and I believe it was Mr. Makely's account of his speculations that kept me awake last night. My brain got running on figures till the dark seemed to be all sown with dollar marks, like the stars in the milky way. I—Ugh! What in the world is it? Oh, you dreadful little things!"

Mrs. Makely passed swiftly from terror to hysterical laughter as the driver pulled up short, and a group of barefooted children broke in front of his horses, and scuttled out of the dust into the roadside bushes like a covey of quails. There seemed to be a dozen of them, nearly all the same in size, but there turned out to be only five or six; or at least no more showed their gleaming eyes and teeth through the underbrush in quiet enjoyment of the lady's alarm.

"Don't you know that you might have got killed?" she demanded with that severity good women feel for people who have just escaped with their lives. "How lovely the dirty little dears are!" she added, in the next wave of emotion. One bold fellow of six showed a half length above the bushes, and she asked, "Don't you know that you oughtn't to play in the road when there are so many teams passing? Are all those your brothers and sisters?"

He ignored the first question. "One's my cousin." I pulled out a half-dozen coppers, and held my hand toward him. "See if there is one for each." They had no difficulty in solving the simple mathematical problem, except the smallest girl, who cried for fear and baffled longing. I tossed the coin to her, and a little fat dog darted out at her feet and caught it up in his mouth.

"Oh, good gracious!" I called out in my light, humorous way. "Do you suppose he's going to spend it for candy?" The little people thought that a famous joke, and they laughed with the gratitude that even small favors inspire. "Bring your sister here," I said to the boldest boy, and when he came up with the little woman, I put another copper into her hand. "Look out that the greedy dog doesn't get it," I said, and my gaiety met with fresh applause. "Where do you live?" I asked with some vague purpose of showing the Altrurian the kindliness that exists between our upper and lower classes.

"Over there," said the boy. I followed the twist of his head, and glimpsed a wooden cottage on the border of the forest, so very new that the sheathing had not yet been covered with clapboards. I stood up in the buckboard and saw that it was a story and a half high, and could have had four or five rooms in it. The bare, curtainless windows were set in the unpainted frames, but the front door seemed not to be hung yet. The people meant to winter there, however, for the sod was banked up against the wooden underpinning; a stove-pipe stuck out of the roof of a little wing behind. While I gazed, a young-looking woman came to the door, as if she had been drawn by our talk with the children, and then she jumped down from the threshold, which still wanted a doorstep, and came slowly out to us. The children ran to her with their coppers, and then followed her back to us.

Mrs. Makely called to her before she reached us, "I hope you weren't frightened. We didn't drive over any of them."

"Oh, I wasn't frightened," said the young woman. "It's a very safe place to bring up children, in the country, and I never feel uneasy about them."

"Yes, if they are not under the horses' feet," said Mrs. Makely, mingling instruction and amusement very judiciously in her reply. "Are they all yours?"

"Only five," said the mother, and she pointed to the alien in her flock. "He's my sister's. She lives just below here." Her children had grouped themselves about her, and she kept passing her hands caressingly over their little heads as she talked. "My sister has nine children, but she has the rest at church with her today."

"You don't speak like an American," Mrs. Makely suggested.

"No, we're English. Our husbands work in the quarry. That's *my* little palace." The woman nodded her head toward the cottage.

"It's going to be very nice," said Mrs. Makely, with an evident perception of her pride in it.

"Yes, if we ever get money to finish it. Thank you for the children!"

"Oh, it was this gentleman." Mrs. Makely indicated me, and I bore the merit of my good action as modestly as I could.

"Then, thank *you*, sir," said the young woman, and she asked Mrs. Makely, "You're not living about here, ma'am?"

"Oh, no, we're staying at the hotel."

"At the hotel! It must be very dear, there."

"Yes, it is expensive," said Mrs. Makely, with a note of that satisfaction in her voice which we all feel in spending a great deal of money.

"But I suppose you can afford it," said the woman, whose eye was running hungrily over Mrs. Makely's pretty costume. "Some are poor, and some are rich. That's the way the world has to be made up, isn't it?"

"Yes," said Mrs. Makely, very dryly, and the talk languished from this point, so that the driver felt warranted in starting up his horses. When we had driven beyond earshot she said, "I knew she was not an American, as soon as she spoke, by her accent, and then those foreigners have no self-respect. That was a pretty bold bid for a contribution to finish up her 'little palace!' I'm glad you didn't give her anything, Mr. Twelvemough. I was afraid your sympathies had been wrought upon."

"Oh, not at all!" I answered. "I saw the mischief I had done with the children."

The Altrurian, who had not asked anything for a long time, but had listened with eager interest to all that passed, now came up smiling with his question: "Will you kindly tell me what harm would have been done by offering the woman a little money to help finish up her cottage?"

I did not allow Mrs. Makely to answer, I was so eager to air my political economy. "The very greatest harm. It would have pauperized her. You have no idea how quickly they give way to the poison of that sort of thing. As soon as they get any sort of help they expect more; they count upon it, and they begin to live upon it. The sight of those coppers which I gave her children —more out of joke than charity—demoralized the woman. She took us for rich people, and wanted us to build her a house. You have to guard against every approach to a thing of that sort."

"I don't believe," said Mrs. Makely, "that an American would have hinted as she did."

"No, an American would not have done that, I'm thankful to say. They take fees, but they don't ask charity, yet." We went on to exult in the noble independence of the American character in all classes, at some length. We talked at the Altrurian, but he did not seem to hear us. At last, he asked with a faint sigh, "Then, in your conditions, a kindly impulse to aid one who needs your help, is something to be guarded against as possibly pernicious?"

"Exactly," I said. "And now you see what difficulties beset us in dealing with the problem of poverty. We cannot let people suffer, for that would be cruel; and we cannot relieve their need without pauperizing them."

"I see," he answered. "It is a terrible quandary."

"I wish," said Mrs. Makely, "that you would tell us just how you manage with the poor in Altruria."

"We have none," he replied.

"But the comparatively poor—you have some people who are richer than others?"

"No. We should regard that as the worst incivism."

"What is incivism?"

I interpreted, "Bad citizenship."

"Well then, if you will excuse me, Mr. Homos," she said, "I think that is simply impossible. There *must* be rich and there *must* be poor. There always have been, and there always will be. That woman said it as well as anybody. Didn't Christ himself say, 'The poor ye have always with you' ?"

VII

THE ALTRURIAN looked at Mrs. Makely with an amazement visibly heightened by the air of complacency she put on after delivering this poser: "Do you really think Christ meant that you *ought* always to have the poor with you?" he asked.

"Why, of course!" she answered triumphantly. "How else are the sympathies of the rich to be cultivated? The poverty of some and the wealth of others, isn't that what forms the great tie of human brotherhood? If we were all comfortable, or all shared alike, there could not be anything like charity, and Paul said 'the greatest of these is charity.' I believe it's 'love,' in the new version, but it comes to the same thing."

The Altrurian gave a kind of gasp and then lapsed into a silence that lasted until we came in sight of the Camp farmhouse. It stood on the crest of a roadside upland, and looked down the beautiful valley, bathed in Sabbath sunlight, and away to the ranges of hills, so far that it was hard to say whether it was sun or shadow that dimmed their distance. Decidedly, the place was what the country people call sightly. The old house, once painted a Brandon red, crouched low to the ground, with its lean-to in the rear, and its flat-arched wood-sheds and wagon-houses, stretching away at the side to the barn, and covering the approach to it with an unbroken roof. There were flowers in the beds along the under-pinning of the house, which stood close to the street, and on one side of the door was a clump of Spanish willow; an old-fashioned June rose climbed over it from the other. An aged dog got stiffly to his feet from the threshold stone, and whimpered, as our buckboard drew up; the poultry picking about the path and among the chips, lazily made way for us, and as our wheels ceased to crunch upon the gravel, we heard hasty steps, and Reuben Camp came round the corner of the house in time to give Mrs. Makely his hand, and help her spring to the ground, which she did very lightly; her remarkable mind had kept her body in a sort of sympathetic activity, and at thirty-five she had the gracile ease and self-command of a girl.

"Ah, Reuben," she sighed, permitting herself to call him by his first name, with the emotion which expressed itself more definitely in the words that followed, "how I envy you all this dear, old, home-like place! I never come here without thinking of my grandfather's farm in Massachusetts, where I used to go every summer when I was a little girl. If I had a place like this, I should never leave it."

"Well, Mrs. Makely," said young Camp, "you can have this place cheap, if you really want it. Or almost any other place in the neighborhood."

"Don't say such a thing!" she returned. "It makes one feel as if the foundations of the great deep were giving way. I don't know what that means, exactly, but I suppose it's equivalent to mislaying George's hatchet, and going back on the Declaration generally; and I don't like to hear you talk so."

Camp seemed to have lost his bitter mood, and he answered pleasantly, "The Declaration is all right, as far as it goes, but it don't help us to compete with the western farm operations."

"Why, you believe every one was born free and equal, don't you?" Mrs. Makely asked.

"Oh, yes, I believe that; but"—

"Then why do you object to free and equal competition?"

The young fellow laughed, and said, as he opened the door for us: "Walk right into the parlor, please. Mother will be ready for you in a minute." He added, "I guess she's putting on her best cap, for you, Mr. Homos. It's a great event for her, your coming here. It is for all of us. We're glad to have you."

"And I'm glad to be here," said the Altrurian, as simply as the other. He looked about the best room of a farmhouse that had never adapted itself to the tastes or needs of the city boarder, and was as stiffly repellant in its upholstery, and as severe in its decoration as haircloth chairs and dark brown wall-paper of a trellis-pattern, with drab roses, could make it. The windows were shut tight, and our host did not offer to open them. A fly or two crossed the doorway into the hall, but made no attempt to penetrate the interior, where we sat in an obscurity that left the high-hung family photographs on the walls vague and uncertain. I made a mental note of it as a place where it would be very characteristic to have a rustic funeral take place; and I was pleased to have Mrs. Makely drop into a sort of mortuary murmur, as she said: "I hope your mother is as well as usual, this morning?" I perceived that this murmur was produced by the sepulchral influence of the room.

"Oh, yes," said Camp, and at that moment a door opened from the room across the hall, and his sister seemed to bring in some of the light from it to us, where we sat. She shook hands with Mrs. Makely, who introduced me to her, and then presented the Altrurian. She bowed very civilly to me, but with a touch of severity, such as country people find necessary for the assertion of their self-respect with strangers. I thought it very pretty, and instantly saw that I could work it into some picture of character; and I was not at all sorry that she made a difference in favor of the Altrurian.

"Mother will be so glad to see you," she said to him, and, "Won't you come right in?" she added to us all.

We followed her and found ourselves in a large, low, sunny room on the southeast corner of the house, which had no doubt once been the living-room, but which was now given up to the bed-ridden invalid; a door opened into the kitchen behind, where the table was already laid for the midday meal, with the plates turned down in the country fashion, and some netting drawn over the dishes to keep the flies away.

Mrs. Makely bustled up to the bedside with her energetic, patronizing cheerfulness. "Ah, Mrs. Camp, I am glad to see you looking so well this morning. I've been meaning to run over for several days past, but I couldn't find a moment till this morning, and I knew you didn't object to Sunday visits." She took the invalid's hand in hers, and with the air of showing how little she felt any inequality between them, she leaned over and kissed her, where Mrs. Camp sat propped against her pillows. She had a large, nobly-moulded face of rather masculine contour, and at the same time the most motherly look in the world. Mrs. Makely bubbled and babbled on, and every one waited patiently till she had done, and turned and said, toward the Altrurian: "I have ventured to bring my friend, Mr. Homos, with me. He is from Altruria." Then she turned to me, and said, "Mr. Twelvemough, you know already through his delightful books;" but although she paid me this perfunctory compliment, it was perfectly apparent to me that in the esteem of this disingenuous woman the distinguished stranger was a far more important person than the distinguished author. Whether Mrs. Camp read my perception of this fact in my face or not, I cannot say, but she was evidently determined that I should not feel a difference in her. She held out her hand to me first, and said that I never could know how many heavy hours I had helped to lighten for her, and then she turned to the Altrurian, and took his hand. "Oh!" she said, with a long, deep, drawn sigh, as if that were the supreme moment of her life. "And are you really from Altruria? It seems too good to be true!" Her devout look and her earnest tone gave the commonplace words a quality that did not inhere in them, but Mrs. Makely took them on their surface.

"Yes, doesn't it?" she made haste to interpose, before the Altrurian could say anything. "That is just the way we all feel about it, Mrs. Camp. I assure you, if it were not for the accounts in the papers, and the talk about it everywhere, I couldn't believe there *was* any such place as Altruria; and if it were not for Mr. Twelvemough here—who has to keep all his inventions for his novels, as a mere matter of business routine,—I might really suspect him and Mr. Homos of—well, *working* us, as my husband calls it."

The Altrurian smiled politely, but vaguely, as if he had not quite caught her meaning, and I made answer for both: "I am sure, Mrs. Makely, if you could understand my peculiar state of mind about Mr. Homos, you would never believe that I was in collusion with him. I find him quite as incredible as you do. There are moments when he seems so entirely subjective with me, that I feel as if he were no more definite or tangible than a bad conscience."

"Exactly!" said Mrs. Makely, and she laughed out her delight in my illustration.

The Altrurian must have perceived that we were joking, though the Camps all remained soberly silent. "I hope it isn't so bad as that," he said, "though I have noticed that I seem to affect you all with a kind of misgiving. I don't know just what it is; but if I could remove it, I should be very glad to do so."

Mrs. Makely very promptly seized her chance: "Well, then, in the first place, my husband and I were talking it over last night, after we left you, and that was one of the things that kept us awake; it turned into money afterwards. It isn't so much that a whole continent, as big as Australia, remained undiscovered till within such a very few years, as it is the condition of things among you: this sort of all living for one another, and not each one for himself. My husband says that is simply moonshine; such a thing never was and never can be; it is opposed to human nature, and would take away incentive, and all motive for exertion and advancement and enterprise. I don't know *what* he didn't say against it; but one thing: he says it's perfectly un-American." The Altrurian remained silent, gravely smiling, and Mrs. Makely added, with her most engaging little manner: "I hope you won't feel hurt, personally or patriotically, by what I've repeated to you. I know my husband is awfully Philistine, though he *is* such a good fellow, and I don't, by any means, agree with him on all those points; but I *would* like to know what you think of them. The trouble is, Mrs. Camp," she said, turning to the invalid, "that Mr. Homos is so dreadfully reticent about his own country, and I am so curious to hear of it at first hands, that I consider it justifiable to use any means to make him open up about it."

"There is no offense," the Altrurian answered for himself, "in what Mr. Makely says, though, from the Altrurian point of view, there is a good deal of error. Does it seem so strange to you," he asked, addressing himself to Mrs. Camp, "that people should found a civilization on the idea of living for one another, instead of each for himself?"

"No, indeed!" she answered. "Poor people have always had to live that way, or they could not have lived at all."

"That was what I understood your porter to say last night," said the Altrurian to me. He added, to the company generally: "I suppose that even in America there are more poor people than there are rich people?"

"Well, I don't know about that," I said. "I suppose there are more people independently rich than there are people independently poor."

"We will let that formulation of it stand. If it is true, I do not see why the Altrurian system should be considered so very un-American. Then, as to whether there is or ever was really a practical altruism, a civic expression of it, I think it cannot be denied that among the first Christians, those who immediately followed Christ, and might be supposed to be directly influenced by his life, there was an altruism practised, as radical as that which we have organized into a national polity and a working economy in Altruria."

"Ah, but you know," said Mrs. Makely, with the air of advancing a point not to be put aside, "they had to drop *that*. It was a dead failure. They found that they couldn't make it go at all, among cultivated people, and that, if Christianity was to advance, they would have to give up all that crankish kind of idolatry of the mere letter. At any rate," she went on, with the satisfaction we all feel in getting an opponent into close quarters, "you must confess that there is a much greater play of individuality here."

Before the Altrurian could reply, young Camp said: "If you want to see American individuality, the real, simon-pure article, you ought to go down to one of our big factory towns, and look at the mill-hands coming home in droves after a day's work, young girls and old women, boys and men, all fluffed over with cotton, and so dead-tired that they can hardly walk. They come shambling along with all the individuality of a flock of sheep."

"Some," said Mrs. Makely, heroically, as if she were one of these, "must be sacrificed. Of course, some are not so individual as others. A great deal depends upon temperament."

"A great deal more depends upon capital," said Camp, with an offensive laugh. "If you have capital in America, you can have individuality; if you haven't, you can't."

His sister, who had not taken part in the talk before, said demurely: "It seems to me you've got a good deal of individuality, Reub, and you haven't got a great deal of capital either," and the two young people laughed together.

Mrs. Makely was one of those fatuous women whose eagerness to make a point, excludes the consideration even of their own advantage. "I'm sure," she said, as if speaking for the upper classes, "*we* haven't got any individuality at all. We are as like as so many peas, or pins. In fact, you have to be so, in society. If you keep asserting your own individuality too much, people avoid you. It's very vulgar, and the greatest bore."

"Then you don't find individuality so desirable, after all," said the Altrurian.

"I perfectly detest it!" cried the lady, and evidently she had not the least notion where she was in the argument. "For my part, I'm never happy, except when I've forgotten myself and the whole individual bother."

Her declaration seemed somehow to close the incident, and we were all silent a moment, which I employed in looking about the room, and taking in with my literary sense, the simplicity and even bareness of its furnishing. There was the bed where the invalid lay, and near the head, a table with a pile of books and a kerosene lamp on it, and I decided that she was a good deal wakeful, and that she read by that lamp, when she could not sleep at night. Then there were the hard chairs we sat on, and some home-made hooked rugs, in rounds and ovals, scattered about the clean floor; there was a small melodeon pushed against the wall; the windows had paper shades, and I recalled that I had not seen any blinds on the outside of the house. Over the head of the bed hung a cavalryman's sword, with its belt; the sword that Mrs. Makely had spoken of. It struck me as a room where a great many things might have happened, and I said: "You can't think, Mrs. Camp, how glad I am to see the inside of your house. It seems to me so typical."

A pleased intelligence showed itself in her face, and she answered: "Yes, it is a real old-fashioned farmhouse. We have never taken boarders and so we have kept it as it was built, pretty much, and only made such changes in it as we needed or wanted for ourselves."

"It's a pity," I went on, following up what I thought a fortunate lead, "that we city people see so little of the farming life, when we come into the country. I have been here now for several seasons, and this is the first time I have been inside a farmer's house."

"Is it possible!" cried the Altrurian, with an air of utter astonishment; and when I found the fact appeared so singular to him, I began to be rather proud of its singularity.

"Yes, I suppose that most city people come and go, year after year, in the country, and never make any sort of acquaintance with the people who live there the year round. We keep to ourselves in the hotels, or if we go out at all, it is to make a call upon some city cottager, and so we do not get out of the vicious circle of our own over-intimacy with ourselves, and our ignorance of others."

"And you regard that as a great misfortune?" asked the Altrurian.

"Why, it's inevitable. There is nothing to bring us together, unless it's some happy accident, like the present. But we don't have a traveller from Altruria to exploit every day, and so we have no business to come into people's houses."

"You would have been welcome in ours, long ago, Mr. Twelvemough," said Mrs. Camp.

"But, excuse me!" said the Altrurian. "What you say really seems dreadful to me. Why, it is as if you were not the same race, or kind of men!"

"Yes," I answered. "It has sometimes seemed to me as if our

big hotel there were a ship, anchored off some strange coast. The inhabitants come out with supplies, and carry on their barter with the ship's steward, and we sometimes see them over the side, but we never speak to them, or have anything to do with them. We sail away at the close of the season, and that is the end of it till next summer."

The Altrurian turned to Mrs. Camp. "And how do you look at it? How does it seem to you?"

"I don't believe we have thought about it very much; but now that Mr. Twelvemough has spoken of it, I can see that it does look that way. And it seems very strange, doesn't it, for we are all the same people, and have the same language, and religion and country—the country that my husband fought for, and I suppose I may say, died for; he was never the same man after the war. It does appear as if we had some interests in common, and might find it out if we ever came together."

"It's a great advantage, the city people going into the country so much as they do now," said Mrs. Makely. "They bring five million dollars into the state of New Hampshire, alone, every summer."

She looked round for the general approval which this fact merited, and young Camp said: "And it shows how worthless the natives are, that they can't make both ends meet, with all that money, but have to give up their farms and go west, after all. I suppose you think it comes from wanting buggies and pianos."

"Well, it certainly comes from something," said Mrs. Makely, with the courage of her convictions.

She was evidently not going to be put down by that sour young fellow, and I was glad of it, though I must say I thought the thing she left to rankle in his mind from our former meeting had not been said in very good taste. I thought, too, that she would not fare best in any encounter of wits with him, and I rather trembled for the result. I said, to relieve the strained situation, "I wish there was some way of our knowing each other better. I'm sure there's a great deal of good will on both sides."

"No, there isn't," said Camp, "or at least I can answer for

our side, that there isn't. You come into the country to get as much for your money as you can, and we mean to let you have as little as we can. That's the whole story, and if Mr. Homos believes anything different, he's very much mistaken."

"I hadn't formed any conclusion in regard to the matter, which is quite new to me," said the Altrurian, mildly. "But why is there no basis of mutual kindness between you?"

"Because it's like everything else with us, it's a question of supply and demand, and there is no room for any mutual kindness in a question of that kind. Even if there were, there is another thing that would kill it. The summer folks, as we call them, look down on the natives, as they call us, and we know it."

"Now, Mr. Camp, I am sure that you cannot say *I* look down on the natives," said Mrs. Makely, with an air of argument.

The young fellow laughed. "Oh, yes, you do," he said, not unamiably, and he added, "and you've got the right to. We're not fit to associate with you, and you know it, and we know it. You've got more money, and you've got nicer clothes, and you've got prettier manners. You talk about things that most natives never heard of, and you care for things they never saw. I know it's the custom to pretend differently, but I'm not going to pretend differently." I recalled what my friend, the banker, said about throwing away cant, and I asked myself if I were in the presence of some such free spirit again. I did not see how young Camp could afford it; but then I reflected that he had really nothing to lose by it, for he did not expect to make anything out of us; Mrs. Makely would probably not give up his sister as seamstress, if the girl continued to work so well and so cheaply as she said. "Suppose," he went on, "that some old native took you at your word, and came to call upon you at the hotel, with his wife, just as one of the city cottagers would do if he wanted to make your acquaintance?"

"I should be perfectly delighted!" said Mrs. Makely. "And I should receive them with the greatest possible cordiality."

"The same kind of cordiality that you would show to the cottagers?"

"I suppose that I should feel that I had more in common with the cottagers. We should be interested in the same things, and we should probably know the same people and have more to talk about"—

"You would both belong to the same class, and that tells the whole story. If you were out west, and the owner of one of those big, twenty thousand acre farms called on you with his wife, would you act toward them as you would toward our natives? You wouldn't! You would all be rich people together, and you would understand each other because you had money."

"Now, that is not so," Mrs. Makely interrupted. "There are plenty of rich people one wouldn't wish to know at all, and who really can't get into society; who are ignorant and vulgar. And then when you come to money, I don't see but what country people are as glad to get it as anybody."

"Oh, gladder," said the young man.

"Well?" demanded Mrs. Makely, as if this were a final stroke of logic. The young man did not reply, and Mrs. Makely continued: "Now I will appeal to your sister to say whether she has ever seen any difference in my manner toward her from what I show to all the young ladies in the hotel." The young girl flushed, and seemed reluctant to answer. "Why, Lizzie!" cried Mrs. Makely, and her tone showed that she was really hurt.

The scene appeared to me rather cruel, and I glanced at Mrs. Camp, with an expectation that she would say something to relieve it. But she did not. Her large, benevolent face expressed only a quiet interest in the discussion.

"You know very well, Mrs. Makely," said the girl, "you don't regard me as you do the young ladies in the hotel."

There was no resentment in her voice or look, but only a sort of regret, as if, but for this grievance, she could have loved the woman from whom she had probably had much kindness. The tears came into Mrs. Makely's eyes, and she turned toward Mrs. Camp. "And is this the way you *all* feel toward us?" she asked.

"Why shouldn't we?" asked the invalid, in her turn. "But, no, it isn't the way all the country people feel. Many of them feel as you would like to have them feel; but that is because they do not think. When they think, they feel as we do. But I don't blame you. You can't help yourselves, any more than we can. We're all bound up together in that, at least."

At this apparent relenting, Mrs. Makely tricked her beams a little, and said, plaintively, as if offering herself for further condolence: "Yes, that is what that woman at the little shanty back there said: some have to be rich, and some have to be poor; it takes all kinds to make a world."

"How would you like to be one of those that have to be poor?" asked young Camp, with an evil grin.

"I don't know," said Mrs. Makely, with unexpected spirit; "but I am sure that I should respect the feelings of all, rich or poor."

"I am sorry if we have hurt yours, Mrs. Makely," said Mrs. Camp, with dignity. "You asked us certain questions, and we thought you wished us to reply truthfully. We could not answer you with smooth things."

"But sometimes you do," said Mrs. Makely, and the tears stood in her eyes again. "And you know how fond I am of you all!"

Mrs. Camp wore a bewildered look. "Perhaps we have said more than we ought. But I couldn't help it, and I don't see how the children could, when you asked them here, before Mr. Homos."

I glanced at the Altrurian, sitting attentive and silent, and a sudden misgiving crossed my mind concerning him. Was he really a man, a human entity, a personality like ourselves, or was he merely a sort of spiritual solvent, sent for the moment to precipitate whatever sincerity there was in us, and show us what the truth was concerning our relations to each other? It was a fantastic conception, but I thought it was one that I might employ in some sort of purely romantic design, and I was professionally grateful for it. I said, with a humorous gaiety: "Yes, we all seem to have been compelled to be much more honest than we like; and if Mr. Homos is going to write an account of his travels, when he gets home, he can't accuse us of hypocrisy, at any rate. And I always used to think it was one of our virtues! What with Mr. Camp, here, and my friend, the banker, at the hotel, I don't think he'll have much reason to complain even of our reticence."

"Well, whatever he says of us," sighed Mrs. Makely, with a pious glance at the sword over the bed, "he will have to say that, in spite of our divisions and classes, we are all Americans, and if we haven't the same opinions and ideas on minor matters, we all have the same country."

"I don't know about that," came from Reuben Camp, with shocking promptness. "I don't believe we all have the same country. America is one thing for you, and it's quite another thing for us. America means ease, and comfort, and amusement for you, year in and year out, and if it means work, it's work that you *wish* to do. For us, America means work that we *have* to do, and hard work, all the time, if we're going to make both ends meet. It means liberty for you; but what liberty has a man got who doesn't know where his next meal is coming from ? Once I was in a strike, when I was working on the railroad, and I've seen men come and give up their liberty for a chance to earn their family's living. They knew they were right, and that they ought to have stood up for their rights; but they had to lie down, and lick the hand that fed them! Yes, we are all Americans, but I guess we haven't all got the same country, Mrs. Makely. What sort of a country has a black-listed man got?"

"A black-listed man?" she repeated. "I don't know what you mean."

"Well, a kind of man I've seen in the mill towns, that the bosses have all got on their books as a man that isn't to be given work on any account; that's to be punished with hunger and cold, and turned into the street, for having offended them; and that's to be made to suffer through his helpless family, for having offended them."

"Excuse me, Mr. Camp," I interposed, "but isn't a black-listed man usually a man who has made himself prominent in some labor trouble?"

"Yes," the young fellow answered, without seeming sensible of the point I had made.

"Ah!" I returned. "Then you can hardly blame the employers for taking it out of him in any way they can. That's human nature."

"Good heavens!" the Altrurian cried out. "Is it possible that in America it is human nature to take away the bread of a man's family, because he has gone counter to your interest or pleasure on some economical question?"

"Well, Mr. Twelvemough seems to think so," sneered the young man. "But whether it's human nature or not, it's a fact that they do it, and you can guess how much a black-listed man must love the country where such a thing can happen to him. What should you call such a thing as black-listing in Altruria?"

"Oh, yes," Mrs. Makely pleaded, "do let us get him to talking about Altruria, on any terms. I think all this about the labor question is so tiresome; don't you, Mrs. Camp?"

Mrs. Camp did not answer; but the Altrurian said, in reply to her son: "We should have no name for such a thing, for with us such a thing would be impossible. There is no crime so heinous, with us, that the punishment would take away the criminal's chance of earning his living."

"Oh, if he was a criminal," said young Camp, "he would be all right, *here*. The state would give him a chance to earn his living, then."

"But if he had no other chance of earning his living, and had committed no offense against the laws"—

"Then the state would let him take to the road. Like that fellow."

He pulled aside the shade of the window, where he sat, and we saw pausing before the house, and glancing doubtfully at the door-step, where the dog lay, a vile and loathsome-looking tramp, a blot upon the sweet and wholesome landscape, a scandal to the sacred day. His rags burlesqued the form which they did not wholly hide; his broken shoes were covered with dust; his coarse hair came in a plume through his tattered hat;

his red, sodden face, at once fierce and timid, was rusty with a fortnight's beard. He offended the eye like a visible stench, and the wretched carrion seemed to shrink away from our gaze, as if he were aware of his loathsomeness.

"Really," said Mrs. Makely, "I thought those fellows were arrested, now. It is too bad to leave them at large. They are dangerous." Young Camp left the room, and we saw him going out toward the tramp. "Ah, that's quite right!" said the lady. "I hope Reuben is going to send him about his business. Why, surely he's not going to feed the horrid creature!" she added, as Camp, after a moment's parley with the tramp, turned with him, and disappeared round the corner of the house. "Now, Mrs. Camp, I think that is really a very bad example. It's encouraging them. Very likely, he'll go to sleep in your barn, and set it on fire with his pipe. What do you do with tramps in Altruria, Mr. Homos?"

The Altrurian seemed not to have heard her. He said to Mrs. Camp: "Then I understand from something your son let fall that he has not always been at home with you, here. Does he reconcile himself easily to the country after the excitement of town life? I have read that the cities in America are draining the country of the young people."

"I don't think he was sorry to come home," said the mother with a touch of fond pride. "But there was no choice for him after his father died; he was always a good boy, and he has not made us feel that we were keeping him away from anything better. When his father was alive we let him go, because then we were not so dependent, and I wished him to try his fortune in the world, as all boys long to do. But he is rather peculiar, and he seems to have got quite enough of the world. To be sure, I don't suppose he's seen the brightest side of it. He first went to work in the mills down at Ponkwasset, but he was laid off there, when the hard times came, and there was so much overproduction, and he took a job of railroading, and was braking on a freight train, when his father left us."

Mrs. Makely said, smiling, "No, I don't think that was the

brightest outlook in the world. No wonder he has brought back such gloomy impressions. I am sure that if he could have seen life under brighter auspices he would not have the ideas he has."

"Very likely," said the mother dryly. "Our experiences have a great deal to do with forming our opinions. But I am not dissatisfied with my son's ideas. I suppose Reuben got a good many of his ideas from his father: he's his father all over again. My husband thought slavery was wrong, and he went into the war to fight against it. He used to say when the war was over that the negroes were emancipated, but slavery was not abolished yet."

"What in the world did he mean by that?" demanded Mrs. Makely.

"Something you wouldn't understand as we do. I tried to carry on the farm after he first went, and before Reuben was large enough to help me much, and ought to be in school, and I suppose I overdid. At any rate that was when I had my first shock of paralysis. I never was very strong, and I presume my health was weakened by my teaching school so much, and studying, before I was married. But that doesn't matter now and hasn't for many a year. The place was clear of debt, then, but I had to get a mortgage put on it. The savings bank down in the village took it, and we've been paying the interest ever since. My husband died paying it, and my son will pay it all my life, and then I suppose the bank will foreclose. The treasurer was an old playmate of my husband's, and he said that as long as either of us lived, the mortgage could lie."

"How splendid of him!" said Mrs. Makely. "I should think you had been very fortunate."

"I said that you would not see it as we do," said the invalid patiently.

The Altrurian asked: "Are there mortgages on many of the farms in the neighborhood?"

"Nearly all," said Mrs. Camp. "We seem to own them, but in fact they own us."

Mrs. Makely hastened to say: "My husband thinks it's the best way to have your property. If you mortgage it close up, you have all your capital free, and you can keep turning it over. That's what you ought to do, Mrs. Camp. But what was the slavery that Captain Camp said was not abolished yet?"

The invalid looked at her a moment without replying, and just then the door of the kitchen opened, and young Camp came in, and began to gather some food from the table on a plate.

"Why don't you bring him to the table Reub?" his sister called to him.

"Oh, he says he'd rather not come in, as long as we have company. He says he isn't dressed for dinner; left his spike-tail in the city."

The young man laughed, and his sister with him.

VIII

YOUNG CAMP carried out the plate of victuals to the tramp, and Mrs. Makely said to his mother, "I suppose you would make the tramp do some sort of work to earn his breakfast on week-days?"

"Not always," Mrs. Camp replied. "Do the boarders at the hotel always work to earn their breakfast?"

"No, certainly not," said Mrs. Makely, with the sharpness of offence. "But they always pay for it."

"I don't think that paying for a thing is earning it. Perhaps some one else earned the money that pays for it. But I believe there is too much work in the world. If I were to live my life over again, I should not work half so hard. My husband and I took this place when we were young married people, and began working to pay for it. We wanted to feel that it was ours, that we owned it, and that our children should own it afterwards. We both worked all day long like slaves, and many a moonlight night we were up till morning, almost, gathering the stones from our fields, and burying them in deep graves that we had dug for them. But we buried our youth and strength, and health in those graves, too, and what for? I don't own the farm that we worked so hard to pay for, and my children won't. That is what it has all come to. We were rightly punished for our greed, I suppose. Perhaps no one has a right to own any portion of the earth. Sometimes I think so, but my husband and I earned this farm, and now the savings bank owns it. That seems strange, doesn't it? I suppose you'll say that the bank paid for it. Well, perhaps so; but the bank didn't earn it. When I think of that I don't always think that a person who pays for his breakfast has the best right to a breakfast."

I could see the sophistry of all this, but I had not the heart to point it out; I felt the pathos of it, too. Mrs. Makely seemed not to see the one nor to feel the other, very distinctly. "Yes, but surely," she said, "if you give a tramp his breakfast without making him work for it, you must see that it is encouraging idleness. And idleness is very corrupting—the sight of it."

"You mean to the country people? Well, they have to stand a good deal of that. The summer folks that spend four or five months of the year here, don't seem to do anything from morning till night."

"Ah, but you must recollect that they are *resting!* You have no idea how hard they all work in town during the winter," Mrs. Makely urged, with an air of argument.

"Perhaps the tramps are resting, too. At any rate, I don't think the sight of idleness in rags, and begging at back doors, is very corrupting to the country people; I never heard of a single tramp who had started from the country; they all come from the cities. It's the other kind of idleness that tempts our young people. The only tramps that my son says he ever envies are the well-dressed, strong young fellows from town, that go tramping through the mountains for exercise every summer."

The ladies both paused. They seemed to have got to the end of their tether; at least Mrs. Makely had apparently nothing else to advance, and I said lightly, "But that is just the kind of tramps that Mr. Homos would most disapprove of. He says that in Altruria they would consider exercise for exercise' sake a wicked waste of force, and little short of lunacy."

I thought my exaggeration might provoke him to denial, but

he seemed not to have found it unjust. "Why, you know," he said to Mrs. Camp, "in Altruria every one works with his hands, so that the hard work shall not all fall to any one class; and this manual labor of each is sufficient to keep the body in health, as well as to earn a living. After the three hours' work, which constitutes a day's work with us, is done, the young people have all sorts of games and sports, and they carry them as late into life as the temperament of each demands. But what I was saying to Mr. Twelvemough—perhaps I did not make myself clear—was that we should regard the sterile putting forth of strength in exercise, if others were each day worn out with hard manual labor, as insane or immoral. But I can account for it differently with you, because I understand that in your conditions a person of leisure could not do any manual labor without taking away the work of some one who needed it to live by; and could not even relieve an overworked laborer, and give him the money for the work without teaching him habits of idleness. In Altruria we can all keep ourselves well by doing each his share of hard work, and we can help those who are exhausted, when such a thing happens, without injuring them materially or morally."

Young Camp entered at this moment, and the Altrurian hesitated. "Oh, do go on!" Mrs. Makely entreated. She added to Camp, "We've got him to talking about Altruria at last, and we wouldn't have him stopped for worlds."

The Altrurian looked round at all our faces, and no doubt read our eager curiosity in them. He smiled, and said, "I shall be very glad I'm sure. But I do not think you will find anything so remarkable in our civilization, if you will conceive of it as the outgrowth of the neighborly instinct. In fact, neighborliness is the essence of Altrurianism. If you will imagine having the same feeling toward all," he explained to Mrs. Makely, "as you have toward your next door neighbor"—

"My next door neighbor!" she cried. "But I don't *know* the people next door! We live in a large apartment house, some forty families, and I assure you I do not know a soul among them."

He looked at her with a puzzled air, and she continued,

"Sometimes it *does* seem rather hard. One day the people on the same landing with us, lost one of their children, and I should never have been a whit the wiser, if my cook hadn't happened to mention it. The servants all know each other; they meet in the back elevator, and get acquainted. I don't encourage it. You can't tell what kind of families they belong to."

"But surely," the Altrurian persisted, "you have friends in the city whom you think of as your neighbors?"

"No, I can't say that I have," said Mrs. Makely. "I have my visiting list, but I shouldn't think of anybody on *that* as a neighbor."

The Altrurian looked so blank and baffled that I could hardly help laughing. "Then I should not know how to explain Altruria to you, I'm afraid."

"Well," she returned lightly, "if it's anything like neighborliness, as I've seen it in small places, deliver me from it! I like being independent. That's why I like the city. You're let alone."

"I was down in New York, once, and I went through some of the streets and houses where the poor people live," said young Camp, "and they seemed to know each other, and to be quite neighborly."

"And would you like to be all messed in with each other, that way?" demanded the lady.

"Well, I thought it was better than living as we do in the country, so far apart that we never see each other, hardly. And it seems to me better than not having any neighbors at all."

"Well, every one to his taste," said Mrs. Makely. "I wish you would tell us how people manage with you, socially, Mr. Homos."

"Why, you know," he began, "we have neither city nor country in your sense, and so we are neither so isolated nor so crowded together. You feel that you lose a great deal, in not seeing each other oftener?" he asked Camp.

"Yes. Folks rust out, living alone. It's human nature to want to get together."

"And I understand Mrs. Makely that it is human nature to want to keep apart?"

"Oh, no, but to come together independently," she answered.

"Well, that is what we have contrived in our life at home. I should have to say, in the first place, that"—

"Excuse me, just one moment, Mr. Homos!" said Mrs. Makely. This perverse woman was as anxious to hear about Altruria as any of us, but she was a woman who would rather hear the sound of her own voice than any other, even if she were dying, as she would call it, to hear the other. The Altrurian stopped politely, and Mrs. Makely went on: "I have been thinking of what Mr. Camp was saying about the black-listed men, and their all turning into tramps"—

"But I didn't say that, Mrs. Makely," the young fellow protested, in astonishment.

"Well, it stands to reason that if the tramps have all been black-listed men"—

"But I didn't say that, either!"

"No matter! What I am trying to get at is this: if a workman has made himself a nuisance to the employers, haven't they a right to punish him in any way they can?"

"I believe there's no law yet, against black-listing," said Camp.

"Very well, then, I don't see what they've got to complain of. The employers surely know their own business."

"They claim to know the men's too. That's what they're always saying; they will manage their own affairs in their own way. But no man, or company, that does business on a large scale, has any affairs that are not partly other folks' affairs, too. All the saying in the world won't make it different."

"Very well, then," said Mrs. Makely, with a force of argument which she seemed to think was irresistible, "I think the workmen had better leave things to the employers, and then they won't get black-listed. It's as broad as it's long." I confess, that although I agreed with Mrs. Makely in regard to what the workmen had better do, her position had been arrived at by such extraordinary reasoning, that I blushed for her; at the same time, I wanted to laugh. She continued, triumphantly, "You see, the employers have ever so much more at stake."

"The men have everything at stake; the work of their hands," said the young fellow.

"Oh, but surely," said Mrs. Makely, "you wouldn't set that against capital? You wouldn't compare the two?"

"Yes, I should," said Camp, and I could see his eye kindle and his jaw stiffen.

"Then, I suppose you would say that a man ought to get as much for his work as an employer gets for his capital. If you think one has as much at stake as the other, you must think they ought to be paid alike."

"That is *just* what I think," said Camp, and Mrs. Makely burst into a peal of amiable laughter.

"Now that is too preposterous!"

"Why is it preposterous?" he demanded, with a quivering nostril.

"Why, simply because it *is*," said the lady, but she did not say why, and although I thought so, too, I was glad she did not attempt to do it, for her conclusions seemed to me much better than her reasons.

The old wooden clock in the kitchen began to strike, and she rose briskly to her feet, and went and laid the books she had been holding in her lap, on the table beside Mrs. Camp's bed. "We must really be going," she said, as she leaned over and kissed the invalid. "It is your dinner time, and we shall barely get back for lunch, if we go by the Loop road; and I want very much to have Mr. Homos see the Witch's Falls, on the way. I have got two or three of the books here that Mr. Makely brought me last night— I sha'n't have time to read them at once—and I'm smuggling in one of Mr. Twelvemough's, that he's too modest to present for himself." She turned a gay glance upon me, and Mrs. Camp thanked me, and a number of civilities followed from all sides. In the process of their exchange, Mrs. Makely's spirits perceptibly rose, and she came away in high good-humor with the whole Camp family. "Well, now, I am sure," she said to the Altrurian, as we began the long ascent of the Loop road, "you must allow that you have seen some very original characters.

But how *warped* people get living alone so much! That is the great drawback of the country. Mrs. Camp thinks the savings bank did her a real injury in taking a mortgage on her place, and Reuben seems to have seen just enough of the outside world to get it all wrong! But they are the best-hearted creatures in the world, and I know you won't misunderstand them. That unsparing country bluntness, don't you think it's perfectly delightful? I do like to stir poor Reuben up, and get him talking. He is a good boy, if he *is* so wrong-headed, and he's the most devoted son and brother in the world. Very few young fellows would waste their lives on an old farm like that; I suppose when his mother dies he will marry and strike out for himself in some growing place."

"He did not seem to think the world held out any very bright inducements for him to leave home," the Altrurian suggested.

"Oh, let him get one of these lively, pushing Yankee girls for a wife, and he will think very differently," said Mrs. Makely.

The Altrurian disappeared that afternoon, and I saw little or nothing of him till the next day at supper. Then he said he had been spending the time with young Camp, who had shown him something of the farm work, and introduced him to several of the neighbors; he was very much interested in it all, because at home he was, at present, engaged in farm work himself, and he was curious to contrast the American and Altrurian methods. We began to talk of the farming interest again, later in the day, when the members of our little group came together, and I told them what the Altrurian had been doing. The doctor had been suddenly called back to town; but the minister was there, and the lawyer, and the professor, and the banker, and the manufacturer. It was the banker who began to comment on what I said, and he seemed to be in the frank humor of the Saturday night before. "Yes," he said, "it's a hard life, and they have to look sharp, if they expect to make both ends meet. I would not like to undertake it myself, with their resources."

The professor smiled, in asking the Altrurian: "Did your agricultural friends tell you anything of the little rural traffic in votes that they carry on about election time? That is one of the side means they have of making both ends meet."

"I don't understand," said the Altrurian.

"Why, you know that you can buy votes among our virtuous yeomen, from two dollars up, at the ordinary elections. When party feeling runs high, and there are vital questions at stake, the votes cost more."

The Altrurian looked round at us all, aghast: "Do you mean that Americans buy votes?"

The professor smiled again. "Oh, no; I only mean that they sell them. Well, I don't wonder that they rather prefer to blink the fact; but it is a fact, nevertheless, and pretty notorious."

"Good heavens!" cried the Altrurian. "And what defense have they for such treason? I don't mean those who sell; from what I have seen of the bareness and hardship of their lives, I could well imagine that there might, sometimes, come a pinch when they would be glad of the few dollars that they could get in that way; but what have those who buy to say?"

"Well," said the professor, "it isn't a transaction that's apt to be talked about, much, on either side."

"I think," the banker interposed, "that there is some exaggeration about that business; but it certainly exists, and I suppose it is a growing evil in the country. I fancy it arises, somewhat, from a want of clear thinking on the subject. Then, there is no doubt but it comes, sometimes, from poverty. A man sells his vote, as a woman sells her person, for money, when neither can turn virtue into cash. They feel that they must live, and neither of them would be satisfied if Dr. Johnson told them he didn't see the necessity. In fact, I shouldn't, myself, if I were in their places. You can't have the good of a civilization like ours, without having the bad; but I am not going to deny that the bad is bad. Some people like to do that; but I don't find my account in it. In either case, I confess that I think the buyer is worse than the seller—incomparably worse. I suppose you are not troubled with either case, in Altruria?"

"Oh, no!" said the Altrurian, with an utter horror, which

no repetition of his words can give the sense of. "It would be unimaginable."

"Still," the banker suggested, "you have cakes and ale, and at times the ginger is hot in the mouth?"

"I don't pretend that we have immunity from error; but upon such terms as you have described, we have none. It would be impossible."

The Altrurian's voice expressed no contempt, but only a sad patience, a melancholy surprise, such as a celestial angel might feel in being suddenly confronted with some secret shame and horror of the Pit.

"Well," said the banker, "with us, the only way is to take the business view and try to strike an average somewhere."

"Talking of business," said the professor, turning to the manufacturer, who had been quietly smoking, "why don't some of you capitalists take hold of farming, here in the east, and make a business of it, as they do in the west?"

"Thank you," said the other, "if you mean me, I would rather not invest." He was silent a moment, and then he went on, as if the notion were beginning to win upon him: "It may come to something like that, though. If it does, the natural course, I should think, would be through the railroads. It would be a very easy matter for them to buy up all the good farms along their lines and put tenants on them, and run them in their own interest. Really, it isn't a bad scheme. The waste in the present method is enormous, and there is no reason why the roads should not own the farms, as they are beginning to own the mines. They could manage them better than the small farmers do, in every way. I wonder the thing hasn't occurred to some smart railroad man."

We all laughed a little, perceiving the semi-ironical spirit of his talk; but the Altrurian must have taken it in dead earnest: "But, in that case, the number of people thrown out of work would be very great, wouldn't it? And what would become of them?"

"Well, they would have whatever their farms brought, to

make a new start with somewhere else; and, besides, that question of what would become of people thrown out of work by a given improvement, is something that capital cannot consider. We used to introduce a bit of machinery, every now and then, in the mill, that threw out a dozen, or a hundred people; but we couldn't stop for that."

"And you never knew what became of them?"

"Sometimes. Generally not. We took it for granted that they would light on their feet, somehow."

"And the state—the whole people—the government—did nothing for them?"

"If it became a question of the poorhouse, yes."

"Or the jail," the lawyer suggested.

"Speaking of the poorhouse," said the professor, "did our exemplary rural friends tell you how they sell out their paupers to the lowest bidder, and get them boarded sometimes as low as a dollar and a quarter a week?"

"Yes, young Mr. Camp told me of that. He seemed to think it was terrible."

"Did he? Well, I'm glad to hear that of young Mr. Camp. From all that I've been told before, he seems to reserve his conscience for the use of capitalists. What does he propose to do about it?"

"He seems to think the state ought to find work for them."

"Oh, paternalism! Well, I guess the state won't."

"That was his opinion, too."

"It seems a hard fate," said the minister, "that the only provision the law makes for people who are worn out by sickness or a life of work should be something that assorts them with idiots and lunatics, and brings such shame upon them that it is almost as terrible as death."

"It is the only way to encourage independence and individuality," said the professor. "Of course, it has its dark side. But anything else would be sentimental and unbusinesslike, and in fact, un-American."

"I am not so sure that it would be un-Christian," the minister timidly ventured, in the face of such an authority on political economy.

"Oh, as to that, I must leave the question to the reverend clergy," said the professor.

A very unpleasant little silence followed. It was broken by the lawyer, who put his feet together, and after a glance down at them, began to say, "I was very much interested this afternoon by a conversation I had with some of the young fellows in the hotel. You know most of them are graduates, and they are taking a sort of supernumerary vacation this summer, before they plunge into the battle of life in the autumn. They were talking of some other fellows, classmates of theirs, who were not so lucky, but had been obliged to begin the fight at once. It seems that our fellows here are all going in for some sort of profession: medicine, or law, or engineering, or teaching, or the church, and they were commiserating those other fellows not only because they were not having the supernumerary vacation, but because they were going into business. That struck me as rather odd, and I tried to find out what it meant, and as nearly as I could find out, it meant that most college graduates would not go into business if they could help it. They seemed to feel a sort of incongruity between their education and the business life. They pitied the fellows that had to go in for it, and apparently the fellows that had to go in for it pitied themselves, for the talk seemed to have begun about a letter that one of the chaps here had got from poor Jack or Jim somebody, who had been obliged to go into his father's business, and was groaning over it. The fellows who were going to study professions were hugging themselves at the contrast between their fate and his, and were making remarks about business that were to say the least unbusinesslike. A few years ago we should have made a summary disposition of the matter, and I believe some of the newspapers still are in doubt about the value of a college education to men who have got to make their way. What do you think?"

The lawyer addressed his question to the manufacturer, who answered with a comfortable satisfaction, that he did not think those young men if they went into business would find that they knew too much.

"But they pointed out," said the lawyer, "that the great American fortunes had been made by men who had never had their educational advantages, and they seemed to think that what we call the education of a gentleman was a little too good for money-making purposes."

"Well," said the other, "they can console themselves with the reflection that going into business isn't necessarily making money; it isn't necessarily making a living, even."

"Some of them seem to have caught on to that fact; and they pitied Jack or Jim partly because the chances were so much against him. But they pitied him mostly because in the life before him he would have no use for his academic training, and he had better not gone to college at all. They said he would be none the better for it, and would always be miserable when he looked back to it."

The manufacturer did not reply, and the professor, after a preliminary hemming, held his peace. It was the banker who took the word. "Well, so far as business is concerned, they were right. It is no use to pretend that there is any relation between business and the higher education. There is no business man who will pretend that there is not often an actual incompatibility, if he is honest. I know that when we get together at a commercial or financial dinner, we talk as if great merchants and great financiers were beneficent geniuses, who evoked the prosperity of mankind by their schemes from the conditions that would otherwise have remained barren. Well, very likely they are, but we must all confess that they do not know it at the time. What they are consciously looking out for then is the main chance. If general prosperity follows, all well and good; they are willing to be given the credit for it. But, as I said, with business as business, the 'education of a gentleman' has nothing to do. That education is always putting the old Ciceronian question: whether the fellow arriving at a starving city with a cargo of grain is bound to tell the people before he squeezes them, that there are half a dozen other fellows with grain just below the horizon. As a gentleman he would have to tell them, because he could not take advantage of their necessities; but as a business man, he would think it bad business to tell them, or no business at all. The principle goes all through; I say, business is business; and I am not going to pretend that business will ever be anything else. In our business battles, we don't take off our hats to the other side, and say, 'Gentlemen of the French Guard, have the goodness to fire.' That may be war, but it is not business. We seize all the advantages we can; very few of us would actually deceive; but if a fellow believes a thing, and we know he is wrong, we do not usually take the trouble to set him right, if we are going to lose anything by undeceiving him. That would not be business. I suppose you think that is dreadful?" He turned smilingly to the minister.

"I wish—I wish," said the minister, gently, "it could be otherwise."

"Well, I wish so, too," returned the banker. "But it isn't. Am I right or am I wrong?" he demanded of the manufacturer, who laughed.

"I am not conducting this discussion. I will not deprive you of the floor."

"What you say," I ventured to put in, "reminds me of the experience of a friend of mine, a brother novelist. He wrote a story where the failure of a business man turned on a point just like that you have instanced. The man could have retrieved himself if he had let some people believe that what was so was not so, but his conscience stepped in and obliged him to own the truth. There was a good deal of talk about the case, I suppose because it was not in real life, and my friend heard divers criticisms. He heard of a group of ministers who blamed him for exalting a case of common honesty, as if it were something extraordinary; and he heard of some business men who talked it over, and said he had worked the case up splendidly, but he was all wrong in the outcome; the fellow would never have told the other fellows. They said it would not have been business."

We all laughed, except the minister and the Altrurian, and the manufacturer said, "Twenty-five years hence, the fellow who is going into business, may pity the fellows who are pitying him for his hard fate now."

"Very possibly, but not necessarily," said the banker. "Of course, the business man is on top, as far as money goes; he is the fellow who makes the big fortunes; the millionaire lawyers, and doctors, and ministers are exceptional. But his risks are tremendous. Ninety-five times out of a hundred he fails. To be sure, he picks up and goes on, but he seldom gets there, after all."

"Then in your system," said the Altrurian, "the great majority of those who go into what you call the battle of life, are defeated?"

"The killed, wounded and missing sum up a frightful total," the banker admitted. "But whatever the end is, there is a great deal of prosperity on the way. The statistics are correct, but they do not tell the whole truth. It is not so bad as it seems. Still, simply looking at the material chances, I don't blame those young fellows for not wanting to go into business. And when you come to other considerations! We used to cut the knot of the difficulty pretty sharply; we said a college education was wrong; or, the hot and hot American spreadeaglers did. Business is the national ideal, and the successful business man is the American type. It is a business man's country."

"Then, if I understand you," said the Altrurian, "and I am very anxious to have a clear understanding of the matter, the effect of the university with you is to unfit a youth for business life."

"Oh, no. It may give him great advantages in it, and that is the theory and expectation of most fathers who send their sons to the university. But, undoubtedly, the effect is to render business-life distasteful. The university nurtures all sorts of lofty ideals, which business has no use for."

"Then the effect is undemocratic?"

"No, it is simply unbusinesslike. The boy is a better democrat when he leaves college, than he will be later, if he goes into business. The university has taught him and equipped him to use his own gifts and powers for his advancement, but the first lesson of business and the last, is to use other men's gifts and powers. If he looks about him at all, he sees that no man gets rich simply by his own labor, no matter how mighty a genius he is, and that if you want to get rich, you must make other men work for you, and pay you for the privilege of doing so. Isn't that true?"

The banker turned to the manufacturer with this question, and the other said, "The theory is, that we give people work," and they both laughed.

The minister said, "I believe that in Altruria, no man works for the profit of another?"

"No; each works for the profit of all," replied the Altrurian.

"Well," said the banker, "you seem to have made it go. Nobody can deny that. But we couldn't make it go here."

"Why? I am very curious to know why our system seems so impossible to you!"

"Well, it is contrary to the American spirit. It is alien to our love of individuality."

"But we prize individuality, too, and we think we secure it under our system. Under yours, it seems to me that while the individuality of the man who makes other men work for him is safe, except from itself, the individuality of the workers"—

"Well, that is their lookout. We have found that, upon the whole, it is best to let every man look out for himself. I know that, in a certain light, the result has an ugly aspect; but, nevertheless, in spite of all, the country is enormously prosperous. The pursuit of happiness, which is one of the inalienable rights secured to us by the Declaration, is, and always has been, a dream; but the pursuit of the dollar yields tangible proceeds, and we get a good deal of excitement out of it, as it goes on. You can't deny that we are the richest nation in the world. Do you call Altruria a rich country?"

I could not quite make out whether the banker was serious or not in all this talk; sometimes I suspected him of a fine mockery, but the Altrurian took him upon the surface of his words.

"I hardly know whether it is or not. The question of wealth does not enter into our scheme. I can say that we all have enough, and that no one is even in the fear of want."

"Yes, that is very well. But we should think it was paying too much for it, if we had to give up the hope of ever having more than we wanted," and at this point the banker uttered his jolly laugh, and I perceived that he had been trying to draw the Altrurian out, and practice upon his patriotism. It was a great relief to find that he had been joking in so much that seemed a dead give-away of our economical position. "In Altruria," he asked, "who is your ideal great man? I don't mean personally, but abstractly."

The Altrurian thought a moment. "With us, there is so little ambition for distinction, as you understand it, that your question is hard to answer. But I should say, speaking largely, that it was some man who had been able, for the time being, to give the greatest happiness to the greatest number—some artist, or poet, or inventor, or physician."

I was somewhat surprised to have the banker take this preposterous statement seriously, respectfully. "Well, that is quite conceivable with your system. What should you say," he demanded of the rest of us, generally, "was our ideal of greatness?"

No one replied at once, or at all, till the manufacturer said, "We will let you continue to run it."

"Well, it is a very curious inquiry, and I have thought it over a good deal. I should say that within a generation our ideal had changed twice. Before the war, and during all the time from the revolution onward, it was undoubtedly the great politician, the publicist, the statesman. As we grew older and began to have an intellectual life of our own, I think the literary fellows had a pretty good share of the honors that were going; that is, such a man as Longfellow was popularly considered a type of greatness. When the war came, it brought the soldier to the front, and there was a period of ten or fifteen years when he dominated the national imagination. That period passed, and the great era of material prosperity set in. The big fortunes began to tower up, and heroes of another sort began to appeal to our admiration. I don't think there is any doubt but the millionaire is now the American ideal. It isn't very pleasant to think so, even for people who have got on, but it can't very hopefully be denied. It is the man with the most money who now takes the prize in our national cake-walk."

The Altrurian turned curiously toward me, and I did my best to tell him what a cake-walk was. When I had finished, the banker resumed, only to say, as he rose from his chair to bid us good-night, "In any average assembly of Americans, the greatest millionaire would take the eyes of all from the greatest states-man, the greatest poet, or the greatest soldier, we ever had. That," he added to the Altrurian, "will account to you for many things, as you travel through our country."

IX

THE NEXT TIME the members of our little group came together, the manufacturer began at once upon the banker:

"I should think that our friend, the professor, here, would hardly like that notion of yours, that business, as business, has nothing to do with the education of a gentleman. If this is a busi-ness man's country, and if the professor has nothing in stock but the sort of education that business has no use for, I should sup-pose that he would want to go into some other line."

The banker mutely referred the matter to the professor, who said, with that cold grin of his which I hated:

"Perhaps we shall wait for business to purge and live cleanly. Then it will have some use for the education of a gentleman."

"I see," said the banker, "that I have touched the quick in both of you, when I hadn't the least notion of doing so. But I shouldn't, really, like to prophesy which will adapt itself to the other: education or business. Let us hope there will be mutual concessions. There are some pessimists who say that business methods, especially on the large scale of the trusts and combinations, have grown worse, instead of better; but this may be merely what is called a 'transition state.' Hamlet must be cruel to be kind; the darkest hour comes before dawn; and so on. Perhaps when business gets the whole affair of life into its hands, and runs the republic, as its enemies now accuse it of doing, the process of purging and living cleanly will begin. I have known lots of fellows who started in life rather scampishly; but when they felt secure of themselves, and believed that they could afford to be honest, they became so. There's no reason why the same thing shouldn't happen on a large scale. We must never forget that we are still a very novel experiment, though we have matured so rapidly in some respects that we have come to regard ourselves as an accomplished fact. We are, really, less so than we were forty years ago, with all the tremendous changes since the war. Before that, we could take certain matters for granted. If a man got out of work, he turned his hand to something else; if a man failed in business, he started in again from some other direction; as a last resort, in both cases, he went west, preëmpted a quarter section of public land, and grew up with the country. Now, the country is grown up; the public land is gone; business is full on all sides, and the hand that turned itself to something else has lost its cunning. The struggle for life has changed from a free fight to an encounter of disciplined forces, and the free fighters that are left get ground to pieces between organized labor and organized capital. Decidedly, we are in a transition state, and if the higher education tried to adapt itself to business needs, there are chances that it might sacrifice itself without helping business. After all, how much education does business need? Were our great fortunes made by educated men, or men of university training? I don't know but these young fellows are right about that."

"Yes, that may all be," I put in. "But it seems to me that you give Mr. Homos, somehow, a wrong impression of our economic life by your generalizations. You are a Harvard man yourself."

"Yes, and I am not a rich man. A million or two, more or less;

but what is that? I have suffered, at the start and all along, from the question as to what a man with the education of a gentleman ought to do in such and such a juncture. The fellows who have not that sort of education have not that sort of question, and they go in and win."

"So you admit, then," said the professor, "that the higher education elevates a business man's standard of morals?"

"Undoubtedly. That is one of its chief drawbacks," said the banker, with a laugh.

"Well," I said, with the deference due even to a man who had only a million or two, more or less, "we must allow *you* to say such things. But if the case is so bad with the business men who have made the great fortunes—the business men who have never had the disadvantage of a university education—I wish you would explain to Mr. Homos why, in every public exigency, we instinctively appeal to the business sense of the community, as if it were the fountain of wisdom, probity and equity. Suppose there were some question of vital interest—I won't say financial, but political, or moral, or social—on which it was necessary to rouse public opinion; what would be the first thing to do? To call a meeting, over the signatures of the leading business men; because no other names appeal with such force to the public. You might get up a call signed by all the novelists, artists, ministers, lawyers and doctors in the state, and it would not have a tithe of the effect, with the people at large, that a call signed by a few leading merchants, bank presidents, railroad men and trust officers, would have. What is the reason? It seems strange that I should be asking you to defend yourself against yourself."

"Not at all, my dear fellow, not at all!" the banker replied, with his caressing bonhomie. "Though I will confess, to begin with, that I do not expect to answer your question to your entire satisfaction. I can only do my best—on the installment plan."

He turned to the Altrurian, and then went on:

"As I said the other night, this is a business man's country. We are a purely commercial people; money is absolutely to the fore; and business, which is the means of getting the most money, is the American ideal. If you like, you may call it the American fetish; I don't mind calling it so myself. The fact that business is our ideal, or our fetish, will account for the popular faith in business men, who form its priesthood, its hierarchy. I don't know, myself, any other reason for regarding business men as solider than novelists, or artists, or ministers, not to mention lawyers and doctors. They are supposed to have long heads; but it appears that ninety-five times out of a hundred they haven't. They are supposed to be very reliable; but it is almost invariably a business man, of some sort, who gets out to Canada while the state examiner is balancing his books, and it is usually the longest-headed business men who get plundered by him. No, it is simply because business is our national ideal, that the business man is honored above all other men among us. In the aristocratic countries they forward a public object under the patronage of the nobility and gentry; in a plutocratic country they get the business men to endorse it. I suppose that the average American citizen feels that they wouldn't endorse a thing unless it was safe; and the average American citizen likes to be safe—he is cautious. As a matter of fact, business men are always taking risks, and business is a game of chance, in a certain degree. Have I made myself intelligible?"

"Entirely so," said the Altrurian; and he seemed so thoroughly well satisfied, that he forbore asking any question farther.

No one else spoke. The banker lighted a cigar, and resumed at the point where he left off when I ventured to enter upon the defense of his class with him. I must say that he had not convinced me at all. At that moment, I would rather have trusted him, in any serious matter of practical concern, than all the novelists I ever heard of. But I thought I would leave the word to him, without further attempt to reinstate him in his self-esteem. In fact, he seemed to be getting along very well without it; or else he was feeling that mysterious control from the Altrurian which I had already suspected him of using. Voluntarily or involuntarily, the banker proceeded with his contribution to the Altrurian's stock of knowledge concerning our civilization:

"I don't believe, however, that the higher education is any more of a failure, as a provision for a business career, than the lower education is for the life of labor. I suppose that the hyper-critical observer might say that in a wholly commercial civilization, like ours, the business man really needed nothing beyond the three R's, and the workingman needed no R at all. As a practical affair, there is a good deal to be said in favor of that view. The higher education is part of the social ideal which we have derived from the past, from Europe. It is part of the provision for the life of leisure, the life of the aristocrat, which nobody of our generation leads, except women. Our women really have some use for the education of a gentleman, but our men have none. How will that do, for a generalization?" the banker asked of me.

"Oh," I admitted, with a laugh, "it is a good deal like one of my own. I have always been struck with that phase of our civilization."

"Well, then," the banker resumed, "take the lower education. This is part of the civic ideal which, I suppose, I may say we evolved from the depths of our inner consciousness of what an American citizen ought to be. It includes instruction in all the R's, and in several other letters of the alphabet. It is given free, by the state, and no one can deny that it is thoroughly socialistic in conception and application."

"Distinctly so," said the professor. "Now that the text-books are furnished by the state, we have only to go a step farther, and provide a good, hot lunch for the children every day, as they do in Paris."

"Well," the banker returned, "I don't know that I should have much to say against that. It seems as reasonable as anything in the system of education which we force upon the working-classes. *They* know, perfectly well, whether we do or not, that the three R's will not make their children better mechanics or laborers, and that, if the fight for a mere living is to go on, from generation to generation, they will have no leisure to apply the little learning they get in the public schools, for their personal culture. In the meantime, we deprive the parents of their children's labor, in order that they may be better citizens for their schooling, as we imagine; I don't know whether they are or not. We offer them no sort of compensation for their time, and I think we ought to feel obliged to them for not wanting wages for their children while we are teaching them to be better citizens."

"You know," said the professor, "that has been suggested by some of their leaders."

"No, really? Well, that is *too* good!" The banker threw back his head, and roared, and we all laughed with him. When we had sobered down again, he said: "I suppose that when a workingman makes all the use he can of his lower education, he becomes a business man, and then he doesn't need the higher. Professor, you seem to be left out in the cold, by our system, whichever way you take it."

"Oh," said the professor, "the law of supply and demand works both ways; it creates the demand, if the supply comes first; and if we keep on giving the sons of business men the education of a gentleman, we may yet make them feel the need of it. We shall evolve a new sort of business man."

"The sort that can't make money, or wouldn't exactly like to, on some terms?" asked the banker. "Well, perhaps we shall work out our democratic salvation in that way. When you have educated your new business man to the point where he can't consent to get rich at the obvious cost of others, you've got him on the way back to work with his hands. He will sink into the ranks of labor, and give the fellow with the lower education a chance. I've no doubt he'll take it. I don't know but you're right, professor."

The lawyer had not spoken, as yet. Now he said: "Then, it is education, after all, that is to bridge the chasm between the classes and the masses, though it seems destined to go a long way round about it. There was a time, I believe, when we expected religion to do that."

"Well, it may still be doing it, for all I know," said the banker. "What do you say?" he asked, turning to the minister. "You ought to be able to give us some statistics on the subject, with that large congregation of yours. You preach to more people than any other pulpit in your city."

The banker named one of the principal cities in the east, and the minister answered, with modest pride: "I am not sure of that; but our society is certainly a very large one."

"Well, and how many of the lower classes are there in it— people who work for their living with their hands?"

The minister stirred uneasily in his chair, and at last he said, with evident unhappiness: "They—I suppose—they have their own churches. I have never thought that such a separation of the classes was right; and I have had some of the very best people— socially and financially—with me in the wish that there might be more brotherliness between the rich and poor among us. But as yet"—

He stopped; the banker pursued: "Do you mean there are *no* working-people in your congregation?"

"I cannot think of any," returned the minister, so miserably that the banker forbore to press the point.

The lawyer broke the awkward pause which followed: "I have heard it asserted that there is no country in the world, where the separation of the classes is so absolute as in ours. In fact, I once heard a Russian revolutionist, who had lived in exile all over Europe, say that he had never seen, anywhere, such a want of kindness or sympathy between rich and poor, as he had observed in America. I doubted whether he was right. But he believed that, if it ever came to the industrial revolution with us, the fight would be more uncompromising than any such fight that the world had ever seen. There was no respect from low to high, he said, and no consideration from high to low, as there were in countries with traditions and old associations."

"Well," said the banker, "there may be something in that. Certainly, so far as the two forces have come into conflict here, there has been no disposition, on either side, to 'make war with the water of roses.' It's astonishing, in fact, to see how ruthless the fellows who have just got up are towards the fellows who are still down. And the best of us have been up only a generation or two—and the fellows who are still down know it."

"And what do you think would be the outcome of such a conflict?" I asked, with my soul divided between fear of it, and the perception of its excellence as material. My fancy vividly sketched the outline of a story which should forecast the struggle and its event, somewhat on the plan of the Battle of Dorking.

"We should beat," said the banker, breaking his cigar-ash off with his little finger; and I instantly cast him, with his ironic calm, for the part of a great patrician leader, in my Fall of the Republic. Of course, I disguised him somewhat, and travestied his worldly bonhomie with the bluff sang-froid of the soldier; these things are easily done.

"What makes you think we should beat?" asked the manufacturer, with a certain curiosity.

"Well, all the good jingo reasons: we have got the materials for beating. Those fellows throw away their strength whenever they begin to fight, and they've been so badly generaled, up to the present time, that they have wanted to fight at the outset of every quarrel. They have been beaten in every quarrel, but still they always want to begin by fighting. That is all right. When they have learned enough to begin by *voting*, then we shall have to look out. But if they keep on fighting, and always putting themselves in the wrong and getting the worst of it, perhaps we can fix the voting so we needn't be any more afraid of that than we are of the fighting. It's astonishing how short-sighted they are. They have no conception of any cure for their grievances, except more wages and fewer hours."

"But," I asked, "do you really think they have any just grievances?"

"Of course not, as a business man," said the banker. "If I were a workingman, I should probably think differently. But we will suppose, for the sake of argument, that their day is too long and their pay is too short. How do they go about to better themselves? They strike. Well, a strike is a fight, and in a fight, now-a-days, it is always skill and money that win. The workingmen can't stop till they have put themselves outside of the public sympathy which the newspapers say is so potent in their behalf; I never saw that it did them the least good. They begin by boycotting, and breaking the heads of the men who want to work. They destroy property, and they interfere with business— the two absolutely sacred things in the American religion. Then we call out the militia, and shoot a few of them, and their leaders declare the strike off. It is perfectly simple."

"But will it be quite as simple," I asked, reluctant in behalf of my projected romance, to have the matter so soon disposed of, "will it be quite so simple if their leaders ever persuade the workingmen to leave the militia, as they threaten to do, from time to time?"

"No, not quite so simple," the banker admitted. "Still, the fight would be comparatively simple. In the first place, I doubt —though I won't be certain about it—whether there are a great many workingmen in the militia now. I rather fancy it is made up, for the most part, of clerks and small tradesmen, and book-keepers, and such employés of business as have time and money for it. I may be mistaken."

No one seemed able to say whether he was mistaken or not; and, after waiting a moment, he proceeded:

"I feel pretty sure that it is so in the city companies and regiments, at any rate, and that if every workingman left them, it would not seriously impair their effectiveness. But when the workingmen have left the militia, what have they done? They have eliminated the only thing that disqualifies it for prompt and unsparing use against strikers. As long as they are in it, we might have our misgivings, but if they were once out of it, we should have none. And what would they gain? They would not be allowed to arm and organize as an inimical force. *That* was settled once for all, in Chicago, in the case of the International Groups. A few squads of policemen would break them up. Why," the banker exclaimed, with his good-humored laugh, "how preposterous they are, when you come to look at it! They are in the majority, the immense majority, if you count the farmers, and they prefer to behave as if they were the hopeless minority. They say they want an eight-hour law, and every now and then they strike, and try to fight it. Why don't they *vote* it? They could *make* it the law in six months, by such overwhelming numbers that no one would dare to evade or defy it. They can make any law they want, but they prefer to break such laws as we have. That 'alienates public sympathy,' the newspapers say, but the spectacle of their stupidity and helpless wilfulness is so lamentable that I could almost pity them. If they chose, it would take only a few years to transform our government into the likeness of anything they wanted. But they would rather not have what they want, apparently, if they can only keep themselves from getting it, and they have to work hard to do that!"

"I suppose," I said, "that they are misled by the un-American principles and methods of the socialists among them."

"Why, no," returned the banker, "I shouldn't say that. As far as I understand it, the socialists are the only fellows among them who propose to vote their ideas into laws, and nothing can be more American than that. I don't believe the socialists stir up the strikes, at least among our workingmen, though the newspapers convict them of it, generally without trying them. The socialists seem to accept the strikes as the inevitable outcome of the situation, and they make use of them as proofs of the industrial discontent. But, luckily for the status, our labor leaders are not socialists, for your socialist, whatever you may say against him, has generally thought himself into a socialist. He knows that until the workingmen stop fighting, and get down to voting— until they consent to be the majority—there is no hope for them. I am not talking of anarchists, mind you, but of socialists, whose philosophy is more law, not less, and who look forward to an order so just that it can't be disturbed."

"And what," the minister faintly said, "do you think will be the outcome of it all?"

"We had that question the other night, didn't we? Our legal friend, here, seemed to feel that we might rub along indefinitely as we are doing, or work out an Altruria of our own; or go back to the patriarchal stage, and own our workingmen. He seemed not to have so much faith in the logic of events as I have. I doubt if it is altogether a woman's logic. *Parole femmine, fatti maschi*, and the logic of events isn't altogether words; it's full of hard knocks, too. But I'm no prophet. I can't forecast the future; I prefer to take it as it comes. There's a little tract of William Morris's though—I forget just what he calls it—that is full of curious and interesting speculation on this point. He thinks that if we keep the road we are now going, the last state of labor will be like its first, and it will be owned."

"Oh, I don't believe that will ever happen in America," I protested.

"Why not?" asked the banker. "Practically, it *is* owned already in a vastly greater measure than we recognize. And where would the great harm be? The new slavery would not be like the old. There needn't be irresponsible whipping and separation of families, and private buying and selling. The proletariat would probably be owned by the state, as it was at one time in Greece; or by large corporations, which would be much more in keeping with the genius of our free institutions; and an enlightened public opinion would cast safeguards about it in the form of law to guard it from abuse. But it would be strictly policed, localized, and controlled. There would probably be less suffering than there is now, when a man may be cowed into submission to any terms through the suffering of his family; when he may be starved out and turned out if he is unruly. You may be sure that nothing of that kind would happen in the new slavery. We have not had nineteen hundred years of Christianity for nothing."

The banker paused, and as the silence continued he broke it with a laugh, which was a prodigious relief to my feelings, and I suppose to the feelings of all. I perceived that he had been joking, and I was confirmed in this when he turned to the Altrurian and laid his hand upon his shoulder. "You see," he said, "I'm a kind of Altrurian myself. What is the reason why we should not found a new Altruria here on the lines I've drawn? Have you never had philosophers—well, call them philanthropists; I don't mind —of my way of thinking among you?"

"Oh, yes," said the Altrurian. "At one time, just before we emerged from the competitive conditions, there was much serious question whether capital should not own labor, instead of labor owning capital. That was many hundred years ago."

"I am proud to find myself such an advanced thinker," said the banker. "And how came you to decide that labor should own capital?"

"We voted it," answered the Altrurian.

"Well," said the banker, "our fellows are still fighting it, and getting beaten."

I found him later in the evening, talking with Mrs. Makely. "My dear sir," I said, "I liked your frankness with my Altrurian friend immensely; and it may be well to put the worst foot foremost; but what is the advantage of not leaving us a leg to stand upon?"

He was not in the least offended at my boldness, as I had feared he might be, but he said with that jolly laugh of his, "Capital! Well, perhaps I have worked my candor a little too hard; I suppose there is such a thing. But don't you see that it leaves me in the best possible position to carry the war into Altruria, when we get him to open up about his native land?"

"Ah! If you can get him to do it."

"Well, we were just talking about that. Mrs. Makely has a plan."

"Yes," said the lady, turning an empty chair near her own, toward me. "Sit down and listen!"

X

I SAT DOWN, and Mrs. Makely continued: "I have thought it all out, and I want you to confess that in all practical matters a woman's brain is better than a man's. Mr. Bullion, here, says it is, and I want you to say so, too."

"Yes," the banker admitted, "when it comes down to business, a woman is worth any two of us."

"And we have just been agreeing," I coincided, "that the only gentlemen among us are women. Mrs. Makely, I admit, without further dispute, that the most unworldly woman is worldlier than the worldliest man; and that in all practical matters we fade into dreamers and doctrinaires beside you. Now, go on!"

But she did not mean to let me off so easily. She began to brag herself up, as women do, whenever you make them the slightest concession.

"Here, you men," she said, "have been trying for a whole week to get something out of Mr. Homos about his country, and you have left it to a poor, weak woman, at last, to think how to manage it. I do believe that you get so much interested in your own talk, when you are with him, that you don't let him get in a word, and that's the reason you haven't found out anything about Altruria, yet, from him."

In view of the manner in which she had cut in at Mrs. Camp's, and stopped Homos on the very verge of the only full and free confession he had ever been near making about Altruria, I thought this was pretty cool, but, for fear of worse, I said:

"You're quite right, Mrs. Makely. I'm sorry to say that there has been a shameful want of self-control among us, and that, if we learn anything at all from him, it will be because you have taught us how."

She could not resist this bit of taffy. She scarcely gave herself time to gulp it, before she said:

"Oh, it's very well to say that, now! But where would you have been, if I hadn't set my wits to work? Now, listen! It just popped into my mind, like an inspiration, when I was thinking of something altogether different. It flashed upon me in an instant: a good object, and a public occasion!"

"Well?" I said, finding this explosive and electrical inspiration rather enigmatical.

"Why, you know, the Union chapel, over in the village, is in a languishing condition, and the ladies have been talking all summer about doing something for it, getting up something—a concert, or theatricals, or a dance, or something—and applying the proceeds to repainting and papering the visible church; it needs it dreadfully. But, of course, those things are not exactly religious, don't you know; and a fair is so much trouble; and *such* a bore, when you get the articles ready, even; and everybody feels swindled; and now people frown on raffles, so there is no use thinking of them. What you want is something striking. We did think of a parlor-reading, or perhaps ventriloquism; but the performers all charge so much that there wouldn't be anything left after paying expenses."

She seemed to expect some sort of prompting at this point; so I said, "Well?"

"Well," she repeated, "that is just where your Mr. Homos comes in."

"Oh! How does he come in there?"

"Why, get him to deliver a Talk on Altruria. As soon as he knows it's for a good object, he will be on fire to do it; and they must live so much in common there, that the public occasion will be just the thing that will appeal to him."

It did seem a good plan to me, and I said so. But Mrs. Makely was so much in love with it, that she was not satisfied with my modest recognition.

"Good? It's magnificent! It's the very thing! And I have thought it out, down to the last detail—"

"Excuse me!" I interrupted. "Do you think there is sufficient general interest in the subject, outside of the hotel, to get a full house for him? I shouldn't like to see him subjected to the mortification of empty benches."

"What in the world are you thinking of? Why, there isn't a farmhouse, anywhere within ten miles, where they haven't heard of Mr. Homos; and there isn't a servant under this roof, or in any of the boarding-houses, who doesn't know something about Altruria and want to know more. It seems that your friend has been much oftener with the porters and the stable boys than he has been with us."

I had only too great reason to fear so. In spite of my warnings and entreaties, he had continued to behave toward every human being he met, exactly as if they were equals. He apparently could not conceive of that social difference which difference of occupation creates among us. He owned that he saw it, and from the talk of our little group, he knew it existed; but when I expostulated with him upon some act in gross violation of society usage, he only answered that he could not imagine that what he saw and knew could actually be. It was quite impossible to keep him from bowing with the greatest deference to our waitress; he shook hands with the head waiter every morning as well as with me; there was a fearful story current in the house, that he had been seen running down one of the corridors to relieve a chambermaid laden with two heavy waterpails, which she was carrying to the rooms to fill up the pitchers. This was probably not true, but I myself saw him helping in the hotel hayfield one afternoon, shirt-sleeved like any of the hired men. He said that it was the best possible exercise, and that he was ashamed he could give no better excuse for it than the fact that without something of the kind he should suffer from indigestion. It was grotesque, and out of all keeping with a man of his cultivation and breeding. He was a gentleman and a scholar, there was no denying, and yet he did things in contravention of good form at every opportunity, and nothing I could say had any effect with him. I was perplexed beyond measure, the day after I had reproached him for his labor in the hayfield, to find him in a group of table-girls, who were listening while the head waiter read aloud to them in the shade of the house; there was a corner looking towards the stables which was given up to them by tacit consent of the guests during a certain part of the afternoon. I feigned not to see him, but I could not forbear speaking to him about it afterwards. He took it in good part, but he said he had been rather disappointed in the kind of literature they liked, and the comments they made on it; he had expected that with the education they had received, and with their experience of the seriousness of life, they would prefer something less trivial. He supposed, however, that a romantic love story, where a poor American girl marries an English lord, formed a refuge for them from the real world which promised them so little and held them so cheap. It was quite useless for one to try to make him realize his behavior in consorting with servants as a kind of scandal.

The worst of it was that his behavior, as I could see, had already begun to demoralize the objects of his misplaced politeness. At first, the servants stared and resented it, as if it were some tasteless joke; but in an incredibly short time, when they saw that he meant his courtesy in good faith they took it as their due. I had always had a good understanding with the head waiter, and I thought I could safely smile with him at the queer conduct of my friend toward himself and his fellow servants. To my astonishment he said, "I don't see why he shouldn't treat them as if they were ladies and gentlemen. Doesn't he treat you and your friends so?"

It was impossible to answer this, and I could only suffer in silence, and hope the Altrurian would soon go. I had dreaded the moment when the landlord should tell me that his room was wanted; now I almost desired it, but he never did. On the contrary, the Altrurian was in high favor with him. He said he liked to see a man make himself pleasant with everybody; and that he did not believe he had ever had a guest in the house who was so popular all round.

"Of course," Mrs. Makely went on, "I don't criticise him—with his peculiar traditions. I presume I should be just so myself if I had been brought up in Altruria, which thank goodness, I wasn't. But Mr. Homos is a perfect dear, and all the women in the house are in love with him, from the cook's helpers, up and down. No, the only danger is that there won't be room in the hotel parlors for all the people that will want to hear him, and we shall have to make the admission something that will be prohibitive in most cases. We shall have to make it a dollar."

"Well," I said, "I think that will settle the question as far as the farming population is concerned. It's twice as much as they ever pay for a reserved seat in the circus, and four times as much as a simple admission. I'm afraid, Mrs. Makely, you're going to be very few, though fit."

"Well, I've thought it all over, and I'm going to put the tickets at one dollar."

"Very good. Have you caught your hare?"

"No, I haven't, yet. And I want you to help me catch him. What do you think is the best way to go about it?"

The banker said he would leave us to the discussion of that question, but Mrs. Makely could count upon him in everything, if she could only get the man to talk. At the end of our conference we decided to interview the Altrurian together.

I shall always be ashamed of the way that woman wheedled the Altrurian, when we found him the next morning, walking up and down the piazza, before breakfast. That is, it was before our breakfast; when we asked him to go in with us, he said he had just had his breakfast and was waiting for Reuben Camp, who had promised to take him up as he passed with a load of hay for one of the hotels in the village.

"Ah, that reminds me, Mr. Homos," the unscrupulous woman began on him, at once. "We want to interest you in a little movement we're getting up for the Union chapel in the village. You know it's the church where all the different sects have their services, alternately. Of course, it's rather an original way of doing, but there *is* sense in it where the people are too poor to go into debt for different churches, and—"

"It's admirable!" said the Altrurian. "I have heard about it from the Camps. It is an emblem of the unity which ought to prevail among Christians of all professions. How can I help you, Mrs. Makely?"

"I knew you would approve of it!" she exulted. "Well, it's simply this: The poor little place has got so shabby that *I'm* almost ashamed to be seen going into it, for one; and want to raise money enough to give it a new coat of paint outside and put on some kind of pretty paper, of an ecclesiastical pattern, on the inside. I declare, those staring white walls, with the cracks in the plastering zigzagging every *which* way, distract me so that I can't put my mind on the sermon. Don't you think that paper, say of a gothic design, would be a great improvement? I'm sure it would; and it's Mr. Twelvemough's idea, too."

I learned this fact now for the first time; but, with Mrs. Makely's warning eye upon me, I could not say so, and I made what sounded to me like a gothic murmur of acquiescence. It sufficed for Mrs. Makely's purpose, at any rate, and she went on, without giving the Altrurian a chance to say what he thought the educational effect of wall paper would be:

"Well, the long and short of it is that we want you to make this money for us, Mr. Homos."

"I?" He started in a kind of horror. "My dear lady, I never made any money in my life! I should think it *wrong* to make money!"

"In Altruria, yes. We all know how it is in your delightful country, and I assure you that no one could respect your conscientious scruples more than I do. But you must remember that you are in America, now. In America you have to make money, or else—get left. And then you must consider the object, and all the good you can do, indirectly, by a little Talk on Altruria."

He answered, blandly: "A little Talk on Altruria? How in the world should I get money by that?"

She was only too eager to explain, and she did it with so much volubility and at such great length, that I, who am good for nothing till I have had my cup of coffee in the morning, almost perished of an elucidation which the Altrurian bore with the sweetest patience.

When she gave him a chance to answer, at last, he said: "I shall be very happy to do what you wish, madam."

"*Will* you?" she screamed. "Oh, I'm *so* glad! You *have* been so slippery about Altruria, you know, that I expected nothing but a point-blank refusal. Of course, I knew you would be kind about it. Oh, I can hardly believe my senses! You can't think what a dear you are." I knew she had got that word from some English people who had been in the hotel; and she was working it rather wildly, but it was not my business to check her. "Well, then, all you have got to do is to leave the whole thing to me, and not bother about it a bit till I send and tell you we are ready to listen. There comes Reuben with his ox-team! Thank you *so* much, Mr. Homos. No one need be ashamed to enter the house of God"—she said Gawd, in an access of piety—"after we get that paint and paper on it; and we shall have them on before two Sabbaths have passed over it."

She wrung the Altrurian's hand; I was only afraid she was going to kiss him.

"There is but one stipulation I should like to make," he began.

"Oh, a thousand," she cut in.

"And that is, there shall be no exclusion from my lecture on account of occupation or condition. That is a thing that I can in no wise countenance, even in America; it is far more abhorrent to me even than money-making, though they are each a part and parcel of the other."

"I thought it was that!" she retorted joyously. "And I can assure you, Mr. Homos, there shall be nothing of that kind. Every one—I don't care who it is, or what they do—shall hear you who buys a ticket. Now, will that do?"

"Perfectly," said the Altrurian, and he let her wring his hand again.

She pushed hers through my arm as we started for the dining-room, and leaned over to whisper jubilantly: "That will fix it! He will see how much his precious lower classes care for Altruria if they have to pay a dollar apiece to hear about it. And I shall keep faith with him to the letter."

I could not feel that she would keep it in the spirit; but I could only groan inwardly and chuckle outwardly at the woman's depravity.

It seemed to me, though I could not approve of it, a capital joke, and so it seemed to all the members of the little group whom I had made especially acquainted with the Altrurian. It is true that the minister was somewhat troubled with the moral question, which did not leave me wholly at peace; and the banker affected to find a question of taste involved, which he said he must let me settle, however, as the man's host; if I could stand it, he could. No one said anything against the plan to Mrs. Makely, and this energetic woman made us take two tickets apiece, as soon as she got them printed, over in the village. She got little hand-bills printed, and had them scattered about through the neighborhood, at all the hotels, boarding-houses and summer cottages, to give notice of the time and place of the Talk on Altruria. She fixed this for the following Saturday after-noon, in our hotel parlor; she had it in the afternoon so as not to interfere with the hop in the evening; she put tickets on sale at the principal houses, and at the village drug-store, and she made me go about with her and help her sell them at some of the cottages in person.

I must say I found this extremely distasteful, especially where the people were not very willing to buy, and she had to urge them. They all admitted the excellence of the object, but they were not so sure about the means. At several places the ladies asked who was this Mr. Homos, anyway; and how did she know he was really from Altruria? He might be an imposter.

Then Mrs. Makely would put me forward, and I would be obliged to give such account of him as I could, and to explain just how and why he came to be my guest; with the cumulative effect of bringing back all the misgivings which I had myself felt at the outset concerning him, and which I had dismissed as too fantastic.

The tickets went off rather slowly, even in our own hotel; people thought them too dear; and some, as soon as they knew the price, said frankly they had heard enough about Altruria already, and were sick of the whole thing.

Mrs. Makely said this was quite what she had expected of those people; that they were horrid, and stingy and vulgar; and she should see what face they would have to ask her to take tickets when *they* were trying to get up something. She began to be vexed with herself, she confessed, at the joke she was playing on Mr. Homos, and I noticed that she put herself rather defiantly *en évidence* in his company, whenever she could in the presence of these reluctant ladies. She told me she had not the courage to ask the clerk how many of the tickets he had sold out of those she had left at the desk. One morning, the third or fourth, as I was going in to breakfast with her, the head waiter stopped her as he opened the door, and asked modestly if she could spare him a few tickets, for he thought he could sell some. To my amazement the unprincipled creature said, "Why, certainly. How many?" and instantly took a package out of her pocket, where she seemed always to have them. He asked, Would twenty be more than she could spare? and she answered, "Not at all! Here are twenty-five," and bestowed the whole package upon him.

That afternoon Reuben Camp came lounging up toward us, where I sat with her on the corner of the piazza, and said that if she would like to let him try his luck with some tickets for the Talk he would see what he could do.

"You can have all you want, Reuben," she said, "and I hope you'll have better luck than I have. I'm perfectly disgusted with people."

She fished several packages out of her pocket this time and he asked, "Do you mean that I can have them all?"

"Every one, and a band of music into the bargain," she answered recklessly. But she seemed a little daunted when he quietly took them. "You know there are a hundred here?"

"Yes, I should like to see what I can do amongst the natives. Then, there is a construction train over at the junction, and I know a lot of the fellows. I guess some of 'em would like to come."

"The tickets are a dollar each, you know," she suggested.

"That's all right," said Camp. "Well, good afternoon."

Mrs. Makely turned to me with a kind of gasp, as he shambled away. "I don't know about that!"

"About having the whole crew of a construction train at the Talk? I dare say it won't be pleasant to the ladies who have bought tickets."

"*Oh!*" said Mrs. Makely with astonishing contempt, "I don't care what *they* think. But Reuben has got all my tickets, and suppose he keeps them so long that I won't have time to sell any, and then throws them back on my hands? *I* know!" she added joyously. "I can go round now, and tell people that my tickets are all gone; and I'll go instantly and have the clerk hold all he has left at a premium."

She came back looking rather blank.

"He hasn't got a single one left. He says an old native came in this morning and took every last one of them—he doesn't remember just how many. I believe they're going to speculate on them; and if Reuben Camp serves me a trick like that— Why!" she broke off, "I believe I'll speculate on them myself! I should like to know why I shouldn't! Oh, I should just *like* to make some of those creatures pay double or treble for the chances they've refused. Ah, Mrs. Bulkham," she called out to a lady who was coming down the veranda toward us, "you'll be glad to know I've got rid of all my tickets! *Such* a relief!"

"You *have*?" Mrs. Bulkham retorted.

"Every one!"

"I thought," said Mrs. Bulkham, "that you understood I wanted one for my daughter and myself, if she came."

"I certainly didn't," said Mrs. Makely, with a wink of concentrated wickedness at me. "But if you do, you will have to say so now, without any ifs or ands about it; and if any of the tickets come back—I let friends have a few on sale—I will give you two."

"Well, I do," said Mrs. Bulkham, after a moment.

"Very well, it will be five dollars for the two. I feel bound to get all I can for the cause. Shall I put your name down?"

"Yes," said Mrs. Bulkham, rather crossly; but Mrs. Makely inscribed her name on her tablets with a radiant amiability, which suffered no eclipse, when within the next fifteen minutes a dozen other ladies hurried up, and bought in at the same rate.

I could not stand it, and I got up to go away, feeling extremely *particeps criminis*. Mrs. Makely seemed to have a conscience as light as air.

"If Reuben Camp or the head waiter don't bring back some

of those tickets I don't know what I shall do. I shall have to put chairs into the aisles, and charge five dollars apiece for as many people as I can crowd in there. I never knew anything so perfectly providential."

"I envy you the ability to see it in that light, Mrs. Makely," I said, faint at heart. "Suppose Camp crowds the place full of his train men, how will the ladies that you've sold tickets to at five dollars apiece like it?"

"Pooh! What do I care how they like it? Horrid things! And for repairs on the house of Gawd, it's the same as being in church, where everybody is equal."

The time passed. Mrs. Makely sold chances to all the ladies in the house; on Friday night Reuben Camp brought her a hundred dollars; the head waiter had already paid in twenty-five.

"I didn't dare to ask them if they speculated on them," she confided to me. "Do you suppose they would have the conscience?"

They had secured the large parlor of the hotel, where the young people danced in the evening, and where entertainments where held, of the sort usually given in summer hotels; we had already had a dramatic reading, a time with the phonograph, an exhibition of necromancy, a concert by a college glee club, and I do not know what else. The room would hold perhaps two hundred people, if they were closely seated, and by her own showing, Mrs. Makely had sold above two hundred and fifty tickets and chances. All Saturday forenoon she consoled herself with the belief that a great many people at the other hotels and cottages had bought seats merely to aid the cause, and would not really come; she estimated that at least fifty would stay away; but if Reuben Camp had sold his tickets among the natives, we might expect every one of them to come and get his money's worth; she did not dare to ask the head waiter how he had got rid of his twenty-five tickets.

The hour set for the Talk to begin was three o'clock, so that people could have their naps comfortably over, after the one o'clock dinner, and be just in the right frame of mind for listening. But long before the appointed time, the people who dine at twelve, and never take an afternoon nap, began to arrive, on foot, in farm-wagons, smart buggies, mud-crusted carryalls, and all manner of ramshackle vehicles. They arrived as if coming to a circus, old husbands and wives, young couples and their children, pretty girls and their fellows, and hitched their horses to the tails of their wagons, and began to make a picnic lunch in the shadow of the grove lying between the hotel and the station. About two, we heard the snorting of a locomotive at a time when no train was due, and a construction train came in view, with the men waving their handkerchiefs from the windows, and apparently ready for all the fun there was to be in the thing. Some of them had a small flag in each hand, the American stars and stripes, and the white flag of Altruria, in compliment to my guest, I suppose. A good many of the farmers came over to the hotel to buy tickets, which they said they expected to get after they came, and Mrs. Makely was obliged to pacify them with all sorts of lying promises. From moment to moment she was in consultation with the landlord, who decided to throw open the dining-room, which connected with the parlor, so as to allow the help and the neighbors to hear, without incommoding the hotel guests. She said that this took a great burden off her mind, and that now she should feel perfectly easy, for now no one could complain about being mixed up with the servants and the natives, and yet everyone could hear perfectly.

She could not rest until she had sent for Homos and told him of this admirable arrangement. I did not know whether to be glad or not, when he instantly told her that, if there was to be any such separation of his auditors, in recognition of our class distinctions, he must refuse to speak at all.

"Then, what in the world are we to do?" she wailed out, and the tears came into her eyes.

"Have you got the money for all your tickets?" he asked, with a sort of disgust for the whole transaction in his tone.

"Yes, and more, too. I don't believe there's a soul, in the

hotel or out of it, that hasn't paid at least a dollar to hear you: and that makes it so very embarrassing. Oh, *dear* Mr. Homos! you won't be so implacably high-principled as all that! Think that you are doing it for the house of Gawd."

The woman made me sick.

"Then, no one," said the Altrurian, "can feel aggrieved, or unfairly used, if I say what I have to say in the open air, where all can listen equally, without any manner of preference or distinction. We will go up to the edge of the grove over-looking the tennis-court, and hold our meeting there, as the Altrurian meetings are always held, with the sky for a roof, and with no walls but the horizon."

"The very thing!" cried Mrs. Makely. "Who would ever have thought you were so practical, Mr. Homos? I don't believe you're an Altrurian, after all; I believe you are an American in disguise."

The Altrurian turned away, without making any response to this flattering attribution of our nationality to him; but Mrs. Makely had not waited for any. She had flown off, and I next saw her attacking the landlord, with such apparent success that he slapped himself on the leg and vanished, and immediately the porters and bell-boys and all the men-servants began carrying out chairs to the tennis-court, which was already well set round with benches. In a little while the whole space was covered, and settees were placed well up the ground toward the grove.

By half past two, the guests of the hotel came out, and took the best seats, as by right, and the different tallyhoes and mountain wagons began to arrive from the other hotels, with their silly hotel-cries, and their gay groups dismounted and dispersed themselves over the tennis-court until all the chairs were taken. It was fine to see how the natives and the trainmen and the hotel servants, with an instinctive perception of the proprieties, yielded these places to their superiors, and, after the summer folks were all seated, scattered themselves on the grass and the pine-needles about the border of the grove. I should have liked to instance the fact to the Altrurian, as a proof that this sort of subordination was a part of human nature, and that a principle which pervaded our civilization, after the democratic training of our whole national life, must be divinely implanted. But there was no opportunity for me to speak with him after the fact had accomplished itself, for by this time he had taken his place in front of a little clump of low pines and was waiting for the assembly to quiet itself before he began to speak. I do not think there could have been less than five hundred present, and the scene had that accidental picturesqueness which results from the grouping of all sorts of faces and costumes. Many of our ladies had pretty hats and brilliant parasols, but I must say that the soberer tone of some of the old farm-wives' brown calicoes and out-dated bonnets contributed to enrich the coloring, and there was a certain gayety in the sunny glisten of the men's straw-hats, everywhere, that was very good.

The sky overhead was absolutely stainless, and the light of the cool afternoon sun dreamed upon the slopes of the solemn mountains to the east. The tall pines in the background blackened themselves against the horizon; nearer they showed more and more decidedly their bluish green, and the yellow of the newly-fallen needles painted their aisles deep into the airy shadows.

A little wind stirred their tops, and for a moment, just before the Altrurian began to speak, drew from them an organ-tone that melted delicately away as his powerful voice rose.

XI

"I COULD NOT give you a clear account of the present state of things in my country," the Altrurian began, "without first telling you something of our conditions before the time of our Evolution. It seems to be the law of all life, that nothing can come to fruition without dying and seeming to make an end. It must be sown in corruption before it can be raised in incorruption. The truth itself must perish to our senses before it can live to our souls; the Son of Man must suffer upon the cross before we can know the Son of God.

"It was so with His message to the world, which we received in the old time as an ideal realized by the earliest Christians, who loved one another and who had all things common. The apostle cast away upon our heathen coasts, won us with the story of this first Christian republic, and he established a commonwealth of peace and goodwill among us in its likeness. That commonwealth perished, just as its prototype perished, or seemed to perish; and long ages of civic and economic warfare succeeded, when every man's hand was against his neighbor, and might was the rule that got itself called right. Religion ceased to be the hope of this world, and became the vague promise of the next. We descended into the valley of the shadow, and dwelt amid chaos for ages, before we groped again into the light.

"The first glimmerings were few and indistinct, but men formed themselves about the luminous points here and there, and when these broke and dispersed into lesser gleams, still men formed themselves about each of them. There arose a system of things, better, indeed, than that darkness, but full of war, and lust, and greed, in which the weak rendered homage to the strong, and served them in the field and in the camp, and the strong in turn gave the weak protection against the other strong. It was a juggle in which the weak did not see that their safety was after all from themselves; but it was an image of peace, however false and fitful, and it endured for a time. It endured for a limited time, if we measure by the life of the race; it endured for an unlimited time if we measure by the lives of the men who were born and died while it endured.

"But that disorder, cruel and fierce and stupid, which endured because it sometimes masked itself as order, did at last pass away. Here and there one of the strong overpowered the rest; then the strong became fewer and fewer, and in their turn they all yielded to a supreme lord, and throughout the land there was one rule, as it was called then, or one misrule, as we should call it now. This rule, or this misrule, continued for ages more; and again, in the immortality of the race, men toiled and struggled, and died without the hope of better things.

"Then the time came when the long nightmare was burst with the vision of a future in which all men were the law, and not one man, or any less number of men than all.

"The poor, dumb beast of humanity rose, and the throne tumbled, and the sceptre was broken, and the crown rolled away into that darkness of the past. We thought that heaven had descended to us, and that liberty, equality and fraternity were ours. We could not see what should again alienate us from one another, or how one brother could again oppress another. With a free field and no favor, we believed we should prosper on together, and there would be peace and plenty for all. We had the republic, again, after so many ages now, and the republic, as we knew it in our dim annals, was brotherhood and universal happiness. All but a very few who prophesied evil of our lawless freedom, were rapt in a delirium of hope. Men's minds and men's hands were suddenly released to an activity unheard of before. Invention followed invention; our rivers and seas became the warp of commerce where the steam-sped shuttles carried the woof of enterprise to and fro with tireless celerity. Machines to save labor multiplied themselves as if they had been procreative forces; and wares of every sort were produced with incredible swiftness and cheapness. Money seemed to flow from the ground; vast fortunes 'rose like an exhalation,' as your Milton says.

"At first we did not know that they were the breath of the nethermost pits of hell, and that the love of money which was becoming universal with us, was filling the earth with the hate of men. It was long before we came to realize that in the depths of our steamships were those who fed the fires with their lives, and that our mines from which we dug our wealth were the graves of those who had died to the free light and air, without finding the rest of death. We did not see that the machines for saving labor were monsters that devoured women and children, and wasted men at the bidding of the power which no man must touch.

"That is, we thought we must not touch it, for it called itself prosperity, and wealth, and the public good, and it said that it gave bread, and it impudently bade the toiling myriads consider what would become of them, if it took away their means of wearing themselves out in its service. It demanded of the state absolute immunity and absolute impunity, the right to do its will wherever and however it would, without question from the people who were the final law. It had its way, and under its rule we became the richest people under the sun. The Accumulation, as we called this power, because we feared to call it by its true name, rewarded its own with gains of twenty, of a hundred, of a thousand per cent., and to satisfy its need, to produce the labor that operated its machines, there came into existence a hapless race of men who bred their kind for its service, and whose little ones were its prey, almost from their cradles. Then the infamy became too great, and the law, the voice of the people, so long guiltily silent, was lifted in behalf of those who had no helper. The Accumulation came under control, for the first time, and could no longer work its slaves twenty hours a day amid perils to life and limb from its machinery and in conditions that forbade them decency and morality. The time of a hundred and a thousand per cent. passed; but still the Accumulation demanded immunity and impunity, and in spite of its conviction of the enormities it had practiced, it declared itself the only means of civilization and progress. It began to give out that it was timid, though its history was full of the boldest frauds and crimes, and it threatened to withdraw itself if it were ruled or even crossed; and again it had its way, and we seemed to prosper more and more. The land was filled with cities where the rich flaunted their splendor in palaces, and the poor swarmed in squalid tenements. The country was drained of its life and force, to feed the centers of commerce and industry. The whole land was bound together with a network of iron roads that linked the factories and foundries to the fields and mines, and blasted the landscape with the enterprise that spoiled the lives of men.

"Then, all at once, when its work seemed perfect and its dominion sure, the Accumulation was stricken with consciousness of the lie always at its heart. It had hitherto cried out for a free field and no favor, for unrestricted competition; but, in truth, it had never prospered, except as a monopoly. Whenever and wherever competition had play, there had been nothing but disaster to the rival enterprises, till one rose over the rest. Then there was prosperity for that one.

"The Accumulation began to act upon its new consciousness. The iron roads united; the warring industries made peace, each kind under a single leadership. Monopoly, not competition, was seen to be the beneficent means of distributing the favors and blessings of the Accumulation to mankind. But as before, there was alternately a glut and dearth of things, and it often happened that when starving men went ragged through the streets, the storehouses were piled full of rotting harvests that the farmers toiled from dawn till dusk to grow, and the warehouses fed the moth with the stuffs that the operative had woven his life into at his loom. Then followed, with a blind and mad succession, a time of famine, when money could not buy the superabundance that vanished, none knew how or why.

"The money itself vanished from time to time, and disappeared into the vaults of the Accumulation, for no better reason than that for which it poured itself out at other times. Our theory was that the people, that is to say the government of the people, made the people's money, but, as a matter of fact, the Accumulation made it, and controlled it, and juggled with it; and now you saw it, and now you did not see it. The government made gold coins, but the people had nothing but the paper money that the Accumulation made. But whether there was scarcity or plenty, the failures went on with a continuous ruin that nothing could check, while our larger economic life proceeded in a series of violent shocks, which we called financial panics, followed by long periods of exhaustion and recuperation. There was no law in our economy, but as the Accumulation had never cared for the nature of law, it did not trouble itself for its name in our order of things. It had always bought the law it needed for its own use, first through the voter at the polls in the more primitive

days, and then, as civilization advanced, in the legislatures and
the courts. But the corruption even of these methods was far
surpassed when the era of consolidation came, and the necessity
for statutes and verdicts and decisions became more stringent.
Then we had such a burlesque of—"

"Look here!" a sharp nasal voice snarled across the rich, full
pipe of the Altrurian, and we all instantly looked there. The
voice came from an old farmer, holding himself stiffly up, with
his hands in his pockets and his lean frame bent toward the
speaker. "When are you goin' to git to Altrury? We know all
about Ameriky."

He sat down again, and it was a moment before the crowd
caught on. Then a yell of delight and a roar of volleyed laughter
went up from the lower classes, in which, I am sorry to say, my
friend, the banker, joined, so far as the laughter was concerned.
"Good! That's it! First-rate!" came from a hundred vulgar
throats.

"Isn't it a perfect shame?" Mrs. Makely demanded. "I think
some of you gentlemen ought to say something! What will Mr.
Homos think of our civilization if we let such interruptions go
unrebuked!"

She was sitting between the banker and myself, and her indignation made him laugh more and more. "Oh, it serves him
right," he said. "Don't you see that he is hoist with his own
petard? Let him alone. He's in the hands of his friends."

The Altrurian waited for the tumult to die away, and then
he said, gently: "I don't understand."

The old farmer jerked himself to his feet again: "It's like this:
I paid my dolla' to hear about a country where there wa'n't no
co'perations, nor no monop'lies, nor no buyin' up cou'ts; and I
ain't agoin' to have no allegory shoved down my throat, instead
of a true history, noways. I know all about how it is *here*. Fi'st,
run their line through your backya'd, and then kill off your
cattle, and keep kerryin' on it up from cou't to cou't, till there
ain't hide or hair on 'em left—"

"Oh, set down, set down! Let the man go on! He'll make it

all right with you," one of the construction gang called out; but the farmer stood his ground, and I could hear him through the laughing and shouting, keep saying something, from time to time, about not wanting to pay no dolla' for no talk about co'perations and monop'lies that we had right under our own noses the whole while, and you might say in your very bread-troughs; till, at last, I saw Reuben Camp make his way towards him, and, after an energetic expostulation, turn to leave him again.

Then he faltered out, "I guess it's all right," and dropped out of sight in the group he had risen from. I fancied his wife scolding him there, and all but shaking him in public.

"I should be very sorry," the Altrurian proceeded, "to have anyone believe that I have not been giving you a bona fide account of conditions in my country before the Evolution, when we first took the name of Altruria in our great, peaceful campaign against the Accumulation. As for offering you any allegory or travesty of your own conditions, I will simply say that I do not know them well enough to do so intelligently. But, whatever they are, God forbid that the likeness which you seem to recognize should ever go so far as the desperate state of things which we finally reached. I will not trouble you with details; in fact, I have been afraid that I had already treated of our affairs too abstractly; but, since your own experience furnishes you the means of seizing my meaning, I will go on as before.

"You will understand me when I explain that the Accumulation had not erected itself into the sovereignty with us unopposed. The workingmen who suffered most from its oppression had early begun to band themselves against it, with the instinct of self-preservation, first trade by trade, and art by art, and then in congresses and federations of the trades and arts, until finally they enrolled themselves in one vast union, which included all the workingmen whom their necessity or their interest did not leave on the side of the Accumulation. This beneficent and generous association of the weak for the sake of the weakest did not accomplish itself fully till the baleful instinct of the Accumulation had reduced the monopolies to one vast monopoly, till the stronger had devoured the weaker among its members, and the supreme agent stood at the head of our affairs, in everything but name our imperial ruler. We had hugged so long the delusion of each man for himself, that we had suffered all realty to be taken from us. The Accumulation owned the land as well as the mines under it and the shops over it; the Accumulation owned the seas and the ships that sailed the seas, and the fish that swam in their depths; it owned transportation and distribution, and the wares and products that were to be carried to and fro; and, by a logic irresistible and inexorable, the Accumulation *was*, and we were *not*.

"But the Accumulation, too, had forgotten something. It had found it so easy to buy legislatures and courts, that it did not trouble itself about the polls. It left us the suffrage, and let us amuse ourselves with the periodical election of the political clay images which it manipulated and moulded to any shape and effect, at its pleasure. The Accumulation knew that it was the sovereignty, whatever figure-head we called president, or governor, or mayor: we had other names for these officials, but I use their analogues for the sake of clearness, and I hope my good friend over there will not think I am still talking about America."

"No," the old farmer called back, without rising, "we hain't got there, quite, yit."

"No hurry," said a trainman. "All in good time. Go on!" he called to the Altrurian.

The Altrurian resumed:

"There had been, from the beginning, an almost ceaseless struggle between the Accumulation and the proletariate. The Accumulation always said that it was the best friend of the proletariate, and it denounced, through the press which it controlled, the proletarian leaders who taught that it was the enemy of the proletariate, and who stirred up strikes and tumults of all sorts, for higher wages and fewer hours. But the friend of the proletariate, whenever occasion served, treated the proletariate like a deadly enemy. In seasons of over-production, as it was called, it locked the workmen out, or laid them off, and left their families to starve, or ran light work, and claimed the credit of public benefactors for running at all. It sought every chance to reduce wages; it had laws passed to forbid or cripple the workmen in their strikes; and the judges convicted them of conspiracy, and wrested the statutes to their hurt in cases where there had been no thought of embarrassing them even among the legislators. God forbid that you should ever come to such a pass in America; but, if you ever should, God grant that you may find your way out as simply as we did at last, when freedom had perished in everything but name among us, and justice had become a mockery.

"The Accumulation had advanced so smoothly, so lightly, in all its steps to the supreme power, and had at last so thoroughly quelled the uprisings of the proletariate, that it forgot one thing: it forgot the despised and neglected suffrage. The ballot, because it had been so easy to annul its effect, had been left in the people's hands; and when, at last, the leaders of the proletariate ceased to counsel strikes, or any form of resistance to the Accumulation that could be tormented into the likeness of insurrection against the government, and began to urge them to attack it in the political way, the deluge that swept the Accumulation out of existence came trickling and creeping over the land. It appeared first in the country, a spring from the ground; then it gathered head in the villages; then it swelled to a torrent in the cities. I cannot stay to trace its course; but suddenly, one day, when the Accumulation's abuse of a certain power became too gross, it was voted out of that power. You will perhaps be interested to know that it was with the telegraphs that the rebellion against the Accumulation began, and the government was forced by the overwhelming majority which the proletariate sent to our parliament, to assume a function which the Accumulation had impudently usurped. Then the transportation of smaller and more perishable wares—"

"Yes," a voice called, "express business. Go on!"

"Was legislated a function of the post-office," the Altrurian went on. "Then all transportation was taken into the hands of the political government, which had always been accused of great corruption in its administration, but which showed itself immaculately pure, compared with the Accumulation. The common ownership of mines necessarily followed, with an allotment of lands to anyone who wished to live by tilling the land; but not a foot of the land was remitted to private hands for purposes of selfish pleasure or the exclusion of any other from the landscape. As all businesses had been gathered into the grasp of the Accumulation, and the manufacture of everything they used and the production of everything that they ate was in the control of the Accumulation, its transfer to the government was the work of a single clause in the statute.

"The Accumulation, which had treated the first menaces of resistance with contempt, awoke to its peril too late. When it turned to wrest the suffrage from the proletariate, at the first election where it attempted to make head against them, it was simply snowed under, as your picturesque phrase is. The Accumulation had no voters, except the few men at its head, and the creatures devoted to it by interest and ignorance. It seemed, at one moment, as if it would offer an armed resistance to the popular will, but, happily, that moment of madness passed. Our Evolution was accomplished without a drop of bloodshed, and the first great political brotherhood, the commonwealth of Altruria, was founded.

"I wish that I had time to go into a study of some of the curious phases of the transformation from a civility in which the people lived *upon* each other to one in which they lived *for* each other. There is a famous passage in the inaugural message of our first Altrurian president, which compares the new civic consciousness with that of a disembodied spirit released to the life beyond this and freed from all the selfish cares and greeds of the flesh. But perhaps I shall give a sufficiently clear notion of the triumph of the change among us, when I say that within half a decade after the fall of the old plutocratic oligarchy one of the chief directors of the Accumulation publicly expressed his gratitude to God that the Accumulation had passed away forever. You will realize the importance of such an expression in recalling the declarations some of your slaveholders have made since the civil war, that they would not have slavery restored for any earthly consideration.

"But now, after this preamble, which has been so much longer than I meant it to be, how shall I give you a sufficiently just conception of the existing Altruria, the actual state from which I come?"

"Yes," came the nasal of the old farmer, again, "that's what we are here fur. I wouldn't give a copper to know all you went through beforehand. It's too dumn like what we have been through ourselves, as fur as heard from."

A shout of laughter went up from most of the crowd, but the Altrurian did not seem to see any fun in it.

"Well," he resumed, "I will tell you, as well as I can, what Altruria is like, but, in the first place, you will have to cast out of your minds all images of civilization with which your experience has filled them. For a time, the shell of the old Accumulation remained for our social habitation, and we dwelt in the old competitive and monopolistic forms after the life had gone out of them. That is, we continued to live in populous cities, and we toiled to heap up riches for the moth to corrupt, and we slaved on in making utterly useless things, merely because we had the habit of making them to sell. For a while we made the old sham things, which pretended to be useful things and were worse than the confessedly useless things. I will give you an illustration from the trades, which you will all understand. The proletariate, in the competitive and monopolistic time, used to make a kind of shoes for the proletariate, or the women of the proletariate, which looked like fine shoes of the best quality. It took just as much work to make these shoes as to make the best fine shoes; but they were shams through and through. They wore out in a week, and the people called them, because they were bought fresh for every Sunday—"

"Sat'd'y night shoes!" screamed the old farmer. "I know 'em. My gals buy 'em. Half dolla' a pai', and not wo'th the money."

"Well," said the Altrurian, "they were a cheat and a lie, in every way, and under the new system it was not possible, when public attention was called to the fact, to continue the falsehood they embodied. As soon as the Saturday night shoe realized itself to the public conscience, an investigation began, and it was found that the principle of the Saturday night shoe underlay half our industries and made half the work that was done. Then an immense reform took place. We renounced, in the most solemn convocation of the whole economy, the principle of the Saturday night shoe, and those who had spent their lives in producing sham shoes—"

"Yes," said the professor, rising from his seat near us, and addressing the speaker, "I shall be very glad to know what became of the worthy and industrious operatives who were thrown out of employment by this explosion of economic virtue."

"Why," the Altrurian replied, "they were set to work making honest shoes; and as it took no more time to make a pair of honest shoes, which lasted a year, than it took to make a pair of dishonest shoes that lasted a week, the amount of labor in shoemaking was at once enormously reduced."

"Yes," said the professor, "I understand that. What became of the shoemakers?"

"They joined the vast army of other laborers who had been employed, directly or indirectly, in the fabrication of fraudulent wares. These shoemakers—lasters, buttonholers, binders, and so on—no longer wore themselves out over their machines. One hour sufficed where twelve hours were needed before, and the operatives were released to the happy labor of the fields, where no one with us toils killingly, from dawn till dusk, but does only as much work as is needed to keep the body in health. We had a continent to refine and beautify; we had climates to change, and seasons to modify, a whole system of meteorology to readjust, and the public works gave employment to the multitudes emancipated from the soul-destroying service of shams. I can scarcely give you a notion of the vastness of the improvements undertaken and carried through, or still in process of accomplishment. But a single one will, perhaps, afford a sufficient illustration. Our southeast coast, from its vicinity to the pole, had always suffered from a winter of antarctic rigor; but our first president conceived the plan of cutting off a peninsula, which kept the equatorial current from making in to our shores; and the work was begun in his term, though the entire strip, twenty miles in width and ninety-three in length, was not severed before the end of the first Altrurian decade. Since that time the whole region of our southeastern coast has enjoyed the climate of your Mediterranean countries.

"It was not only the makers of fraudulent things who were released to these useful and wholesome labors, but those who had spent themselves in contriving ugly and stupid and foolish things were set free to the public employments. The multitude of these monstrosities and iniquities was as great as that of the shams—"

Here I lost some words, for the professor leaned over and whispered to me: "He has got *that* out of William Morris. Depend upon it, the man is a humbug. He is not an Altrurian at all."

I confess that my heart misgave me; but I signalled the professor to be silent, and again gave the Altrurian—if he was an Altrurian—my whole attention.

XII

"AND SO," the Altrurian continued, "when the labor of the community was emancipated from the bondage of the false to the free service of the true, it was also, by an inevitable implication, dedicated to beauty and rescued from the old slavery to the ugly, the stupid and the trivial. The thing that was honest and useful became by the operation of a natural law, a beautiful thing. Once we had not time enough to make things beautiful, we were so overworked in making false and hideous things to sell; but now we had all the time there was, and a glad emulation arose among the trades and occupations to the end that everything done should be done finely as well as done honestly. The artist, the man of genius, who worked from the love of his work became the normal man, and in the measure of his ability and of his calling each wrought in the spirit of the artist. We got back the pleasure of doing a thing beautifully, which was God's primal blessing upon all his working children, but which we had lost in the horrible days of our need and greed. There is not a working-man within the sound of my voice, but has known this divine delight, and would gladly know it always if he only had the time. Well, now we had the time, the Evolution had given us the time, and in all Altruria there was not a furrow driven or a swarth mown, not a hammer struck on house or on ship, not a stitch sewn or a stone laid, not a line written or a sheet printed, not a temple raised or an engine built, but it was done with an eye to beauty as well as to use.

"As soon as we were freed from the necessity of preying upon one another, we found that *there was no hurry*. The good work would wait to be well done; and one of the earliest effects of the Evolution was the disuse of the swift trains which had traversed the continent, night and day, that one man might overreach another, or make haste to undersell his rival, or seize some advantage of him, or plot some profit to his loss. Nine-tenths of the railroads, which in the old times had ruinously competed, and then in the hands of the Accumulation had been united to impoverish and oppress the people, fell into disuse. The commonwealth operated the few lines that were necessary for the collection of materials and the distribution of manufactures, and for pleasure travel and the affairs of state; but the roads that had been built to invest capital, or parallel other roads, or 'make work,' as it was called, or to develop resources, or boom localities, were suffered to fall into ruin; the rails were stripped from the landscape, which they had bound as with shackles, and the road-beds became highways for the use of kindly neighborhoods, or nature recovered them wholly and hid the memory of their former abuse in grass and flowers and wild vines. The ugly towns that they had forced into being, as Frankenstein was fashioned, from the materials of the charnel, and that had no life in or from the good of the community, soon tumbled into decay. The administration used parts of them in the construction of the villages in which the Altrurians now mostly live; but generally these towns were built of materials so fraudulent, in form so vile, that it was judged best to burn them. In this way their sites were at once purified and obliterated.

"We had, of course, a great many large cities under the old egoistic conditions, which increased and fattened upon the country, and fed their cancerous life with fresh infusions of its blood. We had several cities of half a million, and one of more than a million; we had a score of them with a population of a hundred thousand or more. We were very proud of them, and vaunted them as a proof of our unparalleled prosperity, though really they never were anything but congeries of millionaires and the wretched creatures who served them and supplied them. Of course, there was everywhere the appearance of enterprise and activity, but it meant final loss for the great mass of the business men, large and small, and final gain for the millionaires. These, and their parasites dwelt together, the rich starving the poor and the poor plundering and misgoverning the rich; and it was the intolerable suffering in the cities that chiefly hastened the fall of the old Accumulation, and the rise of the Commonwealth.

"Almost from the moment of the Evolution the competitive and monopolistic centers of population began to decline. In the clear light of the new order it was seen that they were not fit dwelling-places for men, either in the complicated and luxurious palaces where the rich fenced themselves from their kind, or in the vast tenements, towering height upon height, ten and twelve stories up, where the swarming poor festered in vice and sickness and famine. If I were to tell you of the fashion of those cities of our egoistic epoch, how the construction was one error from the first, and every correction of an error bred a new defect, I should make you laugh, I should make you weep. We let them fall to ruin as quickly as they would, and their sites are still so pestilential, after the lapse of centuries, that travellers are publicly guarded against them. Ravening beasts and poisonous reptiles lurk in those abodes of the riches and the poverty that are no longer known to our life. A part of one of the less malarial of the old cities, however, is maintained by the commonwealth in the form of its prosperity, and is studied by antiquarians for the instruction, and by moralists for the admonition it affords. A section of a street is exposed, and you see the foundations of the houses; you see the filthy drains that belched into the common sewers, trapped and retrapped to keep the poison gases down; you see the sewers that rolled their loathsome tides under the streets, amidst a tangle of gas pipes, steam pipes, water pipes, telegraph wires, electric lighting wires, electric motor wires and grip-cables; all without a plan, but makeshifts, expedients, devices, to repair and evade the fundamental mistake of having any such cities at all.

"There are now no cities in Altruria, in your meaning, but there are capitals, one for each of the Regions of our country, and one for the whole commonwealth. These capitals are for the transaction of public affairs, in which every citizen of Altruria is schooled, and they are the residences of the administrative officials, who are alternated every year, from the highest to the lowest. A public employment with us is of no greater honor or profit than any other, for with our absolute economic equality, there can be no ambition, and there is no opportunity for one citizen to outshine another. But as the capitals are the centers of all the arts, which we consider the chief of our public affairs, they are oftenest frequented by poets, actors, painters, sculptors, musicians and architects. We regard all artists, who are in a sort creators, as the human type which is likest the divine, and we try to conform our whole industrial life to the artistic temperament. Even in the labors of the field and shop, which are obligatory upon all, we study the inspirations of this temperament, and in the voluntary pursuits we allow it full control. Each, in these, follows his fancy as to what he shall do, and when he shall do it, or whether he shall do anything at all. In the capitals are the universities, theaters, galleries, museums, cathedrals, laboratories and conservatories, and the appliances of every art and science, as well as the administration buildings; and beauty as well as use is studied in every edifice. Our capitals are as clean and quiet and healthful as the country, and these advantages are secured simply by the elimination of the horse, an animal which we should be as much surprised to find in the streets of a town as the plesiosaurus or the pterodactyl. All transportation in the capitals, whether for pleasure or business, is by electricity, and swift electrical expresses connect the capital of each region with the villages which radiate from it to the cardinal points. These expresses run at the rate of a hundred and fifty miles an hour, and they enable the artist, the scientist, the literary man, of the remotest hamlet, to visit the capital (when he is not actually resident there in some public use) every day, after the hours of the obligatory industries; or, if he likes, he may remain there a whole week or fortnight, giving six hours a day instead of three to the obligatories, until the time is made up. In case of very evident merit, or for the purpose of allowing him to complete some work requiring continuous application, a vote of the local agents may release him from the obligatories indefinitely. Generally, however, our artists prefer not to ask this, but avail themselves of the stated means we have of allowing them to work at the obligatories, and get the needed exercise and variety of occupation, in the immediate vicinity of the capital.

"We do not think it well to connect the hamlets on the different lines of radiation from the capital, except by the good country roads which traverse each region in every direction. The villages are mainly inhabited by those who prefer a rural life; they are farming villages; but in Altruria it can hardly be said that one man is more a farmer than another. We do not like to distinguish men by their callings; we do not speak of the poet This or the shoemaker That, for the poet may very likely be a shoemaker in the obligatories, and the shoemaker a poet in the voluntaries. If it can be said that one occupation is honored above another with us, it is that which we all share, and that is

the cultivation of the earth. We believe that this, when not followed slavishly, or for gain, brings man into the closest relations
to the deity, through a grateful sense of the divine bounty, and
that it not only awakens a natural piety in him, but that it endears
to the worker that piece of soil which he tills, and so strengthens
his love of home. The home is the very heart of the Altrurian
system, and we do not think it well that people should be away
from their homes very long or very often. In the competitive and
monopolistic times men spent half their days in racing back and
forth across our continent; families were scattered by the chase
for fortune, and there was a perpetual paying and repaying of
visits. One-half the income of those railroads which we let fall
into disuse came from the ceaseless unrest. Now a man is born
and lives and dies among his own kindred, and the sweet sense
of neighborhood, of brotherhood, which blessed the golden age
of the first Christian republic is ours again. Every year the people
of each Region meet one another on Evolution day, in the
regionic capital; once in four years they all visit the national
capital. There is no danger of the decay of patriotism among us;
our country is our mother, and we love her as it is impossible to
love the stepmother that a competitive or monopolistic nation
must be to its citizens.

"I can only touch upon this feature and that of our system, as
I chance to think of it. If any of you are curious about others, I
shall be glad to answer questions as well as I can. We have, of
course," the Altrurian proceeded, after a little indefinite pause,
to let any speak who liked, "no money in your sense. As the whole
people control affairs, no man works for another, and no man
pays another. Every one does his share of labor, and receives his
share of food, clothing and shelter, which is neither more nor less
than another's. If you can imagine the justice and impartiality
of a well-ordered family, you can conceive of the social and
economic life of Altruria. We are, properly speaking, a family
rather than a nation like yours.

"Of course, we are somewhat favored by our insular, or continental position; but I do not know that we are more so than you

are. Certainly, however, we are self-sufficing in a degree unknown to most European countries; and we have within our borders the materials of every comfort and the resources of every need. We have no commerce with the egoistic world, as we call that outside, and I believe that I am the first Altrurian to visit foreign countries avowedly in my national character, though we have always had emissaries living abroad incognito. I hope that I may say without offense that they find it a sorrowful exile, and that the reports of the egoistic world, with its wars, its bankruptcies, its civic commotions and its social unhappiness, do not make us discontented with our own condition. Before the Evolution we had completed the round of your inventions and discoveries, impelled by the force that drives you on; and we have since disused most of them as idle and unfit. But we profit, now and then, by the advances you make in science, for we are passionately devoted to the study of the natural laws, open or occult, under which all men have their being. Occasionally an emissary returns with a sum of money, and explains to the students of the national university the processes by which it is lost and won; and at a certain time there was a movement for its introduction among us, not for its use as you know it, but for a species of counters in games of chance. It was considered, however, to contain an element of danger, and the scheme was discouraged.

"Nothing amuses and puzzles our people more than the accounts our emissaries give of the changes of fashion in the outside world, and of the ruin of soul and body which the love of dress often works. Our own dress, for men and for women, is studied in one ideal of use and beauty, from the antique; caprice and vagary in it would be thought an effect of vulgar vanity. Nothing is worn that is not simple and honest in texture; we do not know whether a thing is cheap or dear, except as it is easy or hard to come by, and that which is hard to come by is forbidden as wasteful and foolish. The community builds the dwellings of the community, and these, too, are of a classic simplicity, though always beautiful and fit in form; the splendors of the arts are lavished upon the public edifices, which we all enjoy in common."

"Isn't this the greatest rehash of Utopia, New Atlantis, and City of the Sun, that you ever imagined?" the professor whispered across me to the banker. "The man is a fraud, and a very bungling fraud at that."

"Well, you must expose him, when he gets through," the banker whispered back.

But the professor could not wait. He got upon his feet, and called out: "May I ask the gentleman from Altruria a question?"

"Certainly," the Altrurian blandly assented.

"Make it short!" Reuben Camp's voice broke in, impatiently. "We didn't come here to listen to your questions."

The professor contemptuously ignored him. "I suppose you occasionally receive emissaries from, as well as send them to the world outside?"

"Yes, now and then castaways land on our coasts, and ships out of their reckonings put in at our ports, for water or provision."

"And how are they pleased with your system?"

"Why, I cannot better answer than by saying that they mostly refuse to leave us."

"Ah, just as Bacon reports!" cried the professor.

"You mean in the New Atlantis?" returned the Altrurian. "Yes; it is astonishing how well Bacon in that book, and Sir Thomas More in his Utopia, have divined certain phases of our civilization and polity."

"I think he rather *has* you, professor," the banker whispered, with a laugh.

"But all those inspired visionaries," the Altrurian continued, while the professor sat grimly silent, watching for another chance, "who have borne testimony of us in their dreams, conceived of states perfect without the discipline of a previous competitive condition. What I thought, however, might specially interest you Americans in Altruria is the fact that our economy was evolved from one so like that in which you actually have your being. I had even hoped you might feel that, in all these points of resemblance, America prophesies another Altruria. I know that to some of you all that I have told of my country will seem a baseless fabric, with no more foundation, in fact, than More's fairy tale of another land where men dealt kindly and justly by one another, and dwelt, a whole nation, in the unity and equality of a family. But why should not a part of that fable have come true in our polity, as another part of it has come true in yours? When Sir Thomas More wrote that book, he noted with abhorrence the monstrous injustice of the fact that men were hanged for small thefts in England; and in the preliminary conversation between its characters he denounced the killing of men for any sort of thefts. Now you no longer put men to death for theft; you look back upon that cruel code of your mother England with an abhorrence as great as his own. We, for our part, who have realized the Utopian dream of brotherly equality, look back with the same abhorrence upon a state where some were rich and some poor, some taught and some untaught, some high and some low, and the hardest toil often failed to supply a sufficiency of the food which luxury wasted in its riots. That state seems as atrocious to us as the state which hanged a man for stealing a loaf of bread seems to you.

"But we do not regret the experience of competition and monopoly. They taught us some things in the operation of the industries. The labor-saving inventions which the Accumulation perverted to money-making, we have restored to the use intended by their inventors and the Creator of their inventors. After serving the advantage of socializing the industries which the Accumulation effected for its own purposes, we continued the work in large mills and shops, in the interest of the workers, whom we wished to guard against the evil effects of solitude. But our mills and shops are beautiful as well as useful. They look like temples, and they are temples, dedicated to that sympathy between the divine and human which expresses itself in honest and exquisite workmanship. They rise amid leafy boscages beside the streams, which form their only power; for we have disused steam altogether, with all the offenses to the eye and ear which its use brought into the world. Our life is so simple and our needs are so few that the handwork of the primitive toilers could easily

supply our wants; but machinery works so much more thoroughly and beautifully, that we have in great measure retained it.
Only, the machines that were once the workmen's enemies and
masters are now their friends and servants; and if any man
chooses to work alone with his own hands, the state will buy
what he makes at the same price that it sells the wares made collectively. This secures every right of individuality.

"The farm work, as well as the mill work and the shop work,
is done by companies of workers; and there is nothing of that
loneliness in our woods and fields which, I understand, is the
cause of so much insanity among you. It is not good for man to be
alone, was the first thought of his Creator when he considered
him, and we act upon this truth in everything. The privacy of the
family is sacredly guarded in essentials, but the social instinct is
so highly developed with us that we like to eat together in large
refectories, and we meet constantly to argue and dispute on
questions of æsthetics and metaphysics. We do not, perhaps,
read so many books as you do, for most of our reading, when not
for special research, but for culture and entertainment, is done
by public readers, to large groups of listeners. We have no social
meetings which are not free to all; and we encourage joking and
the friendly give and take of witty encounters."

"A little hint from Sparta," suggested the professor.

The banker leaned over to whisper to me, "From what I have
seen of your friend when offered a piece of American humor, I
should fancy the Altrurian article was altogether different. Upon
the whole I would rather not be present at one of their witty
encounters, if I were obliged to stay it out."

The Altrurian had paused to drink a glass of water, and now
he went on. "But we try, in everything that does not inconvenience or injure others, to let everyone live the life he likes
best. If a man prefers to dwell apart and have his meals in
private for himself alone, or for his family, it is freely permitted;
only, he must not expect to be served as in public, where service
is one of the voluntaries; private service is not permitted; those
wishing to live alone must wait upon themselves, cook their own

food and care for their own tables. Very few, however, wish to withdraw from the public life, for most of the discussions and debates take place at our midday meal, which falls at the end of the obligatory labors, and is prolonged indefinitely, or as long as people like to chat and joke, or listen to the reading of some pleasant book.

"In Altruria *there is no hurry*, for no one wishes to outstrip another, or in any wise surpass him. We are all assured of enough, and are forbidden any and every sort of superfluity. If anyone, after the obligatories, wishes to be entirely idle, he may be so, but I cannot now think of a single person without some voluntary occupation; doubtless there are such persons, but I do not know them. It used to be said, in the old times, that 'it was human nature' to shirk, and malinger and loaf, but we have found that it is no such thing. We have found that it is human nature to work cheerfully, willingly, eagerly, at the tasks which all share for the supply of the common necessities. In like manner we have found out that it is not human nature to hoard and grudge, but that when the fear, and even the imagination, of want is taken away, it is human nature to give and to help generously. We used to say, 'A man will lie, or a man will cheat in his own interest; that is human nature,' but that is no longer human nature with us, perhaps because no man has any interest to serve; he has only the interests of others to serve, while others serve his. It is in nowise possible for the individual to separate his good from the common good; he is prosperous and happy only as all the rest are so; and therefore it is not human nature with us for any one to lie in wait to betray another or seize an advantage. That would be ungentlemanly, and in Altruria every man is a gentleman, and every woman a lady. If you will excuse me here, for being so frank, I would like to say something by way of illustration, which may be offensive if you take it personally."

He looked at our little group, as if he were addressing himself more especially to us, and the banker called out jollily: "Go on! I guess we can stand it," and "Go ahead!" came from all sides, from all kinds of listeners.

"It is merely this: that as we look back at the old competitive conditions we do not see how any man could be a gentleman in them, since a gentleman must think first of others, and these conditions *compelled* every man to think first of himself."

There was a silence broken by some conscious and hardy laughter, while we each swallowed this pill as we could.

"What are competitive conditions?" Mrs. Makely demanded of me.

"Well, ours are competitive conditions," I said.

"Very well, then," she returned, "I don't think Mr. Homos is much of a gentleman to say such a thing to an American audience. Or, wait a moment! Ask him if the same rule applies to women!"

I rose, strengthened by the resentment I felt, and said, "Do I understand that in your former competitive conditions it was also impossible for a woman to be a lady?"

The professor gave me an applausive nod as I sat down. "I envy you the chance of that little dig," he whispered.

The Altrurian was thoughtful a moment, and then he answered: "No, I should not say it was. From what we know historically of those conditions in our country, it appears that the great mass of women were not directly affected by them. They constituted an altruistic dominion of the egoistic empire and except as they were tainted by social or worldly ambitions, it was possible for every woman to be a lady, even in competitive conditions. Her instincts were unselfish, and her first thoughts were nearly always of others."

Mrs. Makely jumped to her feet, and clapped violently with her fan on the palm of her left hand. "Three cheers for Mr. Homos!" she shrieked, and all the women took up the cry, supported by all the natives and the construction gang. I fancied these fellows gave their support largely in a spirit of burlesque; but they gave it robustly, and from that time on, Mrs. Makely led the applause, and they roared in after her.

It is impossible to follow closely the course of the Altrurian's account of his country, which grew more and more incredible as he went on, and implied every insulting criticism of ours. Some one asked him about war in Altruria, and he said, "The very name of our country implies the absence of war. At the time of the Evolution our country bore to the rest of our continent the same relative proportion that your country bears to your continent. The egoistic nations to the north and the south of us entered into an offensive and defensive alliance to put down the new altruistic commonwealth, and declared war against us. Their forces were met at the frontier by our entire population in arms, and full of the martial spirit bred of the constant hostilities of the competitive and monopolistic epoch just ended. Negotiations began in the face of the imposing demonstration we made, and we were never afterwards molested by our neighbors, who finally yielded to the spectacle of our civilization and united their political and social fate with ours. At present, our whole continent is Altrurian. For a long time we kept up a system of coast defenses, but it is also a long time since we abandoned these; for it is a maxim with us that where every citizen's life is a pledge of the public safety, that country can never be in danger of foreign enemies.

"In this, as in all other things, we believe ourselves the true followers of Christ, whose doctrine we seek to make our life, as He made it His. We have several forms of ritual, but no form of creed, and our religious differences may be said to be æsthetic and temperamental rather than theologic and essential. We have no denominations, for we fear in this as in other matters to give names to things lest we should cling to the names instead of the things. We love the realities, and for this reason we look at the life of a man rather than his profession for proof that he is a religious man.

"I have been several times asked, during my sojourn among you, what are the sources of compassion, of sympathy, of humanity, of charity with us, if we have not only no want, or fear of want, but not even any economic inequality. I suppose this is because you are so constantly struck by the misery arising from economic inequality, and want, or the fear of want, among yourselves, that you instinctively look in that direction. But have you ever seen sweeter compassion, tenderer sympathy, warmer humanity, heavenlier charity, than that shown in the family, where all are economically equal, and no one can want while any other has to give? Altruria, I say again, is a family, and as we are mortal, we are still subject to those nobler sorrows which God has appointed to men, and which are so different from the squalid accidents that they have made for themselves. Sickness and death call out the most angelic ministries of love; and those who wish to give themselves to others may do so without hindrance from those cares, and even those duties, resting upon men where each must look out first for himself and for his own. Oh, believe me, believe me, you can know nothing of the divine rapture of self-sacrifice while you must dread the sacrifice of another in it! You are not *free*, as we are, to do everything for others, for it is your *duty* to do rather for those of your own household!

"There is something," he continued, "which I hardly know how to speak of," and here we all began to prick our ears. I prepared myself as well as I could for another affront, though I shuddered when the banker hardily called out: "Don't hesitate to say anything you wish, Mr. Homos. I, for one, should like to hear you express yourself fully."

It was always the unexpected, certainly, that happened from the Altrurian. "It is merely this," he said. "Having come to live rightly upon earth, as we believe, or having at least ceased to deny God in our statutes and customs, the fear of death, as it once weighed upon us, has been lifted from our souls. The mystery of it has so far been taken away that we perceive it as something just and natural. Now that all unkindness has been banished from among us, we can conceive of no such cruelty as death once seemed. If we do not know yet the full meaning of death, we know that the Creator of it and of us meant mercy and blessing by it. When one dies, we grieve, but not as those without hope. We do not say that the dead have gone to a better place, and then selfishly bewail them; for we have the kingdom of heaven upon earth, already, and we know that wherever they go they will be homesick for Altruria, and when we think of the years that may pass before we meet them again, our hearts ache, as they must. But the presence of the risen Christ in our daily lives is our assurance that no one ceases to be, and that we shall see our dead again. I cannot explain this to you; I can only affirm it."

The Altrurian spoke very solemnly, and a reverent hush fell upon the assembly. It was broken by the voice of a woman, wailing out: "Oh, do you suppose, if *we* lived so, we should feel so, too? That I should *know* my little girl was living?"

"Why not?" asked the Altrurian.

To my vast astonishment, the manufacturer, who sat the farthest from me in the same line with Mrs. Makely, the professor and the banker, rose and asked tremulously: "And have—have you had any direct communication with the other world? Has any disembodied spirit returned to testify of the life beyond the grave?"

The professor nodded significantly across Mrs. Makely to me, and then frowned and shook his head. I asked her if she knew what he meant. "Why, didn't you know that spiritualism was that poor man's foible? He lost his son in a railroad accident, and ever since—"

She stopped and gave her attention to the Altrurian, who was replying to the manufacturer's question.

"We do not need any such testimony. Our life here makes us sure of the life there. At any rate, no externation of the supernatural, no objective miracle, has been wrought in our behalf. We have had faith to do what we prayed for, and the prescience of which I speak has been added unto us."

The manufacturer asked, as the bereaved mother had asked: "And if I lived so, should I feel so?"

Again the Altrurian answered: "Why not?"

The poor woman quavered: "Oh, do believe it! I just *know* it must be true!"

The manufacturer shook his head sorrowfully, and sat down, and remained there, looking at the ground.

"I am aware," the Altrurian went on, "that what I have said as to our realizing the kingdom of heaven on the earth must seem boastful and arrogant. That is what you pray for every day, but you do not believe it possible for God's will to be done on earth as it is done in heaven; that is, you do not if you are like the competitive and monopolistic people we once were. We once regarded that petition as a formula vaguely pleasing to the Deity, but we no more expected His kingdom to come than we expected Him to give us each day our daily bread; we knew that if we wanted something to eat we should have to hustle for it, and get there first; I use the slang of that far-off time, which, I confess, had a vulgar vigor.

"But now everything is changed, and the change has taken place chiefly from one cause, namely, the disuse of money. At first, it was thought that some sort of circulating medium *must* be used, that life could not be transacted without it. But life began to go on perfectly well, when each dwelt in the place assigned him, which was no better and no worse than any other; and when, after he had given his three hours a day to the obligatory labors, he had a right to his share of food, light, heat and raiment; the voluntary labors, to which he gave much time or little, brought him no increase of those necessaries, but only credit and affection. We had always heard it said that the love of money was the root of all evil, but we had taken this for a saying, merely; now we realized it as an active, vital truth. As soon as money was abolished, the power to purchase was gone, and even if there had been any means of buying beyond the daily needs, with overwork, the community had no power to sell to the individual. No man owned anything, but every man had the right to anything that he could use; when he could not use it, his right lapsed.

"With the expropriation of the individual, the whole vast catalogue of crimes against property shrank to nothing. The thief could only steal from the community; but if he stole, what was he to do with his booty? It was still possible for a depredator to destroy, but few men's hate is so comprehensive as to include all other men, and when the individual could no longer hurt some other individual in his property, destruction ceased.

"All the many murders done from love of money, or of what money could buy, were at an end. Where there was no want, men no longer bartered their souls, or women their bodies, for the means to keep themselves alive. The vices vanished with the crimes, and the diseases almost as largely disappeared. People were no longer sickened by sloth and surfeit, or deformed and depleted by overwork and famine. They were wholesomely housed in healthful places, and they were clad fitly for their labor and fitly for their leisure; the caprices of vanity were not suffered to attaint the beauty of the national dress.

"With the stress of superfluous social and business duties, and the perpetual fear of want which all classes felt, more or less; with the tumult of the cities and the solitude of the country, insanity had increased among us till the whole land was dotted with asylums, and the mad were numbered by hundreds of thousands. In every region they were an army, an awful army of anguish and despair. Now they have decreased to a number so small, and are of a type so mild, that we can hardly count insanity among our causes of unhappiness.

"We have totally eliminated chance from our economic life. There is still a chance that a man will be tall or short, in Altruria, that he will be strong or weak, well or ill, gay or grave, happy or unhappy in love, but none that he will be rich or poor, busy or idle, live splendidly or meanly. These stupid and vulgar accidents of human contrivance cannot befall us; but I shall not be able to tell you just how or why, or to detail the process of eliminating chance. I may say, however, that it began with the nationalization of telegraphs, expresses, railroads, mines and all large industries operated by stock companies. This at once struck a fatal blow at the speculation in values, real and unreal, and at the stock exchange, or bourse; we had our own name for that gambler's paradise, or gambler's hell, whose baleful influence penetrated every branch of business.

"There were still business fluctuations, as long as we had

business, but they were on a smaller and smaller scale, and with the final lapse of business they necessarily vanished; all economic chance vanished. The founders of the commonwealth understood perfectly that business was the sterile activity of the function interposed between the demand and the supply; that it was nothing structural; and they intended its extinction, and expected it from the moment that money was abolished."

"This is all pretty tiresome," said the professor, to our immediate party. "I don't see why we oblige ourselves to listen to that fellow's stuff. As if a civilized state could exist for a day without money or business!"

He went on to give his opinion of the Altrurian's pretended description, in a tone so audible that it attracted the notice of the nearest group of railroad hands, who were listening closely to Homos, and one of them sang out to the professor: "Can't you wait and let the first man finish?" and another yelled: "Put him out!" and then they all laughed, with a humorous perception of the impossibility of literally executing the suggestion.

By the time all was quiet again I heard the Altrurian saying: "As to our social life, I cannot describe it in detail, but I can give you some notion of its spirit. We make our pleasures civic and public as far as possible, and the ideal is inclusive, and not exclusive. There are, of course, festivities which all cannot share, but our distribution into small communities favors the possibility of all doing so. Our daily life, however, is so largely social that we seldom meet by special invitation or engagement. When we do, it is with the perfect understanding that the assemblage confers no social distinction, but is for a momentary convenience. In fact, these occasions are rather avoided, recalling as they do the vapid and tedious entertainments of the competitive epoch, the receptions and balls and dinners of a semi-barbaric people striving for social prominence by shutting a certain number in and a certain number out, and overdressing, overfeeding and overdrinking. Anything premeditated in the way of a pleasure we think stupid and mistaken; we like to meet suddenly, or on the spur of the moment, out of doors, if possible, and arrange a picnic, or a dance, or a play; and let people come and go without ceremony. No one is more host than guest; all are hosts and guests. People consort much according to their tastes—literary, musical, artistic, scientific, or mechanical—but these tastes are made approaches, not barriers; and we find out that we have many more tastes in common than was formerly supposed.

"But, after all, our life is serious, and no one among us is quite happy, in the general esteem, unless he has dedicated himself, in some special way, to the general good. Our ideal is not rights, but duties."

"Mazzini!" whispered the professor.

"The greatest distinction which anyone can enjoy with us is to have found out some new and signal way of serving the community; and then it is not good form for him to seek recognition. The doing any fine thing is the purest pleasure it can give; applause flatters, but it hurts, too, and our benefactors, as we call them, have learned to shun it.

"We are still far from thinking our civilization perfect; but we are sure that our civic ideals are perfect. What we have already accomplished is to have given a whole continent perpetual peace; to have founded an economy in which there is no possibility of want; to have killed out political and social ambition; to have disused money and eliminated chance; to have realized the brotherhood of the race, and to have outlived the fear of death."

The Altrurian suddenly stopped with these words, and sat down. He had spoken a long time, and with a fullness which my report gives little notion of; but, though most of his cultivated listeners were weary, and a good many ladies had left their seats and gone back to the hotel, not one of the natives, or the workpeople of any sort, had stirred; now they remained a moment motionless and silent, before they rose from all parts of the field, and shouted: "Go on! Don't stop! Tell us all about it!"

I saw Reuben Camp climb the shoulders of a big fellow near where the Altrurian had stood; he waved the crowd to silence with outspread arms. "He isn't going to say anything more; he's tired. But if any man don't think he's got his dollar's worth, let him walk up to the door and the ticket-agent will refund him his money."

The crowd laughed, and some one shouted: "Good for you, Reub!"

Camp continued: "But our friend here will shake the hand of any man, woman or child, that wants to speak to him; and you needn't wipe it on the grass, first, either. He's a *man!* And I want to say that he's going to spend the next week with us, at my mother's house, and we shall be glad to have you call."

The crowd, the rustic and ruder part of it, cheered and cheered till the mountain echoes answered; then a railroader called for three times three, with a tiger, and got it. The guests of the hotel broke away and went toward the house, over the long shadows of the meadow. The lower classes pressed forward, on Camp's invitation.

"Well, did you ever hear a more disgusting rigmarole?" asked Mrs. Makely, as our little group halted indecisively about her.

"With all those imaginary commonwealths to draw upon, from Plato, through More, Bacon, and Campanella, down to Bellamy and Morris, he has constructed the shakiest effigy ever made of old clothes stuffed with straw," said the professor.

The manufacturer was silent. The banker said: "I don't know. He grappled pretty boldly with your insinuations. That frank declaration that Altruria was all these pretty soap-bubble worlds solidified, was rather fine."

"It was splendid!" cried Mrs. Makely. The lawyer and the minister came towards us from where they had been sitting together. She called out to them: "Why in the world didn't one of you gentlemen get up and propose a vote of thanks?"

"The difficulty with me is," continued the banker, "that he has rendered Altruria incredible. I have no doubt that he is an Altrurian, but I doubt very much if he comes from anywhere in particular, and I find this quite a blow, for we had got Altruria nicely located on the map, and were beginning to get accounts of it in the newspapers."

"Yes, that is just exactly the way I feel about it," sighed Mrs. Makely. "But still, don't you think there ought to have been a vote of thanks, Mr. Bullion?"

"Why, certainly. The fellow was immensely amusing, and you must have got a lot of money by him. It was an oversight not to make him a formal acknowledgment of some kind. If we offered him money, he would have to leave it all behind him here when he went home to Altruria."

"Just as *we* do when we go to heaven," I suggested; the banker did not answer, and I instantly felt that in the presence of the minister my remark was out of taste.

"Well, then, don't you think," said Mrs. Makely, who had a leathery insensibility to everything but the purpose possessing her, "that we ought at least to go and say something to him personally?"

"Yes, I think we ought," said the banker, and we all walked up to where the Altrurian stood, still thickly surrounded by the lower classes, who were shaking hands with him, and getting in a word with him, now and then.

One of the construction gang said, carelessly: "No all-rail route to Altruria, I suppose?"

"No," answered Homos, "it's a far sea voyage."

"Well, I shouldn't mind working my passage, if you think they'd let me stay after I got there."

"Ah, you mustn't go to Altruria! You must let Altruria come to *you*," returned Homos, with that confounded smile of his that always won my heart.

"Yes," shouted Reuben Camp, whose thin face was red with excitement, "that's the word! Have Altruria right here, and right now!"

The old farmer, who had several times spoken, cackled out: "I didn't know, one while, when you was talk'n' about not havin' no money, but what some on us had had Altrury here for quite a spell, already. I don't pass more'n fifty dolla's through my hands, most years."

A laugh went up, and then, at sight of Mrs. Makely heading

our little party, the people round Homos civilly made way for us. She rushed upon him, and seized his hand in both of hers; she dropped her fan, parasol, gloves, handkerchief and vinaigrette in the grass to do so. "Oh, Mr. Homos!" she fluted, and the tears came into her eyes, "it was beautiful, *beautiful*, every word of it! I sat in a perfect trance from beginning to end, and I felt that it was all as true as it was beautiful. People all round me were breathless with interest, and I don't know how I can ever thank you enough."

"Yes, indeed," the professor hastened to say, before the Altrurian could answer, and he beamed malignantly upon him through his spectacles while he spoke, "it was like some strange romance."

"I don't know that I should go so far as that," said the banker, in his turn, "but it certainly seemed too good to be true."

"Yes," the Altrurian responded simply, but a little sadly, "now that I am away from it all, and in conditions so different, I sometimes had to ask myself, as I went on, if my whole life had not hitherto been a dream, and Altruria were not some blessed vision of the night."

"Then you know how to account for a feeling which I must acknowledge, too?" the lawyer asked, courteously. "But it was most interesting."

"The kingdom of God upon earth," said the minister, "it ought not to be incredible; but that, more than anything else you told us of, gave me pause."

"You, of all men?" returned the Altrurian, gently.

"Yes," said the minister, with a certain dejection, "when I remember what I have seen of men, when I reflect what human nature is, how can I believe that the kingdom of God will ever come upon the earth?"

"But in heaven, where He reigns, who is it does His will? The spirits of men?" pursued the Altrurian.

"Yes, but, conditioned as men are here—"

"But if they were conditioned as men are there?"

"Now, I can't let you two good people get into a theological dispute," Mrs. Makely pushed in. "Here is Mr. Twelvemough dying to shake hands with Mr. Homos and compliment his distinguished guest!"

"Ah, Mr. Homos knows what I must have thought of his talk without my telling him," I began, skilfully. "But I am sorry that I am to lose my distinguished guest so soon!"

Reuben Camp broke out: "That was my blunder, Mr. Twelvemough. Mr. Homos and I had talked it over, conditionally, and I was not to speak of it till he had told you; but it slipped out in the excitement of the moment."

"Oh, it's all right," I said, and I shook hands cordially with both of them. "It will be the greatest possible advantage for Mr. Homos to see certain phases of American life at close range, and he couldn't possibly see them under better auspices than yours, Camp."

"Yes, I'm going to drive him through the hill country, after haying, and then I'm going to take him down and show him one of our big factory towns."

I believe this was done, but finally the Altrurian went on to New York, where he was to pass the winter. We parted friends; I even offered him some introductions; but his acquaintance had become more and more difficult, and I was not sorry to part with him. That taste of his for low company was incurable, and I was glad that I was not to be responsible any longer for whatever strange thing he might do next. I think he remained very popular with the classes he most affected; a throng of natives, construction hands and table-girls saw him off on his train; and he left large numbers of such admirers in our house and neighborhood, devout in the faith that there was such a commonwealth as Altruria, and that he was really an Altrurian. As for the more cultivated people who had met him, they continued of two minds upon both points.

LETTERS OF AN ALTRURIAN TRAVELLER

I

New York, September 1st, 1893.

MY DEAR CYRIL:

I hoped before this to have seen you again in Altruria, and given you by word of mouth some account of my experiences and observations in this country; but I have now been here more than a year, and I find myself still lingering here in a kind of fascination. At times I seem to myself to have been in a fantastic dream since I landed on its shores, with the spectacle of so many things before me happening without law and without reason, as things do in sleep; and then, again, it is as if I were carried by some enchantment back to the old competitive period in our own country; for, after all, America is like a belated Altruria, tardily repeating in the nineteenth century the errors which we committed in the tenth. In fact, if you could imagine an Altruria where the millennium had never yet come, you would have some conception of America; and, perhaps, I had better leave you with this suggestion, and not attempt farther to generalize from my impressions, but give you these at first hand and let you form your own idea of the American civilization from them.

I say civilization, because one has to use some such term to describe a state which has advanced beyond the conditions of cannibalism, tribalism, slavery, serfdom and feudalism; but, of course, no Altrurian would think America a civilized country, though many of the Americans are as truly civilized as ourselves.

We should not think it a democratic country, though many of the Americans are really democrats, and they are all proud of their republican form of government, though it is now little but a form. Far less should we think it a Christian country, though it abounds in good people, who love one another, and lead lives of continual self-sacrifice. The paradox is intelligible when you reflect that these Americans are civilized, and democratic and Christian, in spite of their conditions and not because of them. In order to do them full justice, you must remember that they are still, socially as well as civically, sunk in the lowest depths of competition, and that, theoretically at least, they prize this principle as the spring of all the personal and public virtues. To us this is a frightful anomaly; but because they do not feel it so, they are often able to do and to will the good, as I have intimated. Nowhere else in the whole world is capitalism now carried to such brutal excess, and yet nowhere else have qualities which we should think impossible in a capitalistic state shown themselves so nobly, so beautifully. It is this fact, in its different aspects, which, I suppose, has formed for me that fascination I have felt almost from the first moment of my arrival.

I had hardly been in the country a week before an illustration of the facility with which human nature adjusts itself to bad conditions and makes them tolerable by its patience, eclipsed all the little instances that were every moment offering themselves to my notice. The great event at Homestead, which our Altrurian papers will have given you some account of, occurred little over a year ago, but it is already forgotten. To the Americans it was not astounding that a force of armed workmen should bloodily fight out their quarrel with the mercenaries of their masters. In many states no change of the laws in respect to the incident has taken place to prevent its repetition, on any larger or smaller scale. None of the legal procedures have resulted in anything, and so far as the arrests for murder on either side are concerned, the whole affair has ended like a comic opera; and the warring interests have left the stage singing the same chorus together. The affair is, in fact, so thoroughly bouffe that

I have to take my imagination in both hands before I can conceive of it as a fact; but the Americans are so used to these private wars between the banded forces of labor and the hirelings of capital, that they accept it as something almost natural, or as a disease inherent in the nature of things, and having its own laws and limitations. The outbreak at Homestead, as you know, was followed by something like a civic convulsion among the miners in Tennessee and in Idaho, and by a strike of railroad employés at Buffalo, which destroyed immense values, delayed traffic, and shed blood on both sides. In this last strike it was thought a great gain that the railroad managers, instead of employing mercenaries to shoot down the strikers, appealed to the state for protection; and it was somehow felt to be a fine effect of patriotism that the militia should occupy the scene of the riot in force and bear themselves toward the strikers like the invaders of an enemy's country.

If it had not all been so tragical in other aspects, the observer must have been amused by the attitude of most Americans towards these affairs. They seemed really to regard them as proofs of the superiority of the plutocracy which they call a republic, and to feel a kind of pride in the promptness and ferocity of the civil and military officials in suppressing symptoms which ought to have appealed to every sane person as signs of the gravest organic disorder. To my mind nothing seems so conclusive against their pretensions to civilization as the fact that these terrible occurrences are accepted as the necessary incidents of civilization.

There was, indeed, a certain small percentage of the people who felt the significance of the disasters; and I am anxious to have you understand that the average of intelligence among the Americans, as well as the average of virtue, is very high, not according to the Altrurian standard, of course, but certainly according to the European standard. Bad as their plutocracy is, it is still the best system known to competitional conditions, except perhaps that of Switzerland, where the initiative and the referendum enable the people to originate and to ultimate legislation,

while the Americans can do neither. Here, the people, as you
know, can only elect representatives; these again delegate their
powers to committees, which in effect make the laws governing
the nation. The American plutocracy is the old oligarchic conception of government in a new phase, and while it is established
and maintained by a community mostly Christian, it is essentially
pagan in its civic ideal. Yet this people, whose civic ideal is
pagan, are, many of them, not only Christian in creed, but
Christian in life, so far as their polity and their society permit
them to think rightly and act generously. There are beautiful and
pathetic instances of approach to our ideal among them which
constantly win my admiration and compassion. That is to say,
certain Americans are good and gentle not because of conditions
that invite them to be so, but in spite of conditions that invite
them to be otherwise, almost with the first economic and social
lessons which they teach. Almost from the beginning the American is taught to look out for himself in business and in society,
and if he looks out for others at the same time it is by a sacrifice
of advantages which are vitally necessary to him in the battle of
life. He may or he may not make these sacrifices; he very often
does, to such effect that the loveliest and lovablest natures I
have known here have been those of unsuccessful Americans,
and the ugliest and hatefullest, those of successful Americans.
But the sad thing, and the droll thing, is that they think their
bad conditions the source of their virtues, and they really believe
that without the inducements to rapacity on every hand there
would be no beauty in yielding and giving.

Certain persons have been instanced to me as embodying certain generous qualities, and when I explain that the man who
had not all these qualities in Altruria would be as exceptional as
the man who has them is here, I have seen that people either did
not believe me or did not understand me. The Americans honor
such qualities as much as we do, and they appreciate gentleness,
unselfishness, and neighborliness as much as we do, but they
expect them only so far as they do not cross a man's self-interest;
when they do that, he is a very unusual man if he continues to

indulge in them, or, as they say, he is not *business*. When I tell them that the man who does not indulge them in Altruria is not business they look blank, or suspect me of a joke. When I try to make them understand that in their sense we have no self-interest in Altruria, and that if they had our conditions they would have no self-interest, it alarms them; they have so long been accustomed to live *upon* one another that they cannot imagine living *for* one another; they think self-interest a very good thing, the best sort of thing, and they ask what merit has a man in being good if he is not good to his disadvantage; they cannot conceive that a man *should* have no merit in being good. As for Christ's coming to do away with the old pagan economics as well as the old pagan ethics, they hoot at the notion.

I will not try, in this letter, to tell you just how all this can be; you will, in some sort, conceive of its possibility from what you know of the competitive world at second hand, but I hope to make it clearer to you by and by. You must always account for a sort of bewilderment in me, inevitable in the presence of a state of things which is the complete inversion of our own, and in which I seem to get the same effect of life that boys sometimes get of the landscape by putting down their heads and looking at it between their legs.

Just at present there is no violent outbreak in the economic world, no bloody collision between labor and capital, no private war to be fought out in the face of the whole acquiescent nation till the inconvenience forces the government to interfere and put down the weaker party. But though there is now an interval of quiet, no one can say how long it will last, and many feel that there is even something ominous in it, that it is something like the calm in the heart of the cyclone. The cyclone is financial, if I may carry out the figure, and it began to blow, no one knows why or whence, several months ago. A great many weather-wiseacres pretended to know, and began to prophesy that if the export of gold to Europe could be stopped, and the coinage of silver could be arrested, and the enormous imposts could be removed, the ship of state would have plain sailing again. But the

outflow of gold ceased without the slightest effect upon the
cyclone; the mere threat of touching the tariff caused the closure
of factories and foundries by the score, and the otiosation of workmen by the hundred thousand; with every prospect that the
coinage of silver would be arrested, there were failures of bank-
ing-houses and business-houses on every hand. It remains to be
seen what effect the actual demonetization of silver will have
upon the situation, but the situation is so chaotic that no one
among all the weather-wiseacres ventures to prophesy when the
storm will cease to rage. Perhaps it has already ceased, but so
far as the logic of events is concerned we might as well be in the
heart of the cyclone, as I suggested.

I am afraid that with all your reading, and with all your
special study of American conditions you would be dismayed if
you could be confronted with the financial ruin which I find
myself in the midst of, but which this extremely amiable and
hopeful people do not seem to think so desperate. Like their
bloody industrial wars, it is of such frequent recurrence that
they have come to look upon it as in the order of nature. Probably they would tell you, if criticised from our point of view,
that it was human nature to go to pieces about once in so often,
and that this sort of disintegration was altogether preferable to
any hard and fast system that held it together by the cohesion of
moral principles. In fact their whole business world is a world
of chance, where nothing happens according to law, but follows
a loose order of accident, which any other order of accident may
change. The question of money is the prime question of American life, and you would think that the issue of money would be
one of the most carefully guarded functions of the government.
But curiously enough, most of the money in the hands of the
American people is not issued by the government at all, but
consists of the promissory notes of a multitude of banks, as was
the case with us in the old competitive days. The government
bonds, which perpetuate the national debt, that their circula-
tion may be based on them, are exempted from taxation as a sort
of reward for the usurpation of the governmental function by

the banks; and these banks are supposed to serve the community by supplying business men with the means of carrying on the commercial warfare. But they do this only at the heaviest rates of interest, and in times of general prosperity: at the first signs of adversity they withhold their favors. You might think that the government which secures their notes would also secure their deposits, but the government does nothing of the kind, and the man who trusts his money to their keeping does so wholly at his own risk. When they choose, or when they are unable, they may cease to pay it back to him, and he has no recourse whatever.

With a financial system resting upon such a basis as this, and with the perpetual gambling in values, nominal and real, and in every kind of produce and manufacture, which goes on throughout the whole country, you can hardly be surprised at the recurrence of the panics which follow each other at irregular intervals in the American business world. Indeed, the Americans are not surprised themselves; they regard them as something that always must be because they always have been, though they own that each successive panic spreads wider disaster and causes deeper suffering. Still, they expect them to come, and they do not dream of contriving a system like ours, in which they are no more possible than human sacrifices. They say, that is all very well for us Altrurians, but it would not do for Americans, and they really seem to believe that misery on so vast a scale as they have it in one of their financial convulsions is a sort of testimony to their national greatness. When they begin to drag themselves up out of the pit of ruin, bewildered and bemired by their fall, they begin to boast of the magnificent recuperative energies of the country. Still, I think that the old American maxim that it will all come out right in the end, has less and less acceptance. Some of them are beginning to fear that it will come out wrong in the end, if they go their old gait, or that it will at least come out Europe in the end. I would not venture to say how common this doubt was, but it certainly exists, and there is no question but that some of the thoughtfulest and best Americans are beginning to look toward Altruria as the only alternative from Europe.

Such Americans see that Europe is already upon them in the conditions of the very rich and the very poor. Poverty is here upon the European terms, and luxury is here upon the European terms. There is no longer the American workingman as he once was; he still gets better wages than the European workingman, but his economic and social status is exactly the same. He has accepted the situation for the present, but what he intends to do about it hereafter, no man knows; he, least of all men, knows. The American plutocrat has accepted the situation even more frankly than the proletarian. He perceives distinctly that there is no American life for the very rich American, and when he does not go abroad to live, as he increasingly does, he lives at home upon the same terms and to the same effect that the Continental noble lives in Europe; for the English noble is usefuller to his country than the rich American. Of course the vast majority of Americans are of the middle class, and with them you can still find the old American life, the old American ideals, the old American principles; and if the old America is ever to prevail, it must be in their love and honor of it. I do not mean to say the American middle class are as a general thing consciously American, but it is valuable that they are even unconsciously so. As a general thing they are simply and frankly bent upon providing for themselves and for their own; but some of them already see that they cannot realize even this low ideal, as things are, and that it will be more and more difficult to do so hereafter. A panic like the present is a great object lesson to them, and teaches the essential insecurity of their system as nothing else could. It shows that no industry, no frugality, no sagacity can be proof against such a storm, and that when it comes, the prudent and the diligent must suffer from it like the imprudent and the indolent. At last some of them are asking themselves if there is not something wrong in the system itself, and if a system based upon self-seeking does not embody recurrent disaster and final defeat. They have heard of the Altrurian system, and they are inquiring whether the sole economic safety is not in some such system. You must not suppose their motive is so low as this makes it seem. They are people of fine courage, and they have accesses of a noble generosity, but they have been born and bred in the presence of the fact that each man can alone save himself and those dear to him, from want; and we must not blame them if they cannot first think of the beauty and the grandeur of saving others from want. For the present, we cannot expect that they will think of anything higher at first than the danger to themselves, respectively; when they grasp the notion of escape from that, they will think of the danger to others, and will be eager to Altrurianize, as they call it, for the sake of the common good as well as the personal good. I may be in error, through my zeal for Altrurian principles, but I think that the Altrurian idea has come to stay, as they say, with this class. At any rate, it is not the very rich or the very poor who are leading reform in our direction, but it is such of the comfortable middle class as have got the light. There is everything to hope from this fact, for it means that if the change comes at all, it will not come superficially and it will not come violently. The comfortable Americans are the most comfortable people in the world, and when they find themselves threatened in their comfort, they will deal with the danger seriously, deliberately, thoroughly.

But whatever the struggle is to be here, whether it will be a wild revolt of the poor against the rich, of laborer against capitalist, with all the sanguinary circumstance of such an outbreak, or whether it will be the quiet opposition of the old American instincts to the recent plutocratic order of things, ending in the overthrow of the pagan ideals and institutions, and the foundation of a commonwealth upon some such basis as ours, I am sure that some sort of conflict is coming. I may be unable to do the proletarians justice, but so far, I do not think they have shown great wisdom in their attitude. If you were here you would sympathize with them, as I do in their strikes; but I think that you too would feel that these were not the means to achieve the ends they seek, and that higher wages and fewer hours were not the solution. The solution is the complete control of the industries by the people, as we know, and the assurance to every man willing to work that he shall not want; yet I must confess that the workingmen in America have not often risen to the conception of this notion. It is from those who have not been forced to toil so exhaustively that they cannot think clearly; it is from the comfortable middle class, which sees itself more and more closely environed by the inimical factors of this so-called civilization that the good time is to come. It is by no means impossible, indeed, if things should now go on as they are going, and the proletarians should be more and more subjected to the plutocrats, that we should find the workingmen arrayed by their enemies against the only principles that can befriend them. This is to be seen already in the case of those small merchants and manufacturers whose business has been destroyed by the trusts and syndicates, but who have been received into the service of their destroyers; the plutocracy has no such faithful allies and followers. But it is not possible for all the small merchants and manufacturers to be disposed of in this way, and it is to such of these as perceive the fact, that the good cause can look for help. They have already fully imagined the situation, and some of them have imagined it actual. It is chiefly they, therefore, who are anxious to Altrurianize America, as the sole means of escape from their encompassing dangers. Their activity is very great and it is incessant; and they were able to shape and characterize the formless desires of a popular movement in the West, so that at the last presidential election twenty-two electoral votes were cast in favor of the Altrurian principles which formed the vital element of the uprising.

Nevertheless, as I have more than once suggested, I do not think any fundamental change is near. The Americans are a very conservative race, and much slower to move than the English, as the more intelligent English have often observed. The Altrurianization of England may take place first, but I do not think I am mistaken in believing that America will yet be entirely Altrurianized. Just at present the whole community is proletarianized, and is made to feel the poor man's concern as to where the next day's bread or the next day's cake is to come from; if a

man is used to having cake he will be as anxious to keep on having cake as the man who is used to having bread alone will be
anxious to keep on having bread. In former times this experience
would probably have been without definite significance or ultimate effect, but now I do not think it will be so. The friends of
Altrurianization will be sure to press its lessons home; and the
people have been so widely awakened to the possibility of escape
from the evils of their system that they will not be so patient of
them as they have been in former times.

You might infer from the apparently unbroken front that the
Americans show on the side of competition in the great conflict
dividing every nation into opposing camps, that there was no
division amongst them. But there is very great division amongst
them, and there is acceptance of one Altrurian principle or
another to such a degree that there may be said to be almost a
universal tendency toward Altrurianization, though, as a whole,
the vast majority of Americans still regard the idea of human
brotherhood with distrust and dislike. No doubt they will now
patch up some sort of financial modus vivendi, and go on as
before; in fact, there is no reason why they should not, in their
conception of things. There was no reason why the panic should
have come, and there is no reason why it should not go; but still,
I do not think it will have come and gone without something
more of question than former panics.

The friends of Altrurianization will not fail to bring before the
American people some question of the very nature of money, and
of the essential evil of it, as they understand money. They will try
to show that accumulated money, as a means of providing
against want, is always more or less a failure in private hands;
that it does not do its office; that it evades the hardest clutch
when its need is greatest. They will teach every man, from his
own experience and conscience, that it is necessarily corrupting;
that it is the source of most vices, and the incentive, direct or
indirect, of almost every crime. They will prove that these are
not the mere accidents of money, but are its essentials; and that
a thing invented to create or to recognize economic inequality

among men can never be otherwise than hurtful to them. They will preach the Altrurian notion of money, as the measure of work done and the warrant of need to be relieved, which in a civilized state can have no use but to issue from the commonwealth to the man who has worked, and return to the commonwealth from the man who has satisfied his wants with it. As yet, most Americans believe that money can be innocently gathered into one man's hands by his cunning and his skill, and as innocently taken from another's through his misfortune or his weakness. This primitive notion of money, which is known to us historically, is of actual effect among them; and though I was aware of the fact before I came to America, as you are now, I had no idea of the infernal variety of the evil.

In Altruria we cannot imagine a starving man in rags, passing the threshold of another man surfeited with every luxury and warranted in his opulence by the same law that dooms the beggar to destitution. But this is a spectacle so common in this great typical American city that no one would turn to look at it. In fact, both the beggar and the millionaire recognize the situation as something almost normal. Charity, the love of man and the fear of God, as the Americans know it, does not propose to equalize the monstrous conditions, or to do more than afford alleviation at the best, until the wretch in the gutter can somehow win from the wretch in the palace the chance to earn a miserable wage. This chance is regarded not as his right; it is his privilege, and it is accorded him usually at the cost of half a dozen other wretches, who are left outcast by it. It is money that creates this evil, and yet the Americans think that money is somehow a good thing; and they think they are the most prosperous people on earth, because they have more moneyed men among them than any other people.

I know, my dear Cyril, how strange all this will seem to you, how impossible, in spite of your study of American conditions. I remember how we used to talk of America together, before I planned my present visit, and how we disputed the general Altrurian notion of this country, as necessarily mistaken, because we said that such things could not be in a republic and a democracy. We had our dreams of a system different from ours, a system which vaunted itself the realization, above all others, of the individuality which we Altrurians prize more than everything else. We felt that our emissaries must have been hasty or mistaken in their observations, but you have only to visit this democratic republic, to understand that they have no such thing as individuality here, and that in conditions where one man depends upon another man for the chance of earning his bread, there can be no more liberty than there is equality.

The Americans still imagine that they have liberty, but as for the equality which we supposed the aim of their democracy, nobody any longer even pretends that it is, or that it can be. With the rich there is a cynical contempt of it; with the poor a cynical despair of it. The division into classes here is made as sharply as in any country of Europe, and the lines are passed only by the gain or the loss of money. I say only, but of course there are exceptions. The career is still open to the talents, and the plebeian rich here are glad to ally themselves with the patrician poor of Europe; but what I say holds good of the vast majority of cases. Every tendency of economic and social life is a tendency to greater and greater difference between the classes; and in New York, which is the most typical of American cities, the tendency is swifter and stronger than in other places.

It is for this reason that I have come here for the winter before I leave these shores, as I hope, forever. My American sojourn has been a passionate disappointment from first to last: it has been a grief which I cannot express to you, for the people are at heart so noble, so generous, so magnanimous, so infinitely better than their conditions that my pity for them has been as great as my detestation of the terms on which they accept life. I cannot convey to you the pathos with which the spectacle of their contradictions fills me; I can only say that if I were an American with nothing but a competitive conception of life, as a warfare in which the strong must perpetually and even involuntarily oppress the weak, as a race in which the swift must seize every

advantage of the slow, as a game in which the shrewd must out-
wit the simple, I would not accept life at all. But, of course, I
speak as an Altrurian, and I warn you that an utter abhorrence
of the situation would ignore a thousand things that are lovely
and of good report. It would ignore the most heroic self-sacrifice,
the most romantic martyrdom, the spectacle of unnumbered
brave and good, who do not the less sublimely lay their hearts
upon the altar, because they lay them futilely there.

It is the exceptional character of what is generous and noble in
the Americans, this accidental, this vicarious nature of their
heroism and their martyrdom, that moves me to a pity for which
there seems no relief but laughter. They pray as we do that God's
will may be done here, and His kingdom come on earth as it is in
heaven, but they reject both because, as they say, they are
against human nature. They do this in spite of those instances of
heavenly goodness among them, which they honor as much as
we do, and admire even more, since these things are not so difficult with us as with them. They fancy that goodness, and
gentleness, and unselfishness, would somehow lose their value if
they were the rule and not the exception, that they would become cheap in becoming common. Perhaps I can best make you
understand all this by an illustration drawn from the æsthetic
aspect of this vast city, which, I suppose, is upon the whole the
ugliest city in the world. Ugliness is the rule in the architecture,
which is for far the greatest part not merely ignoble and mean but
positively offensive, insulting the eye by every conceivable or
inconceivable stupidity and vulgarity of form. But in the midst
of the chaotic ugliness there is from time to time, and from space
to space, a beautiful edifice erected by some artist who has been
able so far to circumvent some millionaire as to turn his money
to that effect. I could instance half a score of exquisite master-
pieces of this sort, but you would not be the wiser for my doing so.
It is in architecture more than in any other art that the Americans
have shown themselves gifted, but they have not shown it to such
effect as to characterize their richest and greatest city with
architectural beauty. On the contrary, so far from redeeming

their environment, these gracious structures are lost and annulled in it. Your pleasure in them is spoiled by the sight of some monstrosity next to them, or by the sea of hideous forms that welters round them and overwhelms them from every side. They do not stand out from the sordid mass; they sink into it and leave you thinking of that, and bruised and quivering from the affront and hurt of it.

Commend me lovingly to all the Altrurians, and believe me, dear Cyril, most affectionately and constantly,

Your friend,

Aristides Homos.

II

———

My dear Cyril:

When I last wrote you, I thought to have settled quietly down in New York for the rest of my stay in America, and given my time wholly to the study of its life, which seemed to me typical of the life of the whole country. I do not know, even now, that I should wish altogether to revise this impression; it still appears to me just, if not so distinct and so decisive, as it appeared before I saw Chicago, or rather the World's Fair City at Chicago, which is what I want to write you of. Chicago, one might say, was after all only a Newer York, an ultimated Manhattan, the realized ideal of that largeness, loudness and fastness, which New York has persuaded the Americans is metropolitan. But after seeing the World's Fair City here, I feel as if I had caught a glimpse of the glorious capitals which will whiten the hills and shores of the east and the borderless plains of the west, when the New York and the Newer York of today shall seem to all the future Americans as impossible as they would seem to any Altrurian now.

To one of our philosophy it will not be wonderful that this Altrurian miracle should have been wrought here in the very heart, and from the very heart, of egoism seven times heated in the fiery competition hitherto the sole joy of this strange people. We know that like produces like only up to a certain point, and that then unlike comes of like since all things are of one essence; that from life comes death at last, and from death comes life

198

again in the final issue. Yet it would be useless trying to persuade most Americans that the World's Fair City was not the effect, the fine flower, of the competition which underlies their economy, but was the first fruits of the principle of emulation which animates our happy commonwealth, and gives men, as no where else on earth, a foretaste of heaven. If I were writing to an American I should have to supply him with proofs and argue facts at every moment, which will be self-evident to you in their mere statement.

I confess that I was very loth to leave New York, which I fancied I was beginning to see whole, after my first fragmentary glimpses of it. But I perceive now that without a sight of the White City (as the Americans with their instant poetry called the official group of edifices at the great Fair) and the knowledge of its history, which I could have realized nowhere but in its presence, New York would have wanted the relief, the projection, in which I shall hereafter be able to study it. For the worst effect of sojourn in an egoistic civilization (I always use this word for lack of a closer descriptive) is that Altrurian motives and efforts become incredible, and almost inconceivable. But the Fair City is a bit of Altruria: it is as if the capital of one of our Regions had set sail and landed somehow on the shores of the vast inland sea, where the Fair City lifts its domes and columns.

Its story, which I need not rehearse to you at any length, records the first great triumph of Altrurian principles among this people in a work of peace; in their mighty civil war they were Altrurian enough; and more than once they have proved themselves capable of a magnificent self-sacrifice in bloodshed, but here for the first time in their pitiless economic struggle, their habitual warfare in which they neither give nor ask quarter, and take no prisoners, the interests submitted to the arts, and lent themselves as frankly to the work as if there had never been a question of money in the world. From the beginning it was believed that there could be no profit in the Fair; money loss was expected and accepted as a necessary part of the greater gain; and when the question passed from how much to how, in

the discussion of the ways and means of creating that beauty
which is the supreme use, the capitalists put themselves into the
hands of the artists. They did not do it at once, and they did not
all do it willingly. It is a curious trait of the American who has
made money that he thinks he can make anything; and the
Chicago millionaires who found themselves authorized by the
nation to spend their money in the creation of the greatest marvel
of the competitive world, thought themselves fully competent to
work the miracle, or to choose the men who would work it according to their ideals. But their clarification, if it was not as
swift as the passage of light, was thorough, and I do not suppose
there is now any group of rich men in Europe or America who
have so luminous a sense of the true relations of the arts and the
interests as they. The notion of a competition among the artists,
which is the practical American's notion of the way to get the
best art, was at length rejected by these most practical Americans, and one mind large enough to conceive the true means and
strong enough to give its conception effect was empowered to
invite the free coöperation of the arts through the foremost artists
of the country. As yet the governmental function is so weak here
that the national part in the work was chiefly obstructive, and
finally null; and when it came to this there remained an opportunity for the arts, unlimited as to means and unhampered
by conditions.

For the different buildings to be erected, different architects
were chosen; and for the first time since the great ages, since the
beauty of antiquity and the elegance of the renaissance, the arts
were reunited. The greatest landscape gardeners, architects,
sculptors and painters, gathered at Chicago for a joyous interchange of ideas and criticisms; and the miracle of beauty which
they have wrought grew openly in their breath and under their
hands. Each did his work and had his way with it, but in this
congress of gifted minds, of sensitive spirits, each profited by the
censure of all, and there were certain features of the work—as
for instance, the exquisite peristyle dividing the city from the
lake—which were the result of successive impulses and sug-

gestions from so many different artists that it would be hard to divide the honor among them with exactness. No one, however, seems to have been envious of another's share, and each one gave his talent as freely as the millionaires gave their money. These great artists willingly accepted a fifth, a tenth, of the gain which they could have commanded in a private enterprise, and lavished their time upon the opportunity afforded them, for the pleasure of it, the pride of it, the pure good of it.

Of the effect, of the visible, tangible result, what better can I say, than that in its presence I felt myself again in Altruria? The tears came, and the pillared porches swam against my vision; through the hard nasal American tones, the liquid notes of our own speech stole to my inner ear; I saw under the care-worn masks of the competitive crowds, the peace, the *rest* of the dear Altrurian face; the gay tints of our own simple costumes eclipsed the different versions of the Paris fashions about me. I was at home once more, and my heart overflowed with patriotic rapture in this strange land, so remote from ours in everything, that at times Altruria really seems to me the dream which the Americans think it.

I first saw the Fair City by night, from one of the electric launches which ply upon the lagoon; and under the dimmed heaven, in the splendor of the hundred moony arc-lamps of the esplanades, and the myriad incandescent bubbles that beaded the white quays, and defined the structural lines of dome and porch and pediment, I found myself in the midst of the Court of Honor, which you will recognize on the general plan and the photographs I enclose. We fronted the beautiful Agricultural building, which I think fitly the finest in the city, though many prefer the perfect Greek of the Art building; and on our right was the Administration building with its coroneted dome, and the magnificent sculptured fountain before it, turned silver in the radiance of the clustered electric jets at either side. On our right was the glorious peristyle, serene, pure, silent, lifting a population of statues against the night, and dividing the lagoon from the lake, whose soft moan came appealingly through the pillared spaces, and added a divine heartache to my ecstacy. Here a group of statuary showed itself prominently on quay or cornice; we caught the flamy curve of a bridge's arch; a pale column lifted its jutting prores into the light; but nothing insisted; all was harmonized to one effect of beauty, as if in symbol of the concentered impulses which had created it. For the moment I could not believe that so foul a thing as money could have been even the means of its creation. I call the effect creation because it is divinely beautiful, but no doubt suggestion would be a better word, since they have here merely sketched in stucco what we have executed in marble in each of our Regionic capitals.

In grandeur of design and freedom of expression, it is perhaps even nobler than the public edifices of some of these, as I had to acknowledge at another moment, when we rounded the shores of the Wooded Island which forms the heart of the lagoon, and the launch slowed while we got the effect of its black foliage against the vast lateral expanse of the Liberal Arts building. Then, indeed, I was reminded of our national capitol, when it shows its mighty mass above the bosks around it, on some anniversary night of our Evolution.

But the illusion of Altruria was very vivid at many moments in the Fair City, where I have spent the happiest days of my stay in America, perhaps because the place is so little American in the accepted sense. It is like our own cities in being a design, the effect of a principle, and not the straggling and shapeless accretion of accident. You will see, from the charts and views I send you, something of the design in detail, but you can form only a dim conception of the skill with which the natural advantages of the site have been turned to account, and even its disadvantages have been transmuted to the beauty which is the highest and last result of all. There was not only the great lake here, which contributes so greatly to this beauty, but there were marshes to be drained and dredged before its pure waters could be invited in. The trees which at different points offer the contrast of their foliage to the white of the edifices, remain from wilding growths which overspread the swamps and sand dunes, and which had to be destroyed in great part before these lovely groves could be evoked from them. The earth itself, which now of all the earth seems the spot best adapted to the site of such a city, had literally to be formed anew for the use it has been put to. There is now no shadow, no hint of the gigantic difficulties of the undertaking, which was carried on in the true Altrurian spirit, so far as the capitalists and artists were concerned, and with a joy like ours in seeing nature yield herself to the enlightened will of man. If I told you how time itself was overcome in this work by the swiftness of modern methods, it would be nothing new to you, for we are used to seeing the powerful machinery of our engineers change the face of the landscape, without stay for the slow processes of other days, when the ax and the saw wrought for years in the destruction of the forests that now vanish in a night. But to the Americans these things are still novel, and they boast of the speed with which the trees were dragged from the soil where they were rooted, and the morasses were effaced, and the wastes of sand made to smile with the verdure that now forms the most enchanting feature of their normal city.

They dwell upon this, and they do not seem to feel as I do the exquisite simplicity with which its life is operated, the perfection with which it is policed, and the thoroughness with which it has been dedicated to health as well as beauty. In fact, I fancy that very few out of the millions who visit this gala town realize that it has its own system of drainage, lighting and transportation, and its own government, which looks as scrupulously to the general comfort and cleanliness, as if these were the private concern of each member of the government. This is, as it is with us, military in form, and the same precision and discipline which give us the ease and freedom of our civic life, proceed here from the same spirit and the same means. The Columbian Guards, as they are called, who are here at every turn, to keep order and to care for the pleasure as well as the welfare of the people, have been trained by officers of the United States army, who still command them, and they are amenable to the rules governing the only body in America whose ideal is not interest but duty. Every night, the whole place is cleansed of the rubbish which the visitors leave behind them, as thoroughly as if it were a camp. It is merely the litter of lunch-boxes and waste paper which has to be looked after, for there is little of the filth resulting in all other American cities from the use of the horse, which is still employed in them so many centuries after it has been banished from ours. The United States mail-carts and the watering-carts are indeed anomalously drawn through the Fair City thoroughfares by horses, but wheeled chairs pushed about by a corps of high school boys and college undergraduates form the means of transportation by land for those who do not choose to walk. On the water, the electric launches are quite of our own pattern, and steam is allowed only on the boats which carry people out into the lake for a view of the peristyle. But you can get this by walking, and as in Venice, which is represented here by a fleet of gondolas, there are bridges that enable you to reach every desirable point on the lagoon.

When I have spoken of all this to my American friends they have not perceived the moral value of it, and when I have insisted upon the practical perfection of the scheme apparent in the whole, they have admitted it, but answered me that it would never do for a business city, where there was something going on besides the pleasure of the eyes and the edification of the mind. When I tell them that this is all that our Altrurian cities are for, they do not understand me; they ask where the money is made that the people live on in such play-cities; and we are alike driven to despair when I try to explain that we have no money, and should think it futile and impious to have any.

I do not believe they quite appreciate the intelligence with which the Fair City proper has been separated, with a view to its value as an object lesson, from all the state and national buildings in the ground. Some of the national buildings, notably those of Germany and Sweden, are very picturesque, but the rest decline through various grades of inferiority, down to the level of the State buildings. Of these, only the California and the New

York buildings have a beauty comparable to that of the Fair City: the California house, as a reminiscence of the Spanish ecclesiastical architecture in which her early history is recorded, and the New York house, as a sumptuous expression of the art which ministers to the luxury of the richest and greatest State of the Union.

By still another remove the competitive life of the present epoch is relegated to the long avenue remotest from the White City, which you will find marked as the Midway Plaisance. Even this, where a hundred shows rival one another in a furious advertisement for the favor of the passer, there is so much of a high interest that I am somewhat loth to instance it as actuated by an inferior principle; and I do so only for the sake of the contrast. In the Fair City, everything is free; in the Plaisance everything must be paid for. You strike at once here the hard level of the outside western world; and the Orient, which has mainly peopled the Plaisance, with its theaters and restaurants and shops, takes the tint of the ordinary American enterprise, and puts on somewhat the manners of the ordinary American hustler. It is not really so bad as that, but it is worse than American in some of the appeals it makes to the American public, which is decent if it is dull, and respectable if it is rapacious. The lascivious dances of the East are here, in the Persian and Turkish and Egyptian theaters, as well as the exquisite archaic drama of the Javanese and the Chinese in their village and temple. One could spend many days in the Plaisance, always entertainingly, whether profitably or unprofitably; but whether one visited the Samoan or Dahomeyan in his hut, the Bedouin and the Lap in their camps, the delicate Javanese in his bamboo cottage, or the American Indian in his tepee, one must be aware that the citizens of the Plaisance are not there for their health, as the Americans quaintly say, but for the money there is in it. Some of the reproductions of historical and foreign scenes are excellent, like the irregular square of Old Vienna, with its quaintly built and quaintly decorated shops; the German village, with its admirably realized castle and chalet; and the Cairene street, with its motley oriental life; but these are all there for the profit to be had from the pleasure of their visitors, who seem to pay as freely as they talk through their noses. The great Ferris wheel itself, with its circle revolving by night and by day in an orbit incomparably vast, is in the last analysis a money-making contrivance.

I have tried to make my American friends see the difference, as I do, between the motive that created the Fair City, and the motive that created the Plaisance, but both seem to them alike the outcome of the principle which they still believe animates their whole life. They think both an effect of the competitive conditions in which they glory, not knowing that their conditions are now purely monopolistic, and not perceiving that the White City is the work of an armistice between the commercial interests ruling them. I expressed this belief to one of them, the banker, whom I met last summer in the country, and whom I ran upon one night during the first week of my visit here; and he said there could certainly be that view of it. But, like the rest, he asked where the money would have come from without the warfare of competitive conditions, and he said he could not make out how we got the money for our public works in Altruria, or, in fact, how we paid the piper. When I answered that as each one of us was secured by all against want, every one could freely give his labor, without money and without price, and the piper could play for the pure pleasure of playing, he looked stupefied and said incredulously, "Oh, come, now!"

"Why, how strange you Americans are," I could not help breaking out upon him, "with your talk about competition! There *is* no competition among you a moment longer than you can help, a moment after one proves himself stronger than another. Then you have monopoly, which even upon the limited scale it exists here is the only vital and fruitful principle, as you all see. And yet you are afraid to have it upon the largest possible scale, the national scale, the scale commensurate with the whole body politic, which implicates care for every citizen as the liege of the collectivity. When you have monopoly of such proportions money will cease to have any office among you, and such a beautiful creation as this will have effect from a consensus of the common wills and wishes."

He listened patiently, and he answered amiably, "Yes, that is what you Altrurians believe, I suppose, and certainly what you preach; and if you look at it in that light, why there certainly is no competition left, except between the monopolies. But you must allow, my dear Homos," he went on, "that at least one of the twin fetishes of our barbarous worship has had something to do with the creation of all this beauty. I'll own that you have rather knocked the notion of competition on the head; the money that made this thing possible never came from competition at all; it came from some sort or shape of monopoly, as all money always does; but what do you say about individuality? You can't say that individuality has had nothing to do with it. In fact, you can't deny that it has had everything to do with it, from the individuality of the several capitalists, up or down, to the individuality of the several artists. And will you pretend in the face of all this wonderful work that individuality is a bad thing?"

"Have I misrepresented myself and country so fatally," I returned, "as to have led you to suppose that the Altrurians thought individuality a bad thing? It seems to us the most precious gift of the Deity, the dearest and holiest possession of his creatures. What I lament in America at every moment, what I lament even here, in the presence of a work so largely Altrurian in conception and execution as this, is the wholesale effacement, the heartbreaking obliteration of individuality. I know very well that you can give me the name of the munificent millionaires— large-thoughted and noble-willed men—whose largesse made this splendor possible, and the name of every artist they freed to such a glorious opportunity. Their individuality is lastingly safe in your memories; but what of the artisans of every kind and degree, whose patience and skill realized their ideals? Where will you find *their* names?"

My companion listened respectfully, but not very seriously, and in his reply he took refuge in that humor peculiar to the Americans: a sort of ether where they may draw breath for a moment free from the stifling despair which must fill every true man among them when he thinks how far short of their ideal their reality has fallen. For they were once a people with the noblest ideal; we were not mistaken about that; they did, indeed, intend the greatest good to the greatest number, and not merely the largest purse to the longest head. They are a proud people, and it is hard for them to confess that they have wandered from the right way, and fallen into a limitless bog, where they can only bemire themselves more and more till its miasms choke them or its foul waters close over them.

"My dear fellow," the banker laughed, "you are very easily answered. You will find *their* names on the pay-rolls, where, I've no doubt, they preferred to have them. Why, there was an army of them; and we don't erect monuments to private soldiers, except in the lump. How would you have managed it in Altruria?"

"In Altruria," I replied, "every man who drove a nail, or stretched a line, or laid a trowel upon such a work, would have had his name somehow inscribed upon it, where he could find it, and point it out to those dear to him and proud of him. Individuality! I find no record of it here, unless it is the individuality of the few. That of the many makes no sign from the oblivion in which it is lost, either in these public works of artistic coöperation, or the exhibits of your monopolistic competition. I have wandered through these vast edifices and looked for the names of the men who wrought the marvels of ingenuity that fill them. But I have not often found the name even of a man who owns them. I have found the styles of the firms, the companies, the trusts which turn them out as impersonally as if no heart had ever ached or glowed in imagining and embodying them. This whole mighty industrial display is in so far dehumanized; and yet you talk of individuality as one of your animating principles!"

"You are hopelessly unbusinesslike, my dear Homos," said the banker, "but I like your unpracticability. There is something charming in it; there is, really; and I enjoy it particularly at this moment because it has enabled me to get back my superiority to

Chicago. I am a Bostonian, you know, and I came out here with all the misgivings which a Bostonian begins to secrete as soon as he gets west of the Back Bay Fens. It is a survival of Puritanism in us. In the old times, you know, every Bostonian, no matter how he prayed and professed, felt it in his bones that he was one of the elect, and we each feel so still; only, then God elected us, and now we elect ourselves. Fancy such a man confronted with such an achievement as this, and unfriended yet by an Altrurian traveller! Why, I have gone about the last three days inwardly bowed down before Chicago in the most humiliating fashion. I've said to myself that our eastern fellows did half the thing, perhaps the best half; but then I had to own it was Chicago that imagined letting them do it, that imagined the thing as a whole, and I had to give Chicago the glory. When I looked at it I had to forgive Chicago Chicago, but now that you've set me right about the matter, and I see that the whole thing is dehumanized, I shall feel quite easy, and I shall not give Chicago any more credit than is due."

I saw that he was joking, but I did not see how far, and I thought it best not to take him in joke at all. "Ah, I don't think you can give her too much credit, even if you take her at the worst. It seems to me, from what I have seen of your country— and, of course, I speak from a foreigner's knowledge only—that no other American city could have brought this to pass."

"You must come and stay with us a while in Boston," said the banker; and he smiled. "One other city could have done it. Boston has the public spirit and Boston has the money, but perhaps Boston has not the ambition. Perhaps we give ourselves in Boston too much to a sense of the accomplished fact. If that is a fault, it is the only fault conceivable of us. Here in Chicago they have the public spirit, and they have the money, and they are still anxious to do; they are not content as we are, simply to be. Of course, they have not so much reason! I don't know," he added thoughtfully, "but it comes in the end to what you were saying, and no other American city but Chicago *could* have brought this to pass. Leaving everything else out of the question,

I doubt if any other community could have fancied the thing in its vastness; and the vastness seems an essential condition of the beauty. You couldn't possibly say it was pretty, for instance; if you admitted it was fine you would have to say it was beautiful. To be sure, if it were possible to have too much of a good thing, there are certain states of one's legs, here, when one could say there was too much of it; but that is not possible. But come, now; be honest for once, my dear fellow, and confess that you really prefer the Midway Plaisance to the Fair City!''

I looked at him with silent reproach, and he broke out laughing, and took me by the arm.

"At any rate," he said, "let us go down there, and get something to eat.

> 'The glory that was Greece,
> And the grandeur that was Rome,'

here, take it out of you so that I find myself wanting lunch about every three hours. It's nearly as long as that now, since I dined, and I feel an irresistible yearning for Old Vienna, where that pinchbeck halberdier of a watchman is just now crying the hour of nine.''

"Oh, is it so late as that?" I began, for I like to keep our Altrurian hours even here, when I can, and I was going to say that I could not go with him when he continued:

"They won't turn us out, if that's what you mean. Theoretically, they do turn people out toward the small hours, but practically, one can stay here all night, I believe. That's a charming thing about the Fair, and I suppose it's rather Chicagoan; if we'd had the Fair in Boston, every soul would have had to leave before midnight. We couldn't have helped turning them out, from the mere oldmaidishness of our Puritanic tradition, and not because we really minded their staying. In New York they would have put them out from Keltic imperiousness, and locked them up in the station-house when they got them out, especially if they were sober and inoffensive.''

I could not follow him in this very well, or in the playful

allusiveness of his talk generally, though I have reported it, to give some notion of his manner; and so I said, by way of bringing him within easy range of my intelligence again, "I have seen no one here who showed signs of drink."

"No," he returned. "What a serious, and peaceable, and gentle crowd it is! I haven't witnessed a rudeness, or even an unkindness, since I've been here, and nobody looks as if anything stronger than apollinaris had passed his lips for a fortnight. They seem, the vast majority of them, to pass their time in the Fair City, and I wish I could flatter myself that they preferred it, as you wish me to think you do, to the Plaisance. Perhaps they are really more interested in the mechanical arts, and even the fine arts, than they are in the muscle dances, but I'm afraid it's partly because there isn't an additional charge for admission to those improving exhibits in the official buildings. Though I dare say that most of the hardhanded folks here, are really concerned in transportation and agricultural implements to a degree that it is difficult for their more cultivated fellow-countrymen to conceive of. Then, the merely instructive and historical features must have an incredible lot to say to them. We people who have had advantages, as we call them, can't begin to understand the state that most of us come here in, the state of enlightened ignorance, as one may call it, when we know how little we know, and are anxious to know more. But I congratulate you, Homos, on the opportunity you have to learn America personally, here; you won't easily have such another chance. I'm glad for your sake, too, that it (the crowd) is mainly a western and southwestern crowd, a Mississippi Valley crowd. You can tell it by their accent. It's a mistake to suppose that New England has a monopoly of the habit of speaking through the nose. We may have invented it, but we have imparted it apparently to the whole west, as the Scotch-Irish of Pennsylvania have lent the twist of their 'r,' and the combined result is something frightful. But it's the only frightful thing about the westerners, as I find them here. Their fashions are not the latest, but they are not only well behaved, they are on the average pretty well dressed, as the clothing store and the paper pattern dress our people. And they look pathetically good! When I think how hard-worked they all are, and what lonely lives most of them live on their solitary farms, I wonder they don't descend upon me with the whoop of savages. You're very fond of equality, my dear Homos! How do you like the equality of the American effect here? It's a vast level, as unbroken as the plains that seemed to widen as I came over them in the cars to Chicago, and that go widening on, I suppose, to the sunset itself. I won't speak of the people, but I *will* say the plains were dreary."

"Yes," I assented, for those plains had made me melancholy, too. They looked so habitable, and they were so solitary, though I could see that they were broken by the lines of cultivated fields, which were being plowed for wheat, or were left standing with their interminable ranks of maize. From time to time one caught sight of a forlorn farmstead, with a windmill beside it, making helpless play with its vanes as if it were vainly struggling to take flight from the monotonous landscape. There was nothing of the cheerfulness of our Altrurian farm villages; and I could understand how a dull uniformity of the human type might result from such an environment, as the banker intimated.

I have made some attempts, here, to get upon speaking terms with these average people, but I have not found them conversible. Very likely they distrusted my advances, from the warnings given them to beware of imposters and thieves at the Fair; it is one of the necessities of daily life in a competitive civilization, that you must be on your guard against strangers lest they cheat or rob you. It is hard for me to understand this, coming from a land where there is no theft and can be none, because there is no private property, and I have often bruised myself to no purpose in attempting the acquaintance of my fellow-visitors of the Fair. They never make any attempt at mine; no one has asked me a favor, here, or even a question; but each remains bent, in an intense preoccupation, upon seeing the most he can in the shortest time for the least money. Of course, there are many of the more cultivated visitors, who are more responsive, and who show themselves at least interested in me as a fellow-stranger; but these, though they are positively many, are, after all, relatively few. The vast bulk, the massed members of that immense equality which fatigued my friend, the banker, by its mere aspect, were shy of me, and I do not feel that I came to know any of them personally. They strolled singly, or in pairs, or by family groups, up and down the streets of the Fair City, or the noisy thoroughfare of the Plaisance, or through the different buildings, quiescent, patient, inoffensive, but reserved and inapproachable, as far as I was concerned. If they wished to know anything they asked the guards, who never failed in their duty of answering them fully and pleasantly.

The people from the different states visited their several State buildings, and seemed to be at home, there, with that instinctive sense of ownership which every one feels in a public edifice, and which is never tainted with the greedy wish to keep others out. They sat in long rows on the benches that lined the avenues, munching the victuals they had mostly brought with them in the lunch-boxes which strewed the place at nightfall, and were gathered up by thousands in the policing of the grounds. If they were very luxurious, they went to the tables of those eating-houses where, if they ordered a cup of tea or coffee, they could spread out the repast from their boxes and enjoy it more at their ease. But in none of these places did I see any hilarity in them, and whether they thought it unseemly or not to show any gayety, they showed none. They were peacefully content within the limits of their equality, and where it ended, as from time to time it must, they betrayed no discontent. That is what always astonishes me in America. The man of the harder lot accepts it unmurmuringly and with no apparent sense of injustice in the easier lot of another. He suffers himself, without a word, to be worse housed, worse clad, worse fed, than his merely luckier brother, who could give him no reason for his better fortune that an Altrurian would hold valid. Here, at the Fair, for example, on the days when the German village is open to the crowd without charge, the crowd streams through without an envious glance at the people dining richly and expensively at the restaurants, with no greater right than the others have to feed poorly and cheaply from their paper boxes. In the Plaisance, weary old farmwives and delicate women of the artisan class make way uncomplainingly for the ladies and gentlemen who can afford to hire wheeled chairs. As meekly and quietly they loiter by the shores of the lagoon and watch those who can pay to float upon their waters in the gondolas and electric launches. Everywhere the economic inequality is as passively accepted as if it were a natural inequality, like difference in height or strength, or as if it were something of immemorial privilege, like birth and title in the feudal countries of Europe. Yet, if one of these economically inferior Americans were told that he was not the peer of any and every other American, he would resent it as the grossest insult, such is the power of the inveterate political illusion in which the nation has been bred.

The banker and I sat long over our supper, in the graveled court of Old Vienna, talking of these things, and enjoying a bottle of delicate Rhenish wine under the mild September moon, not quite put out of countenance by the electric lamps. The gay parties about us broke up one after another, till we were left almost alone, and the watchman in his mediæval dress, with a halberd in one hand, and a lantern in the other, came round to call the hour for the last time. Then my friend beckoned to the waiter for the account, and while the man stood figuring it up, the banker said to me: "Well, you must come to Boston a hundred years hence, to the next Columbian Fair, and we will show you every body trundled about and fed at the public expense. I suppose that's what you would like to see?"

"It is what we always see in Altruria," I answered. "I haven't the least doubt it will be so with you in much less than a hundred years."

The banker was looking at the account the waiter handed him. He broke into an absent laugh, and then said to me, "I beg your pardon! You were saying?"

"Oh, nothing," I answered, and then, as he took out his

pocket-book to pay, he laid the bill on the table, and I could not help seeing what our little supper had cost him. It was twelve dollars; and I was breathless; it seemed to me that two would have been richly enough.

"They give you a good meal here, don't you think?" he said. "But the worst of having dined or supped well is reflecting that if you hadn't you could have given ten or twelve fellows, who will have to go to bed supperless, a handsome surfeit; that you could have bought twenty-five hungry men a full meal each; that you could have supplied forty-eight with plenty; that you could have relieved the famine of a hundred and twenty-four. But what is the use? If you think of these things you have no peace of your life!"

I could not help answering, "We don't have to think of them in Altruria."

"Ah, I dare say," answered the banker, as he tossed the waiter a dollar, and we rose and strolled out into the Plaisance. "If all men were unselfish, I should agree with you that Altrurianism was best."

"You can't have unselfishness till you have Altrurianism," I returned. "You can't put the cart before the horse."

"Oh, yes, we can," he returned in his tone of banter. "We always put the cart before the horse in America, so that the horse can see where the cart is going."

We strolled up and down the Plaisance, where the crowd had thinned to a few stragglers like ourselves. Most of the show villages were silenced for the night. The sob of the Javanese water-wheel was hushed; even the hubbub of the Chinese theater had ceased. The Samoans slept in their stucco huts; the Bedouins were folded to slumber in their black tents. The great Ferris wheel hung motionless with its lamps like a planetary circle of fire in the sky. It was a moment that invited to musing, that made a tacit companionship precious. By an impulse to which my own feeling instantly responded, my friend passed his arm through mine.

"Don't let us go home at all! Let us go over and sleep in the peristyle. I have never slept in a peristyle, and I have a fancy for trying it. Now, don't tell me you always sleep in peristyles in Altruria!"

I answered that we did not habitually, at least, and he professed that this was some comfort to him; and then he went on to talk more seriously about the Fair, and the effect that it must have upon American civilization. He said that he hoped for an æsthetic effect from it, rather than any fresh impulse in material enterprise, which he thought the country did not need. It had inventions enough, millionaires enough, prosperity enough; the great mass of the people lived as well and travelled as swiftly as they could desire. Now what they needed was some standard of taste, and this was what the Fair City would give them. He thought that it would at once have a great influence upon architecture, and sober and refine the artists who were to house the people; and that one might expect to see everywhere a return to the simplicity and beauty of the classic forms, after so much mere wandering and maundering in design, without authority or authenticity.

I heartily agreed with him in condemning the most that had yet been done in architecture in America, but I tried to make him observe that the simplicity of Greek architecture came out of the simplicity of Greek life, and the preference given in the Greek state to the intellectual over the industrial, to art over business. I pointed out that until there was some enlightened municipal or national control of the matter, no excellence of example could avail, but that the classicism of the Fair City would become, among a wilful and undisciplined people, a fad with the rich and a folly with the poor, and not a real taste with either class. I explained how with us the state absolutely forbade any man to aggrieve or insult the rest by the exhibition of his ignorance in the exterior of his dwelling, and how finally architecture had become a government function, and fit dwellings were provided for all by artists who approved themselves to the public criticism. I ventured so far as to say that the whole competitive world, with the exception of a few artists, had indeed lost the sense of beauty, and I even added that the Americans as a people seemed never to have had it at all.

He was not offended, as I had feared he might be, but asked me with perfect good nature what I meant.

"Why, I mean that the Americans came into the world too late to have inherited that influence from the antique world which was lost even in Europe, when in mediæval times the picturesque barbarously substituted itself for the beautiful, and a feeling for the quaint grew up in place of love for the perfect."

"I don't understand, quite," he said, "but I'm interested. Go on!"

"Why," I went on, "I have heard people rave over the beauty of the Fair City, and then go and rave over the beauty of the German village, or of Old Vienna, in the Plaisance. They were cultivated people, too; but they did not seem to know that the reproduction of a feudal castle or of a street in the taste of the middle ages, could not be beautiful, and could at the best be only picturesque. Old Vienna is no more beautiful than the Javanese village, and the German village outrivals the Samoan village only in its greater adaptability to the purposes of the painter. There is in your modern competitive world very little beauty anywhere, but there is an abundance of picturesqueness, of forms that may be reflected upon canvas, and impart the charm of their wild irregularity to all who look at the picture, though many who enjoy it there would fail of it in a study of the original. I will go so far as to say that there are points in New York, intrinsically so hideous that it makes me shudder to recall them—"

"*Don't* recall them!" he pleaded.

"Which would be much more capable of pictorial treatment than the Fair City, here," I continued. We had in fact got back to the Court of Honor, in the course of our talk, which I have only sketched here in the meagerest abstract. The incandescent lamps had been quenched, and the arc-lights below and the moon above flooded the place with one silver, and the absence of the crowds that had earlier thronged it, left it to a solitude indescribably solemn and sweet. In that light, it was like a ghost of the antique world witnessing a loveliness lost to modern times everywhere but in our own happy country.

I felt that silence would have been a fitter tribute to it than any words of mine, but my companion prompted me with an eager, "Well!" and I went on.

"This beauty that we see here is not at all picturesque. If a painter were to attempt to treat it picturesquely, he must abandon it in despair, because the charm of the picturesque is in irregularity, and the charm of the beautiful is in symmetry, in just proportion, in equality. You Americans do not see that the work of man, who is the crown of animate life, can only be beautiful as it approaches the regularity expressive of beauty in that life. Any breathing thing that wants perfect balance of form or feature is in so far ugly; it is offensive and ridiculous, just as a perfectly balanced tree or hill would be. Nature is picturesque, but what man creates should be beautiful, or else it is inferior. Since the Greeks, no people have divined this but the Altrurians, until now; and I do not believe that you would have begun to guess at it as you certainly have here, but for the spread of our ideas among you, and I do not believe this example will have any lasting effect with you unless you become Altrurianized. The highest quality of beauty is a spiritual quality."

"I don't know precisely how far I have followed you," said my companion, who seemed struck by a novelty in truisms which are so trite with us, "but I certainly feel that there is something in what you say. You are probably right in your notion that the highest quality of beauty is a spiritual quality, and I should like very much to know what you think that spiritual quality is here."

"The quality of self-sacrifice in the capitalists who gave their money, and in the artists who gave their talent without hope of material return, but only for the pleasure of authorizing and creating beauty that shall last forever in the memory of those it has delighted."

The banker smiled compassionately.

"Ah, my dear fellow, you must realize that this was only a spurt. It could be done once, but it couldn't be kept up."

"Why not?" I asked.

"Because people have got to live, even capitalists and artists have got to live, and they couldn't live by giving away wealth and giving away work, in our conditions."

"But you will change the conditions!"

"I doubt it," said the banker with another laugh. One of the Columbian guards passed near us, and faltered a little in his walk. "Do you want us to go out?" asked my friend.

"No," the young fellow hesitated. "Oh no!" and he continued his round.

"He hadn't the heart to turn us out," said the banker, "he would hate so to be turned out himself. I wonder what will become of all the poor fellows who are concerned in the government of the Fair City when they have to return to earth! It will be rough on them." He lifted his head, and cast one long look upon the miracle about us. "Good heavens!" he broke out, "And when they shut up shop, here, will all this beauty have to be destroyed, this fabric of a vision demolished? It would be infamous, it would be sacrilegious! I have heard some talk of their burning it, as the easiest way, the only way of getting rid of it. But it musn't be, it can't be."

"No, it can't be," I responded fervently. "It may be rapt from sight in the flames like the prophet in his chariot of fire; but it will remain still in the hearts of your great people. An immortal principle, higher than use, higher even than beauty, is expressed in it, and the time will come when they will look back upon it, and recognize in it the first embodiment of the Altrurian idea among them, and will cherish it forever in their history, as the earliest achievement of a real civic life."

I believe this, my dear Cyril, and I leave it with you as my final word concerning the great Columbian Fair.

Yours in all brotherly affection,

A. Homos.

III

A BIT OF ALTRURIA IN NEW YORK

New York, October 24, 1893.
WELL, MY DEAR CYRIL, I have returned to this Babylon, you
see, from my fortnight's stay in that vision of Altruria at the
great Fair in Chicago. I can, perhaps, give you some notion of
the effect with me by saying that it is as if I were newly exiled and
were exposing myself a second time to the shock of American
conditions, stripped of the false hopes and romantic expectations
which, in some sort, softened the impression at first. I knew what
I had to look forward to when my eyes lost the last glimpse of the
Fair City, and I confess that I had not much heart for it. If it had
only been to arrive here, and at once take ship for home, I could
have borne it; but I had denied myself this, in the interest of the
studies of plutocratic civilization which I wish to make, and this
purpose could not support me under the burden that weighed
my spirits down. I had seen what might be, in the Fair City, and
now I was to see again what the Americans say must be, in New
York, and I shrank not only from the moral, but the physical
ugliness of the thing.

But, in fact, do not the two kinds of ugliness go together? I
asked myself the question as I looked about me in the ridiculous
sleeping-car I had taken passage in from Chicago. Money had
been lavished upon its appointments, as if it had been designed
for the state progress of some barbarous prince through his
dominions, instead of the conveyance of simple republican citizens from one place to another, on business. It was as expensively

upholstered as the bad taste of its designer could contrive, and a rich carpet under foot caught and kept whatever disease-germs were thrown off by the slumbering occupants in their long journey; on the floor, at every seat, a silver-plated spittoon ministered to the filthy national habit. The interior was of costly foreign wood, which was everywhere covered with a foolish and meaningless carving; mirrors framed into the panels reflected the spendthrift absurdity through the whole length of the saloon. Of course, this waste in the equipment and decoration of the car meant the exclusion of the poorer sort of travellers, who were obliged to sit up all night in the day-cars, when they might have been lodged, for a fifth of what I paid, in a sleeping-car much more tasteful, wholesome and secure than mine, which was destined, sooner or later, in the furious risks of American travel, to be whirled over the side of an embankment, or plunged through a broken bridge, or telescoped in a collision, or piled in a heap of shattered and ruined splendors like its own, and consumed in a holocaust to the American god Hustle.

For not only are the comforts of travel here made so costly that none but the very well-to-do can afford them, but the service of the insufficiently manned trains and lines is overworked and underpaid. Even the poor negroes who make up the beds in the sleepers are scrimped of half a living by the companies which declare handsome dividends, and leave them to the charity of the fleeced and imperilled passengers. The Americans are peculiarly proud of their sleeping-car system, though I can hardly believe that when he is pinned into a broken seat, the most infatuated American can get much pleasure, while the flames advance swiftly upon him, out of the carving of the woodwork, or even the brass capitals of the onyx columns supporting nothing at either end of the car-roof. But until he is placed in some such predicament, the American hears with acquiescence, if not complacence, of the railroad slaughters which have brought the mortality of travel to and from the Fair during the past month up to a frightful sum. Naturally, if he does not mind the reports of these disasters, where his own name may any day appear in the list of killed or wounded, he is not vividly concerned in the fate of the thirty thousand trainmen who are annually mangled or massacred. He regards these dire statistics, apparently, as another proof of the immense activity of his country, and he does not stop, as he is hurled precariously over its continental spaces, and shot out of his train at his journey's end, from two to six hours late, to consider whether a public management of public affairs is not as well in economics as in politics.

I was fortunate in my journey to New York; I arrived only two hours behind time, and I arrived safe and sound. The Americans are quite satisfied with the large average of people who arrive safe and sound, in spite of the large numbers who do neither; and from time to time their newspapers print exultant articles to show how many get home in the full enjoyment of life and limb. I do not see that they celebrate so often the seasonable arrival of the surviving travellers, and, in fact, my experience of railroads in America is that the trains seldom bring me to my journey's end at the appointed hour. On each great through-road there is one very rapid train, which has precedence of all other travel and traffic, and which does arrive at the hour fixed; but the other trains, swift or slow, seem to come lagging in at all sorts of intervals after their schedule-time. If I instance my experience and observation of this fact, my friends are inclined to doubt it; and if I insist upon matching it with their own, they allege the irregularity of the government trains in Germany, without seeming to know more about them than they know of their own trains. They at once begin to talk largely of the celerity and frequency of these, and to express their wonder that the companies should come so near keeping their word to the public as they sometimes do.

However, I was thankful for my safety and my soundness, when I found myself again in New York, though I felt so loth to be here. If I could fitly have done so I would very willingly have turned and taken the next train back to Chicago, since I must not take the next steamer on to Altruria. But if I had gone back, it could only have been for a fortnight more, since at the end of the month now so far spent, they must begin to destroy the beauty they have created in the Fair City there. I tried to console myself with this fact, but the sense of an irreparable loss, of banishment, of bereavement, remained with me for days, and is only now beginning to wear itself away into a kind of impersonal sorrow, and to blend with the bruise of my encounter with the brute ugliness of this place, which is none the less brute, because it is so often kindly. It is like the ugliness of some great unwieldy monster, which looks so helpless and so appealing, that you cannot quite abhor it, but experience a sort of compassion for its unloveliness. I had thought of it in that way at a distance, but when I came to see it again, I found that, even in this aspect it was hard to bear. So I came up from the station to this hotel where I am now lodged, and where my windows overlook the long reaches of the beautiful Central Park at such a height that unless I drop my glance, none of the shapeless bulks of the city intrude themselves between me and the effect of a vast forest. My hotel is itself one of the most preposterous of the structures which disfigure the city, if a city without a sky-line can be said to be disfigured by any particular structure. With several others as vast or as high, it forms a sort of gateway to the Park, from whose leafy depths, these edifices swaggering upward unnumbered stories, look like detached cliffs in some broken and jagged mountain range. They are built with savage disregard to one another, or to the other buildings about them, and with no purpose, apparently, but to get the most money out of the narrowest space of ground. Any objective sense of them is to the last degree painful, as any objective sense of the American life is, in its inequality and disproportion; but subjectively they are not so bad as that is, not so bad from the inside. At great cost they offer you an incomparable animal comfort, and they realize for the average American an ideal of princely magnificence, such as he has been instructed by all his traditions to regard as the chief good of success.

But for me the best thing about my hotel is that I can leave it when I will and descend to the level of the street below, where I can at once lose myself in woods as sweet and friendly as our groves at home, and wander through their aisles unmolested by the crowds that make them their resort so harmlessly that even the sylvan life there is unafraid. This morning, as I sat on a bench in one of the most frequented walks, I could almost have touched the sparrows on the sprays about me; a squirrel foraging for nuts, climbed on my knees, as if to explore my pockets. Of course, there is a policeman at every turn to see that no wrong is done these pretty creatures, and that no sort of trespass is committed by any in the domain of all; but I like to think that the security and immunity of the Park is proof of something besides the vigilance of its guardians; that it is a hint of a growing sense in the Americans that what is common is the personal charge of everyone in the community.

In the absence of the private interest here, I get back again to the Fair City, and the yet fairer cities of our own Altruria; and I hope that, if you cannot quite excuse my self-indulgence, in placing myself near the Park, you will at least be able to account for it. You must remember the perpetual homesickness gnawing at my heart, and you must realize how doubly strange an Altrurian finds himself in any country of the plutocratic world; and then, I think, you will understand why I spend, and even waste, so much of my time lingering in this lovely place. As I turn from my page and look out upon it, I see the domes and spires of its foliage beginning to feel the autumn and taking on those wonderful sunset tints of the American year in its decline; when I stray through its pleasant paths, I feel the pathos of the tender October air; but, better than these sensuous delights, in everything of it and in it, I imagine a prophecy of the truer state which I believe America is destined yet to see established. It cannot be that the countless thousands who continually visit it, and share equally in its beauty, can all come away insensible of the meaning of it; here and there someone must ask himself, and then ask others, why the whole of life should not be as generous and as just as this part of it; why he should not have a country as palpably his own as the Central Park is, where his ownership excludes the ownership of no other.

Some workman out of work, as he trudges aimlessly through its paths, must wonder why the city cannot minister to his need as well as his pleasure, and not hold aloof from him till he is thrown a pauper on its fitful charities. If it can give him this magnificent garden for his forced leisure, why cannot it give him a shop where he can earn his bread?

I may be mistaken. His thoughts may never take this turn at all. The poor are slaves of habit, they bear what they have borne, they suffer on from generation to generation, and seem to look for nothing different. But this is what I think for the poor people in the Park, not alone for the workman recently out of work, but for the workman so long out of it that he has rotted into one of the sodden tramps whom I meet now and then, looking like some forlorn wild beast, in the light of the autumnal leaves. That is the great trouble, here, my dear Cyril: you cannot anywhere get away from the misery of life. You would think that the rich for their own sakes would wish to see conditions bettered so that they might not be confronted at every turn by the mere loathliness of poverty. But they likewise are the slaves of habit, and go the way the rich have gone since the beginning of time in those unhappy countries where there are rich and poor. Sometimes I think that as Shakespeare says of the living and the dead, the rich and the poor here are "but as pictures" to one another, without vital reality. It is only a luckless exile from Altruria like myself who sees them in their dreadful verity, and has a living sense of them; and I, too, lose this at times.

Sometimes I am glad to lose it, and this is why I would rather walk in the pathways of the Park than in the streets of the city, for the contrasts here are not so frequent, if they are glaring still. I do get away from them now and then, for a moment or two, and give myself wholly up to the delight of the place. It has been treated with an artistic sense which finds its best expression here, as with us, in the service of the community, but I do not think the Americans understand this, the civic spirit is so weak in them yet; and I doubt if the artists themselves are conscious of it, they are so rarely given the chance to serve the community. But somehow, when this chance offers, it finds the right man to profit by it, as in the system of parks at Chicago, the gardened spaces at Washington, and the Central Park in New York. Some of the decorative features here are bad, the sculpture is often foolish or worse, and the architecture is the outgrowth of a mood, where it is not merely puerile. The footways have been asphalted, and this is out of keeping with the rustic character of the place, but the whole design, and much of the detail in the treatment of the landscape, bears the stamp of a kindly and poetic genius. The Park is in nowise taken away from nature, but is rendered back to her, when all has been done to beautify it, an American woodland, breaking into meadows, here and there, and brightened with pools and ponds lurking among rude masses of rock, and gleaming between leafy knolls and grassy levels. It stretches and widens away, mile after mile, in the heart of the city, a memory of the land as it was before the havoc of the city began, and giving to the city-prisoned poor an image of what the free country still is, everywhere. It is all penetrated by well-kept drives and paths; and it is in these paths that I find my pleasure. They are very simple woodland paths but for the asphalt; though here and there an effect of art is studied with charming felicity; once I mounted some steps graded in the rock, and came upon a plinth supporting the bust of a poet, as I might have done in our gardens at home. But there is otherwise very little effect of gardening except near the large fountain by the principal lake where there is some flare of flowers on the sloping lawns. I send you a photograph of this point, and you will see the excess of the viaduct, with its sweeping stairways, and carven free-stone massiveness; —but it is charming in a way, too, and the basin of the fountain is full of lotoses and papyrus reeds, so that you do not much notice the bronze angel atop, who seems to be holding her skirt to one side and picking her steps, and to be rather afraid of falling into the water. There is, in fact, only one thoroughly good piece of sculpture in the Park, which I was glad to find in sympathy with the primeval suggestiveness of the landscape gardening: an American Indian hunting with his dog, as the Indians must have hunted through the wilds here before the white men came.

This group is always a great pleasure to me, from whatever point I come upon it, or catch a glimpse of it; and I like to go and find the dog's prototype in the wolves at the menagerie here which the city offers free to the wonder of the crowds constantly thronging its grounds and houses. The captive brutes seem to be of that solidarity of good fellowship which unites all the frequenters of the Park; the tigers and the stupidly majestic lions have an air different to me, at least, from tigers and lions shown for profit. Among the milder sorts, I do not care so much for the wallowing hippopotamuses, and the lumbering elephants, and the supercilious camels which one sees in menageries everywhere, as for those types which represent a period as extinct as that of the American pioneers: I have rather a preference for going and musing upon the ragged bison pair as they stand with their livid mouths open at the pale of their paddock, expecting the children's peanuts, and unconscious of their importance as survivors of the untold millions of their kind, which a quarter of a century ago blackened the western plains for miles and miles. There are now only some forty or fifty left; for of all the forces of the plutocratic conditions, so few are conservative that the American buffalo is as rare as the old-fashioned American mechanic, proud of his independence, and glorying in his citizenship.

In some other enclosures are pairs of the beautiful native deer, which I wish might be enlarged to the whole extent of the Park, as we have them in our Regionic parks at home. But I can only imagine them on the great sweeps of grass, which recall the savannahs and prairies, though there is a very satisfactory flock of sheep which nibbles the herbage there, when these spaces are not thrown open to the ball-players who are allowed on certain days of the week. I like to watch them, and so do great numbers of other frequenters of the Park, apparently; and when I have walked far up beyond the reservoirs of city-water, which serve the purpose of natural lakes in the landscape, I like to come upon that expanse in the heart of the woods where the tennis-players have stretched their nets over a score of courts, and the art students have set up their easels on the edges of the lawns, for what effect of the autumnal foliage they have the luck or the skill to get. It is all very sweet and friendly, and in keeping with the purpose of the Park, and its frank and simple treatment throughout.

From an Altrurian point of view I think this treatment is best for the greatest number of those who visit the place, and for whom the aspect of simple nature is the thing to be desired. Their pleasure in it, as far as the children are concerned, is visible and audible enough, but I like, as I stroll along, to note the quiet comfort which the elder people take in this domain of theirs, as they sit on the benches in the woodland ways, or under the arching trees of the Mall, unmolested by the company of some of the worst of all the bad statues in the plutocratic world. They are mostly foreigners, I believe, but I find every now and then an American among them, who has released himself, or has been forced by want of work, to share their leisure for the time; I fancy he has always a bad conscience, if he is taking the time off, for there is a continual pressure of duty here, to add dollar to dollar, and provide for the future as well as the present need. The foreigner, who has been bred up without the American's hope of advancement, has not his anxiety, and is a happier man, so far as that goes; but the Park imparts something of its peace to every one, even to some of the people who drive, and form a spectacle for those who walk.

For me they all unite to form a spectacle I never cease to marvel at, with a perpetual hunger of conjecture as to what they really think of one another. Apparently, they are all, whether they walk or whether they drive, willing collectively, if not individually, to go on forever in the economy which perpetuates their inequality, and makes a mock of the polity which assures them their liberty. I cannot get used to the difference which money creates among men here, and whenever I take my eyes from it the thing ceases to be credible; yet this difference is what the vast majority of Americans have agreed to accept forever as right and justice. If I were to go and sit beside some poor man in the Park, and ask him why a man no better than he was driving before him in a luxurious carriage, he would say that the other man had the money to do it; and he would really think he had given me a reason; the man in the carriage himself could not regard the answer as more full and final than the man on the bench. They have both been reared in the belief that it is a sufficient answer, and they would both regard me with the same misgiving, if I ventured to say that it was not a reason; for if their positions were to be at once reversed, they would both acquiesce in the moral outlawry of their inequality. The man on foot would think it had simply come his turn to drive in a carriage and the man whom he ousted would think it was rather hard luck, but he would realize that it was what, at the bottom of his heart, he had always expected.

I have sometimes ventured to address a man walking or sitting by my side, if he appeared more than commonly intelligent, in the hope of getting at some personal philosophy, instead of this conventional acceptance of the situation, but I have only had short or suspicious answers, or a bewildered stare for my pains. Only once have I happened to find any one who questioned the situation from a standpoint outside of it, and that was a shabbily dressed man whom I overheard talking to a poor woman in one of those pleasant arbors which crown certain points of rising ground in the Park. She had a paper bundle on the seat beside her, and she looked like some workingwoman out of place, with that hapless, wistful air, which such people often have. Her poor little hands, which lay in her lap, were stiffened and hardened with work, but they were clean, except for the black of the nails, and she was very decently clad in garments beginning to fray into rags; she had a good, kind, faithful face, and she listened without rancor to the man as he unfolded the truth to her concerning the conditions in which they lived, if it may be called living. It was the wisdom of the poor, hopeless, joyless, as it now and then makes itself heard in the process of the years and ages in the plutocratic world, and then sinks again into silence. He showed her how she had no permanent place in the economy, not because she had momentarily lost work, but because in the nature of things as the Americans have them, it could only be a question of time when she must be thrown out of any place she found. He blamed no one; he only blamed the conditions, and with far more leniency than you or I should. I do not know whether his wisdom made the friendless woman happier, but I could not gainsay it, when he saw me listening, and asked me, "Isn't that the truth?" I left him talking sadly on, and I never saw him again. He looked very threadbare, but he too was cleanly and decent in his dress, and not at all of that type of agitators of whom the Americans have made an effigy like nothing I have ever found here, as if merely for the childish pleasure of reviling it.

The whole incident was infinitely pathetic to me; and yet I warn you, my dear Cyril, that you must not romance the poor, here, or imagine that they are morally better than the rich; you must not fancy that a poor man, when he ceases to be a poor man, would be kinder for having been poor. He would perhaps oftener, and certainly more logically, be unkinder, for there would be mixed with his vanity of possession a quality of cruel fear, an apprehension of loss, which the man who had always been rich would not feel. The self-made man in America, when he has made himself of money, seems to have been deformed by his original destitution, and I think that if I were in need I would rather take my chance of pity from the man who had never been poor. Of course, this is generalization, and there are instances to the contrary, which at once occur to me. But what is absolutely true, is that plutocratic prosperity, the selfish joy of having, at the necessary cost of those who cannot have, is blighted by the feeling of insecurity, which every man here has in his secret soul, and which the man who has known want must have in greater measure than the man who has never known want.

There is, indeed, no security for wealth, which the Americans think the chief good of life, in the system that warrants it. When a man has gathered his millions, he cannot be reduced to want, probably; but while he is amassing them, while he is in the midst of the fight, or the game, as most men are here, there are ninety-five chances out of a hundred that he will be beaten. Perhaps it is best so, and I should be glad it was so, if I could be sure that the common danger bred a common kindness between the rich and the poor here, but it seems not to do so. As far as I can see, the rule of chance, which they all live under, does nothing more than reduce them to a community of anxieties.

To the eye of the stranger they have the monotony of the sea, where some tenth wave runs a little higher than the rest, but sinks at last, or breaks upon the rocks or sands, as inevitably as the other nine. Their inequality is without picturesqueness and without distinction. The people in the carriages are better dressed than those on foot, especially the women; but otherwise they do not greatly differ from the most of these. The spectacle of the driving in the Park has none of that dignity which, our emissaries tell us, characterizes such spectacles in European capitals. This may be because many people of the finest social quality are still in the country, or it may be because the differences growing out of money can never have the effect of those growing out of birth; that a plutocracy can never have the last wicked grace of an aristocracy. It would be impossible, for instance, to weave any romance about the figures you see in the carriages here; they do not even suggest the poetry of ages of prescriptive wrong; they are of today, and there is no guessing whether they will be of tomorrow or not.

In Europe, this sort of tragicomedy is at least well played; but in America, you always have the feeling that the performance is that of second-rate amateurs, who, if they would really live out the life implied by America, would be the superiors of the whole world. I have, my dear Cyril, not a very keen sense of humor, as you know; but even I am sometimes moved to laughter by some of the things I see among them. Or, you perhaps think that I ought to be awed by the sight of a little, lavishly dressed lady, lolling in the corner of a ponderous landau, with the effect of holding fast lest she should be shaken out of it, while two powerful horses, in jingling, silver-plated harness, with the due equipment of coachman and footman, seated on their bright-buttoned overcoats on the box together, get her majestically over the ground at a slow trot. This is what I sometimes see, with not so much reverence as I feel for the simple mother pushing her baby-carriage on the asphalt beside me and doubtless envying the wonderful creature in the landau. Sometimes it is a fat old man in the landau; or a husband and wife, not speaking; or a pair of grim old ladies, who look as if they had lived so long aloof from their unluckier sisters that they could not be too severe with the mere sight of them. Generally speaking, the people in the carriages do not seem any happier for being there, though I have sometimes seen a jolly party of strangers in a public carriage, drawn by those broken-kneed horses which seem peculiarly devoted to this service.

The best place to see the driving is at a point where the different driveways converge, not far from the Egyptian obelisk which the Khedive gave the Americans some years ago, and which they have set up here in one of the finest eminences of the Park. He had of course no moral right to rob his miserable land of any one of its characteristic monuments, but I do not know that it is not as well in New York as in Alexandria. If its heart of aged stone could feel the terrible continuity of conditions in the world outside of Altruria, it must be aware of the essential unity of the civilizations beside the Nile and beside the Hudson; and if Cleopatra's needle had really an eye to see, it must perceive that there is nothing truly civic in either. As the great tide of dissatisfied and weary wealth rolls by its base here, in the fantastic variety of its equipages, does it discern so much difference between their occupants and the occupants of the chariots that swept beneath it in the capital of the Ptolemies two thousand years ago? I can imagine it at times winking such an eye and cocking in derision the gilded cap with which the New Yorkers have lately crowned it. They pass it in all kinds of vehicles, and there are all kinds of people in them, though there are sometimes no people at all, as when the servants have been sent out to exercise the horses, for nobody's good or pleasure, and in the spirit of that atrocious waste which runs through the whole plutocratic life. I have now and then seen a gentleman driving a four-in-hand, with everything to minister to his vanity in the exact imitation of a nobleman driving a four-in-hand over English roads, and with no one to be drawn by his crop-tailed bays or blacks, except himself and the solemn-looking groom on his perch; I have wondered how much more nearly equal they were in their aspirations and instincts than either of them imagined. A gentleman driving a pair, abreast or tandem, with a groom on the rumble, for no purpose except to express his quality, is a common sight enough; and sometimes you see a lady illustrating her consequence in like manner. A lady driving, while a gentleman occupies the seat behind her, is a sight which always affects me like the sight of a man taking a woman's arm, in walking, as the man of an underbred sort is apt to do here.

Horsey-looking women, who are, to ladies at least, what horsey-looking men are to gentlemen, drive together; often they are really ladies, and sometimes they are nice young girls, out for an innocent dash and chat. They are all very much and very unimpressively dressed, whether they sit in state behind the regulation coachman and footman, or handle the reins themselves. Now and then you see a lady with a dog on the seat beside her, for an airing, but not often a child; once or twice I have seen one with a large spaniel seated comfortably in front of her, and I have asked myself what would happen if, instead of the dog, she had taken into her carriage some pale woman or weary old man, such as I sometimes see gazing patiently after her. The thing would be possible in Altruria; but I assure you, my dear Cyril, it would be altogether impossible in America. I should be the first to feel the want of keeping in it; for, however recent wealth may be here, it has equipped itself with all the apparatus of long inherited riches, which it is as strongly bound to maintain intact as if it were really old and hereditary—perhaps more strongly. I must say that, mostly, its owners look very tired of it, or of something, in public, and that the American plutocrats, if they have not the distinction of an aristocracy, have at least the ennui.

But these stylish turnouts form only a part of the spectacle in the Park driveways, though they form, perhaps, the larger part. Bicyclers weave their dangerous and devious way everywhere through the roads, and seem to be forbidden the bridle-paths, where from point to point you catch a glimpse of the riders. There are boys and girls in village carts, the happiest of all the people you see; and there are cheap-looking buggies, like those you meet in the country here, with each a young man and young girl in them, as if they had come in from some remote suburb; turnouts shabbier yet, with poor old horses, poke about with some elderly pair, like a farmer and his wife. There are family carryalls, with friendly looking families, old and young, getting the good of the Park together in a long, leisurely jog; and open buggies with yellow wheels and raffish men in them behind their wide-spread trotters; or with some sharp-faced young fellow getting all the speed out of a lively span that the mounted policemen, stationed at intervals along the driveways, will allow. The finer vehicles are of all types, patterned like everything else that is fine in America, upon something fine in Europe; but just now a very high-backed phaeton appears to be most in favor; and in fact I get a great deal of pleasure out of these myself, as I do not have to sit stiffly up in them. They make me think somehow of those eighteenth-century English novels, which you and I used to delight in so much, and which filled us with a romantic curiosity concerning the times when young ladies like Evelina drove out in phaetons, and were the passionate pursuit of Lord Orvilles and Sir Clement Willoughbys.

You will be curious to know how far the Americans publicly carry their travesty of the European aristocratic life; and here I am somewhat at a loss, for I only know that life from the relations of our emissaries, and from the glimpses I had of it in my brief sojourn in England on my way here. But I should say, from what I have seen of the driving in the Park, where I suppose I have not yet seen the parody at its height, it does not err on the side of excess. The equipages, when they are fine, are rather simple; and the liveries are such as express a proprietary grandeur in coat buttons, silver or gilt, and in a darker or lighter drab of the cloth the servants wear; they are often in brown or dark green. Now and then you see the tightly cased legs and top boots and cockaded hat of a groom, but this is oftenest on a four-in-hand coach, or the rumble of a tandem cart; the soul of the free-born republican is rarely bowed before it on the box of a family carriage. I have seen nothing like an attempt at family colors in the trappings of the coachman and horses.

Yes, I should say that the imitation was quite within the bounds of good taste. The bad taste is in the wish to imitate Europe at all; but with the abundance of money, the imitation is simply inevitable. As I have told you before, and I cannot insist too much upon the fact, there is no American life for wealth; there is no native formula for the expression of social superiority; because America, like Altruria, means equality if it means any-thing, in the last analysis. But without economic equality there can be no social equality, and, finally, there can be no political equality; for money corrupts the franchise, the legislature and the judiciary here, just as it used to do with us in the old days before the Evolution. Of all the American fatuities, none seems to me more deplorable than the pretension that with their con-ditions it can ever be otherwise, or that simple manhood can assert itself successfully in the face of such power as money wields over the very soul of man. At best, the common man can only break from time to time, into insolent defiance, pending his chance to make himself an uncommon man with money. In all this show here on the Park driveways, you get no effect so vivid as the effect of sterility in that liberty without equality which seems to satisfy the Americans. A man may come into the Park with any sort of vehicle, so that it is not for the carriage of merchandise, and he is free to spoil what might be a fine effect with the intrusion of whatever squalor of turnout he will. He has as much right there as any one, but the right to be shabby in the presence of people who are fine is not one that we should envy him. I do not think that he can be comfortable in it, for the superiority around him puts him to shame, as it puts the poor man to shame here at every turn in life, though some Americans, with an impudence that is pitiable, will tell you that it does not put him to shame; that he feels himself as good as any one. They are always talking about human nature and what it is, and what it is not; but they try in their blind worship of inequality, to refuse the first and simplest knowledge of human nature, which testifies of itself in every throb of their own hearts, as they try even to refuse a knowledge of the Divine nature, when they attribute to the Father of all a design in the injustice they have themselves created.

To me the lesson of Central Park is that where it is used in the spirit of fraternity and equality, the pleasure in it is pure and fine, and that its frequenters have for the moment a hint of the beauty which might be perpetually in their lives; but where it is invaded by the plutocratic motives of the strife that raves all round it in the city outside, its joys are fouled with contempt and envy, the worst passions that tear the human heart. Ninety-nine Americans out of a hundred, have never seen a man in livery; they have never dreamt of such a display as this in the Park; the sight of it would be as strange to them as it would be to all the Altrurians. Yet with their conditions, I fear that at sight of it, ninety-nine Americans out of every hundred, would lust for their turn of the wheel, their throw of the dice, so that they might succeed to a place in it, and flaunt their luxury in the face of poverty, and abash humility with their pride. They would not feel, as we should, the essential immorality of its deformity; they would not perceive that its ludicrous disproportion was the outward expression of an inward ugliness.

A. Homos.

IV

ASPECTS AND IMPRESSIONS OF A PLUTOCRATIC CITY

New York, October 30, 1893.

MY DEAR CYRIL:

If you will look at a plan of New York, you will see that Central Park is really in the center of the place, if a thing which has length only, or is so nearly without breadth or thickness, can be said to have a center. South of the Park, the whole island is dense with life and business—it is pretty solidly built up on either side; but to the northward the blocks of houses are no longer of a compact succession; they struggle up, at irregular intervals, from open fields, and sink again, on the streets pushed beyond them into the simple country, where even a suburban character is lost. It can only be a few years, at most, before all the empty spaces will be occupied, and the town, such as it is, and such as it seems to have been ever since the colonial period, will have anchored itself fast in the rock that underlies the larger half of it, and imparted its peculiar effect to every street—an effect of arrogant untidiness, of superficial and formal gentility, of immediate neglect and overuse.

You will see more of the neglect and overuse in the avenues which penetrate the city's mass from north to south, and more of the superficial and formal gentility in the streets that cross these avenues from east to west; but the arrogant untidiness you will find nearly everywhere, except in some of the newest quarters westward from the Park, and still further uptown. These are really very clean; but they have a bare look, as if they were not yet inhabited, and, in fact, many of the houses are still empty. Lower down, the streets are often as shabby and as squalid as the avenues that run parallel with the river sides; and at least two of the avenues are as decent as the decentest cross-street. But all are more or less unkempt; the sweepings lie in little heaps in the gutters for days; and in a city without alleys barrels of ashes and kitchen offal line the curbstones and offer their offense to the nose and eye everywhere.

Of late, a good many streets and several avenues have been asphalted, and the din of wheels on the rough pavement no longer torments the ear so cruelly; but there is still the sharp clatter of the horses' iron shoes everywhere; and their pulverized manure, which forms so great a part of the city's dust, and is constantly taken into people's stomachs and lungs, seems to blow more freely about on the asphalt than on the old-fashioned pavements; scraps of paper, straw, fruit-peel, and all manner of minor waste and rubbish, litter both. Every city of the plutocratic world must be an outrage to Altrurian senses, as you already understand, but I doubt if I could ever make you understand the abominable condition of the New York streets during the snowy months of the past winter, when for weeks no attempt was made to remove their accumulated filth. At their best, they would be intolerable to us; at their worst, they are inconceivable and wholly indescribable. The senses witness their condition, but the mind refuses to receive the evidence of the senses; and nothing can be more pathetic, more comic, than the resolution of the New Yorkers in ignoring it.

But if I were once to go into detail, in my effort to make New York intelligible to you, there would be no end to it, and I think I had better get back to my topographical generalities. I have given you some notion of my position at the gate of Central Park, and you must imagine all my studies of the city beginning and ending here. I love to linger near it, because it affords a hope for New York that I feel so distinctly nowhere else in New York, though certain traits of the city's essentially transitional and experimental nature sometimes also suggest that it may be the

first city of America to Altrurianize. The upper classes are at
least used to the political sway of the lower classes, and when they
realize that they never can have any hope but in bettering the lot
of their rulers, the end will not be far off, for it will then be seen
that this can be lastingly done only through a change of the
economic conditions.

In the meantime, the Park, which is the physical heart of New
York, is Altrurian already. In the contrasts of rich and poor,
which you can no more escape there than you can in the city
streets, you are, indeed, afflicted with that sense of absurdity, of
impossibility, so comforting to the American when he strives to
imagine Altrurian conditions, and gets no farther than to imagine
the creatures of a plutocratic civilization in them. He imagines
that, in an Altrurian state, people must have the same motives,
interests, anxieties, which he has always known them to have,
and which they carry with them into Central Park, and only lay
aside for a moment in response to the higher appeal which its
equal opportunities make. But then, at moments these care-
worn, greed-worn souls do put off the burden of their inequality,
their superiority or their inferiority, and meet on the same broad
level of humanity; and I wish, my dear Cyril, that you would
always keep its one great oasis in your thoughts, as you follow
me in my wanderings through this vast commercial desert. It is
the token, if not the pledge, of happier things, and, while I
remain here, it will be always to me a precious image of home.

When I leave it I usually take one of the avenues southward,
and then turn eastward or westward on one of the cross-streets
whose perspective appeals to my curiosity, and stroll through it
to one of the rivers. The avenues, as you will see, are fifteen or
sixteen in number, and they stretch, some farther than others, up
and down the island, but most of them end in the old town, where
its irregularity begins, at the south, and several are interrupted
by the different parks at the north. Together with the streets that
intersect them between the old town and Central Park, they
form one of the most characteristic parts of modern New York.
Like the streets, they are numbered, as you know, rather than

named, from a want of imagination, or from a preference of mere convenience to the poetry and associations that cluster about a name, and can never cling to a number, or from a business impatience to be quickly done with the matter. This must rather defeat itself, however, when a hurried man undertakes to tell you that he lives at three hundred and seventy-five on One Hundred and Fifty-seventh street. Towards the rivers the avenues grow shabbier and shabbier, though this statement must be qualified, like all general statements. Seventh avenue, on the west, is pleasanter than Sixth avenue, and Second avenue, on the east, is more agreeable than Third avenue. In fact, the other afternoon, as I strayed over to the East river, I found several blocks of Avenue A, which runs nearest it, very quiet, built up with comfortable dwellings, and even clean, as cleanliness is understood in New York.

But it is Fifth avenue which divides the city lengthwise nearest the middle, and it is this avenue which affords the norm of style and comfort to the other avenues on either hand, and to all the streets that intersect it. Madison avenue is its rival, and has suffered less from the invasion of shops and hotels, but a long stretch of Fifth avenue is still the most aristocratic quarter of the city, and is upon the whole its finest thoroughfare. I need not say that we should not, in Altruria, think any New York street fine; but, generally, Fifth avenue and the cross-streets in its better part have a certain regularity in their mansions of brownstone, which recalls to one, if it does not actually give again, the pleasure we get from the symmetry at home. They are at least not so chaotic as they might be, and though they always suggest money more than taste, I cannot at certain moments, and under the favor of an evening sky, deny them a sort of unlovely and forbidding beauty.

There are not many of these cross-streets which have remained intact from the business of the other avenues. They have always a drinking saloon, or a provision store, or an apothecary's shop, at the corners where they intersect; the modistes find lodgment in them almost before the residents are aware. Beyond Sixth avenue, or Seventh at furthest, on the west, and Fourth avenue or Lexington, on the east, they lose their genteel character; their dwellings degenerate into apartment-houses, and then into tenement-houses of lower and lower grade till the rude traffic and the offensive industries of the river shores are reached.

But once more I must hedge, for sometimes a street is respectable almost to the water on one side or the other; and there are whole neighborhoods of pleasant dwellings far down town, which seem to have been forgotten by the enterprise of business, or neglected by its caprice, and to have escaped for a time at least the contagion of poverty. Business and poverty are everywhere slowly or swiftly eating their way into the haunts of respectability, and destroying its pleasant homes. They already have the whole of the old town to themselves. In large spaces of it no one dwells but the janitors with their families, who keep the sky-scraping edifices where business frets the time away; and by night, in the streets where myriads throng by day, no one walks but the outcast and the watch.

Many of these business streets are the handsomest in the city, with a good sky line, and an architectural ideal too good for the sordid uses of commerce. This is often realized in antipathetic iron, but often there is good honest work in stone, and an effect better than the best of Fifth avenue. But this is stupid and wasteful, as everything necessarily is in the plutocratic conditions. It is for the pleasure of no one's taste or sense; the business men who traffic in these edifices have no time for their beauty, or no perception of it; the porters and truckmen and expressmen, who toil and moil in these thoroughfares, have no use for the grandeur that catches the eye of a chance passer from Altruria.

Other spaces are abandoned to the poverty which festers in the squalid houses and swarms day and night in the squalid streets; but business presses closer and harder upon these refuges of its foster-child, not to say its offspring, and it is only a question of time before it shall wholly possess them. It is only a question of time before all the comfortable quarters of the city, northward from the old town to the Park, shall be invaded, and the people driven to the streets building up on the west and east of it for a little longer sojourn. Where their last stay shall be, heaven knows; perhaps they will be forced into the country; or before that happens they may be rescued from themselves by the advance of Altrurianization.

In this sort of invasion, however, it is poverty that seems mostly to come first, and it is business that follows and holds the conquest, though this is far from being always the case. Whether it is so or not, however, poverty is certain at some time to impart its taint; for it is perpetual here, from generation to generation, like death itself. In the plutocratic conditions, poverty is incurable; the very hope of cure is laughed to scorn by those who cling the closest to these conditions; it may be better at one time, and worse at another; but it must always be, somehow, till time shall be no more. It is from everlasting to everlasting, they say, with an unconscious blasphemy of the ever-enduring Good, and, unless the conditions change, I must confess that they have reason for their faith in evil.

When I come home from these walks of mine, heart-sick, as I usually do, I have a vision of the wretched quarters through which I have passed, as blotches of disease upon the civic body, as loathsome sores, destined to eat deeper and deeper into it; and I am haunted by this sense of them, until I plunge deep into the Park, and wash my consciousness clean of it all for a while. But when I am actually in these leprous spots, I become hardened, for the moment, to the deeply underlying fact of human discomfort. I feel their picturesqueness, with a devilish indifference to that ruin, or that defect, which must so largely constitute the charm of the picturesque. A street of tenement-houses is always more picturesque than a street of brownstone residences, which the same thoroughfare usually is before it slopes to either river. The fronts of the edifices are decorated with the iron balconies and ladders of the fire-escapes, and have in the perspective a false air of gayety, which is travestied in their rear by the lines thickly woven from the windows to the tall poles set between the backs of the houses, and fluttering with drying clothes as with banners.

The sidewalks swarm with children, and the air rings with their clamor, as they fly back and forth at play; on the thresholds, the mothers sit nursing their babes, and the old women gossip together; young girls lean from the casements, alow and aloft, or flirt from the doorways with the hucksters who leave their carts in the street, while they come forward with some bargain in fruit or vegetables, and then resume their leisurely progress and their jarring cries. The place has all the attraction of close neighborhood, which the poor love, and which affords them for nothing the spectacle of the human drama, with themselves for actors. In a picture it would be most pleasingly effective, for then you could be in it, and yet have the distance on it which it needs. But to be in it, and not have the distance, is to inhale the stenches of the neglected street, and to catch that yet fouler and dreadfuller poverty-smell which breathes from the open doorways. It is to see the children quarrelling in their games, and beating each other in the face, and rolling each other in the gutter, like the little savage outlaws they are. It is to see the work-worn look of the mothers, the squalor of the babes, the haggish ugliness of the old women, the slovenly frowziness of the young girls. All this makes you hasten your pace down to the river, where the tall buildings break and dwindle into stables and shanties of wood, and finally end in the piers, commanding the whole stretch of the mighty waterway with its shipping, and the wooded heights of its western bank.

I am supposing you to have walked down a street of tenement-houses to the North river, as the New Yorkers call the Hudson; and I wish I could give you some notion of the beauty and majesty of the stream. You must turn to the photographs I send you for that beauty and majesty, and for some sense of the mean and ignoble effect of the city's invasion of the hither shore. The ugliness is, indeed, only worse in degree, but not in kind, than that of all city waterfronts in plutocratic countries. Instead of pleasant homes, with green lawns and orchards sloping to the brink, as we have them in Altruria, they have here the inexorable self-assertion of business, which is first in the people's thoughts, and must necessarily be given the first place in their cities. Huge factories and foundries, lumber yards, breweries, slaughterhouses and warehouses, abruptly interspersed with stables and hovels, and drinking saloons, disfigure the shore, and in the nearest avenue, the freight trains come and go on lines of railroads, in all this middle portion of New York. South of it, in the business section, the poverty section, the river region is a mere chaos of industrial and commercial strife and pauper wretchedness. North of it there are gardened driveways following the shore; and even at many points between, when you finally reach the river, there is a kind of peace, or at least a truce to the frantic activities of business. To be sure, the heavy trucks grind up and down the long piers, but on either side the docks are full of leisurely canal-boats, and if you could come with me in the late afternoon, you would see the smoke curling upward from their cabin roofs, as from the chimneys of so many rustic cottages, and smell the evening meal cooking within, while the canal-wives lounged at the gangway hatches for a breath of the sunset air, and the boatmen smoked on the gunwales or indolently plied the long sweeps of their pumps. All the hurry and turmoil of the city is lost among these people, whose clumsy craft recall the grassy inland levels remote from the metropolis, and the slow movement of life in the quiet country ways. Some of the mothers from the tenement-houses stroll down on the piers with their babies in their arms, and watch their men-kind, of all ages, fishing along the sides of the dock, or casting their lines far out into the current at the end. They do not seem to catch many fish, and never large ones, but they silently enjoy the sport, which they probably find leisure for in the general want of work in these hard times; if they swear a little at their luck, now and then, it is, perhaps, no more than their luck deserves. Some do not even fish, but sit with their legs dangling over the water, and watch the swift tugs, or the lagging sloops that pass, with now and then a larger sail, or a towering passenger steamboat. Far down the stream they can see the forests of masts, fringing either shore, and following the point of the island round and up into the great channel called the East river. These ships seemed as multitudinous as the houses that spread everywhere from them over the shore further than the eye can reach. They bring the commerce of the world to this mighty city, which, with all its riches, is the parent of such misery, and with all its traffic abounds in idle men who cannot find work. The ships look happy and free, in the stream, but they are of the plutocratic world, too, as well the houses; and let them spread their wings ever so widely, they still bear with them the slavery of the poor, as we know too well from the sorrowful tales of the castaways on our coast.

You must lose the thought of what is below the surface everywhere and in everything in America, if you would possess your soul from the pain perpetually threatening it; and I am afraid, my dear Cyril, that if you could be suddenly transported to my side, and behold what underlies all life here, with your fresh Altrurian eyes, you would not be more shocked at the sight than at me, who, knowing it all, can ever have a moment's peace in my knowledge. But I do have many moments' peace, through the mere exhaustion of consciousness, and I must own with whatever shame you would have me feel, that sometimes I have moments of pleasure. The other evening I walked over to the East river through one of those tenement streets, and I reached the waterside just as the soft night was beginning to fall in all its autumnal beauty. The afterglow died from the river, while I hung upon a parapet over a gulf ravened out of the bank for a street, and experienced that artistic delight which cultivated people are often proud of feeling here, in the aspect of the long prison island which breaks the expanse of the channel. I knew the buildings on it were prisons, and that the men and women in them, bad before, could only come out of them worse than before, and doomed to a life of outlawry and of crime. I was aware that they were each an image of that loveless and hopeless perdition which the cruelty of men imagines God has prepared for the souls of the damned, but I could not see the barred windows of those hells in the waning light. I could only see the trees along their walks; their dim lawns and gardens, and the castellated

forms of the prisons; and the esthetic sense, which in these unhappy lands is careful to keep itself pure from pity, was tickled
with an agreeable impression of something old and fair. The dusk
thickened, and the vast steamboats which ply between the city
and the New England ports on Long Island Sound, and daily
convey whole populations of passengers between New York and
Boston, began to sweep by silently, swiftly, luminous masses on
the black water. Their lights aloft at bow and stern, floated with
them like lambent planets; the lights of lesser craft dipped by,
and came and went in the distance; the lamps of the nearer and
farther shores twinkled into sight, and a peace that ignored all
the sorrow of it, fell upon the scene.

It was such peace as can alone come to you in a life like this. If
you would have any rest you must ignore a thousand facts,
which, if you recognize them, turn and rend you, and instil their
poison into your lacerated soul. In your pleasures you must forget
the deprivation which your indulgence implies; if you feast, you
must shut out the thought of them that famish; when you lie down
in your bed, you cannot sleep if you remember the houseless who
have nowhere to lay their heads. You are everywhere belea-
guered by the armies of want and woe, and in the still watches
of the night you can hear their invisible sentinels calling to one
another, "All is ill! All is ill!" and hushing their hosts to the
apathy of despair.

Yes, if you would have any comfort of your life here, you must
have it in disregard of your fellowmen, your kindred, your
brothers, made like yourself and fashioned to the same enjoy-
ments and sufferings, whose hard lot forbids them comfort. This
is a fact, however, which the civilization of all plutocratic countries is resolute to deny, and the fortunate children of that
civilization try to live in a fiction of the demerit of the unfortunate: they feign that these are more indolent or vicious than
themselves, and so are, somehow, condemned by the judgments
of God to their abasement and destitution. But at the bottom of
their hearts they know that this pretense is false, and that it is a
mere chance they are not themselves of the unfortunate. They

must shut their minds to this knowledge as they must shut them to the thought of all the misery which their prosperity is based on, or, as I say, they can have no peace.

You can reason to the effect upon character among them, among the best of them. It is a consequence which you would find unspeakably shocking, yet which, if you personally knew their conditions, you would be lenient to, for you would perceive that, while the conditions endure, there is no help, no hope for them. The wonder is that, in such circumstances as theirs, they ever permit their sympathies the range that these sometimes take, only to return upon them in an anguish of impotency. None but the short-sighted and thoughtless in a plutocracy can lastingly satisfy themselves even with a constant giving, for the thoughtful know that charity corrupts and debases, and that finally it is no remedy. So these take refuge from themselves in a wilful ignorance, sometimes lasting, sometimes transient, of the things in their life that disturb and displease them. It is the only thing to do here, my dear Cyril, and I will not deny that I have come to do it, like the rest. Since I cannot relieve the wrong I see, I have learned often to shut my eyes to it, with the effect, which most Americans experience, that, since there seems to be no way of righting the wrong, the wrong must be a sort of right. Yes, this infernal juggle of the mind operates itself in me, too, at times, so that I doubt the reality of my whole happy life in the past, I doubt Altruria, I doubt you.

I beseech you, therefore, to write me as often as you can, and as fully and vividly. Tell me of our country, remind me of the state where men dwell together as brothers; use every device to make it living and real to me; for here I often lose the memory and the sense of it, and at all times I have a weakened sense of the justice and mercy that I once thought ruled this world, but which the Americans think rules only the world to come.

A. Homos.

V

PLUTOCRATIC CONTRASTS AND CONTRADICTIONS

New York, November 15, 1893.

MY DEAR CYRIL:

In my last I tried to give you some notion of the form and structure of this strange city, but I am afraid that I did it very vaguely and insufficiently. I do not suppose that I could ever do it fully, and perhaps the attempt was foolish. But I hope that I may, without greater folly, at least offer to share with you the feeling I have concerning American life, and most of all concerning New York life, that it is forever on the way, and never arrives. This is the effect that I constantly receive in the streets here and especially in the avenues, which are fitly named so far as avenue means approach merely. They are roadways which people get back and forth by, in their haste from nowhere to nowhere, as it would seem to us. Of course they do physically reach their places of business downtown in the morning, and their places of eating and sleeping uptown in the evening; but morally they are forever in transition. Whether they are bent upon business, or bent upon pleasure, the Americans, or certainly the New Yorkers, perpetually postpone the good of life, as we know it in Altruria, and as it is known in some tranquiller countries even of the plutocratic world. They make money, but they do not have money, for there is no such thing as the sensible possession of money, and hardly of the things that money can buy. They seek enjoyment and they find excitement, for joy is the blessing of God, and like every good gift comes unsought, and

248

flies pursuit. They know this, as well as we do, and in certain moments of dejection, in the hours of pain, in the days of sorrow, they realize it, but at other times they ignore it. If they did not ignore it they could not live, they say, and they appear to think that by ignoring it they do live, though to me there is nothing truly vital in their existence.

The greatest problem of their metropolis is not how best to be in this place or that, but how fastest to go from one to the other, and they have made guesses at the riddle, bad and worse, on each of the avenues, which, in their character of mere roadways, look as if the different car-tracks had been in them first, and the buildings, high and low, had chanced along their sides afterwards. This is not the fact, of course, and it is not so much the effect on Fifth avenue, and Madison avenue, and Lexington avenue, which are streets of dwellings, solidly built up, like the cross streets. But it is undoubtedly the effect on all the other avenues, in great part of their extent. They vary but little in appearance otherwise, from east to west, except so far as the elevated railroads disfigure them, if thoroughfares so shabby and repulsive as they mostly are, can be said to be disfigured, and not beautified by whatever can be done to hide any part of their ugliness. Where this is left to make its full impression upon the spectator, there are lines of horse-cars perpetually jingling up and down except on Fifth avenue, where they have stages, as the New Yorkers call the unwieldly and unsightly vehicles that ply there, and on Second avenue, where they have electric cars, something like our own, in principle. But the horse-cars run even under the elevated tracks, and you have absolutely no experience of noise in the Altrurian life which can enable you to conceive of the hellish din that bursts upon the sense, when at some corner two cars encounter on the parallel tracks below, while two trains roar and shriek and hiss on the rails overhead, and a turmoil of rattling express wagons, heavy drays and trucks, and carts, hacks, carriages and huge vans rolls itself between and beneath the prime agents of the uproar. The noise is not only deafening, it is bewildering; you cannot know which side the danger threatens

most, and you literally take your life in your hand when you cross
in the midst of it. Broadway, which traverses the district I am
thinking of, in a diagonal line till it loses its distinctive character
beyond the Park, is the course of the cable cars. These are pro-
pelled by an endless chain running underneath the pavement
with a silent speed that is more dangerous even than the tumul-
tuous rush on the avenues. Now and then the apparatus for grip-
ping the chain will not release it, and then the car rushes wildly
over the track, running amuck through everything in its way,
and spreading terror on every hand. When under control the
long saloons advance swiftly, from either direction, at intervals
of half a minute, with a monotonous alarum of their gongs, and
the foot passenger has to look well to his way if he ventures across
the track, lest in avoiding one car another roll him under its
wheels.

Apparently, the danger is guarded as well as it can be, and it
has simply to be taken into the account of life in New York, for it
cannot be abated, and no one is to be blamed for what is the fault
of everyone. It is true that there ought not, perhaps, to be any
track in such a thoroughfare, but it would be hard to prove that
people could get on without it, as they did before the theft of the
street for the original horse-car track. Perhaps it was not a theft;
but at all events, and at the best, the street was given away by the
city to an adventurer who wished to lay the tracks in it for his
private gain, and none of the property owners along the line
could help themselves. There is nothing that the Americans hold
so dear, you know, or count so sacred, as private property; life
and limb are cheap in comparison; but private enterprise is
allowed to violate the rights of private property, from time to
time here, in the most dramatic way.

I do not speak, now, of the railroad companies, which have
gridironed the country, in its whole length and breadth, and
which are empowered by their franchises to destroy the homes of
the living and desecrate the graves of the dead, in running their
lines from point to point. These companies do pay something, as
little as they may, or as much as they must; but the street-car

company which took possession of Broadway never paid the abuttors anything, I believe; and the elevated railroad companies are still resisting payment of damages on the four avenues which they occupied for their way up and down the city without offering compensation to the property owners along their route. If the community had built these roads, it would have indemnified everyone, for the community is always just when it is the expression of the common honesty here; and if it is ever unjust, it is because the uncommon dishonesty has contrived to corrupt it.

Yet the Americans trust themselves so little in their civic embodiment that the movement for the public ownership of the railroads makes head slowly against an inconceivable prejudice. Last winter, when the problem of rapid transit pressed sorely upon the New Yorkers, the commission in charge could find no way to solve it but by offering an extension of franchise to the corporation which has already the monopoly of it. There was no question of the city's building the roads, and working them at cost; and if there had been, there would have been no question of submitting the project to those whose interests are involved. They have no such thing here as the referendum, and the Americans who are supposed to make their own laws, merely elect their representatives, and have no voice themselves in approving or condemning legislation.

The elevated roads and the cable road had no right to be, on the terms that the New Yorkers have them, but they are by far the best means of transit in the city, and I must say that if they were not abuses, they would offer great comfort and great facility to the public. This is especially true of the elevated roads, which, when you can put their moral offense out of your mind, are always delightful in their ease and airy swiftness. The tracks are lifted upon iron piers, from twenty to fifty feet above the street, according to the inequality of the surface, and you fly smoothly along between the second and third story windows of the houses, which are shops below and dwellings above, on the avenues. The stations, though they have the prevailing effect of over-use, and look dirty and unkempt, are rather pretty in themselves; and you reach them, at frequent intervals, by flights of not ungraceful iron steps. The elevated roads are always picturesque, with here and there a sweeping curve that might almost be called beautiful.

They darken the avenues, of course, and fill them with an abominable uproar. Yet traffic goes underneath, and life goes on alongside and overhead, and the city has adjusted itself to them, as a man adjusts himself to a chronic disease. I do not know whether they add to the foulness of the streets they pass through or not; I hardly think they do. The mud lies longer, after a rain, in the interminable tunnels which they form over the horse-car tracks in the middle of the avenues, and which you can look through for miles; but the mud does not blow into your nose and mouth as the dust does, and that is, so far, a positive advantage. A negative advantage, which I have hinted, is that they hide so much of the street from sight, and keep you from seeing all its foulness and shabbiness, pitilessly open to the eye in the avenues which have only horse-car tracks in them. In fact, now that the elevated railroads are built, and the wrong they have done to persons is mainly past recall, perhaps the worst that can be said of them is that they do not serve their purpose. Of course, in plutocratic conditions, where ten men are always doing the work of one man in rivalry with each other, the passage of people to and from business is enormous: the passage of men to get money, and the passage of women to spend it; and at the hours of the morning and the afternoon when the volume of travel is the greatest, the trains of the elevated roads offer a spectacle that is really incredible.

Every seat in them is taken, and every foot of space in the aisle between the seats is held by people standing, and swaying miserably to and fro by the leather straps dangling from the roofs. Men and women are indecently crushed together, without regard for that personal dignity which we prize, but which the Americans seem to know nothing of and care nothing for. The multitude overflows from the car, at either end, and the passengers are as tightly wedged on the platforms without as they are within. The long trains follow each other at intervals of two or three minutes, and at each station they make a stop of but a few seconds, when those who wish to alight fight their way through the struggling mass. Those who wish to mount fight their way into the car or onto the platform, where the guard slams an iron gate against the stomachs and in the faces of those arriving too late. Sometimes horrible accidents happen; a man clinging to the outside of the gate has the life crushed out of his body against the posts of the station as the train pulls out. But in this land, where people have such a dread of civic collectivism of any kind, lest individuality should suffer, the individual is practically nothing in the regard of the corporate collectivities which abound.

It is not only the corporations which outrage personal rights, in America; where there is a question of interest, there seems to be no question of rights between individuals. They prey upon one another and seize advantages by force and by fraud in too many ways for me to hope to make the whole situation evident to you, but I may at least give you some notion of the wrong they do. The avenues to the eastward and westward have not grown up solidly and continuously in obedience to any law of order, or in pursuance of any meditated design. They have been pushed along given lines, in fragments, as builders saw their interest in offering buyers a house or a row of houses, or as they could glut or trick the greed of land-owners clinging to their land, and counting upon some need of it, in the hope of extorting an unearned profit from it. In one place you will see a vast and lofty edifice, of brick or stone, and on each side of it or in front of it, a structure one-fourth as high, or a row of scurvy hovels, left there till a purchaser comes, not to pay the honest worth of the land for it, but to yield the price the owner wants. In other places you see long stretches of high board fence, shutting in vacant lots, usually the best lots on the street, which the landlord holds for the rise destined to accrue to him from the building all round and beyond his property. In the meantime he pays a low tax on his land compared with the tax which the improved property pays, and gets some meager return for the use of his fence by the Italian fruiterers who build their stalls into it, and by the bill-posters who cover it with a medley of theatrical announcements, picturing the scenes of the different plays and the persons of the players. To the Altrurian public the selfishness of a man willing idly to benefit by the industry and energy of others in giving value to his possessions would be unimaginable. Yet this is so common here that it is accepted and honored as a proof of business sagacity; and the man who knows how to hold onto his land, until the very moment when it can enrich him most, though he has neither plowed nor sown it, or laid the foundation of a human dwelling upon it, is honored as a longheaded and solid citizen, who deserves well of his neighbors. There are many things which unite to render the avenues unseemly and unsightly, such as the apparently desperate tastelessness and the apparently instinctive uncleanliness of the New Yorkers. But as I stand at some point commanding a long stretch of one of their tiresome perspectives, which is architecturally like nothing so much as a horse's jawbone, with the teeth broken or dislodged at intervals, I can blame nothing so much for the hideous effect as the rapacity of the land-owner holding on for a rise, as it is called. It is he who breaks the sky-line, and keeps the street, mean and poor at the best in design, a defeated purpose, and a chaos come again.

Even when the owners begin to build, to improve their real estate, as the phrase is, it is without regard to the rights of their neighbors, or the feelings or tastes of the public, so far as the public may be supposed to have any. This is not true of the shabbier avenues alone, but of the finest, and of all the streets. If you will look, for instance, at the enclosed photograph of the street facing the southern limit of the Park, you will get some notion of what I mean, and I hope you will be willing to suffer by a little study of it. At the western end you will see a vacant lot, with its high board fence covered with painted signs, then a tall mass of apartment houses; then a stretch of ordinary New York dwellings of the old commonplace brownstone sort; then a stable, and a wooden liquor saloon at the corner. Across the next avenue there rises far aloof the compact bulk of a series of apartment houses, which in color and design are the pleasantest in the city, and are so far worthy of their site. Beyond them to the eastward the buildings decline and fall, till they sink into another wooden drinking-shop on the corner of another avenue, where you will see the terminus of one of the elevated roads. Beyond this avenue is the fence of a large vacant lot, covered, as usual, with theatrical posters, and then there surges skyward another series of apartment houses. The highest of these is nearly fifty feet higher than its nearest neighbors, which sink again, till you suddenly drop from their nondescript monotony to the gothic façade of a house of a wholly different color, in its pale sandstone, from the red of their brick fronts.

A vacant lot yawns here again, with a flare of theatrical posters on its fence, and beyond this, on the corner, is a huge hotel, the most agreeable of the three that tower above the fine square at the gate of the Park. With that silly American weakness for something foreign, this square is called the Plaza; I believe that it is not at all like a Spanish plaza, but the name is its least offense. An irregular space in the center is planted with trees, in whose shade the broken-kneed hacks of the public carriages droop their unhappy heads, without the spirit to bite the flies that trouble their dreams; and below this you get a glimpse of the conventional cross-street terminating the Plaza. At the eastern corner of the avenue is a vacant lot, with pictorial advertisements painted on its fence, and then you come to the second of the great hotels which give the Plaza such character as it has. It is of a light-colored stone, and it towers far above the first, which is of brick. It is thirteen stories high, and it stops abruptly in a flat roof. On the next corner north is another hotel, which rises six or seven stories higher yet, and terminates in a sort of mansard, topping a romanesque cliff of yellow brick and red sandstone. I seek a term for the architectural order, but it may not be the right one. There is no term for the civic disorder of what succeeds. From the summit of this enormous acclivity there is a precipitous fall of twelve stories to the roof of the next edifice, which is a grocery; and then to the florist's and photographer's next is another descent of three stories; on the corner is a drinking-saloon, one story in height, with a brick front and a wooden side. I will not ask you to go farther with me; the avenue continues northward and southward in a delirium of lines and colors, a savage anarchy of shapes, which I should think the general experience of the beauty of the Fair City at Chicago would now render perceptible even to the dull American sense. What exists is the necessary and inexorable effect of that uncivic individuality which the Americans prize, and which can manifest itself only in harm and wrong; but if you criticised it you would surprise and alarm them almost as much as if you attacked the atrocious economic inequality it springs from.

There are other points on Fifth avenue nearly as bad as this, but not quite, and there are long stretches of it, which, if dull, have at least a handsome uniformity. I have told you already that it is still upon the whole, the best of the avenues, in the sense of being the abode of the best, that is the richest people; the Americans habitually use best in this sense. Madison avenue stretches northwest farther than the eye can reach, an interminable perspective of brownstone dwellings, as yet little invaded by business. Lexington avenue is of the same character, but of a humbler sort. On Second avenue, down town, there are large old mansions of the time when Fifth avenue was still the home of the parvenus; and at different points on such other avenues as are spared by the elevated roads, there are blocks of decent and comfortable dwellings; but for the most part they are wholly given up to shops. Of course, these reiterate with the insane wastefulness of the competitive system the same business, the same enterprise, a thousand times. The Americans have no conception of our distribution; and though nearly everything they now use is made in large establishments, their wares are dispersed and sold in an infinitude of small stores.

One hears a good deal about the vast emporiums which are gathering the retail trade into themselves, and devastating the minor commerce, but there are perhaps a score of these at most, in New York; and on the shabbier avenues and cross-streets there are at least a hundred miles of little shops, where an immense population of little dealers levy tribute on the public through the profit they live by. Until you actually see this, you can hardly conceive of such a multitude of people taken away from the labor due to all from all, and solely devoted to marketing the things made by people who are overworked in making them. But bad as this is, and immoral as it is in Altrurian eyes, it is really harmless beside a traffic which is the most conspicuous on these avenues; I mean the traffic in intoxicating liquors, sold and drunk on the premises. I need not tell you that I still hold our national principles concerning the use of alcohol, but I have learned here to be lenient to its use, in a measure which you would not perhaps excuse. I perceive that as long as there is poverty there must be drunkenness, until the State interferes and sells a man only so much as he can safely drink. Yet, knowing as I do from the daily witness of the press and the courts, that drink is the source of most of the crimes and vices which curse this people, I find the private traffic in alcohol infinitely shocking, and the spectacle of it incredible. There is scarcely a block on any of the poorer avenues which has not its liquor store, and generally there are two; wherever a street crosses them there is a saloon on at least one of the corners; sometimes on two, sometimes on three, sometimes even on all four. I had one day the curiosity to count the saloons on Sixth avenue, between the Park, and the point down town where the avenue properly ends. In a stretch of some two miles I counted ninety of them, besides the eating houses where you can buy drink with your meat; and this avenue is probably far less infested with the traffic than some others.

You may therefore safely suppose that out of the hundred miles of shops, there are ten, or fifteen, or twenty miles of saloons. They have the best places on the avenues, and on the whole they make the handsomest show. They all have a cheerful and inviting look, and if you step within, you find them cosy, quiet, and for New York, clean. There are commonly tables set about in them, where their frequenters can take their beer or whisky at their ease, and eat the free lunch which is often given in them; in a rear room you see a billiard table. In fact, they form the poor man's clubhouses and if he might resort to them with his family, and be in the control of the State as to the amount he should spend and drink there, I could not think them without their rightful place in an economy which saps the vital forces of the laborer with overwork, or keeps him in a fever of hope or a fever of despair, as to the chances of getting or not getting work when he has lost it. We at home, have so long passed the sad necessity to which such places minister, that we sometimes forget it, but you know how in our old competitive days, this traffic was one of the first to be taken out of private hands, and assumed by the State, which continued to manage it without a profit so long as the twin crazes of competition and drunkenness endured among us. If you suggested this to the average American, however, he would be horror-struck. He would tell you that what you proposed was little better than anarchy; that in a free country you must always leave private persons free to debauch men's souls and bodies with drink, and make money out of their ruin; that anything else was contrary to human nature, and an invasion of the sacred rights of the individual. Here in New York, this valuable principle is so scrupulously respected, that the saloon controls the municipality, and the New Yorkers think this is much better than for the municipality to control the saloon. It is from the saloon that their political bosses rise to power; it is in the saloon that all the election frauds are planned and fostered; and it would be infinitely comic, if it were not so pathetic, to read the solemn homilies on these abuses in the journals which hold by the good old American doctrine of private trade in drink as one of the bulwarks of their constitution, and a chief defense against the advance of Altrurian ideas.

Without it, there would be far less poverty than there is, but poverty is a good old American institution, too; there would inevitably be less inequality, but inequality is as dear to the American heart as liberty itself. In New York the inequality has that effect upon the architecture which I have tried to give you some notion of; but in fact it deforms life here at every turn, and in nothing more than in the dress of the people, high and low. New

York is, on the whole, without doubt, the best dressed community in America, or at least there is a certain number of people here, more expensively and scrupulously attired than you will find anywhere else in the country. I do not say beautifully, for their dress is of the fashion which you have seen in our Regionic museum, where we used to laugh over it together when we fancied people in it, and is a modification of the fashions that prevail everywhere in plutocratic Christendom. The rich copy the fashion set for them in Paris or in London, and then the less rich, and the still less rich, down to the poor, follow them as they can, until you arrive at the very poorest, who wear the cast-off and tattered fashions of former years, and masquerade in a burlesque of the fortunate that never fails to shock and grieve me. They must all somehow be clothed; the climate and the custom require it; but sometimes I think their nakedness would be less offensive; and when I meet a wretched man, with his coat out at elbows, or split up the back, in broken shoes, battered hat, and frayed trousers, or some old woman or young girl in a worn-out, second-hand gown and bonnet, tattered and threadbare and foul, I think that if I were an American, as I am an Altrurian, I would uncover my head to them, and ask their forgiveness for the system that condemns some one always to such humiliation as theirs.

The Americans say such people are not humiliated, that they do not mind it, that they are used to it; but if they ever look these people in the eye, and see the shrinking, averted glance of their shame and tortured pride, they must know that what they say is a cruel lie. At any rate, the presence of these outcasts must spoil the beauty of any dress near them, and there is always so much more penury than affluence that the sight of the crowd in the New York streets must give more pain than pleasure. The other day on Fifth avenue, it did not console me to meet a young and lovely girl, exquisitely dressed in the last effect of Paris, after I had just parted from a young fellow who had begged me to give him a little money to get something to eat, for he had been looking for work a week and had got nothing. I suppose I ought to have doubted his word, he was so decently clad, but I had a present vision of him in rags, and I gave to the frowzy tramp he must soon become.

Of course, this social contrast was extreme, like some of those architectural contrasts I have been noting, but it was by no means exceptional, as those were not. In fact, I do not know but I may say that it was characteristic of the place, though you might say that the prevalent American slovenliness was also characteristic of the New York street crowds; I mean the slovenliness of the men; the women, of whatever order they are, are always as much dandies as they can be. But most American men are too busy to look much after their dress, and when they are very well to do they care very little for it. You see few men dressed with the distinction of the better class of Londoners, and when you do meet them, they have the air of playing a part, as in fact they are: they are playing the part of men of leisure in a nation of men whose reality is constant work, whether they work for bread or whether they work for money, and who, when they are at work, outdo the world, but sink, when they are at leisure, into something third rate and fourth rate. The commonness of effect in the street crowds, is not absent from Fifth avenue or from Madison avenue any more than it is from First avenue or Tenth avenue; and the tide of wealth and fashion that rolls up and down the better avenues in the splendid carriages, makes the shabbiness of the foot-passenger, when he is shabby, as he often is, the more apparent. On the far east side, and on the far west side, the horse-cars, which form the only means of transit, have got the dirt and grime of the streets and the dwellings on them and in them, and there is one tone of foulness in the passengers and the vehicles. I do not wish to speak other than tenderly of the poor but it is useless to pretend that they are other than offensive in aspect, and I have to take my sympathy in both hands when I try to bestow it upon them. Neither they nor the quarter they live in has any palliating quaintness; and the soul, starved of beauty, will seek in vain to feed itself with the husks of picturesqueness in their aspect.

As I have said before, the shabby avenues have a picturesqueness of their own, but it is a repulsive picturesqueness, as I have already suggested, except at a distance. There are some differences of level, on the avenues near the rivers, that give them an advantage of the more central avenues, and there is now and then a break of their line by the water, which is always good. I noticed this particularly on the eastern side of the city, which is also the older part, and which has been less subject to the changes perpetually going on elsewhere, so that First avenue has really a finer sky-line, in many parts, than most parts of Fifth avenue. There are certain bits, as the artists say, in the old quarters of the town once forming Greenwich village, which, when I think of them, make me almost wish to take back what I have said of the absence even of quaintness in New York. If I recall the aspect of Mulberry Bend and Elizabeth street, on a mild afternoon, when their Italian denizens are all either on the pavement or have their heads poked out of the windows, I am still more in doubt of my own words. But I am sure, at least, that there is no kindliness in the quaintness, such as you are said to find in European cities. It has undergone the same sort of malign change here that has transformed the Italians from the friendly folk we are told they are at home, to the surly race, and even savage race they mostly show themselves here: shrewd for their advancement in the material things, which seem the only good things to the Americanized aliens of all races, and fierce for their full share of the political pottage. The Italians have a whole region of the city to themselves, and they might feel at home in it if something more than the filth of their native environment could repatriate them.

As you pass through these streets, there is much to appeal to your pity in the squalid aspect of the people and the place, but nothing to take your fancy; and perhaps this is best, for I think that there is nothing more infernal than the juggle that transmutes for the tenderest hearted people here the misery of their fellows into something comic or poetic. Only very rarely have I got any relief from the sheer distress which the prevalent poverty gives; and perhaps you will not be able to understand how I could find this in the sight of some chickens going to roost on a row of carts drawn up by the street side, near a little hovel where some old people lived in a temporary respite from the building about them; or from a cottage in outlying suburban fields, with a tar-roofed shanty for a stable, and an old horse cropping the pasturage of the enclosure, with a brood of turkeys at his heels.

But in New York you come to be glad of anything that will suggest a sweeter and a gentler life than that which you mostly see. The life of the poor here seemed to me symbolized in a waste and ruined field that I came upon the other day in one of the westward avenues, which had imaginably once been the grounds about a pleasant home, or perhaps a public square. Till I saw this I did not think any piece of our mother earth could have been made to look so brutal and desolate amidst the habitations of men. But every spear of grass had been torn from it; the hardened and barren soil was furrowed and corrugated like a haggard face, and it was all strewn with clubs and stones, as if it had been a savage battleground. A few trees, that seemed beaten back, stood aloof from the borders next the streets, where some courses of an ancient stone wall rose in places above the pavement. I found the sight of it actually depraving; it made me feel ruffianly, and I mused upon it in helpless wonder as to the influence its ugliness must have had amidst the structural ugliness all about it, if some wretch had turned to it in hopes of respite.

But probably none ever does. Probably the people on the shabby streets and avenues are no more sensible of their hideousness than the people in the finer streets and avenues are aware of their dulness or their frantic disproportion. I have never heard a New Yorker speak of these things, and I have no doubt that if my words could come to the eyes of the average cultivated New Yorker he would be honestly surprised that any one should find his city so ugly as it is. Dirty he would cheerfully allow it to be, and he would be rather proud of telling you how much New York spent every year for not having herself cleaned; but that she was ludicrously and wilfully ugly he could not believe. As for that first lesson of civilization which my words implicate, a civic control of the private architecture of the place, he would shrink from it with about as much horror as from civic control of the liquor trade. If he did not, he would still be unable to understand how the individual liberty that suffers a man to build offensively to his neighbor or to the public at large, is not liberty, but is a barbarous tyranny, which puts an end instantly to beauty, and extinguishes the common and the personal rights of every one who lives near the offender or passes by his edifice. The Americans are yet so far lost in the dark ages as to suppose that there is freedom where the caprice of one citizen can interfere with the comfort or pleasure of the rest.

A. Homos.

THROUGH THE EYE OF THE NEEDLE

INTRODUCTION

Aristides Homos, an Emissary of the Altrurian Common-wealth, visited the United States during the summer of 1893 and the fall and winter following. For some weeks or months he was the guest of a well-known man of letters at a hotel in one of our mountain resorts; in the early autumn he spent several days at the great Columbian Exhibition in Chicago; and later he came to New York, where he remained until he sailed, rather suddenly, for Altruria, taking the circuitous route by which he came. He seems to have written pretty constantly throughout his sojourn with us to an intimate friend in his own country, giving freely his impressions of our civilization. His letters from New York appear to have been especially full, and, in offering the present synopsis of these to the American reader, it will not be impertinent to note certain peculiarities of the Altrurian attitude which the temperament of the writer has somewhat modified. He is entangled in his social sophistries regarding all the competitive civilizations; he cannot apparently do full justice to the superior heroism of charity and self-sacrifice as practised in countries where people live *upon* each other as the Americans do, instead of *for* each other as the Altrurians do; but he has some glimmerings of the beauty of our living, and he has undoubtedly the wish to be fair to our ideals. He is unable to value our devotion to the spirit of Christianity amid the practices which seem to deny it; but he evidently wishes to recognize the possibility of such a thing. He at least accords us the virtues of our defects, and, among the many visitors who have censured us, he has not seen us with his censures prepared to fit the instances; in fact, the very reverse has been his method.

Many of the instances which he fits with his censures are such as he could no longer note, if he came among us again. That habit of celebrating the munificence of the charitable rich, on which he spends his sarcasm, has fallen from us through the mere superabundance of occasion. Our rich people give so continuously for all manner of good objects that it would be impossible for our press, however vigilant, to note the successive benefactions, and millions are now daily bestowed upon needy educational institutions, of which no mention whatever is made in the newspapers. If a millionaire is now and then surprised in a good action by a reporter of uncommon diligence, he is able by an appeal to their common humanity to prevail with the witness to spare him the revolting publicity which it must be confessed would once have followed his discovery; the right hand which is full to overflowing is now as skilled as the empty right hand in keeping the left hand ignorant of its doings. This has happened through the general decay of snobbishness among us, perhaps. It is certain that there is no longer the passion for a knowledge of the rich and the smart, which made us ridiculous to Mr. Homos. Ten or twelve years ago, our newspapers abounded in intelligence of the coming and going of social leaders, of their dinners and lunches and teas, of their receptions and balls, and the guests who were bidden to them. But this sort of unwholesome and exciting gossip, which was formerly devoured by their readers with inappeasable voracity, is no longer supplied, simply because the taste for it has wholly passed away.

Much the same might be said of the social hospitalities which raised our visitor's surprise. For example, many people are now asked to dinner who really need a dinner, and not merely those who revolt from the notion of dinner with loathing, and go to it with abhorrence. At the tables of our highest social leaders one now meets on a perfect equality persons of interesting minds and uncommon gifts who would once have been excluded because they were hungry, or were not in the hostess's set, or had not a new gown or a dress-suit. This contributes greatly to the pleasure of the time, and promotes the increasing kindliness between the rich and poor for which our status is above all things notable.

The accusation which our critic brings that the American spirit has been almost Europeanized away, in its social forms, would be less grounded in the observance of a later visitor. The customs of good society must be the same everywhere in some measure, but the student of the competitive world would now find European hospitality Americanized, rather than American hospitality Europeanized. The careful research which has been made into our social origins has resulted in bringing back many of the aboriginal usages; and, with the return of the old American spirit of fraternity, many of the earlier dishes as well as amenities have been restored. A Thanksgiving dinner in the year 1906 would have been found more like a Thanksgiving dinner in 1806 than the dinner to which Mr. Homos was asked in 1893, and which he has studied so interestingly, though not quite without some faults of taste and discretion. The prodigious change for the better in some material aspects of our status which has taken place in the last twelve years could nowhere be so well noted as in the picture he gives us of the housing of our people in 1893. His study of the evolution of the apartment-house from the old flat-house, and the still older single dwelling, is very curious, and, upon the whole, not incorrect. But neither of these last differed so much from the first as the apartment-house now differs from the apartment-house of his day. There are now no dark rooms opening on airless pits for the family, or black closets and dismal basements for the servants. Every room has abundant light and perfect ventilation, and as nearly a southern exposure as possible. The appointments of the houses are no longer in the spirit of profuse and vulgar luxury which it must be allowed once characterized them. They are simply but tastefully finished, they are absolutely fireproof, and, with their less expensive decoration, the rents have been so far lowered that in any good position a quarter of nine or ten rooms, with as many baths, can be had for from three thousand to fifteen thousand dollars. This fact alone must attract to our metropolis the best of our population, the bone and sinew which have no longer any use for themselves where they have been expended in rearing colossal fortunes, and now demand a metropolitan repose.

The apartments are much better fitted for a family of generous size than those which Mr. Homos observed. Children, who were once almost unheard of, and quite unheard, in apartment-houses, increasingly abound under favor of the gospel of race preservation. The elevators are full of them, and in the grassy courts round which the houses are built, the little ones play all day long, or paddle in the fountains, warmed with steam-pipes in the winter, and cooled to an agreeable temperature in a summer which has almost lost its terrors for the stay-at-home New-Yorker. Each child has his or her little plot of ground in the roof-garden, where they are taught the once wellnigh forgotten art of agriculture.

The improvement of the tenement-house has gone hand in hand with that of the apartment-house. As nearly as the rate of interest on the landlord's investment will allow, the housing of the poor approaches in comfort that of the rich. Their children are still more numerous, and the playgrounds supplied them in every open space and on every pier are visited constantly by the better-to-do children, who exchange with them lessons of form and fashion for the scarcely less valuable instruction in practical life which the poorer little ones are able to give. The rents in the tenement-houses are reduced even more notably than those in the apartment-houses, so that now, with the constant increase in wages, the tenants are able to pay their rents promptly. The evictions once so common are very rare; it is doubtful whether a nightly or daily walk in the poorer quarters of the town would develop, in the coldest weather, half a dozen cases of families set out on the sidewalk with their household goods about them.

The Altrurian Emissary visited this country when it was on the verge of the period of great economic depression extending from 1894 to 1898, but, after the Spanish War, Providence marked the divine approval of our victory in that contest by renewing in unexampled measure the prosperity of the Republic. With the downfall of the trusts, and the release of our industrial and commercial forces to unrestricted activity, the condition of every form of labor has been immeasurably improved, and it is now united with capital in bonds of the closest affection. But in no phase has its fate been so brightened as in that of domestic service. This has occurred not merely through the rise of wages, but through a greater knowledge between the employing and employed. When, a few years since, it became practically impossible for mothers of families to get help from the intelligence-offices, and ladies were obliged through lack of cooks and chambermaids to do the work of the kitchen and the chamber and parlor, they learned to realize what such work was, how poorly paid, how badly lodged, how meanly fed. From this practical knowledge it was impossible for them to retreat to their old supremacy and indifference as mistresses. The servant problem was solved, once for all, by humanity, and it is doubtful whether, if Mr. Homos returned to us now, he would give offence by preaching the example of the Altrurian ladies, or would be shocked by the contempt and ignorance of American women where other women who did their household drudgery were concerned.

As women from having no help have learned how to use their helpers, certain other hardships have been the means of good. The flattened wheel of the trolley, banging the track day and night, and tormenting the waking and sleeping ear, was, oddly enough, the inspiration of reforms which have made our city the quietest in the world. The trolleys now pass unheard; the elevated train glides by overhead with only a modulated murmur; the subway is a retreat fit for meditation and prayer, where the passenger can possess his soul in a peace to be found nowhere else; the automobile, which was unknown in the day of the Altrurian Emissary, whirs softly through the most crowded thoroughfare, far below the speed limit, with a sigh of gentle satisfaction in its own harmlessness, and, "like the sweet South, taking and giving odor." The streets that he saw so filthy and unkempt in 1893 are now at least as clean as they are quiet. Asphalt has universally replaced the cobble-stones and Belgian blocks of his day, and, though it is everywhere full of holes, it is still asphalt, and may some time be put in repair.

There is a note of exaggeration in his characterization of our men which the reader must regret. They are not now the intellectual inferior of our women, or at least not so much the inferiors. Since his day they have made a vast advance in the knowledge and love of literature. With the multitude of our periodicals, and the swarm of our fictions selling from a hundred thousand to half a million each, even our business-men cannot wholly escape culture, and they have become more and more cultured, so that now you frequently hear them asking what this or that book is all about. With the mention of them, the reader will naturally recur to the work of their useful and devoted lives —the accumulation of money. It is this accumulation, this heaping-up of riches, which the Altrurian Emissary accuses in the love-story closing his study of our conditions, but which he might not now so totally condemn.

As we have intimated, he has more than once guarded against a rash conclusion, to which the logical habit of the Altrurian mind might have betrayed him. If he could revisit us we are sure that he would have still greater reason to congratulate himself on his forbearance, and would doubtless profit by the lesson which events must teach all but the most hopeless doctrinaires. The evil of even a small war (and soldiers themselves do not deny that wars, large or small, are evil) has, as we have noted, been overruled for good in the sort of Golden Age, or Age on a Gold Basis, which we have long been enjoying. If our good-fortune should be continued to us in reward of our public and private virtue, the fact would suggest to so candid an observer that in economics, as in other things, the rule proves the exception, and that as good times have hitherto always been succeeded by bad times, it stands to reason that our present period of prosperity will never be followed by a period of adversity.

It would seem from the story continued by another hand in

the second part of this work, that Altruria itself is not absolutely logical in its events, which are subject to some of the anomalies governing in our own affairs. A people living in conditions which some of our dreamers would consider ideal, are forced to discourage foreign emigration, against their rule of universal hospitality, and in at least one notable instance are obliged to protect themselves against what they believe an evil example by using compulsion with the wrong-doers, though the theory of their life is entirely opposed to anything of the kind. Perhaps, however, we are not to trust to this other hand at all times, since it is a woman's hand, and is not to be credited with the firm and unerring touch of a man's. The story, as she completes it, is the story of the Altrurian's love for an American woman, and will be primarily interesting for that reason. Like the Altrurian's narrative, it is here compiled from a succession of letters, which in her case were written to a friend in America, as his were written to a friend in Altruria. But it can by no means have the sociological value which the record of his observations among ourselves will have for the thoughtful reader. It is at best the record of desultory and imperfect glimpses of a civilization fundamentally alien to her own, such as would attract an enthusiastic nature, but would leave it finally in a sort of misgiving as to the reality of the things seen and heard. Some such misgiving attended the inquiries of those who met the Altrurian during his sojourn with us, but it is a pity that a more absolute conclusion should not have been the effect of this lively lady's knowledge of the ideal country of her adoption. It is, however, an interesting psychological result, and it continues the tradition of all the observers of ideal conditions from Sir Thomas More down to William Morris. Either we have no terms for conditions so unlike our own that they cannot be reported to us with absolute intelligence, or else there is in every experience of them an essential vagueness and uncertainty.

Part First

I

IF I SPOKE with Altrurian breadth of the way New Yorkers live, my dear Cyril, I should begin by saying that the New Yorkers did not live at all. But outside of our happy country, one learns to distinguish, and to allow that there are several degrees of living, all indeed hateful to us, if we knew them, and yet none without some saving grace in it. You would say that in conditions where men were embattled against one another by the greed, and the envy, and the ambition which these conditions perpetually appeal to here, there could be no grace in life; but we must remember that men have always been better than their conditions, and that otherwise they would have remained savages without the instinct or the wish to advance. Indeed, our own state is testimony of a potential civility in all states, which we must keep in mind when we judge the peoples of the plutocratic world, and especially the American people, who are above all others the devotees and exemplars of the plutocratic ideal, without limitation by any aristocracy, theocracy, or monarchy. They are purely commercial, and the thing that cannot be bought and sold, has logically no place in their life. But life is not logical, outside of Altruria; we are the only people in the world, my dear Cyril, who are privileged to live reasonably; and again I say we must put by our own criterions if we wish to understand the Americans, or to recognize that measure of loveliness which their warped, and stunted, and perverted lives certainly show, in spite of theory and in spite of conscience, even. I can make this clear to you, I think,

275

by a single instance, say that of the American who sees a case of distress, and longs to relieve it. If he is rich, he can give relief with a good conscience, except for the harm that may come to his beneficiary from being helped; but if he is not rich, or not finally rich, and especially if he has a family dependent upon him, he cannot give in anything like the measure Christ bade us give, without wronging those dear to him, immediately or remotely. That is to say, in conditions which oblige every man to look out for himself, a man cannot be a Christian without remorse; he cannot do a generous action without self-reproach; he cannot be nobly unselfish without the fear of being a fool. You would think that this predicament must deprave, and so without doubt it does; and yet it is not wholly depraving. It often has its effect in character of a rare and pathetic sublimity; and many Americans take all the cruel risks of doing good, reckless of the evil that may befall them, and defiant of the upbraidings of their own hearts. This is something that we Altrurians can scarcely understand: it is like the munificence of a savage who has killed a deer and shares it with his starving tribesmen, forgetful of the hungering little ones who wait his return from the chase with food; for life in plutocratic countries is still a chase, and the game is wary and sparse, as the terrible average of failures witnesses.

Of course, I do not mean that Americans may not give at all without sensible risk, or that giving among them is always followed by a logical regret; but as I said, life with them is in nowise logical. They even applaud one another for their charities, which they measure by the amount given, rather than by the love that goes with the giving. The widow's mite has little credit with them, but the rich man's million has an acclaim that reverberates through their newspapers long after his gift is made. It is only the poor in America who do charity as we do by giving help where it is needed; the Americans are mostly too busy, if they are at all prosperous, to give anything but money; and the more money they give, the more charitable they esteem themselves. From time to time some man with twenty or thirty millions gives one of them away, usually to a public institution of some sort, where it will have no effect with the people who are underpaid for their work, or cannot get work; and then his deed is famed throughout the continent as a thing really beyond praise. Yet any one who thinks about it must know that he never earned the millions he kept, or the million he gave, but somehow made them from the labor of others; that with all the wealth left him, he cannot miss the fortune he lavishes any more than if the check which conveyed it were a withered leaf, and not in anywise so much as an ordinary workingman might feel the bestowal of a postage stamp.

But in this study of the plutocratic mind, always so fascinating to me, I am getting altogether away from what I meant to tell you. I meant to tell you not how Americans live in the spirit, illogically, blindly, and blunderingly, but how they live in the body, and more especially how they house themselves in this city of New York. A great many of them do not house themselves at all, but that is a class which we cannot now consider, and I will speak only of those who have some sort of a roof over their heads.

II

FORMERLY the New Yorker lived in one of three different ways: in private houses, or boarding-houses, or hotels; there were few restaurants or public tables outside of the hotels, and those who had lodgings, and took their meals at eating-houses were but a small proportion of the whole number. The old classification still holds in a measure, but within the last thirty years, or ever since the Civil War, when the enormous commercial expansion of the country began, several different ways of living have been opened. The first and most noticeable of these is housekeeping in flats, or apartments of three or four rooms or more, on the same floor, as in all the countries of Europe except England; though the flat is now making itself known in London, too. Before the war, the New Yorker who kept house did so in a separate house, three or four stories in height, with a street door of its own. Its pattern within was fixed by long usage, and seldom varied; without, it was of brown-stone before, and brick behind, with an open space there for drying clothes, which was sometimes gardened or planted with trees and vines. The rear of the city blocks which these houses formed was more attractive than the front, as you may still see in the vast succession of monotonous cross-streets not yet invaded by poverty or business; and often the perspective of these rears is picturesque and pleasing. But with the sudden growth of the population when peace came, and through the acquaintance the hordes of American tourists had made with European fashions of living, it became easy, or at least simple, to divide the floors of many of these private dwellings into apartments, each with its own kitchen and all the apparatus of house-keeping. The apartments then had the street entrance and the stairways in common, and they had in common the cellar and the furnace for heating; they had in common the disadvantage of being badly aired and badly lighted. They were dark, cramped and uncomfortable, but they were cheaper than separate houses, and they were more homelike than boarding-houses or hotels. Large numbers of them still remain in use, and when people began to live in flats, in conformity with the law of evolution, many buildings were put up and subdivided into apartments in imitation of the old dwellings which had been changed.

But the apartment as the New Yorkers now mostly have it, was at the same time evolving from another direction. The poorer class of New York work-people had for a long period before the war lived, as they still live, in vast edifices, once thought prodigiously tall, which were called tenement houses. In these a family of five or ten persons is commonly packed in two or three rooms, and even in one room, where they eat and sleep, without the amenities and often without the decencies of life, and of course without light and air. The buildings in case of fire are death-traps; but the law obliges the owners to provide some apparent means of escape, which they do in the form of iron balconies and ladders giving that festive air to their façades which I have already noted. The bare and dirty entries and stair-cases are really ramifications of the filthy streets without, and each tenement opens upon a landing as if it opened upon a public thoroughfare. The rent extorted from the inmates is sometimes a hundred per cent., and is nearly always cruelly out of proportion to the value of the houses, not to speak of the wretched shelter afforded; and when the rent is not paid the family in arrears is set with all its poor household gear upon the sidewalk, in a pitiless indifference to the season and the weather, which you could not realize without seeing it, and which is incredible even of plutocratic nature. Of course, landlordism, which you have read so much of, is at its worst in the case of the tenement houses. But you must understand that comparatively few people in New York own the roofs that shelter them. By far the greater number live, however they live, in houses owned by others, by a class who prosper and grow rich, or richer, simply by owning the roofs over other men's heads. The landlords have, of course, no human relation with their tenants, and really no business relations, for all the affairs between them are transacted by agents. Some have the reputation of being better than others; but they all live, or expect to live, without work, on their rents. They are very much respected for it; the rents are considered a just return from the money invested. You must try to conceive of this as an actual fact, and not merely as a statistical statement. I know it will not be easy for you; it is not easy for me, though I have it constantly before my face.

III

THE TENEMENT HOUSE, such as it is, is the original of the apartment house, which perpetuates some of its most characteristic features on a scale and in material undreamt of in the simple philosophy of the inventor of the tenement house. The worst of these features is the want of light and air, but as much more space, and as many more rooms are conceded as the tenant will pay for. The apartment house, however, soars to heights that the tenement house never half reached, and is sometimes ten stories high. It is built fire-proof, very often, and is generally equipped with an elevator, which runs night and day, and makes one level of all the floors. The cheaper sort, or those which have departed less from the tenement house original, have no elevators, but the street door in all is kept shut and locked, and is opened only by the tenant's latchkey, or by the janitor having charge of the whole building. In the finer houses, there is a page whose sole duty it is to open and shut this door, and who is usually brass buttoned to one blinding effect of livery with the elevator boy. Where this page or hall-boy is found, the elevator carries you to the door of any apartment you seek; where he is not found, there is a bell and a speaking-tube in the lower entry, for each apartment, and you ring up the occupant, and talk to him as many stories off as he happens to be. But people who can afford to indulge their pride will not live in this sort of apartment house, and the rents in them are much lower than in the finer sort. The finer sort are vulgarly fine for the most part, with a gaudy splendor of mosaic pavement, marble stairs, frescoed ceilings, painted walls, and cabinet wood work. But there are many that are fine in a good taste, in the things that are common to the inmates. Their fittings for house-keeping are of all degrees of perfection, and except for the want of light and air, life in them has a high degree of gross luxury. They are heated throughout with pipes of steam or hot water, and they are sometimes lighted with both gas and electricity, which the inmate uses at will, though of course at his own cost. Outside, they are the despair of architecture, for no style has yet been invented which enables the artist to characterize them with beauty, and wherever they lift their vast bulks they deform the whole neighborhood, throwing the other buildings out of scale, and making it impossible for future edifices to assimilate themselves to the intruder.

There is no end to the apartment houses for multitude, and there is no street or avenue free from them. Of course the better sort are to be found on the fashionable avenues and the finer cross-streets, but others follow the course of the horse-car lines on the eastern and western avenues, and the elevated roads on the avenues which these have invaded. In such places they are shops below and apartments above, and I cannot see that the inmates seem at all sensible that they are unfitly housed in them. People are born and married, and live and die in the midst of an uproar so frantic that you would think they would go mad of it; and I believe the physicians really attribute something of the growing prevalence of neurotic disorders to the wear and tear of the nerves from the rush of the trains passing almost momently, and the perpetual jarring of the earth and air from their swift transit. I once spent an evening in one of these apartments, which a friend had taken for a few weeks last spring (you can get them out of season for any length of time), and as the weather had begun to be warm, we had the windows open, and so we had the full effect of the railroad operated under them. My friend had become accustomed to it, but for me it was an affliction which I cannot give you any notion of. The trains seemed to be in the room with us, and I sat as if I had a locomotive in my lap. Their shrieks and groans burst every sentence I began, and if I had not been master of that visible speech which we use so much at home, I never should have known what my friend was saying. I cannot tell you how this brutal clamor insulted me, and made the mere exchange of thought a part of the squalid struggle which is the plutocratic conception of life; I came away after a few hours of it, bewildered and bruised, as if I had been beaten upon with hammers.

Some of the apartments on the elevated lines are very good, as such things go; they are certainly costly enough to be good; and they are inhabited by people who can afford to leave them during the hot season when the noise is at its worst; but most of them belong to people who must dwell in them summer and winter, for want of money and leisure to get out of them, and who must suffer incessantly from the noise I could not endure for a few hours. In health it is bad enough, but in sickness it must be horrible beyond all parallel. Imagine a mother with a dying child in such a place; or a wife bending over the pillow of her husband to catch the last faint whisper of farewell, as a train of five or six cars goes roaring by the open window! What horror, what profanation!

IV

THE NOISE is bad everywhere in New York, but in some of the finer apartment houses on the better streets, you are as well out of it as you can be anywhere in the city. I have been a guest in these at different times, and in one of them I am such a frequent guest that I may be said to know its life intimately. In fact, my hostess (women transact society so exclusively in America that you seldom think of your host) in the apartment I mean to speak of, invited me to explore it one night when I dined with her, so that I might, as she said, tell my friends when I got back to Altruria how people lived in America; and I cannot feel that I am violating her hospitality in telling you now. She is that Mrs. Makely, whom I met last summer in the mountains, and whom you thought so strange a type from the account of her I gave you, but who is not altogether uncommon here. I confess that with all her faults, I like her, and I like to go to her house. She is, in fact, a very good woman, perfectly selfish by tradition as the American women must be, and wildly generous by nature, as they nearly always are; and infinitely superior to her husband in cultivation, as is commonly the case with them. As he knows nothing but business, he thinks it is the only thing worth knowing, and he looks down on the tastes and interests of her more intellectual life, with amiable contempt, as something almost comic. She respects business, too, and so she does not despise his ignorance as you would suppose; it is at least the ignorance of a business man, who must have something in him beyond her ken, or else he would not be able to make money as he does.

With your greater sense of humor, I think you would be amused if you could see his smile of placid self-satisfaction as he listens to our discussion of questions and problems which no more enter his daily life than they enter the daily life of an Eskimo; but I do not find it altogether amusing myself, and I could not well forgive it, if I did not know that he was at heart so simple and good, in spite of his commerciality. But he *is* sweet and kind, as the American men so often are, and he thinks his wife is the delightfullest creature in the world, as the American husband nearly always does. They have several times asked me to dine with them *en famille*; and, as a matter of form, he keeps me a little while with him after dinner, when she has left the table, and smokes his cigar, after wondering why we do not smoke in Altruria; but I can see that he is impatient to get to her in their drawing-room, where we find her reading a book in the crimson light of the canopied lamp, and where he presently falls silent, perfectly happy to be near her. The drawing-room is of a good size itself, and it has a room opening out of it, called the library, with a case of books in it, and Mrs. Makely's pianoforte. The place is rather too richly and densely rugged, and there is rather more curtaining and shading of the windows than we should like; but Mrs. Makely is too well up to date, as she would say, to have much of the bric-a-brac about which she tells me used to clutter people's houses here. There are some pretty good pictures on the walls, and a few vases and bronzes, and she says she has produced a greater effect of space by quelling the furniture; she means, having few pieces and having them as small as possible. There is a little stand with her afternoon tea-set in one corner, and there is a pretty writing-desk in the library; I remember a sofa, and some easy chairs, but not too many of them. She has a table near one of the windows, with books and papers on it. She tells me that she sees herself that the place is kept just as she wishes it, for she has rather a passion for neatness, and you never can trust servants not to stand the books on their heads, or study a vulgar symmetry in the arrangements. She never allows them in there, she says, except when they are at work under her eye; and she never allows anybody there except her guests, and her husband after he has smoked. Of course her dog must be there; and one evening after her husband fell asleep in the armchair near her, the dog fell asleep on the fleece at her feet, and we heard them softly breathing in unison.

She made a pretty little mocking mouth when the sound first became audible, and said that she ought really to have sent Mr. Makely out with the dog, for the dog ought to have the air every day, and she had been kept indoors; but sometimes Mr. Makely came home from business so tired that she hated to send him out, even for the dog's sake, though he was so apt to become dyspeptic. "They won't let you have dogs in some of the apartment houses, but I tore up the first lease that had that clause in it, and I told Mr. Makely that I would rather live in a house all my days, than any flat where my dog wasn't as welcome as I was. Of course, they're rather troublesome."

The Makelys had no children, but it is seldom that the occupants of apartment houses of a good class have children, though there is no clause in the lease against them. I verified this fact from Mrs. Makely herself, by actual inquiry, for in all the times that I had gone up and down in the elevator to her apartment, I had never seen any children. She seemed at first to think I was joking, and not to like it, but when she found that I was in earnest, she said that she did not suppose all the families living under that roof had more than four or five children among them. She said that it would be inconvenient; and I could not allege the tenement houses in the poor quarters of the city, where children seemed to swarm, for it is but too probable that they do not regard convenience in such places, and that neither parents nor children are more comfortable for their presence.

V

COMFORT is the American ideal, in a certain way, and comfort is certainly what is studied in such an apartment as the Makelys inhabit. We got to talking about it, and the ease of life in such conditions, and it was then she made me that offer to show me her flat, and let me report to the Altrurians concerning it. She is all impulse, and she asked, how would I like to see it *now?* and when I said I should be delighted, she spoke to her husband, and told him that she was going to show me through the flat. He roused himself promptly, and went before us, at her bidding, to turn up the electrics in the passages and rooms, and then she led the way out through the dining-room.

"This and the parlors count three, and the kitchen here is the fourth room of the eight," she said, and as she spoke she pushed open the door of a small room, blazing with light, and dense with the fumes of the dinner and the dishwashing which was now going on in a closet opening out of the kitchen.

She showed me the set range, at one side, and the refrigerator in an alcove, which she said went with the flat, and "Lena," she said to the cook, "this is the Altrurian gentleman I was telling you about, and I want him to see your kitchen. Can I take him into your room?"

The cook said, "Oh, yes, ma'am," and she gave me a good stare, while Mrs. Makely went to the kitchen window, and made me observe that it let in the outside air, though the court that it opened into was so dark that one had to keep the electrics going in the kitchen night and day. "Of course, it's an expense," she said, as she closed the kitchen door after us. She added in a low, rapid tone, "You must excuse my introducing the cook. She has read all about you in the papers—you didn't know, I suppose, that there were reporters, that day of your delightful talk in the mountains, but I had them—and she was wild, when she heard you were coming, and made me promise to let her have a sight of you somehow. She says she wants to go and live in Altruria, and if you would like to take home a cook, or a servant of any kind, you wouldn't have much trouble. Now here," she ran on, without a moment's pause, while she flung open another door, "is what you won't find in every apartment house, even very good ones, and that's a back-elevator. Sometimes there are only stairs, and they make the poor things climb the whole way up from the basement, when they come in, and all your marketing has to be brought up that way, too; sometimes they send it up on a kind of dumb-waiter, in the cheap places, and you give your orders to the marketmen down below through a speaking-tube. But here we have none of that bother, and this elevator is for the kitchen and housekeeping part of the flat. The grocer's and the butcher's man, and anybody who has packages for you, or trunks, or that sort of thing, use it, and of course it's for the servants, and they appreciate not having to walk up, as much as anybody."

"Oh, yes," I said, and she shut the elevator door, and opened another a little beyond it.

"This is our guest-chamber," she continued, as she ushered me into a very pretty room, charmingly furnished. "It isn't very light by day, for it opens on a court, like the kitchen and the servants' room here," and with that she whipped out of the guest-chamber and into another doorway, across the corridor. This room was very much narrower, but there were two small beds in it, very neat and clean, with some furnishings that were in keeping, and a good carpet under foot. Mrs. Makely was clearly proud of it, and expected me to applaud it; but I waited for her to speak, which upon the whole she probably liked as well.

"I only keep two servants, because in a flat there isn't really room for more, and I put out the wash and get in cleaning-women when it's needed. I like to use my servants well, because it pays, and I hate to see anybody imposed upon. Some people put in a double-decker, as they call it—a bedstead with two tiers, like the berths on a ship—but I think that's a shame, and I give them two regular beds, even if it does crowd them a little more, and the beds have to be rather narrow. This room has outside air, from the court, and though it's always dark, it's very pleasant, as you see." I did not say that I did not see, and this sufficed Mrs. Makely.

"Now," she said, "I'll show you *our* rooms," and she flew down the corridor toward two doors that stood open side by side, and flashed into them before me. Her husband was already in the first she entered, smiling in supreme content with his wife, his belongings and himself.

"This is a southern exposure, and it has a perfect gush of sun from morning till night. Some of the flats have the kitchen at the end, and that's stupid; you can have a kitchen in any sort of hole, for you can keep on the electrics, and with them the air's perfectly good. As soon as I saw these chambers, and found out that they would let you keep a dog, I told Mr. Makely to sign the lease instantly, and I would see to the rest."

She looked at me, and I praised the room and its dainty tastefulness to her heart's content, so that she said: "Well, it's some satisfaction to show you anything, Mr. Homos, you are so appreciative. I'm sure you'll give a good account of us to the Altrurians. Well, now we'll go back to the pa—drawing-room. This is the end of the story."

"Well," said her husband, with a wink at me, "I thought it was to be continued in our next," and he nodded toward the door that opened from his wife's bower into the room adjoining.

"Why, you poor old fellow!" she shouted. "I forgot all about *your* room," and she dashed into it before us and began to show it off. It was equipped with every bachelor luxury, and with every appliance for health and comfort. "And here," she said, "he can smoke, or anything, as long as he keeps the door shut. . . . Oh, good gracious! I forgot the bath-room," and they both united in showing me this, with its tiled floor and walls and its porcelain tub; and then Mrs. Makely flew up the corridor before us. "Put out the electrics, Dick!" she called back over her shoulder.

VI

WHEN WE WERE again seated in the drawing-room, which she had been so near calling a parlor, she continued to bubble over with delight in herself and her apartment. "Now, isn't it about perfect?" she urged, and I had to own that it was indeed very convenient and very charming; and in the rapture of the moment, she invited me to criticise it.

"I see very little to criticise," I said, "from your point of view; but I hope you won't think it indiscreet if I ask a few questions?"

She laughed. "Ask anything, Mr. Homos! I hope I got hardened to your questions in the mountains."

"She said you used to get off some pretty tough ones," said her husband, helpless to take his eyes from her, although he spoke to me.

"It is about your servants," I began.

"Oh, of course! Perfectly characteristic! Go on!"

"You told me that they had no natural light either in the kitchen or their bedroom. Do they never see the light of day?"

The lady laughed heartily. "The waitress is in the front of the house several hours every morning at her work, and they both have an afternoon off once a week. Some people only let them go once a fortnight; but I think they are human beings as well as we are, and I let them go *every* week."

"But except for that afternoon once a week, your cook lives in electric light perpetually?"

"Electric light is very healthy, and it doesn't heat the air!" the lady triumphed. "I can assure you that she thinks she's very well off; and so she is." I felt a little temper in her voice, and I was silent, until she asked me, rather stiffly: "Is there any *other* inquiry you would like to make?"

"Yes," I said, "but I do not think you would like it."

"Now, I assure you, Mr. Homos, you were never more mistaken in your life. I perfectly delight in your naïveté. I know that the Altrurians don't think as we do about some things, and I don't expect it. What is it you would like to ask?"

"Well, why should you require your servants to go down on a different elevator from yourselves?"

"Why, good gracious!" cried the lady—"aren't they different from us in *every* way? To be sure they dress up in their ridiculous best when they go out, but you couldn't expect us to let them use the *front* elevator? I don't want to go up and down with my own cook, and I certainly don't with my neighbor's cook!"

"Yes, I suppose you would feel that an infringement of your social dignity. But if you found yourself beside a cook in a horse-car or other public conveyance, you would not feel personally affronted?"

"No, that is a very different thing. That is something we cannot control. But thank goodness we *can* control our elevator, and if I were in a house where I had to ride up and down with the servants, I would no more stay in it than I would in one where I couldn't keep a dog. I should consider it a perfect outrage. I cannot understand you, Mr. Homos! You are a gentleman, and you must have the traditions of a gentleman, and yet you ask me such a thing as that!"

I saw a cast in her husband's eye which I took for a hint not to press the matter, and so I thought I had better say, "It is only that in Altruria we hold serving in peculiar honor."

"Well," said the lady scornfully, "if you went and got your servants from an intelligence office, and had to look up their references, you wouldn't hold them in very much honor. I tell you they look out for their interests as sharply as we do for ours, and it's nothing between us but a question of—"

"Business," suggested her husband.

"Yes," she assented, as if this clinched the matter.

"That's what I'm always telling you, Dolly, and yet you *will* try to make them your friends, as soon as you get them into your house. You want them to love you, and you know that sentiment hasn't got anything to do with it."

"Well, I can't help it, Dick. I can't live with a person without trying to like them, and wanting them to like me. And then, when the ungrateful things are saucy, or leave me in the lurch as they do half the time, it almost breaks my heart. But I'm thankful to say that in these hard times they won't be apt to leave a good place without a good reason."

"Are there many seeking employment?" I asked this because I thought it was safe ground.

"Well, they just stand around in the office as *thick!*" said the lady. "And the Americans are trying to get places as well as the foreigners. But I won't have Americans. They are too uppish, and they are never half so well trained as the Swedes or the Irish. They still expect to be treated as one of the family. I suppose," she continued, with a lingering ire in her voice, "that in Altruria, you do treat them as one of the family?"

"We have no servants, in the American sense," I answered as inoffensively as I could.

Mrs. Makely irrelevantly returned to the question that had first provoked her indignation. "And I should like to know how much worse it is to have a back elevator for the servants than it is to have the basement door for the servants, as you always do when you live in a separate house?"

"I should think it was no worse," I admitted, and I thought this a good chance to turn the talk from the dangerous channel it had taken. "I wish, Mrs. Makely, you would tell me something about the way people live in separate houses in New York."

She was instantly pacified. "Why, I should be delighted. I only wish my friend Mrs. Bellington Strange was back from Europe; then I could show you a model house. I mean to take you there, as soon as she gets home. She's a kind of Altrurian herself, you know. She was my dearest friend at school, and it almost broke my heart when she married Mr. Strange, so much older, and her inferior in every way. But she's got his money now, and oh, the good she does do with it! I know you'll like each other, Mr. Homos. I do wish Eva was at home!"

I said that I should be very glad to meet an American Altrurian, but that now I wished she would tell me about the normal New York house, and what was its animating principle, beginning with the basement door.

She laughed and said, "Why it's just like any other house!"

VII

I can never insist enough, my dear Cyril, upon the illogicality of American life. You know what the plutocratic principle is, and what the plutocratic civilization should logically be. But the plutocratic civilization is much better than it should logically be, bad as it is; for the personal equation constantly modifies it, and renders it far less dreadful than you would reasonably expect. That is, the potentialities of goodness implanted in the human heart by the Creator forbid the plutocratic man to be what the plutocratic scheme of life implies. He is often merciful, kindly and generous, as I have told you already, in spite of conditions absolutely egoistical. You would think that the Americans would be abashed in view of the fact that their morality is often in contravention of their economic principles, but apparently they are not so, and I believe that for the most part they are not aware of the fact. Nevertheless, the fact is there, and you must keep it in mind, if you would conceive of them rightly. You can in no other way account for the contradictions which you will find in my experiences among them; and these are often so bewildering, that I have to take myself in hand, from time to time, and ask myself what mad world I have fallen into, and whether, after all, it is not a ridiculous nightmare. I am not sure, that when I return, and we talk these things over together, I shall be able to overcome your doubts of my honesty, and I think that when I no longer have them before my eyes, I shall begin to doubt my own memory. But for the present, I can only set down what I at least seem to see, and trust you to accept it, if you cannot understand it.

Perhaps I can aid you by suggesting that, logically, the Americans should be what the Altrurians are, since their polity embodies our belief that all men are born equal, with the right to life, liberty, and the pursuit of happiness; but that illogically they are what the Europeans are, since they still cling to the economical ideals of Europe, and hold that men are born socially unequal, and deny them the liberty and happiness which can come from equality alone. It is in their public life and civic life that Altruria prevails; it is in their social and domestic life that Europe prevails; and here, I think, is the severest penalty they must pay for excluding women from political affairs; for women are at once the best and the worst Americans: the best because their hearts are the purest, the worst because their heads are the idlest. "Another contradiction!" you will say, and I cannot deny it; for with all their cultivation, the American women have no real intellectual interests, but only intellectual fads; and while they certainly think a great deal, they reflect little, or not at all. The inventions and improvements which have made their household work easy, the wealth that has released them in such vast numbers from work altogether, has not enlarged them to the sphere of duties which our Altrurian women share with us, but has left them, with their quickened intelligences, the prey of the trivialities which engross the European women, and which have formed the life of the sex hitherto in every country where women have an economical and social freedom without the political freedom that can alone give it dignity and import. They have a great deal of beauty, and they are inconsequently charming; I need not tell you that they are romantic and heroic, or that they would go to the stake for a principle, if they could find one, as willingly as any martyr of the past; but they have not much more perspective than children, and their reading and their talk about reading seem not to have broadened their mental horizons beyond the old sunrise and the old sunset of the kitchen and the parlor.

In fine, the American house as it is, the American household, is what the American woman makes it, and wills it to be, whether she wishes it to be so or not; for I often find that the American woman wills things that she in nowise wishes. What the normal New York house is, however, I had great difficulty in getting Mrs. Makely to tell me, for, as she said quite frankly, she could not imagine my not knowing. She asked me if I really wanted her to begin at the beginning, and when I said that I did, she took a little more time to laugh at the idea, and then she said: "I suppose you mean a brownstone, four-story house in the middle of a block?"

"Yes, I think that is what I mean," I said.

"Well," she began, "those high steps that they all have, unless they're English basement-houses, really give them another story, for people used to dine in the front room of their basements. You've noticed the little front yard, about as big as a handkerchief, generally, and the steps leading down to the iron gate, which is kept locked, and the basement door inside the gate? Well, that's what you might call the back-elevator of a house, for it serves the same purpose: the supplies are brought in there, and marketmen go in and out, and the ashes, and the swill, and the servants—that you object to so much. We have no alleys in New York, the blocks are so narrow, north and south; and, of course, we have no back doors; so we have to put the garbage out on the sidewalk; and it's nasty enough, goodness knows. Underneath the sidewalk, there are bins where people keep their coal and kindling. You've noticed the gratings in the pavements?"

I said yes, and I was ashamed to own that at first I had thought them some sort of registers for tempering the cold in winter; this would have appeared ridiculous in the last degree to my hostess, for the Americans have as yet no conception of publicly modifying the climate, as we do.

"Back of what used to be the dining-room, and what is now used for a laundry, generally, is the kitchen, with closets between, of course, and then the back yard, which some people make very pleasant with shrubs and vines; the kitchen is usually dark and close, and the girls can only get a breath of fresh air in the yard; I like to see them; but generally it's taken up with clothes-lines, for people in houses nearly all have their washing done at home. Over the kitchen is the dining-room, which takes up the whole of the first floor, with the pantry, and it almost always has a bay-window out of it; of course, that overhangs the kitchen, and darkens it a little more, but it makes the dining-room so pleasant. I tell my husband that I should be almost willing to live in a house again, just on account of the dining-room bay-window. I had it full of flowers in pots, for the southern sun came in; and then the yard was so nice for the dog; you didn't have to take him out for exercise, yourself; he chased the cats there and got plenty of it. I must say that the cats on the back fences were a drawback at night; to be sure, we have them here, too; it's seven stories down, but you do hear them, along in the spring. The parlor, or drawing-room, is usually rather long, and runs from the dining-room to the front of the house, though where the house is very deep, they have a sort of middle-room, or back-parlor. Dick, get some paper and draw it! Wouldn't you like to see a plan of the floor?"

I said that I should, and she bade her husband make it like their old house in West Thirty-third Street. We all looked at it together.

"This is the front door," Mrs. Makely explained, "where people come in, and then begins the misery of a house: *stairs!* They mostly go up straight, but sometimes they have them curve a little, and in the new houses the architects have all sorts of little dodges for squaring them and putting landings. Then on the second floor—draw it, Dick!—you have two nice large chambers, with plenty of light and air, before and behind. I do miss the light and air in a flat, there's no denying it."

"You'll go back to a house yet, Dolly," said her husband.

"Never!" she almost shrieked, and he winked at me, as if it were the best joke in the world. "Never, as long as houses have stairs!"

"Put in an elevator," he suggested.

"Well, that is what Eveleth Strange has, and she lets the servants use it, too," and Mrs. Makely said, with a look at me: "I suppose that would please *you*, Mr. Homos. Well, there's a nice side-room over the front door here, and a bath-room at the rear. Then you have more stairs, and large chambers, and two side-rooms. That makes plenty of chambers for a small family. I used to give two of the third-story rooms to my two girls. I ought really to have made them sleep in one; it seemed such a shame to let the cook have a whole large room to herself; but I had nothing else to do with it, and she did take such comfort in it, poor old thing. You see, the rooms came wrong in our house, for it fronted north, and I had to give the girls sunny rooms, or else give them front rooms, so that it was as broad as it was long. I declare, I was perplexed about it the whole time we lived there, it seemed so perfectly anomalous."

"And what is an English basement-house like?" I ventured to ask, in interruption of the retrospective melancholy she had fallen into.

"Oh, *never* live in an English basement-house, if you value your spine!" cried the lady. "An English basement-house is nothing *but* stairs. In the first place, it's only one room wide, and it's a story higher than the high-stoop house. It's one room forward and one back, the whole way up; and in an English basement it's always *up*, and *never* down. If I had my way, there wouldn't one stone be left upon another in the English basements in New York."

I have suffered Mrs. Makely to be nearly as explicit to you as she was to me; for the kind of house she described is of the form ordinarily prevailing in all American cities, and you can form some idea from it how city people live here. I ought perhaps to tell you that such a house is fitted with every housekeeping convenience, and that there is hot and cold water throughout, and gas everywhere. It has fireplaces in all the rooms, where fires are often kept burning for pleasure; but it is really heated from a furnace in the basement, through large pipes carried to the different stories, and opening into them by some such registers as we use. The separate houses sometimes have steam-heating, but not often. They each have their drainage into the sewer of the street, and this is trapped and trapped again, as in the houses of our old plutocratic cities, to keep the poison of the sewer from getting into the houses.

VIII

YOU WILL BE curious to know something concerning the cost of living in such a house, and you may be sure that I did not fail to question Mrs. Makely on this point. She was at once very volubly communicative; she told me all she knew, and, as her husband said, "a great deal more."

"Why, of course," she began, "you can spend all you have, in New York, if you like, and people do spend fortunes every year. But I suppose you mean the average cost of living in a brownstone house, in a good block, that rents for $1800 or $2000 a year, with a family of three or four children, and two servants. Well, what should you say, Dick?"

"Ten or twelve thousand a year—fifteen," answered her husband.

"Yes, fully that," she answered, with an effect of disappointment in his figures. "We had just ourselves, and we never spent less than seven, and we didn't dress, and we didn't entertain, either, to speak of. But you have to live on a certain scale, and generally you live up to your income."

"Quite," said Mr. Makely.

"I don't know what makes it cost so. Provisions are cheap enough, and they say people live in as good style for a third less in London. There used to be a superstition that you could live for less in a flat, and they always talk to you about the cost of a furnace, and a man to tend it, and keep the snow shovelled off your sidewalk, but that is all stuff. Five hundred dollars will make up the whole difference, and more. You pay quite as much rent for a decent flat, and then you don't get half the room. No, if it wasn't for the stairs, I wouldn't live in a flat for an instant. But that makes all the difference."

"And the young people," I urged; "those who are just starting in life, how do they manage? Say when the husband has $1500 or $2000 a year?"

"Poor things!" she returned. "I don't know how they manage. They board, till they go distracted, or they dry up, and blow away; or else the wife has a little money, too; and they take a small flat, and ruin themselves. Of course, they want to live nicely, and like other people."

"But if they didn't?"

"Why, then they could live delightfully. My husband says he often wishes he was a master-mechanic in New York, with a thousand a year, and a flat for twelve dollars a month; he would have the best time in the world."

Her husband nodded his acquiescence. "Fighting-cock wouldn't be in it," he said. "Trouble is, we all want to do the swell thing."

"But you can't all do it," I ventured, "and from what I see of the simple, out-of-the-way neighborhoods in my walks, you don't all try."

"Why, no," he said. "Some of us were talking about that the other night at the club, and one of the fellows was saying that he believed there was as much old-fashioned, quiet, almost countrified life in New York, among the great mass of the people, as you'd find in any city in the world. Said you met old codgers that took care of their own furnaces, just as you would in a town of five thousand inhabitants."

"Yes, that's all very well," said his wife. "But they wouldn't be nice people. Nice people want to live nicely. And so they live beyond their means, or else they scrimp and suffer. I don't know which is worst."

"But there is no obligation to do either?" I asked.

"Oh, yes, there is," she returned. "If you've been born in a certain way, and brought up in a certain way, you can't get out of it. You simply can't. You have got to keep in it till you drop. Or a woman has."

"That means the woman's husband, too," said Mr. Makely, with his wink for me. "Always die together."

In fact, there is the same competition in the social world as in the business world; and it is the ambition of every American to live in some such house as the New York house, and as soon as a village begins to grow into a town, such houses are built. Still, the immensely greater number of the Americans necessarily live so simply and cheaply, that such a house would be almost as strange to them as to an Altrurian. But while we should regard its furnishings as vulgar and unwholesome, most Americans would admire and covet its rich rugs or carpets, its papered walls, and thickly curtained windows, and all its foolish ornamentation, and most American women would long to have a house like the ordinary high-stoop New York house, that they might break their backs over its stairs, and become invalids, and have servants about them to harass them and hate them.

Of course, I put it too strongly, for there is often, illogically, a great deal of love between the American women and their domestics, though why there should be any at all I cannot explain, except by reference to that mysterious personal equation which modifies all conditions here. You will have made your reflection that the servants, as they are cruelly called, (I have heard them called so in their hearing, and wondered they did not fly tooth and nail at the throat that uttered the insult), form really no part of the house, but are aliens in the household and the family life. In spite of this fact, much kindness grows up between them and the family, and they do not always slight the work that I cannot

understand their ever having any heart in. Often they do slight
it, and they insist unsparingly upon the scanty privileges which
their mistresses seem to think a monstrous invasion of their own
rights. The habit of oppression grows upon the oppressor, and
you would find tenderhearted women here, gentle friends, devoted wives, loving mothers, who would be willing that their
domestics should remain indoors, week in and week out, and,
where they are confined in the ridiculous American flat, never
see the light of day. In fact, though the Americans do not know
it, and would be shocked to be told it, their servants are really
slaves, who are none the less slaves, because they cannot be
beaten, or bought and sold except by the week or month, and for
the price which they fix themselves, and themselves receive in the
form of wages. They are social outlaws, so far as the society of the
family they serve is concerned, and they are restricted in the visits
they receive and pay among themselves. They are given the
worst rooms in the house, and they are fed with the food that they
have prepared, only when it comes cold from the family table;
in the wealthier houses, where many of them are kept, they are
supplied with a coarser and cheaper victual bought and cooked
for them apart from that provided for the family. They are subject, at all hours, to the pleasure or caprice of the master or
mistress. Every circumstance of their life is an affront to that just
self-respect which even Americans allow is the right of every
human being. With the rich, they are said to be sometimes indolent, dishonest, mendacious, and all that Plato long ago explained that slaves must be; but in the middle-class families they
are mostly faithful, diligent, and reliable in a degree that would
put to shame most men who hold positions of trust, and would
leave many ladies whom they relieve of work without ground for
comparison.

IX

AFTER MRS. MAKELY had told me about the New York house,
we began to talk of the domestic service, and I ventured to hint
some of the things that I have so plainly said to you. She frankly

consented to my whole view of the matter, for if she wishes to make an effect or gain a point, she has a magnanimity that stops at nothing short of self-devotion. "I know it," she said. "You are perfectly right; but here we are, and what are we to do? What do you do in Altruria, I should like to know?"

I said that in Altruria we all worked, and that personal service was honored among us like medical attendance in America; I did not know what other comparison to make; but I said that any one in health would think it as unwholesome and as immoral to let another serve him as to let a doctor physic him. At this Mrs. Makely and her husband laughed so that I found myself unable to go on for some moments, till Mrs. Makely, with a final shriek, shouted to him, "Dick, do stop, or I shall die! Excuse me, Mr. Homos, but you are so deliciously funny, and I know you're just joking. You *won't* mind my laughing. Do go on!"

I tried to give her some notion as to how we manage, in our common life, which we have simplified so much beyond anything that this barbarous people dream of; and she grew a little soberer as I went on, and seemed at least to believe that I was not, as her husband said, stuffing them; but she ended, as they always do here, by saying that it might be all very well in Altruria, but it would never do in America, and that it was contrary to human nature to have so many things done in common. "Now, I'll tell you," she said. "After we broke up housekeeping in Thirty-third street, we stored our furniture—"

"Excuse me!" I said. "How, stored?"

"Oh, I dare say you never store your furniture in Altruria. But here we have hundreds of storage warehouses of all sorts and sizes, packed with furniture that people put into them when they go to Europe, or get sick to death of servants and the whole bother of housekeeping; and that's what we did; and, then, as my husband says, we browsed about for a year or two. First, we tried hotelling it, and we took a hotel apartment furnished, and dined at the hotel table, until I certainly thought I should go off, I got so tired of it. Then, we hired a suite in one of the family hotels that there are so many of, and got out enough of our things to furnish it, and had our meals in our rooms; they let you do that for the same price, often they are *glad* to have you, for the dining-room is so packed. But everything got to tasting just the same as everything else, and my husband had the dyspepsia so bad he couldn't half attend to business, and I suffered from indigestion myself, cooped up in a few small rooms, that way; and the dog almost died; and finally, we gave that up, and took an apartment, and got out our things—the storage cost as much as the rent of a small house—and put them into it, and had a caterer send in the meals, as they do in Europe. But it isn't the same here as it is in Europe, and we got so sick of it in a month that I thought I should scream when I saw the same old dishes coming on the table, day after day. We had to keep one servant—excuse me, Mr. Homos; *domestic*—anyway, to look after the table and the parlor and chamber work, and my husband said we might as well be hung for a sheep as a lamb, and so we got in a cook; and bad as it is, it's twenty million times better than anything else you can do. Servants are a plague, but you have got to have them, and so I have resigned myself to the will of Providence. If they don't like it, neither do I, and so I fancy it's about as broad as it's long."

I have found this is a favorite phrase of Mrs. Makely's, and that it seems to give her a great deal of comfort.

"And you don't feel that there's any harm in it?" I ventured to ask.

"Harm in it?" she repeated. "Why, aren't the poor things glad to get the work? What would they do without it?"

"From what I see of your conditions I should be afraid that they would starve," I said.

"Yes, they can't all get places in shops or restaurants, and they have to do something, or starve, as you say," she said; and she seemed to think what I had said was a concession to her position.

"But if it were your own case?" I suggested. "If you had no alternatives but starvation and domestic service, you would think there was harm in it, even although you were glad to take a servant's place?"

I saw her flush, and she answered haughtily, "You must excuse me if I refuse to imagine myself taking a servant's place, even for the sake of argument."

"And you are quite right," I said. "Your American instinct is too strong to brook even in imagination the indignities which seem daily, hourly and momently inflicted upon servants in your system."

To my great astonishment she seemed delighted by this conclusion. "Yes," she said, and she smiled radiantly, "and now you understand how it is that American girls won't go out to service, though the pay is so much better and they are so much better housed and fed; and everything. Besides," she added, with an irrelevance which always amuses her husband, though I should be alarmed by it for her sanity if I did not find it so characteristic of women here, who seem to be mentally characterized by the illogicality of the civilization, "they're not half so good as the foreign servants. They've been brought up in homes of their own, and they're uppish, and they have no idea of anything but third-rate boarding-house cooking, and they're always hoping to get married, so that, really, you have no peace of your life with them."

"And it never seems to you that the whole relation is wrong?" I asked.

"What relation?"

"That between maid and mistress, the hirer and the hireling."

"Why, good gracious!" she burst out. "Didn't Christ himself say that the laborer was worthy of his hire? And how would you get your work done, if you didn't pay for it?"

"It might be done for you, when you could not do it yourself, from affection."

"From affection!" she returned, with the deepest derision. "Well, I rather think I *shall* have to do it myself if I want it done from affection! But I suppose you think I *ought* to do it myself, as the Altrurian ladies do? I can tell you that in America it would be impossible for a lady to do her own work, and there are no intelligence offices where you can find girls that want to work for love. It's as broad as it's long."

"It's simply business," her husband said.

They were right, my dear friend, and I was wrong, strange as it must appear to you. The tie of service, which we think as sacred as the tie of blood, can be here only a business relation, and in these conditions service must forever be grudgingly given and grudgingly paid. There is something in it, I do not quite know what, for I can never place myself precisely in an American's place, that degrades the poor creatures who serve, so that they must not only be social outcasts, but must leave such a taint of dishonor on their work, that one cannot even do it for oneself without a sense of outraged dignity. You might account for this in Europe, where ages of prescriptive wrong have distorted the relation out of all human wholesomeness and Christian loveliness; but in America, where many, and perhaps most, of those who keep servants and call them so, are but a single generation from fathers who earned their bread by the sweat of their brows, and from mothers who nobly served in all household offices, it is in the last degree bewildering. I can only account for it by that bedevilment of the entire American ideal through the retention of the English economy when the English polity was rejected. But at the heart of America there is this ridiculous contradiction, and it must remain there until the whole country is Altrurianized. There is no other hope; but I did not now urge this point, and we turned to talk of other things, related to the matters we had been discussing.

"The men," said Mrs. Makely, "get out of the whole bother very nicely, as long as they are single, and even when they're married, they are apt to run off to the club, when there's a prolonged upheaval in the kitchen."

"*I* don't, Dolly," suggested her husband.

"No, *you* don't, Dick," she returned, fondly. "But there are not many like you."

He went on, with a wink at me: "I never live at the club, except in summer, when you go away to the mountains."

"Well, you know I can't very well take you with me," she said.

"Oh, I couldn't leave my business, anyway," he said, and he laughed.

X

I HAD NOTICED the vast and splendid club-houses in the best places in the city, and I had often wondered about their life, which seemed to me a blind groping towards our own, though only upon terms that forbade it to those who most needed it. The clubs here are not like our groups, the free association of sympathetic people, though one is a little more literary, or commercial, or scientific, or political than another; but the entrance to each is more or less jealously guarded; there is an initiation fee, and there are annual dues, which are usually heavy enough to exclude all but the professional and business classes, though there are, of course, successful artists and authors in them. During the past winter I visited some of the most characteristic, where I dined and supped with the members, or came alone when one of these put me down, for a fortnight or a month.

They are equipped with kitchens and cellars, and their wines and dishes are of the best. Each is, in fact, like a luxurious private house on a large scale; outwardly they are palaces, and inwardly they have every feature and function of a princely residence complete, even to a certain number of guest-chambers, where members may pass the night, or stay indefinitely, in some cases, and actually live at the club. The club, however, is known only to the cities and larger towns, in this highly developed form; to the ordinary, simple American, of the country, or of the country town of five or ten thousand people, a New York club would be as strange as it would be to any Altrurian.

"Do many of the husbands left behind in the summer live at the club?" I asked.

"All that *have* a club, do," he said. "Often there's a very good table d'hôte dinner that you couldn't begin to get for the same price anywhere else; and there are a lot of good fellows there, and you can come pretty near forgetting that you're homeless, or even that you're married."

He laughed, and his wife said: "You ought to be ashamed, Dick; and me worrying about you all the time I'm away, and wondering what the cook gives you here. Yes," she continued, addressing me, "that's the worst thing about the clubs. They make the men so comfortable that they say it's one of the principal obstacles to early marriages. The young men try to get lodgings near them, so that they can take their meals there, and they know they get much better things to eat than they could have in a house of their own at a great deal more expense, and so they simply don't think of getting married. Of course," she said with that wonderful, unintentional, or at least unconscious, frankness of hers, "I don't blame the clubs altogether. There's no use denying that girls are expensively brought up, and that a young man has to think twice before taking one of them out of the kind of home she's used to, and putting her into the kind of home he can give her. If the clubs have killed early marriages, the women have created the clubs."

"Do women go much to them?" I asked, choosing this question as a safe one.

"*Much!*" she screamed. "They don't go at all! They *can't!* They won't *let* us! To be sure, there are some that have rooms where ladies can go with their friends who are members, and have lunch or dinner; but as for seeing the inside of the clubhouse proper, where these great creatures"—she indicated her husband—"are sitting up, smoking and telling stories, it isn't to be dreamed of."

Her husband laughed. "You wouldn't like the smoking, Dolly."

"Nor the stories, some of them," she retorted.

"Oh, the stories are always first rate," he said, and he laughed more than before.

"And they never gossip, at the clubs, Mr. Homos, never!" she added.

"Well, hardly ever," said her husband, with an intonation that I did not understand. It seemed to be some sort of catch-phrase.

"All I know," said Mrs. Makely, "is that I like to have my husband belong to his club. It's a nice place for him in summer;

and very often in winter, when I'm dull, or going out somewhere that he hates, he can go down to his club, and smoke a cigar, and come home just about the time I get in, and it's much better than worrying through the evening with a book. He hates books, poor Dick!" She looked fondly at him, as if this were one of the greatest merits in the world. "But I confess, I shouldn't like him to be a mere club man, like some of them."

"But how?" I asked.

"Why, belonging to five or six, or more, even; and spending their whole time at them, when they're not at business."

There was a pause, and Mr. Makely put on an air of modest worth, which he carried off with his usual wink toward me. I said, finally, "And if the ladies are not admitted to the men's clubs, why don't they have clubs of their own?"

"Oh, they have,—several, I believe. But who wants to go and meet a lot of women? You meet enough of them in society, goodness knows. You hardly meet any one else, especially at afternoon teas. They bore you to death."

Mrs. Makely's nerves seemed to lie in the direction of a prolongation of this subject, and I asked my next question a little away from it. "I wish you would tell me, Mrs. Makely, something about your way of provisioning your household. You said that the grocer's and butcher's man came up to the kitchen with your supplies—"

"Yes, and the milkman and the iceman; the iceman always puts the ice into the refrigerator; it's very convenient, and quite like your own house."

"But you go out and select the things yourself, the day before, or in the morning?"

"Oh, not at all! The men come and the cook gives the order; she knows pretty well what we want on the different days, and I never meddle with it from one week's end to the other, unless we have friends. The tradespeople send in their bills at the end of the month, and that's all there is of it." Her husband gave me one of his queer looks, and she went on: "When we were younger, and just beginning housekeeping, I used to go out and order the things myself; I used even to go to the big markets, and half kill myself, trying to get things a little cheaper at one place and another, and waste more car-fare, and lay up more doctor's bills than it would all come to, ten times over. I used to fret my life out, remembering the prices; but now, thank goodness, that's all over. I don't know any more what beef is a pound than my husband does; if a thing isn't good, I send it straight back, and that puts them on their honor, you know, and they have to give me the best of everything. The bills average about the same, from month to month; a little more if we have company; but if they're too outrageous, I make a fuss with the cook, and she scolds the men, and then it goes better for a while. Still, it's a great bother."

I confess that I did not see what the bother was, but I had not the courage to ask, for I had already conceived a wholesome dread of the mystery of an American lady's nerves. So I merely suggested, "And that is the way that people usually manage?"

"Why," she said, "I suppose that some old-fashioned people still do their marketing, and people that have to look to their outgoes, and know what every mouthful costs them. But their lives are not worth having. Eveleth Strange does it—or she did do it when she was in the country; I dare say she won't when she gets back—just from a sense of duty, and because she says that a housekeeper ought to know about her expenses. But I ask her who will care whether she knows or not; and as for giving the money to the poor that she saves by spending economically, I tell her that the butchers and the grocers have to live, too, as well as the poor, and so it's as broad as it's long."

XI

I COULD NOT make out whether Mr. Makely approved of his wife's philosophy or not; I do not believe he thought much about it. The money probably came easily with him, and he let it go easily, as an American likes to do. There is nothing penurious or sordid about this curious people, so fierce in the pursuit of riches.

When these are once gained, they seem to have no value to the man who has won them, and he has generally no object in life but to see his womankind spend them.

This is the season of the famous Thanksgiving, which has now become the national holiday, but has no longer any savor in it of the grim Puritanism it sprang from. It is now appointed by the president and the governors of the several States, in proclamations enjoining a pious gratitude upon the people for their continued prosperity as a nation and a public acknowledgment of the divine blessings. The blessings are supposed to be of the material sort, grouped in the popular imagination as good times, and it is hard to see what they are when hordes of men and women of every occupation are feeling the pinch of poverty in their different degrees. It is not merely those who have always the wolf at their doors, who are now suffering, but those whom the wolf never threatened before; those who amuse, as well as those who serve the rich, are alike anxious and fearful, where they are not already in actual want; thousands of poor players, as well as hundreds of thousands of poor laborers, are out of employment; and the winter threatens to be one of dire misery. Yet you would not imagine from the smiling face of things, as you would see it in the better parts of this great city, that there was a heavy heart or an empty stomach anywhere below it. In fact, people here are so used to seeing other people in want that it no longer affects them as reality; it is merely dramatic, or hardly so lifelike as that—it is merely histrionic. It is rendered still more spectacular to the imaginations of the fortunate by the melodrama of charity they are invited to take part in by endless appeals, and their fancy is flattered by the notion that they are curing the distress they are only slightly relieving by a gift from their superfluity. The charity, of course, is better than nothing, but it is a fleeting mockery of the trouble at the best. If it were proposed that the city should subsidize a theater at which the idle players could get employment in producing good plays at a moderate cost to the people, the notion would not be considered more ridiculous than that of founding municipal works for the different sorts of idle workers;

and it would not be thought half so nefarious, for the proposition to give work by the collectivity is supposed to be in contravention of the sacred principle of monopolistic competition so dear to the American economist, and it would be denounced as an approximation to the surrender of the city to anarchism and destruction by dynamite.

But as I have so often said, the American life is in nowise logical, and you will not be surprised, though you may be shocked or amused to learn that the festival of Thanksgiving is now so generally devoted to witnessing a game of foot-ball between the Elevens of two great universities, that the services at the churches are very scantily attended. The Americans are practical, if they are not logical, and this preference of foot-ball to prayer and praise on Thanksgiving day has gone so far that now a principal church in the city holds its services on Thanksgiving eve, so that the worshippers may not be tempted to keep away from their favorite game.

There is always a heavy dinner at home after the game, to console the friends of those who have lost, and to heighten the joy of the winning side, among the comfortable people. The poor recognize the day largely as a sort of carnival. They go about in masquerade on the eastern avenues, and the children of the foreign races who populate that quarter, penetrate the better streets, blowing horns, and begging of the passers. They have probably no more sense of its difference from the old carnival of Catholic Europe than from the still older Saturnalia of pagan times. Perhaps you will say that a masquerade is no more pagan than a foot-ball game; and I confess that I have a pleasure in that innocent misapprehension of the holiday on the East side. I am not more censorious of it than I am of the displays of festival cheer at the provision stores, or green-groceries throughout the city at this time. They are almost as numerous on the avenues as the drinking saloons, and thanks to them, the wasteful house-keeping is at least convenient in a high degree. The waste is inevitable with the system of separate kitchens, and it is not in provisions alone, but in labor and in time, a hundred cooks doing the work of one; but the Americans have no conception of our coöperative housekeeping, and so the folly goes on.

Meantime, the provision stores add much to their effect of crazy gayety on the avenues. The variety and harmony of colors is very great, and this morning I stood so long admiring the arrangement in one of them, that I am afraid I rendered myself a little suspicious to the policeman guarding the liquor store on the nearest corner; there seems always to be a policeman assigned to this duty. The display was on either side of the provisioner's door, and began on one hand with a basal line of pumpkins well out on the sidewalk. Then it was built up with the soft white and cool green of cauliflowers, and open boxes of red and white grapes, to the window that flourished in banks of celery and rosy apples. On the other side, gray-green squashes formed the foundation, and the wall was sloped upward with the delicious salads you can find here, the dark red of beets, the yellow of carrots, and the blue of cabbages. The association of colors was very artistic and even the line of mutton carcasses overhead, with each a brace of grouse, or half a dozen quail in its embrace, and flanked with long sides of beef at the four ends of the line, was picturesque, though the sight of the carnage at the provision stores here would always be dreadful to an Altrurian; in the great markets it is intolerable. This sort of business is mostly in the hands of the Germans, who have a good eye for such effects as may be studied in it; but the fruiterers are nearly all Italians, and their stalls are charming. I always like, too, the cheeriness of the chestnut and peanut ovens of the Italians; the pleasant smell and friendly smoke that rise from them suggest a simple and homelike life, which there are so many things in this great, weary, heedless city to make one forget.

XII

BUT I AM allowing myself to wander too far from Mrs. Makely and her letter, which reached me only two days before Thanksgiving.

My dear Mr. Homos:

Will you give me the pleasure of your company, at dinner, on Thanksgiving Day, at eight o'clock, very informally. My friend, Mrs. Bellington Strange, has unexpectedly returned from Europe, within the week, and I am asking a few friends, whom I can trust to excuse this very short notice, to meet her.

With Mr. Makely's best regards,

Yours cordially,
Dorothea Makely.

The Sphinx,
November the twenty-sixth,
Eighteen hundred and
Ninety-three.

I must tell you that it has been a fad with the ladies here to spell out their dates, and though the fashion is waning, Mrs. Makely is a woman who would remain in such an absurdity among the very last. I will let you make your own conclusions concerning this, for though, as an Altrurian, I cannot respect her, I like her so much, and have so often enjoyed her generous hospitality, that I cannot bring myself to criticise her except by the implication of the facts. She is anomalous, but to our way of thinking, all the Americans I have met are anomalous, and she has the merits that you would not logically attribute to her character. Of course, I cannot feel that her evident regard for me is the least of these, though I like to think that it is founded on more reason than the rest.

I have by this time become far too well versed in the polite insincerities of the plutocratic world to imagine, that because she asked me to come to her dinner, very informally, I was not to come in all the state I could put into my dress. You know what the evening dress of men is, here, from the costumes in our museum, and you can well believe that I never put on those ridiculous black trousers without a sense of their grotesqueness, that scrap of waistcoat reduced to a mere rim, so as to show the whole white breadth of the starched shirt bosom, and that coat chopped away till it seems nothing but tails and lapels. It is true that I might go out to dinner in our national costume; in fact, Mrs. Makely has often begged me to wear it, for she says the Chinese wear theirs; but I have not cared to make the sensation which I must if I wore it; my outlandish views of life, and my frank study of their customs signalize me quite sufficiently among the Americans.

At the hour named, I appeared in Mrs. Makely's drawing-room in all the formality that I knew her invitation, to come very informally, really meant. I found myself the first, as I nearly always do, but I had only time for a word or two with my hostess before the others began to come. She hastily explained that as soon as she knew Mrs. Strange was in New York, she had dis-patched a note telling her that I was still here; and that as she could not get settled in time to dine at home, she must come and take Thanksgiving dinner with her. "She will have to go out with Mr. Makely; but I am going to put you next to her at table, for I want you both to have a good time. But don't you forget that you are going to take *me* out." I said that I should certainly not forget it, and I showed her the envelope with my name on the outside, and hers on a card inside, which the serving man at the door had given me in the hall, as the first token that the dinner was to be unceremonious. She laughed, and said: "I've had the luck to pick up two or three other agreeable people that I know will be glad to meet you. Usually, it's such a scratch lot at Thanksgiving, for everybody dines at home that can, and you have to trust to the highways and the byways for your guests, if you give a dinner. But I did want to bring Mrs. Strange and you together, and so I chanced it. Of course, it's a sent-in dinner, as you must have inferred from the man at the door; I've given my servants a holiday, and had Claret's people do the whole thing. It's as broad as it's long, and as my husband says, you might as well be hung for a sheep as a lamb; and it saves bother. Everybody will know it's sent in, so that nobody will be deceived. There'll be a turkey in it somewhere, and cranberry sauce; I've insisted on that: but it won't be a regular American Thanksgiving dinner, and I'm rather sorry, on your account, for I wanted you to see one, and I meant to have had you here, just with ourselves; but Eveleth Strange's coming back put a new face on things, and so I've gone in for this affair, which isn't at all what you would like. That's the reason I tell you at once, it's sent in."

XIII

I AM SO OFTEN at a loss for the connection in Mrs. Makely's ideas that I am more patient with her incoherent jargon than you will be, I am afraid. It went on to much the effect that I have tried to report, until the moment she took the hand of the guest who came next. They arrived, until there were eight of us in all; Mrs. Strange coming last, with excuses for being late. I had somehow figured her as a person rather mystical and recluse in appearance, perhaps on account of her name, and I had imagined her tall and superb. But she was, really, rather small, though not below the woman's average, and she had a face more round than otherwise, with a sort of businesslike earnestness, but a very charming smile, and presently, as I saw, an American sense of humor. She had brown hair and gray eyes, and teeth not too regular to be monotonous; her mouth was very sweet, whether she laughed, or sat gravely silent. She at once affected me like a person who had been sobered beyond her nature by responsibilities, and had steadily strengthened under the experiences of life. She was dressed with a sort of personal taste, in a rich gown of black lace, which came up to her throat; and she did not subject me to that embarrassment I always feel in the presence of a lady who is much décolleté, when I sit next her, or face to face with her: I cannot always look at her without a sense of taking an immodest advantage. Sometimes I find a kind of pathos in this sacrifice of fashion, which affects me as if the poor lady were wearing that sort of gown because she thought she really ought, and then I keep my eyes firmly on hers, or avert them altogether; but there are other cases which have not this appealing quality. Yet in the very worst of the cases it would be a mistake to suppose that there was a display personally meant of the display personally made.

Even then it would be found that the gown was worn so because the dressmaker had made it so, and, whether she had made it in this country or in Europe, that she had made it in compliance with a European custom. In fact, all the society customs of the Americans follow some European original, and usually some English original; and it is only fair to say that in this particular custom they do not go to the English extreme.

We did not go out to dinner at Mrs. Makely's by the rules of English precedence, because there are nominally no ranks here, and we could not; but I am sure it will not be long before the Americans will begin playing at precedence just as they now play at the other forms of aristocratic society. For the present, however, there was nothing for us to do but to proceed, when dinner was served, in such order as offered itself, after Mr. Makely gave his arm to Mrs. Strange, though, of course, the white shoulders of the other ladies went gleaming out before the white shoulders of Mrs. Makely shone beside my black ones. I have now become so used to these observances that they no longer affect me as they once did, and as I suppose my account of them must affect you, painfully, comically. But I have always the sense of having a part in amateur theatricals, and I do not see how the Americans can fail to have the same sense, for there is nothing spontaneous in them, and nothing that has grown even dramatically out of their own life.

Often when I admire the perfection of the stage-setting, it is with a vague feeling that I am derelict in not offering it an explicit applause. In fact, this is permitted in some sort and measure, as now when we sat down at Mrs. Makely's exquisite table, and the ladies frankly recognized her touch in it. One of them found a phrase for it at once, and pronounced it a symphony in chrysanthemums; for the color and the character of these flowers played through all the appointments of the table, and rose to a magnificent finale in the vast group in the middle of the board, infinite in their caprices of tint and design. Another lady said that it was a dream, and then Mrs. Makely said: "No, a memory," and confessed that she had studied the effect from her recollection of some tables at a chrysanthemum show held here year before last, which seemed failures because they were so simply and crudely adapted in the china and napery to merely one kind and color of the flower.

"Then," she added, "I wanted to do something very chrysanthemummy, because it seems to me the Thanksgiving flower, and belongs to Thanksgiving quite as much as holly belongs to Christmas."

Everybody applauded her intention, and they hungrily fell to upon the excellent oysters, with her warning that we had better make the most of everything in its turn, for she had conformed her dinner to the brevity of the notice she had given her guests.

XIV

Just what the dinner was I will try to tell you, for I think that it will interest you to know what people here think a very simple dinner. That is, people of any degree of fashion; for the unfashionable Americans, who are innumerably in the majority, have no more than the Altrurians seen such a dinner as Mrs. Makely's. This sort generally sit down to a single dish of meat, with two or three vegetables, and they drink tea or coffee, or water only, with their dinner. Even when they have company, as they say, the things are all put on the table at once; and the average of Americans who have seen a dinner served in courses, after the Russian manner, invariable in the fine world here, is not greater than those who have seen a serving-man in livery. Among these the host piles up his guest's plate with meat and vegetables, and it is passed from hand to hand till it reaches him; his drink arrives from the hostess by the same means. One maid serves the table in a better class, and two maids in a class still better; it is only when you reach people of very decided form that you find a man in a black coat behind your chair; Mrs. Makely, mindful of the informality of her dinner in everything, had two men.

I should say the difference between the Altrurians and the unfashionable Americans, in view of such a dinner as she gave us, would be that, while it would seem to us abominable for its extravagance, and revolting in its appeals to appetite, it would seem to most of such Americans altogether admirable and enviable, and would appeal to their ambition to give such a dinner themselves as soon as ever they could.

Well, with our oysters, we had a delicate French wine, though I am told that formerly Spanish wines were served. A delicious soup followed the oysters, and then we had fish, with sliced cucumbers dressed with oil and vinegar, like a salad; and I suppose you will ask what we could possibly have eaten more. But this was only the beginning, and next there came a course of sweetbreads with green peas. With this the champagne began at once to flow, for Mrs. Makely was nothing if not original, and she had champagne very promptly. One of the gentlemen praised her for it, and said you could not have it too soon, and he had secretly hoped it would have begun with the oysters. Next, we had a remove, a tenderloin of beef, with mushrooms, fresh, and not of the canned sort which it is usually accompanied with. This fact won our hostess more compliments from the gentlemen, which could not have gratified her more if she had dressed and cooked the dish herself. She insisted upon our trying the stewed terrapin, for if it did come in a little by the neck and shoulders, it was still in place at a Thanksgiving dinner, because it was so American; and the stuffed peppers, which, if they were not American, were at least Mexican, and originated in the kitchen of a sister republic. There were one or two other side-dishes, and with all the burgundy began to be poured out.

Mr. Makely said that claret all came now from California, no matter what French château they named it after, but burgundy you could not err in. His guests were now drinking the different wines, and to much the same effect, I should think, as if they had mixed them all in one cup; though I ought to say that several of the ladies took no wine, and kept me in countenance after the first taste I was obliged to take of each, in order to pacify my host.

You must know that all the time there were plates of radishes, olives, celery, and roasted almonds set about that every one ate of without much reference to the courses. The talking and the feasting were at their height, but there was a little flagging of the appetite, perhaps, when it received the stimulus of a water-ice flavored with rum. After eating it, I immediately experienced an extraordinary revival of my hunger (I am ashamed to confess that I was gorging myself like the rest), but I quailed inwardly when one of the men-servants set down before Mr. Makely a roast turkey that looked as large as an ostrich. It was received with cries of joy, and one of the gentlemen said, "Ah, Mrs. Makely, I was waiting to see how you would interpolate the turkey, but you never fail. I knew you would get it in somewhere. But where," he added in a burlesque whisper, behind his hand, "are the—"

"Canvasback duck?" she asked, and at that moment the servant set before the anxious inquirer a platter of these renowned birds, which you know something of already from the report our emissaries have given of their cult among the Americans.

Every one laughed, and after the gentleman had made a despairing flourish over them with a carving knife in emulation of Mr. Makely's emblematic attempt upon the turkey, both were taken away, and carved at a sideboard. They were then served in slices, the turkey with cranberry sauce, and the ducks with currant jelly; and I noticed that no one took so much of the turkey that he could not suffer himself to be helped also to the duck. I must tell you that there was a salad with the duck, and after that there was an ice-cream, with fruit and all manner of candied fruits, and candies, different kinds of cheese, coffee, and liqueurs to drink after the coffee.

"Well, now," Mrs. Makely proclaimed, in high delight with her triumph, "I must let you imagine the pumpkin pie. I meant to have it, because it isn't really Thanksgiving without it. But I couldn't, for the life of me, see where it would come in."

XV

THE SALLY of the hostess made them all laugh, and they began to talk about the genuine American character of the holiday, and what a fine thing it was to have something truly national. They praised Mrs. Makely for thinking of so many American dishes, and the facetious gentleman said that she rendered no greater tribute than was due to the overruling Providence which had so abundantly bestowed them upon the Americans as a people. "You must have been glad, Mrs. Strange," he said, to the lady at my side, "to get back to our American oysters. There seems nothing else so potent to bring us home from Europe."

"I'm afraid," she answered, "that I don't care so much for the American oyster as I should. But I am certainly glad to get back."

"In time for the turkey, perhaps?"

"No, I care no more for the turkey than for the oyster of my native land," said the lady.

"Ah, well, say the canvasback duck then. The canvasback duck is no alien. He is as thoroughly American as the turkey, or as any of us."

"No, I should not have missed him, either," persisted the lady.

"What could one have missed," the gentleman said, with a bow to the hostess, "in the dinner Mrs. Makely has given us? If there had been nothing, I should not have missed it," and when the laugh at his drolling had subsided, he asked Mrs. Strange: "Then, if it is not too indiscreet, might I inquire what in the world has lured you again to our shores, if it was not the oyster, nor the turkey, nor yet the canvasback?"

"The American dinner-party," said the lady, with the same burlesque.

"Well," he consented, "I think I understand you. It is different from the English dinner-party in being a festivity rather than a solemnity; though after all the American dinner is only a condition of the English dinner. Do you find us much changed, Mrs. Strange?"

"I think we are every year a little more European," said the lady. "One notices it on getting home."

"I supposed we were so European already," returned the gentleman, "that a European landing among us would think he had got back to his starting point in a sort of vicious circle. I am

myself so thoroughly Europeanized in all my feelings and instincts, that do you know, Mrs. Makely, if I may confess it
without offence—"

"Oh, by all means!" cried the hostess.

"When that vast bird which we have been praising, that
colossal roast turkey, appeared, I felt a shudder go through my
delicate substance, such as a refined Englishman might have experienced at the sight, and I said to myself, quite as if I were not
one of you, 'Good heavens! now they will begin talking through
their noses and eating with their knives. It's what I might have
expected!'"

It was impossible not to feel that this gentleman was talking at
me; if the Americans have a foreign guest, they always talk at
him more or less; and I was not surprised when he said, "I think
our friend, Mr. Homos, will conceive my fine revolt from the
crude period of our existence which the roast turkey marks as
distinctly as the *graffiti* of the cave-dweller proclaim his epoch."

"No," I protested, "I am afraid that I have not the documents
for the interpretation of your emotion. I hope you will take pity
on my ignorance, and tell me just what you mean."

The others said they none of them knew either, and would like
to know, and the gentleman began by saying that he had been
going over the matter in his mind on his way to dinner, and he
had really been trying to lead up to it ever since we sat down.
"I've been struck, first of all, by the fact, in our evolution, that
we haven't socially evolved from ourselves; we've evolved from
the Europeans, from the English. I don't think you'll find a single
society rite with us now that had its origin in our peculiar national
life, if we have a peculiar national life; I doubt it, sometimes. If
you begin with the earliest thing in the day, if you begin with
breakfast, as society gives breakfasts, you have an English breakfast, though American people and provisions."

"I must say, I think they're both much nicer," said Mrs.
Makely.

"Ah, there I am with you! We borrow the form, but we infuse
the spirit. I am talking about the form, though. Then, if you

come to the society lunch, which is almost indistinguishable from the society breakfast, you have the English lunch, which is really an undersized English dinner. The afternoon tea is English again, with its troops of eager females and stray, reluctant males; though I believe there are rather more men at the English teas, owing to the larger leisure class in England. The afternoon tea and the 'at home' are as nearly alike as the breakfast and the lunch. Then, in the course of time, we arrive at the great society function, the dinner; and what is the dinner with us but the dinner of our mother-country?"

"It is livelier," suggested Mrs. Makely, again.

"Livelier, I grant you, but I am still speaking of the form, and not of the spirit. The evening reception, which is gradually fading away, as a separate rite, with its supper and its dance, we now have as the English have it, for the people who have not been asked to dinner. The ball, which brings us round to breakfast again, is again the ball of our Anglo-Saxon kin beyond the seas. In short, from the society point of view we are in everything their mere rinsings."

"Nothing of the kind!" cried Mrs. Makely. "I won't let you say such a thing! On Thanksgiving Day, too! Why, there is the Thanksgiving dinner itself! If that isn't purely American, I should like to know what is."

"It is purely American, but it is strictly domestic; it is not society. Nobody but some great soul like you, Mrs. Makely, would have the courage to ask any body to a Thanksgiving dinner, and even you ask only such easy-going house-friends as we are proud to be. You wouldn't think of giving a dinner-party on Thanksgiving?"

"No, I certainly shouldn't. I should think it was very presuming; and you are all as nice as you can be to have come to-day; I am not the only great soul at the table. But that is neither here nor there. Thanksgiving is a purely American thing, and it's more popular than ever. A few years ago you never heard of it outside of New England."

The gentleman laughed. "You are perfectly right, Mrs.

Makely, as you always are. Thanksgiving is purely American. So is the corn-husking, so is the apple-bee, so is the sugar-party, so is the spelling-match, so is the church-sociable; but none of these have had their evolution in our society entertainments. The New Year's call was also purely American, but that is now as extinct as the dodo, though I believe the other American festivities are still known in the rural districts."

"Yes," said Mrs. Makely, "and I think it's a great shame that we can't have some of them in a refined form in society. I once went to a sugar-party up in New Hampshire, when I was a girl, and I never enjoyed myself so much in my life. I should like to make up a party to go to one somewhere in the Catskills, in March. Will you all go? It would be something to show Mr. Homos. I should like to show him something really American before he goes home. There's nothing American left in society!"

"You forget the American woman," suggested the gentleman. "She is always American, and she is always in society."

"Yes," returned our hostess, with a thoughtful air, "you're quite right in that. One always meets more women than men in society. But it's because the men are so lazy, and so comfortable at their clubs, they won't go. They enjoy themselves well enough in society after they get there, as I tell my husband, when he grumbles over having to dress."

"Well," said the gentleman, "a great many things, the daytime things, we really can't come to, because we don't belong to the aristocratic class, as you ladies do, and we are busy down town. But I don't think we are reluctant about dinner; and the young fellows are nearly always willing to go to a ball, if the supper's good, and it's a house where they don't feel obliged to dance. But what do *you* think, Mr. Homos?" he asked. "How does your observation coincide with my experience?"

I answered that I hardly felt myself qualified to speak, for though I had assisted at the different kinds of society rites he had mentioned, thanks to the hospitality of my friends in New York, I knew the English functions only from a very brief stay in England on my way here, and from what I had read of them in

English fiction, and in the relations of our emissaries. He inquired into our emissary system, and the company appeared greatly interested in such account of it as I could briefly give.

"Well," he said, "that would do while you kept to yourselves; but now that your country is known to the plutocratic world, your public documents will be apt to come back to the countries your emissaries have visited, and make trouble. The first thing you know some of our bright reporters will get on to one of your emissaries, and interview him, and then we shall get what you think of us at first hand. By-the-by, have you seen any of those primitive social delights which Mrs. Makely regrets so much?"

"I?" our hostess protested. But, then, she perceived that he was joking, and she let me answer.

I said that I had seen them nearly all, during the past year, in New England and in the West, but they appeared to me inalienably of the simpler life of the country, and that I was not surprised they should not have found an evolution in the more artificial society of the cities.

"I see," he returned, "that you reserve your *opinion* of our more artificial society; but you may be sure that our reporters will get it out of you yet, before you leave us."

"Those horrid reporters!" one of the ladies irrelevantly sighed.

The gentleman resumed: "In the meantime, I don't mind saying how it strikes me. I think you are quite right about the indigenous American things being adapted only to the simpler life of the country and the smaller towns. It is so everywhere. As soon as people become at all refined, they look down upon what is their own as something vulgar. But it is peculiarly so with us. We have nothing national that is not connected with the life of work, and when we begin to live the life of pleasure, we must borrow from the people abroad, who have always lived the life of pleasure."

"Mr. Homos, you know," Mrs. Makely explained for me, as if this were the aptest moment, "thinks we all ought to work. He thinks we oughtn't to have any servants."

"Oh, no, my dear lady," I put in. "I don't think that of you, as you *are*. None of you could see more plainly than I do, that in your conditions you *must* have servants, and that you cannot possibly work, unless poverty obliges you."

The other ladies had turned upon me with surprise and horror at Mrs. Makely's words, but they now apparently relented, as if I had fully redeemed myself from the charge made against me. Mrs. Strange alone seemed to have found nothing monstrous in my supposed position. "Sometimes," she said, "I wish we had to work, all of us, and that we could be freed from our servile bondage to servants."

Several of the ladies admitted that it was the greatest slavery in the world, and that it would be comparative luxury to do one's own work. But they all asked, in one form or another, what were they to do, and Mrs. Strange owned that she did not know. The facetious gentleman asked me how the ladies did in Altruria, and when I told them, as well as I could, they were, of course, very civil about it, but I could see that they all thought it impossible, or, if not impossible, then ridiculous. I did not feel bound to defend our customs, and I knew very well that each woman there was imagining herself in our conditions with the curse of her plutocratic tradition still upon her. They could not do otherwise, any of them, and they seemed to get tired of such effort as they did make.

Mrs. Makely rose, and the other ladies rose with her, for the Americans follow the English custom in letting the men remain at table after the women have left. But on this occasion I found it varied, by a pretty touch from the French custom, and the men, instead of merely standing up while the women filed out, gave each his arm, as far as the drawing-room, to the lady he had brought in to dinner. Then we went back, and what is the pleasantest part of the dinner to most men began for us.

XVI

I MUST SAY, to the credit of the Americans, that although the eating and drinking among them appear gross enough to an

Altrurian, you are not revolted by the coarse stories which the English sometimes tell as soon as the ladies have left them. If it is a men's dinner, or more especially a men's supper, these stories are pretty sure to follow the coffee; but when there have been women at the board, some sense of their presence seems to linger in the more delicate American nerves, and the indulgence is limited to two or three things off color, as the phrase is here, told with anxious glances at the drawing-room doors, to see if they are fast shut.

I do not remember just what brought the talk back from these primrose paths, to that question of American society forms, but presently some one said he believed the church sociable was the thing in most towns beyond the apple-bee and sugar-party stage, and this opened the inquiry as to how far the church still formed the social life of the people in cities. Some one suggested that in Brooklyn it formed it altogether, and then they laughed, for Brooklyn is always a joke with the New Yorkers; I do not know exactly why, except that this vast city is so largely a suburb, and that it has a great number of churches, and is comparatively cheap. Then another told of a lady who had come to New York (he admitted, twenty years ago,) and was very lonely, as she had no letters, until she joined a church. This at once brought her a general acquaintance, and she began to find herself in society; but as soon as she did so, she joined a more exclusive church where they took no notice of strangers. They all laughed at that bit of human nature, as they called it, and they philosophized the relation of women to society as a purely business relation. The talk ranged to the mutable character of society, and how people got into it, or were of it, and how it was very different from what it once was, except that with women it was always business. They spoke of certain new rich people with affected contempt; but I could see that they were each proud of knowing such millionaires as they could claim for acquaintance, though they pretended to make fun of the number of men-servants you had to run the gauntlet of in their houses before you could get to your hostess.

One of my commensals said he had noticed that I took little or no wine, and when I said that we seldom drank it in Altruria, he answered that he did not think I could make that go in America, if I meant to dine much. "Dining, you know, means overeating," he explained, "and if you wish to overeat, you must overdrink. I venture to say that you will pass a worse night than any of us, Mr. Homos, and that you will be sorrier to-morrow than I shall." They were all smoking, and I confess that their tobacco was secretly such an affliction to me that I was at one moment in doubt whether I should take a cigar myself, or ask leave to join the ladies.

The gentleman who had talked so much already said: "Well, I don't mind dining, a great deal, especially with Makely, here, but I do object to supping, as I have to do now and then, in the way of pleasure. Last Saturday night I sat down at eleven o'clock to blue-point oysters, consommé, stewed terrapin—yours was very good, Makely; I wish I had taken more of it—lamb chops with peas, redhead duck with celery mayonnaise, Nesselrode pudding, fruit, cheese, and coffee, with sausages, caviare, radishes, celery, and olives interspersed wildly, and drinkables and smokables ad libitum; and I can assure you that I felt very devout when I woke up after churchtime in the morning. It is this turning night into day that is killing us. We men, who have to go to business the next morning, ought to strike, and say that we won't go to anything later than eight o'clock dinner."

"Ah, then the women would insist upon our making it four o'clock tea," said another.

Our host seemed to be reminded of something by the mention of the women, and he said, after a glance at the state of the cigars, "Shall we join the ladies?"

One of the men-servants had evidently been waiting for this question. He held the door open, and we all filed into the drawing-room.

Mrs. Makely hailed me with, "Ah, Mr. Homos, I'm so glad you've come! We poor women have been having a most dismal time!"

"Honestly," asked the funny gentleman, "don't you always, without us?"

"Yes, but this has been worse than usual. Mrs. Strange has been asking us how many people we supposed there were in this city, within five minutes' walk of us, who had no dinner to-day. Do you call that kind?"

"A little more than kin, and less than kind, perhaps," the gentleman suggested. "But what does she propose to do about it?"

He turned toward Mrs. Strange, who answered, "Nothing. What does any one propose to do about it?"

"Then, why do you think about it?"

"I don't. It thinks about itself. Do you know that poem of Longfellow's, 'The Challenge'?"

"No, I never heard of it."

"Well, it begins in his sweet old way, about some Spanish king, who was killed before a city he was besieging, and one of his knights sallies out of the camp, and challenges the people of the city, the living and the dead, as traitors. Then the poet breaks off, *apropos de rien*:

> 'There is a greater army
>   That besets us round with strife,
> A numberless, starving army,
>   At all the gates of life.
> The poverty-stricken millions
>   Who challenge our wine and bread,
> And impeach us all for traitors,
>   Both the living and the dead.
> And whenever I sit at the banquet,
>   Where the feast and song are high,
> Amid the mirth and the music
>   I can hear that fearful cry.
> And hollow and haggard faces
>   Look into the lighted hall,
> And wasted hands are extended
>   To catch the crumbs that fall.
> For within there is light and plenty,
>   And odors fill the air;
> But without there is cold and darkness,
>   And hunger and despair.

> And there, in the camp of famine,
>   In wind and cold and rain,
> Christ, the great Lord of the Army,
>   Lies dead upon the plain.' "

"Ah," said the facetious gentleman, "that is fine! We really forget how fine Longfellow was. It is so pleasant to hear you quoting poetry, Mrs. Strange. That sort of thing has almost gone out; and it's a pity."

XVII

OUR FASHION of offering hospitality on the impulse, would be as strange here as offering it without some special inducement for its acceptance. The inducement is, as often as can be, a celebrity or eccentricity of some sort, or some visiting foreigner; and I suppose that I have been a good deal used myself in one quality or the other. But when the thing has been done, fully and guardedly at all points, it does not seem to have been done for pleasure, either by the host or the guest. The dinner is given in payment of another dinner; or out of ambition by people who are striving to get forward in society; or by great social figures who give regularly a certain number of dinners every season. In either case it is eaten from motives at once impersonal and selfish. I do not mean to say that I have not been at many dinners where I felt nothing perfunctory either in host or guest, and where as sweet and gay a spirit ruled as at any of our own simple feasts. Still, I think our main impression of American hospitality would be that it was thoroughly infused with the plutocratic principle, and that it meant business.

I am speaking now of the hospitality of society people, who number, after all, but a few thousands out of the many millions of American people. These millions are so far from being in society, even when they are very comfortable, and on the way to great prosperity, if they are not already greatly prosperous, that if they were suddenly confronted with the best society of the great eastern cities they would find it almost as strange as so many Altrurians. A great part of them have no conception of entertaining except upon an Altrurian scale of simplicity, and they know nothing and care less for the forms that society people value themselves upon. When they begin in the ascent of the social scale to adopt forms, it is still to wear them lightly and with an individual freedom and indifference; it is long before anxiety concerning the social law renders them vulgar.

Yet from highest to lowest, from first to last, one invariable fact characterizes them all, and it may be laid down as an axiom that in a plutocracy the man who needs a dinner, is the man who is never asked to dine. I do not say that he is not given a dinner. He is very often given a dinner, and for the most part he is kept from starving to death; but he is not suffered to sit at meat with his host, if the person who gives him a meal can be called his host. His need of the meal stamps him with a hopeless inferiority, and relegates him morally to the company of the swine at their husks, and of Lazarus whose sores the dogs licked. Usually, of course, he is not physically of such a presence as to fit him for any place in good society short of Abraham's bosom; but even if he were entirely decent, or of an inoffensive shabbiness, it would not be possible for his benefactors, in any grade of society, to ask him to their tables. He is sometimes fed in the kitchen; where the people of the house feed in the kitchen themselves, he is fed at the back door.

We were talking of this the other night at the house of that lady whom Mrs. Makely invited me specially to meet on Thanksgiving Day. It happened then, as it often happens here, that although I was asked to meet her, I saw very little of her. It was not so bad as it sometimes is, for I have been asked to meet people, very informally, and passed the whole evening with them, and yet not exchanged a word with them. Mrs. Makely really gave me a seat next Mrs. Strange at table, and we had some unimportant conversation; but there was a lively little creature vis-à-vis of me, who had a fancy of addressing me so much of her talk, that my acquaintance with Mrs. Strange rather languished through the dinner, and she went away so soon after the men rejoined the ladies in the drawing-room, that I did not speak to her there. I was rather surprised, then, to receive a note from her a few days later, asking me to dinner; and I finally went, I am ashamed to own, more from curiosity than from any other motive. I had been, in the meantime, thoroughly coached concerning her, by Mrs. Makely, whom I told of my invitation, and who said, quite frankly, that she wished Mrs. Strange had asked her, too. "But Eveleth Strange wouldn't do that," she explained, "because it would have the effect of paying me back. I'm so glad, on your account, that you're going, for I do want you to know at least one American woman that you can unreservedly approve of; I know you don't *begin* to approve of *me*; and I was so vexed that you really had no chance to talk with her that night you met her here; it seemed to me as if she ran away early, just to provoke me; and, to tell you the truth, I thought she had taken a dislike to you. I wish I could tell you just what sort of a person she is, but it would be perfectly hopeless, for you haven't got the documents, and you never could get them. I used to be at school with her, and even then she wasn't like any of the other girls. She was always so original, and did things from such a high motive, that afterwards, when we were all settled, I was perfectly thunderstruck at her marrying old Bellington Strange, who was twice her age, and had nothing but his money; he was not related to the New York Bellingtons at all, and nobody knows how he got the name; nobody ever heard of the Stranges. In fact, people say that he used to be plain Peter B. Strange, till he married Eveleth, and she made him drop the Peter, and blossom out in the Bellington, so that he could seem to have a social as well as a financial history. People who dislike her insisted that they were not in the least surprised at her marrying him; that the high-motive business was just her pose; and that she had jumped at the chance of getting him. But I always stuck up for her,—and I know that she did it for the sake of her family, who were all as poor as poor, and were dependent on her after her father went to smash in his business. She was always as high-strung and romantic as she could be, but I don't believe that even then she would have taken Mr. Strange, if there had been anybody else. I don't suppose any one else ever looked at her, for the young men are pretty sharp nowadays, and are not going to marry girls without a cent, when there are so many rich girls, just as charming every way: you can't expect them to. At any rate, whatever her motive was, she had her reward, for Mr. Strange died within a year of their marriage, and she got all his money. There was no attempt to break the will, for Mr. Strange seemed to be literally of no family; and she's lived quietly on in the house he bought her, ever since, except when she's in Europe, and that's about two-thirds of the time. She has her mother with her, and I suppose that her sisters, and her cousins, and her aunts, come in for outdoor aid. She's always helping somebody. They say that's her pose, now; but if it is, I don't think it's a bad one; and certainly if she wanted to get married again, there would be no trouble, with her three millions. I advise you to go to her dinner, by all means, Mr. Homos. It will be something worth while, in every way, and perhaps you'll convert her to Altrurianism; she's as hopeful a subject as *I* know."

XVIII

I WAS ONE of the earliest of the guests, for I cannot yet believe that people do not want me to come exactly when they say they do. I perceived, however, that one other gentleman had come before me, and I was both surprised and delighted to find that this was my acquaintance, Mr. Bullion, the Boston banker. He professed as much pleasure at our meeting as I certainly felt; but after a few words he went on talking with Mrs. Strange, while I was left to her mother, an elderly woman of quiet and even timid bearing, who affected me at once as born and bred in a wholly different environment. In fact, every American of the former generation is almost as strange to it in tradition, though not in principle, as I am; and I found myself singularly at home with this sweet lady, who seemed glad of my interest in her. I was taken from her side to be introduced to a lady, on the opposite side of the room, who said she had been promised my acquaintance by a friend of hers, whom I had met in the mountains,—Mr.

Twelvemough; did I remember him? She gave a little cry while still speaking, and dramatically stretched her hand toward a gentleman who entered at the moment, and whom I saw to be no other than Mr. Twelvemough himself. As soon as he had greeted our hostess he hastened up to us, and barely giving himself time to press the still outstretched hand of my companion, shook mine warmly, and expressed the greatest joy at seeing me. He said that he had just got back to town, in a manner, and had not known I was here, till Mrs. Strange had asked him to meet me. There were not a great many other guests, when they all arrived, and we sat down, a party not much larger than at Mrs. Makely's.

I found that I was again to take out my hostess, but I was put next the lady with whom I had been talking; she had come without her husband, who was, apparently, of a different social taste from herself, and had an engagement of his own; there was an artist and his wife whose looks I liked; some others whom I need not specify, were there, I fancied, because they had heard of Altruria, and were curious to see me. As Mr. Twelvemough sat quite at the other end of the table, the lady on my right could easily ask me whether I liked his books. She said, tentatively, people liked them because they felt sure when they took up one of his novels they had not got hold of a tract on political economy in disguise.

It was this complimentary close of a remark which scarcely began with praise, that made itself heard across the table, and was echoed with a heartfelt sigh from the lips of another lady.

"Yes," she said, "that is what I find such a comfort in Mr. Twelvemough's books."

"We were *speaking* of Mr. Twelvemough's books," the first lady triumphed, and several began to extol them for being fiction pure and simple, and not dealing with anything but loves of young people.

Mr. Twelvemough sat looking as modest as he could under the praise, and one of the ladies said that in a novel she had lately read there was a description of a surgical operation, that made her feel as if she had been present at a clinic. Then the author said that he had read that passage, too, and found it extremely well done. It was fascinating, but it was not art.

The painter asked, "Why was it not art?"

The author answered, "Well, if such a thing as that was art, then anything that a man chose to do in a work of imagination was art."

"Precisely," said the painter, "art *is* choice."

"On that ground," the banker interposed, "you could say that political economy was a fit subject for art, if an artist chose to treat it."

"It would have its difficulties," the painter admitted, "but there are certain phases of political economy, dramatic moments, human moments, which might be very fitly treated in art. For instance, who would object to Mr. Twelvemough's describing an eviction from an East side tenement-house on a cold winter night, with the mother and her children huddled about the fire the father had kindled with pieces of the household furniture?"

"*I* should object very much, for one," said the lady who had objected to the account of the surgical operation. "It would be too creepy. Art should give pleasure."

"Then you think a tragedy is not art?" asked the painter.

"I think that these harrowing subjects are brought in altogether too much," said the lady. "There are enough of them in real life, without filling all the novels with them. It's terrible the number of beggars you meet on the street, this winter. Do you want to meet them in Mr. Twelvemough's novels, too?"

"Well, it wouldn't cost me any money, there. I shouldn't have to give."

"You oughtn't to give money in real life," said the lady. "You ought to give charity tickets. If the beggars refuse them, it shows they are impostors."

"It's some comfort to know that the charities are so active," said the elderly young lady, "even if half the letters one gets *do* turn out to be appeals from them."

"It's very disappointing to have them do it, though," said the artist, lightly. "I thought there was a society to abolish poverty. That doesn't seem to be so active as the charities this winter. Is it possible they've found it a failure?"

"Well," said Mr. Bullion, "perhaps they have suspended during the hard times."

They tossed the ball back and forth with a lightness the Americans have, and I could not have believed, if I had not known how hardened people become to such things here, that they were almost in the actual presence of hunger and cold. It was within five minutes' walk of their warmth and surfeit; and if they had lifted the window and called, "Who goes there?" the houselessness that prowls the night could have answered them from the street below, "Despair!"

"I had an amusing experience," Mr. Twelvemough began, "when I was doing a little visiting for the charities in our ward, the other winter."

"For the sake of the literary material?" the artist suggested.

"Partly for the sake of the literary material; you know we have to look for our own everywhere. But we had a case of an old actor's son, who had got out of all the places he had filled, on account of rheumatism, and could not go to sea, or drive a truck, or even wrap gas-fixtures in paper any more."

"A checkered employ," the banker mused aloud.

"It was not of a simultaneous nature," the novelist explained. "So he came on the charities, and as I knew the theatrical profession a little, and how generous it was with all related to it, I said that I would undertake to look after his case. You know the theory is that we get work for our patients, or clients, or whatever they are, and I went to a manager whom I knew to be a good fellow, and I asked him for some sort of work. He said, Yes, send the man round, and he would give him a job copying parts for a new play he had written."

The novelist paused, and nobody laughed.

"It seems to me that your experience is instructive, rather than amusing," said the banker. "It shows that something can be done, if you try."

"Well," said Mr. Twelvemough, "I thought that was the moral, myself, till the fellow came afterwards to thank me. He said that he considered himself very lucky, for the manager had told him that there were six other men had wanted that job."

Everybody laughed, now, and I looked at my hostess in a little bewilderment. She murmured, "I suppose the joke is that he had befriended one man at the expense of six others."

"Oh," I returned, "is that a joke?"

No one answered, but the lady at my right asked: "How do you manage with poverty in Altruria?"

I saw the banker fix a laughing eye on me, but I answered, "In Altruria we have no poverty."

"Ah, I knew you would say that!" he cried out. "That's what he always does," he explained to the lady. "Bring up any one of our little difficulties, and ask how they get over it in Altruria, and he says they have nothing like it. It's very simple."

They all began to ask me questions, but with a courteous incredulity, which I could feel well enough, and some of my answers made them laugh, all but my hostess, who received them with a gravity that finally prevailed. But I was not disposed to go on talking of Altruria then, though they all protested a real interest, and murmured against the hardship of being cut off with so brief an account of our country as I had given them.

"Well," said the banker at last, "if there is no cure for our poverty, we might as well go on and enjoy ourselves."

"Yes," said our hostess, with a sad little smile, "we might as well enjoy ourselves."

XIX

THE TALK at Mrs. Strange's table took a far wider range than my meager notes would intimate, and we sat so long that it was almost eleven before the men joined the ladies in the drawing-room. You will hardly conceive of remaining two, three, or four hours at dinner, as one often does here, in society; out of society, the meals are dispatched with a rapidity unknown to the Altrurians. Our habit of listening to lectors, especially at the evening repast, and then of reasoning upon what we have heard, prolongs our stay at the board; but the fondest listener, the greatest talker among us, would be impatient of the delay eked out here by the great number, and the slow procession of the courses served. Yet the poorest American would find his ideal realized rather in the long-drawn-out gluttony of the society dinner here, than in our temperate simplicity.

At such a dinner it is very hard to avoid a surfeit, and I have to guard myself very carefully, lest, in the excitement of the talk, I gorge myself with everything, in its turn. Even at the best, my overloaded stomach often joins with my conscience in reproaching me for what you would think a shameful excess at table. Yet, wicked as my riot is, my waste is worse, and I have to think with contrition, not only of what I have eaten, but of what I have left uneaten, in a city where so many wake and sleep in hunger.

The ladies made a show of lingering, after we joined them in the drawing-room; but there were furtive glances at the clock, and presently her guests began to bid Mrs. Strange good-night. When I came up, and offered her my hand, she would not take it, but murmured, with a kind of passion: "Don't go! I mean it! Stay, and tell us about Altruria,—my mother and me!"

I was by no means loth, for I must confess that all I had seen and heard of this lady interested me in her more and more. I felt at home with her, too, as with no other society woman I have met; she seemed to me not only good, but very sincere, and very good-hearted, in spite of the world she lived in. Yet I have met so many disappointments here, of the kind that our civilization wholly fails to prepare us for, that I should not have been surprised to find that Mrs. Strange had wished me to stay, not that she might hear me talk about Altruria, but that I might hear her talk about herself. You must understand that the essential vice of a system which concenters a human being's thoughts upon his own interests, from the first moment of responsibility, colors and qualifies every motive with egotism. All egotists are unconscious, for otherwise they would be intolerable to themselves; but some are subtler than others; and as most women have finer natures than most men, everywhere, and in America most women have finer minds than most men, their egotism usually takes the form of pose. This is usually obvious, but in some cases it is so delicately managed that you do not suspect it, unless some other woman gives you a hint of it, and even then you cannot be sure of it, seeing the self-sacrifice, almost to martyrdom, which the poseuse makes for it. If Mrs. Makely had not suggested that some people attributed a pose to Mrs. Strange, I should certainly never have dreamed of looking for it, and I should have been only intensely interested, when she began, as soon as I was left alone with her and her mother:

"You may not know how unusual I am in asking this favor of you, Mr. Homos; but you might as well learn from me as from others, that I am rather unusual in everything. In fact, you can report in Altruria, when you get home, that you found at least one woman in America, whom fortune had smiled upon in every way, and who hated her smiling fortune almost as much as she hated herself. I'm quite satisfied," she went on, with a sad mockery, "that fortune is a man, and an American; when he has given you all the materials for having a good time, he believes that you must be happy, because there is nothing to hinder. It isn't that I want to be happy in the greedy way that men think we do, for then I could easily be happy. If you have a soul which is not above buttons, buttons are enough. But if you expect to be of real use, to help on, and to help out, you will be disappointed. I have not the faith that they say upholds you Altrurians in trying to help out, if I don't see my way out. It seems to me that my reason has some right to satisfaction, and that, if I am a woman grown, I can't be satisfied with the assurances they would give to little girls, that everything is going on well. Any one can see that things are not going on well. There is more and more wretchedness of every kind, not hunger of body alone, but hunger of soul. If you escape one, you suffer the other, because, if you *have* a soul, you must long to help, not for a time, but for all time. I suppose," she asked, abruptly, "that Mrs. Makely has told you something about me?"

"Something," I admitted.

"I ask," she went on, "because I don't want to bore you with a statement of my case, if you know it already. Ever since I heard you were in New York, I have wished to see you, and to talk with you about Altruria; I did not suppose that there would be any chance at Mrs. Makely's, and there wasn't; and I did not suppose there would be any chance here, unless I could take courage to do what I have done, now. You must excuse it, if it seems as extraordinary a proceeding to you as it really is; I wouldn't at all have you think it is usual for a lady to ask one of her guests to stay after the rest, in order, if you please, to confess herself to him. It's a crime without a name."

She laughed, not gaily, but humorously, and then went on, speaking always with a feverish eagerness, which I find it hard to give you a sense of, for the women here have an intensity quite beyond our experience of the sex at home:

"But you are a foreigner, and you come from an order of things so utterly unlike ours, that perhaps you will be able to condone my offense. At any rate, I have risked it." She laughed again, more gaily, and recovered herself in a cheerfuller and easier mood. "Well, the long and the short of it is, that I have come to the end of my tether. I have tried, as truly as I believe any woman ever did, to do my share, with money and with work, to help make life better for those whose life is bad, and though one mustn't boast of good works, I may say that I have been pretty thorough, and if I've given up, it's because I see, in our state of things, *no* hope of curing the evil. It's like trying to soak up the drops of a rainstorm. You do dry up a drop here and there; but the clouds are full of them, and the first thing you know, you stand, with your blotting-paper in your hand, in a puddle over your shoe-tops. There is nothing but charity, and charity is a failure, except for the moment. If you think of the misery around you, that must remain around you, forever and ever, as long as you live, you have your choice—to go mad, and be put into an asylum, or go mad, and devote yourself to society."

XX

WHILE MRS. STRANGE talked on, her mother listened quietly, with a dim, submissive smile, and her hands placidly crossed in her lap. She now said:

"It seems to be very different now from what it was in my time. There are certainly a great many beggars, and we used never to have one. Children grew up, and people lived and died, in large towns, without ever seeing one. I remember, when my husband first took me abroad, how astonished we were at the beggars. Now, I meet as many in New York, as I met in London, or in Rome. But if you don't do charity, what can you do? Christ enjoined it, and Paul says—"

"Oh, people *never* do the charity that Christ meant," said Mrs. Strange; "and, as things are now, how *could* they? Who would dream of dividing half her frocks and wraps with poor women, or selling *all*, and giving to the poor? That is what makes it so hopeless. We *know* that Christ was perfectly right, and that he was perfectly sincere in what he said to the good young millionaire; but we all go away exceeding sorrowful, just as the good young millionaire did. We have to, if we don't want to come on charity ourselves. How do *you* manage about that?" she asked me; and then she added, "But, of course, I forgot that you have no need of charity."

"Oh, yes, we have," I returned; and I tried, once more, as I have tried so often with Americans, to explain how the heavenly need of giving the self continues with us, but on terms that do not harrow the conscience of the giver, as self-sacrifice always must here, at its purest and noblest. I sought to make her conceive of our nation as a family, where every one was secured against want by the common provision, and against the degrading and depraving inequality which comes from want. The "dead-level of equality" is what the Americans call the condition in which all would be as the angels of God, and they blasphemously deny that He ever meant His creatures to be alike happy, because some, through a long succession of unfair advantages, have inherited more brain, or brawn, or beauty, than others. I found that this gross and impious notion of God darkened even the clear intelligence of a woman like Mrs. Strange; and, indeed, it prevails here so commonly, that it is one of the first things advanced as an argument against the Altrurianization of America.

I believe I did, at last, succeed in showing her how charity still continues among us, but in forms that bring neither a sense of inferiority to him who takes, nor anxiety to him who gives. I said that benevolence here often seemed to involve, essentially, some such risk as a man should run if he parted with a portion of the vital air which belonged to himself and his family, in succoring a fellow-being from suffocation; but that with us, where it was no more possible for one to deprive himself of his share of the common food, shelter, and clothing, than of the air he breathed, one could devote one's self utterly to others, without that foul alloy of fear, which I thought must basely qualify every good deed in plutocratic conditions.

She said that she knew what I meant, and that I was quite right in my conjecture, as regarded men, at least; a man who did not stop to think what the effect, upon himself and his own, his giving must have, would be a fool or a madman; but women could often give as recklessly as they spent, without any thought of consequences, for they did not know how money came.

"Women," I said, "are exterior to your conditions, and they can sacrifice themselves without wronging any one."

"Or, rather," she continued, "without the sense of wronging any one. Our men like to keep us in that innocence, or ignorance; they think it is pretty, or they think it is funny; and as long as a girl is in her father's house, or a wife is in her husband's, she knows no more of money-earning, or money-making, than a child. Most grown women, among us, if they had a sum of money in the bank, would not know how to get it out. They would not know how to endorse a check, much less draw one. But there are plenty of women who are inside the conditions, as much as men are: poor women who have to earn their bread, and rich women who have to manage their property. I can't speak for the poor women; but I can speak for the rich, and I can confess for them that what you imagine is true. The taint of unfaith and distrust is on every dollar that you dole out, so that, as far as the charity of the rich is concerned, I would read Shakespeare:

'It curseth him that gives, and him that takes.'

"Perhaps that is why the rich give comparatively so little! The poor can never understand how much the rich value their money, how much the owner of a great fortune dreads to see it less! If it were not so, they would surely give more than they do; for a man who has ten millions could give eight of them, without feeling the loss; the man with a hundred could give ninety, and be no nearer want. Ah, it's a strange mystery! My poor husband and I used to talk of it a great deal, in the long year that he lay dying; and I think I hate my superfluity the more because I know he hated it so much."

A little trouble had stolen into her impassioned tones, and there was a gleam, as of tears, in the eyes she dropped for a moment. They were shining still, when she lifted them again to mine.

"I suppose," she said, "that Mrs. Makely told you something of my marriage?"

"Eveleth!" her mother protested, with a gentle murmur.

"Oh, I think I can be frank with Mr. Homos! He is not an American, and he will understand, or, at least, he will not misunderstand. Besides, I dare say I shall not say anything worse than Mrs. Makely has said already! My husband was much older than I, and I ought not to have married him; a young girl ought never to marry an old man, or even a man who is only a good many years her senior. But we both faithfully tried to make the best of our mistake, not the worst, and I think this effort helped us to respect each other, when there couldn't be any question of more. He was a rich man, and he had made his money out of nothing, or, at least, from a beginning of utter poverty. But in his last years he came to a sense of its worthlessness, such as few men who have made their money ever have. He was a

common man, in a great many ways; he was imperfectly educated, and he was ungrammatical, and he never was at home in
society; but he had a tender heart, and an honest nature, and I
revere his memory, as no one would believe I could without
knowing him as I did. His money became a burden and a terror
to him; he did not know what to do with it, and he was always
morbidly afraid of doing harm with it; he got to thinking that
money was an evil in itself."

"That is what we think," I ventured.

"Yes, I know. But he had thought this out for himself, and yet
he had times when his thinking about it seemed to him a kind of
craze, and, at any rate, he distrusted himself so much that he died
leaving it all to me. I suppose he thought that, perhaps, I could
learn how to give it without hurting; and then he knew that, in
our state of things, I must have some money to keep the wolf from
the door. And I am afraid to part with it, too. I have given, and
given; but there seems some evil spell on the principal, that
guards it from encroachment, so that it remains the same, and,
if I do not watch, the interest grows in the bank, with that frightful life dead money seems endowed with, as the hair of dead
people grows in the grave."

"Eveleth!" her mother murmured again.

"Oh, yes," she answered, "I dare say my words are wild. I
dare say they only mean that I loathe my luxury from the bottom
of my soul, and long to be rid of it, if I only could, without harm
to others, and with safety to myself."

XXI

IT SEEMED TO ME that I became suddenly sensible of this luxury
for the first time. I had certainly been aware that I was in a large
and stately house, and that I had been served and banquetted
with a princely pride and profusion. But there had, somehow,
been through all a sort of simplicity, a sort of quiet, so that I had
not thought of the establishment, and its operation, even so much
as I had thought of Mrs. Makely's far inferior scale of living; or,

else, what with my going about so much in society, I was ceasing to be so keenly observant of the material facts as I had been at first. But I was better qualified to judge of what I saw, and I had now a vivid sense of the costliness of Mrs. Strange's environment. There were thousands of dollars in the carpets underfoot; there were tens of thousands in the pictures on the walls. In a bronze group that withdrew itself into a certain niche, with a faint relucence, there was the value of a skilled artisan's wage for five years of hard work; in the bindings of the books that showed from the library shelves, there was almost as much money as most of the authors had got for writing them. Every fixture, every movable, was an artistic masterpiece; a fortune, as fortunes used to be counted even in this land of affluence, had been lavished in the mere furnishing of a house which the palaces of nobles and princes of other times had contributed to embellish.

"My husband," Mrs. Strange went on, "bought this house for me, and let me furnish it after my own fancy. After it was all done, we neither of us liked it, and when he died, I felt as if he had left me in a tomb here."

"Eveleth," said her mother, "you ought not to speak so before Mr. Homos. He will not know what to think of you, and he will go back to Altruria with a very wrong idea of American women."

At this protest, Mrs. Strange seemed to recover herself a little. "Yes," she said, "you must excuse me. I have no right to speak so. But one is often much franker with foreigners than with one's own kind, and, besides, there is something—I don't know what! —that will not let me keep the truth from you."

She gazed at me entreatingly, and then, as if some strong emotion swept her from her own hold, she broke out:

"He thought he would make some sort of atonement to me, as if I owed none to him! His money was all he had to do it with, and he spent that upon me in every way he could think of, though he knew that money could not buy anything that was really good, and that, if it bought anything beautiful, it uglified it with the sense of cost, to every one who could value it in dollars and cents. He was a good man, far better than people ever imagined, and very simple-hearted and honest, like a child, in his contrition for his wealth, which he did not dare to get rid of; and though I know that, if he were to come back, it would be just as it was, his memory is as dear to me as if—"

She stopped, and pressed in her lip with her teeth, to stay its tremor. I was painfully affected. I knew that she had never meant to be so open with me, and was shocked and frightened at herself. I was sorry for her, and yet I was glad, for it seemed to me that she had given me a glimpse, not only of the truth in her own heart, but of the truth in the hearts of a whole order of prosperous people in these lamentable conditions, whom I shall hereafter be able to judge more leniently, more justly.

I began to speak of Altruria, as if that were what our talk had been leading up to, and she showed herself more intelligently interested concerning us, than any one I have yet seen in this country. We appeared, I found, neither incredible nor preposterous to her; our life, in her eyes, had that beauty of right living which the Americans so feebly imagine, or imagine not at all. She asked what route I had come by to America, and she seemed disappointed and aggrieved that we placed the restrictions we have felt necessary upon visitors from the plutocratic world. Were we afraid, she asked, that they would corrupt our citizens, or mar our content with our institutions? She seemed scarcely satisfied when I explained, as I have explained so often here, that the measures we had taken were rather in the interest of the plutocratic world, than of the Altrurians; and alleged the fact that no visitor from the outside had ever been willing to go home again, as sufficient proof that we had nothing to fear from the spread of plutocratic ideals among us. I assured her, and this she easily imagined, that the better known these became, the worse they appeared to us; and that the only concern our Priors felt, in regard to them, was that our youth could not conceive of them in their enormity, but, in seeing how estimable plutocratic people often were, they would attribute to their conditions the inherent good of human nature. I said our own life was so directly reasoned from its economic premises, that they could hardly believe the plutocratic life was often an absolute *non sequitur* of the pluto-cratic premises. I confessed that this error was at the bottom of my own wish to visit America, and study those premises.

"And what has your conclusion been?" she said, leaning eagerly toward me, across the table between us, laden with the maps and charts we had been examining for the verification of the position of Altruria, and my own course here, by way of England.

A slight sigh escaped Mrs. Gray, which I interpreted as an expression of fatigue; it was already past twelve o'clock, and I made it the pretext for escape.

"You have seen the meaning and purport of Altruria so clearly," I said, "that I think I can safely leave you to guess the answer to that question."

She laughed, and did not try to detain me, now, when I offered my hand for good-night. I fancied her mother took leave of me coldly, and with a certain effect of inculpation.

XXII

IT IS LONG since I wrote you, and you have had reason enough to be impatient of my silence. I submit to the reproaches of your letter, with a due sense of my blame; whether I am altogether to blame, you shall say after you have read this.

I cannot yet decide whether I have lost a great happiness, the greatest that could come to any man, or escaped the worst mis-fortune that could befall me. But such as it is, I will try to set the fact honestly down.

I do not know whether you had any conjecture, from my repeated mention of a lady whose character greatly interested me, that I was in the way of feeling any other interest in her than my letters expressed. I am no longer young, though at thirty-five an Altrurian is by no means so old as an American at the same age. The romantic ideals of the American women which I had formed from the American novels had been dissipated; if I had any sentiment toward them, as a type, it was one of distrust,

which my very sense of the charm in their inconsequence, their
beauty, their brilliancy, served rather to intensify. I thought myself doubly defended by that difference between their civilization
and ours, which forbade reasonable hope of happiness in any
sentiment for them, tenderer than that of the student of strange
effects in human nature. But we have not yet, my dear Cyril,
reasoned the passions, even in Altruria.

After I last wrote you, a series of accidents, or what appeared
so, threw me more and more constantly into the society of Mrs.
Strange. We began to laugh at the fatality with which we met
everywhere, at teas, at lunches, at dinners, at evening receptions,
and even at balls, where I have been a great deal, because, with
all my thirty-five years, I have not yet outlived that fondness for
dancing which has so often amused you in me. Wherever my
acquaintance widened among cultivated people, they had no
inspiration but to ask us to meet each other, as if there were really
no other woman in New York who could be expected to understand me. "You must come to lunch (or tea, or dinner, whichever
it might be), and we will have her. She will be so much interested
to meet you."

But perhaps we should have needed none of these accidents
to bring us together. I, at least, can look back, and see that, when
none of them happened, I sought occasions for seeing her, and
made excuses of our common interest in this matter and in that,
to go to her. As for her, I can only say that I seldom failed to find
her at home, whether I called upon her nominal day or not, and
more than once the man who let me in said he had been charged
by Mrs. Strange to say that, if I called, she was to be back very
soon; or, else, he made free to suggest that, though Mrs. Strange
was not at home, Mrs. Gray was; and then I found it easy to stay
until Mrs. Strange returned. The good old lady had an insatiable
curiosity about Altruria, and, though I do not think she ever
quite believed in our reality, she at least always treated me kindly,
as if I were the victim of an illusion that was thoroughly benign.

I think she had some notion that your letters, which I used
often to take with me, and read to Mrs. Strange and herself, were

inventions of mine; and the fact that they bore only an English postmark, confirmed her in this notion, though I explained that in our present passive attitude toward the world outside, we had as yet no postal relations with other countries, and, as all our communication at home was by electricity, that we had no letter post of our own. The very fact that she belonged to a purer and better age in America disqualified her to conceive of Altruria; her daughter, who had lived into a full recognition of the terrible anarchy in which the conditions have ultimated here, could far more vitally imagine us, and to her, I believe, we were at once a living reality. Her perception, her sympathy, her intelligence, became more and more to me, and I escaped to them oftener and oftener, from a world where an Altrurian must be so painfully at odds. In all companies here, I am aware that I have been regarded either as a good joke, or a bad joke, according to the humor of the listener, and it was grateful to be taken seriously.

From the first, I was sensible of a charm in her, different from that I felt in other American women, and impossible in our Altrurian women. She had a deep and almost tragical seriousness, masked with a most winning gaiety, a light irony, a fine scorn that was rather for herself than for others. She had thought herself out of all sympathy with her environment; she knew its falsehood, its vacuity, its hopelessness; but she necessarily remained in it, and of it. She was as much at odds in it as I was, without my poor privilege of criticism and protest, for, as she said, she could not set herself up as a censor of things that she must keep on doing as other people did. She could have renounced the world, as there are ways and means of doing, here; but she had no vocation to the religious life, and she could not feign it, without a sense of sacrilege. In fact, this generous, and magnanimous, and gifted woman was without that faith, that trust in God, which comes to us from living His law, and which I wonder any American can keep. She denied nothing; but she had lost the strength to affirm anything. She no longer tried to do good from her heart, though she kept on doing charity in what she said was a mere mechanical impulse from the belief of other days, but always with the ironical doubt that she was doing harm. Women are nothing by halves, as men can be, and she was in a despair which no man can realize, for we have always some if or and, which a woman of the like mood casts from her in wild rejection. Where she could not clearly see her way to a true life, it was the same to her as an impenetrable darkness.

You will have inferred something of all this, from what I have written of her before, and from words of hers that I have reported to you. Do you think it so wonderful, then, that in the joy I felt at the hope, the solace which my story of our life seemed to give her, she should become more and more precious to me? It was not wonderful, either, I think, that she should identify me with that hope, that solace, and should suffer herself to lean upon me, in a reliance infinitely sweet and endearing. But what a fantastic dream it now appears!

XXIII

I CAN HARDLY tell you just how we came to own our love to each other; but one day I found myself alone with her mother, with the sense that Eveleth had suddenly withdrawn from the room, at the knowledge of my approach. Mrs. Gray was strongly moved by something; but she governed herself, and, after giving me a tremulous hand, bade me sit.

"Will you excuse me, Mr. Homos," she began, "if I ask you whether you intend to make America your home, after this?"

"Oh, no!" I answered, and I tried to keep out of my voice the despair with which the notion filled me. I have sometimes had nightmares, here, in which I thought that I was an American by choice, and I can give you no conception of the rapture of awakening to the fact that I could still go back to Altruria, that I had not cast my lot with this wretched people. "How could I do that?" I faltered; and I was glad to perceive that I had imparted to her no hint of the misery which I had felt at such a notion.

"I mean, by getting naturalized, and becoming a citizen, and taking up your residence amongst us."

"No," I answered, as quietly as I could, "I had not thought of that."

"And you still intend to go back to Altruria?"

"I hope so; I ought to have gone back long ago, and if I had not met the friends I have in this house—" I stopped, for I did not know how I should end what I had begun to say.

"I am glad you think we are your friends," said the lady, "for we have tried to show ourselves your friends. I feel as if this had given me the right to say something to you, that you may think very odd."

"Say anything to me, my dear lady," I returned. "I shall not think it unkind, no matter how odd it is."

"Oh, it's nothing. It's merely that—that when you are not here with us, I lose my grasp on Altruria; and—and I begin to doubt—"

I smiled. "I know! People here have often hinted something of that kind to me. Tell me, Mrs. Gray, do Americans generally take me for an impostor?"

"Oh, no!" she answered, fervently. "Everybody that I have heard speak of you has the highest regard for you, and believes you perfectly sincere. But—"

"But what?" I entreated.

"They think you may be mistaken."

"Then they think I am out of my wits—that I am in an hallucination!"

"No, not that," she returned. "But it is so very difficult for us to conceive of a whole nation living, as you say you do, on the same terms as one family, and no one trying to get ahead of another, or richer, and having neither inferiors nor superiors, but just one dead level of equality, where there is no distinction, except by natural gifts, and good deeds, or beautiful works. It seems impossible, it seems ridiculous."

"Yes," I confessed, "I know that it seems so to the Americans."

"And I must tell you something else, Mr. Homos, and I hope you won't take it amiss. The first night when you talked about Altruria, here, and showed us how you had come, by way of

England, and the place where Altruria ought to be on our maps,
I looked them over, after you were gone, and I could make
nothing of it. I have often looked at the map since, but I could
never find Altruria; it was no use."

"Why," I said, "if you will let me have your atlas—"

She shook her head. "It would be the same again, as soon as
you went away." I could not conceal my distress, and she went
on: "Now, you mustn't mind what I say. I'm nothing but a silly
old woman, and Eveleth would never forgive me if she could
know what I've been saying."

"Then Mrs. Strange isn't troubled, as you are, concerning
me?" I asked, and I confess my anxiety attenuated my voice
almost to a whisper.

"She won't admit that she is. It might be better for her if she
would. But Eveleth is very true to her friends, and that—that
makes me all the more anxious that she should not deceive
herself."

"Oh, Mrs. Gray!" I could not keep a certain tone of reproach
out of my words.

She began to weep. "There! I knew I should hurt your feelings.
But you mustn't mind what I say. I beg your pardon! I take it all
back—"

"Ah, I don't want you to take it back! But what proof shall I
give you that there is such a land as Altruria! If the darkness
implies the day, America must imply Altruria. In what way do I
seem false, or mad, except that I claim to be the citizen of a country where people love one another as the first Christians did?"

"That is just it," she returned. "Nobody can imagine the first
Christians, and do you think we can imagine anything like them
in our own day?"

"But Mrs. Strange—she imagines us, you say?"

"She thinks she does; but I am afraid she only thinks so, and
I know her better than you do, Mr. Homos. I know how enthusiastic she always was, and how unhappy she has been since
she has lost her hold on faith, and how eagerly she has caught
at the hope you have given her of a higher life on earth than we

live here. If she should ever find out that she was wrong, I don't know what would become of her. You mustn't mind me; you mustn't let me wound you by what I say!"

"You don't wound me, and I only thank you for what you say; but I entreat you to believe in me. Mrs. Strange has not deceived herself, and I have not deceived her. Shall I protest to you, by all I hold sacred, that I am really what I told you I was; that I am not less, and that Altruria is infinitely more, happier, better, gladder, than any words of mine can say? Shall I not have the happiness to see your daughter to-day? I had something to say to her—and now I have so much more! If she is in the house, won't you send to her? I can make her understand—"

I stopped at a certain expression which I fancied I saw in Mrs. Gray's face.

"Mr. Homos," she began, so very seriously that my heart trembled with a vague misgiving, "sometimes I think you had better not see my daughter any more."

"Not see her any more?" I gasped.

"Yes; I don't see what good can come of it, and it's all very strange, and uncanny. I don't know how to explain it; but, indeed, it isn't anything personal. It's because you are of a state of things so utterly opposed to human nature, that I don't see how—I am afraid that—"

"But I am not uncanny to *her*?" I entreated. "I am not unnatural, not incredible—"

"Oh, no; that is the worst of it. But I have said too much; I have said a great deal more than I ought. But you must excuse it: I am an old woman. I am not very well, and I suppose it's that that makes me talk so much."

She rose from her chair, and I perforce rose from mine, and made a movement toward her.

"No, no," she said, "I don't need any help. You must come again soon, and see us, and show that you've forgotten what I've said." She gave me her hand, and I could not help bending over it, and kissing it. She gave a little, pathetic whimper. "Oh, I *know* I've said the most dreadful things to you."

"You haven't said anything that takes your friendship from
me, Mrs. Gray, and that is what I care for." My own eyes filled
with tears, I do not know why, and I groped my way from the
room. Without seeing any one in the obscurity of the hallway,
where I found myself, I was aware of some one there, by that sort
of fine perception which makes us know the presence of a spirit.

"You are going?" a whisper said. "Why are you going?" And
Eveleth had me by the hand, and was drawing me gently into
the dim drawing-room that opened from the place. "I don't
know all my mother has been saying to you. I had to let her say
something; she thought she ought. I knew you would know how
to excuse it."

"Oh, my dearest!" I said, and why I said this I do not know,
or how we found ourselves in each other's arms.

"What are we doing?" she murmured.

"You don't believe I am an impostor, an illusion, a visionary!"
I besought her, straining her closer to my heart.

"I believe in you, with all my soul!" she answered.

We sat down, side by side, and talked long. I did not go away
the whole day. With a high disdain of convention, she made me
stay. Her mother sent word that she would not be able to come
to dinner, and we were alone together at table, in an image of
what our united lives might be. We spent the evening in that
happy interchange of trivial confidences that lovers use in symbol
of the unutterable raptures that fill them. We were there in what
seemed an infinite present, without a past, without a future.

XXIV

SOCIETY had to be taken into our confidence, and Mrs. Makely
saw to it that there were no reserves with society. Our engagement was not quite like that of two young persons, but people
found in our character and circumstance an interest far tran-
scending that felt in the engagement of the most romantic lovers.
Some note of the fact came to us by accident, as one evening
when we stood near a couple, and heard them talking. "It must

be very weird," the man said; "something like being engaged to a materialization." "Yes," said the girl, "quite the Demon Lover business, I should think." She glanced round, as people do, in talking, and, at sight of us, she involuntarily put her hand over her mouth. I looked at Eveleth; there was nothing expressed in her face but a generous anxiety for me. But so far as the open attitude of society toward us was concerned, nothing could have been more flattering. We could hardly have been more asked to meet each other than before; but now there were entertainments in special recognition of our betrothal, which Eveleth said could not be altogether refused, though she found the ordeal as irksome as I did. In America, however, you get used to many things. I do not know why it should have been done, but in the society columns of several of the great newspapers, our likenesses were printed, from photographs procured I cannot guess how, with descriptions of our persons as to those points of coloring, and carriage, and stature, which the pictures could not give, and with biographies such as could be ascertained in her case and imagined in mine. In some of the society papers, paragraphs of a surprising scurrility appeared, attacking me as an impostor, and aspersing the motives of Eveleth in her former marriage, and treating her as a foolish crank, or an audacious flirt. The goodness of her life, her self-sacrifice and works of benevolence counted for no more against these wanton attacks than the absolute inoffensiveness of my own; the writers knew no harm of her, and they knew nothing at all of me; but they devoted us to the execration of their readers simply because we formed apt and ready themes for paragraphs. You may judge of how wild they were in their aim when some of them denounced me as an Altrurian plutocrat!

We could not escape this storm of notoriety; we had simply to let it spend its fury. When it began, several reporters of both sexes came to interview me, and questioned me, not only as to all the facts of my past life, and all my purposes in the future, but as to my opinion of hypnotism, eternal punishment, the Ibsen drama, and the tariff reform. I did my best to answer them seriously, and certainly I answered them civilly; but it seemed from what they printed that the answers I gave did not concern them, for they gave others for me. They appeared to me for the most part kindly and well-meaning young people, though vastly ignorant of vital things. They had apparently visited me with minds made up, or else their reports were revised by some controlling hand, and a quality injected more in the taste of the special journals they represented, than in keeping with the facts. When I realized this, I refused to see any more reporters, or to answer them, and then they printed the questions they had prepared to ask me, in such form that my silence was made of the same damaging effect as a full confession of guilt upon the charges.

The experience was so strange and new to me that it affected me in a degree I was unwilling to let Eveleth imagine. But she divined my distress, and when she divined that it was chiefly for her, she set herself to console and reassure me. She told me that this was something every one here expected, in coming willingly or unwillingly before the public; and that I must not think of it at all, for certainly no one else would think twice of it. This, I found, was really so, for when I ventured to refer tentatively to some of these publications, I found that people, if they had read them, had altogether forgotten them; and that they were, with all the glare of print, of far less effect with our acquaintance, than something said under the breath in a corner. I found that some of our friends had not known the effigies for ours which they had seen in the papers; others made a joke of the whole affair, as the Americans do with so many affairs, and said that they supposed the pictures were those of people who had been cured by some patent medicine, they looked so strong and handsome. This, I think, was a piece of Mr. Makely's humor in the beginning; but it had a general vogue, long after the interviews and the illustrations were forgotten.

XXV

I LINGER a little upon these trivial matters because I shrink from what must follow. They were scarcely blots upon our happiness; rather they were motes in the sunshine which had no other cloud.

It is true that I was always somewhat puzzled by a certain manner in Mrs. Gray, which certainly was from no unfriendliness for me: she could not have been more affectionate to me, after our engagement, if I had been really her own son; and it was not until after our common kindness had confirmed itself upon the new footing that I felt this perplexing qualification on it. I felt it first one day when I found her alone, and I talked long and freely to her of Eveleth, and opened to her my whole heart of joy in our love. At one point she casually asked me how soon we should expect to return from Altruria after our visit; and at first I did not understand.

"Of course," she explained, "you will want to see all your old friends, and so will Eveleth, for they will be her friends, too; but if you want me to go with you, as you say, you must let me know when I shall see New York again."

"Why," I said, "you will always be with us!"

"Well, then," she pursued with a smile, "when shall *you* come back?"

"Oh, never!" I answered. "No one ever leaves Altruria, if he can help it, unless he is sent on a mission."

She looked a little mystified, and I went on: "Of course, I was not officially authorized to visit the world outside, but I was permitted to do so, to satisfy a curiosity the Priors thought useful; but I have now had quite enough of it, and I shall never leave home again."

"You won't come to live in America?"

"God forbid!" said I, and I am afraid I could not hide the horror that ran through me at the thought. "And when you once see our happy country, you could no more be persuaded to return to America than a disembodied spirit could be persuaded to return to the earth."

She was silent, and I asked: "But, surely, you understood this, Mrs. Gray?"

"No," she said, reluctantly. "Does Eveleth?"

"Why, certainly!" I said. "We have talked it over a hundred times. Hasn't she—"

"I don't know," she returned, with a vague trouble in her voice and eyes. "Perhaps I haven't understood her exactly. Perhaps—but I shall be ready to do whatever you and she think best. I am an old woman, you know; and you know, I was born here, and I should feel the change."

Her words conveyed to me a delicate reproach; I felt for the first time that, in my love of my own country, I had not considered her love of hers. It is said that the Icelanders are homesick when they leave their world of lava and snow; and I ought to have remembered that an American might have some such tenderness for his atrocious conditions, if he were exiled from them forever. I suppose it was the large and wide mind of Eveleth, with its openness to a knowledge and appreciation of better things, that had suffered me to forget this. She seemed always so eager to see Altruria, she imagined it so fully, so lovingly, that I had ceased to think of her as an alien; she seemed one of us, by birth as well as by affinity.

Yet, now, the words of her mother, and the light they threw upon the situation, gave me pause. I began to ask myself questions I was impatient to ask Eveleth, so that there should be no longer any shadow of misgiving in my breast; and yet I found myself dreading to ask them, lest by some perverse juggle I had mistaken our perfect sympathy for a perfect understanding.

XXVI

LIKE ALL COWARDS who wait a happy moment for the duty that should not be suffered to wait at all, I was destined to have the affair challenge me, instead of seizing the advantage of it that instant frankness would have given me. Shall I confess that I let several days go by, and still had not spoken to Eveleth, when, at the end of a long evening—the last long evening we passed together—she said:

"What would you like to have me do with this house while we are gone?"

"Do with this house?" I echoed; and I felt as if I were standing on the edge of an abyss.

"Yes; shall we let it, or sell it; or what? Or give it away?" I drew a little breath at this; perhaps we had not misunderstood each other, after all. She went on: "Of course, I have a peculiar feeling about it, so that I wouldn't like to get it ready, and let it furnished, in the ordinary way. I would rather lend it to some one, if I could be sure of any one who would appreciate it; but I can't. Not one! And it's very much the same when one comes to think about selling it. Yes, I should like to give it away for some good purpose, if there is any in this wretched state of things! What do you say, Aristide?"

She always used the French form of my name, because she said it sounded ridiculous in English, for a white man, though I told her that the English was nearer the Greek in sound.

"By all means, give it away," I said. "Give it for some public purpose. That will at least be better than any private purpose, and put it somehow in the control of the State, beyond the reach of individuals or corporations. Why not make it the foundation of a free school for the study of the Altrurian polity?"

She laughed at this, as if she thought I must be joking. "It would be droll, wouldn't it, to have Tammany appointees teaching Altrurianism?" Then she said, after a moment of reflection: "Why not? It needn't be in the hands of Tammany. It could be in the hands of the United States; I will ask my lawyer if it couldn't; and I will endow it with money enough to support the school handsomely. Aristide, you have hit it!"

I began: "You can give *all* your money to it, my dear—" But I stopped at the bewildered look she turned on me.

"All?" she repeated. "But what should we have to live on, then?"

"We shall need no money to live on, in Altruria," I answered.

"Oh, in Altruria! But when we come back to New York?"

It was an agonizing moment, and I felt that shutting of the heart which blinds the eyes and makes the brain reel. "Eveleth," I gasped, "did you expect to return to New York?"

"Why, certainly!" she cried. "Not at once, of course. But after you had seen your friends, and made a good, long visit— Why

surely, Aristide, you don't understand that I— You didn't mean
to *live* in Altruria?"

"Ah!" I answered. "Where else could I live? Did you think
for an instant that I could live in such a land as this?" I saw that
she was hurt, and I hastened to say, "I know that it is the best
part of the world outside of Altruria; but, oh, my dear, you cannot imagine how horrible the notion of living here seems to me.
Forgive me! I am going from bad to worse. I don't mean to
wound you. After all, it is your country, and you must love it.
But, indeed, I could not think of living here. I could not take the
burden of its wilful misery on my soul. I must live in Altruria, and
you, when you have once seen my country, *our* country, will
never consent to live in any other!"

"Yes," she said, "I know it must be very beautiful; but I
hadn't supposed—and yet I ought—"

"No, dearest, no! It was I who was to blame, for not being
clearer from the first. But that is the way with us! We can't
imagine any people willing to live anywhere else when once
they have seen Altruria; and I have told you so much of it, and
we have talked of it together so often, that I must have forgotten
you had not actually known it. But listen, Eveleth! We will
agree to this. After we have been a year in Altruria, if you wish
to return to America, I will come back and live with you here."

"No, indeed!" she answered, generously. "If you are to be my
husband," and here she began with the solemn words of the
Bible, so beautiful in their quaint English, " 'whither thou goest,
I will go, and I will not return from following after thee. Thy
country shall be my country, and thy God my God.' "

I caught her to my heart, in a rapture of tenderness, and the
evening that had begun for us so forbiddingly, ended in a happiness such as not even our love had known before. I insisted upon
the conditions I had made, as to our future home, and she agreed
to them gaily, at last, as a sort of reparation which I might make
my conscience, if I liked, for tearing her from a country which
she had willingly lived out of for the far greater part of the last
five years.

But when we met again, I could see that she had been thinking seriously.

"I won't give the house absolutely away," she said. "I will keep the deed of it myself, but I will establish that sort of school of Altrurian doctrine in it, and I will endow it, and when we come back here, for our experimental sojourn, after we've been in Altruria a year, we'll take up our quarters in it,—I won't give the whole house to the school,—and we will lecture on the later phases of Altrurian life to the pupils. How will that do?"

She put her arms round my neck, and I said that it would do admirably; but I had a certain sinking of the heart, for I saw how hard it was even for Eveleth to part with her property.

"I'll endow it," she went on, "and I'll leave the rest of my money at interest here; unless you think that some Altrurian securities—"

"No; there are no such things!" I cried.

"That was what I thought," she returned; "and as it will cost us nothing while we are in Altruria, the interest will be something very handsome by the time we get back, even in United States bonds."

"Something handsome!" I cried. "But, Eveleth, haven't I heard you say yourself that the growth of interest from dead money was like—"

"Oh, yes; that!" she returned. "But you know you have to take it. You can't let the money lie idle; that would be ridiculous; and then, with the good purpose we have in view, it is our *duty* to take the interest. How should we keep up the school, and pay the teachers, and everything?"

I saw that she had forgotten the great sum of the principal, or that, through life-long training and association, it was so sacred to her that she did not even dream of touching it. I was silent, and she thought that I was persuaded.

"You are perfectly right in theory, dear, and I feel just as you do about such things; I'm sure I've suffered enough from them; but if we didn't take interest for your money, what should we have to live on?"

"Not *my* money, Eveleth!" I entreated. "Don't say *my* money!"

"But whatever is mine is yours," she returned, with a wounded air.

"Not your money; but I hope you will soon have none. We should need no money to live on in Altruria. Our share of the daily work of all will amply suffice for our daily bread and shelter."

"In Altruria, yes. But how about America? And you have promised to come back here in a year, you know. Ladies and gentlemen can't share in the daily toil, here, even if they could *get* the toil, and where there are so many out of work, it isn't probable they could."

She dropped upon my knee, as she spoke, laughing, and put her hand under my chin, to lift my fallen face.

"Now, you mustn't be a goose, Aristide, even if you *are* an angel! Now, listen! You *know*, don't you, that I hate money just as badly as you?"

"You have made me think so, Eveleth," I answered.

"I hate it and loathe it. I think it's the source of all the sin and misery in the world; but you can't get rid of it at a blow. For if you gave it away, you might do more harm than good with it."

"You could destroy it," I said.

"Not unless you were a crank," she returned. "And that brings me just to the point. I know that I'm doing a very queer thing to get married, when we know so little, really, about you," and she accented this confession with a laugh that was also a kiss. "But I want to show people that we are just as practical as anybody; and if they can know that I have left my money in United States bonds, they'll respect us, no matter what I do with the interest. Don't you see? We can come back, and preach and teach Altrurianism, and as long as we pay our way, nobody will have a right to say a word. Why, Tolstoy himself doesn't destroy his money, though he wants other people to do it. His wife keeps it, and supports the family. You *have* to do it."

"He doesn't do it willingly."

"No. And *we* won't. And after a while—after we've got back, and compared Altruria and America from practical experience, if we decide to go and live there altogether, I will let you do what you please with the hateful money. I suppose we couldn't take it there with us."

"No more than you could take it to heaven with you," I answered solemnly; but she would not let me be altogether serious about it.

"Well, in either case, we could get on without it, though we certainly could not get on without it, here. Why, Aristide, it is essential to the influence we shall try to exert for Altrurianism; for if we came back here, and preached the true life without any money to back us, no one would pay any attention to us. But if we have a good house waiting for us, and are able to entertain nicely, we can attract the best people, and—and—really do some good."

<h3 style="text-align:center">XXVII</h3>

I ROSE in a distress which I could not hide. "Oh, Eveleth, Eveleth!" I cried. "You are like all the rest, poor child. You are the creature of your environment, as we all are. You cannot escape what you have been. It may be that I was wrong to wish or expect you to cast your lot with me in Altruria, at once and forever. It may be that it is my duty to return here with you after a time, not only to let you see that Altruria is best, but to end my days in this unhappy land, preaching and teaching Altrurianism; but we must not come as prophets to the comfortable people, and entertain nicely. If we are to renew the evangel, it must be in the life and the spirit of the First Altrurian: we must come poor to the poor; we must not try to win any one, save through his heart and conscience; we must be as simple and humble as the least of those that Christ bade follow Him. Eveleth, perhaps you have made a mistake! I love you too much to wish you to suffer even for your good. Yes, I am so weak as that! I did not think that this would be the sacrifice for you that it seems, and I will not ask it of you. I am sorry that we have not understood each other, as I supposed we had. I could never become an American; perhaps you could never become an Altrurian. Think of it, dearest! Think well of it, before you take the step which you cannot recede from. I hold you to no promise; I love you so dearly that I cannot let you hold yourself. But you must choose between me and your money—no; not me!—but between love and your money. You cannot keep both."

She had stood listening to me; now she cast herself on my heart, and stopped my words with an impassioned kiss. "Then there is no choice for me. My choice is made, once for all." She set her hands against my breast, and pushed me from her. "Go, now! But come again to-morrow. I want to think it all over again. Not that I have any doubt; but because you wish it—you wish it, don't you?—and because I will not let you ever think I acted upon an impulse, and that I regretted it."

"That is right, Eveleth! That is like *you*," I said, and I took her into my arms for good-night.

The next day, I came for her decision, or rather for her confirmation of it. The man who opened the door to me, met me with a look of concern and embarrassment. He said Mrs. Strange was not at all well, and had told him he was to give me the letter he handed me. I asked, in taking it, if I could see Mrs. Gray, and he answered that Mrs. Gray had not been down yet, but he would go and see. I was impatient to read my letter, and I made I know not what vague reply, and I found myself, I know not how, on the pavement, with the letter open in my hand. It began abruptly without date or address:

"You will believe that I have not slept, when you read this.

"I have thought it all over again, as you wished, and it is all over between us.

"I am what you said, the creature of my environment. I cannot detach myself from it; I cannot escape from what I have been.

"I am writing this with a strange coldness, like the chill of death in my very soul. I do not ask you to forgive me; I have your forgiveness already. Do not forget me; that is what I ask. Remember me as the unhappy woman who was not equal to her chance when heaven was opened to her: who could not choose the best, when the best came to her.

"There is no use writing; if I kept on forever, it would always be the same cry of shame, of love.

"EVELETH STRANGE."

I reeled as I read the lines. The street seemed to weave itself into a circle around me. But I knew that I was not dreaming, that this was no delirium of my sleep.

It was three days ago, and I have not tried to see her again. I have written her a line, to say that I shall not forget her, and to take the blame upon myself. I expected the impossible of her.

I have yet two days before me until the steamer sails; we were to have sailed together, and now I shall sail alone.

I will try to leave it all behind me forever; but while I linger out these last long hours here, I must think, and I must doubt.

Was she, then, the poseuse that they said? Had she really no heart in our love? Was it only a pretty drama she was playing, and were those generous motives, those lofty principles which seemed to actuate her, the poetical qualities of the play, the graces of her pose? I cannot believe it. I believe that she was truly what she seemed, for she had been that even before she met me. I believe that she was pure and lofty in soul as she appeared; but that her life was warped to such a form by the false conditions of this sad world, that, when she came to look at herself again, after she had been confronted with the sacrifice before her, she feared that she could not make it without in a manner ceasing to be.

She—

But I shall soon see you again; and, until then, farewell.

END OF PART I

Part Second

I

I COULD hardly have believed, my dear Dorothea, that I should be so late in writing to you from Altruria, but you can easily believe that I am thoroughly ashamed of myself for my neglect. It is not for want of thinking of you, or talking of you, that I have seemed so much more ungrateful than I am. My husband and I seldom have any serious talk which doesn't somehow come round to you. He admires you and likes you as much as I do, and he does his best, poor man, to understand you; but his not understanding you is only a part of his general failure to understand how any American can be kind and good in conditions which he considers so abominable as those of the capitalistic world. He is not nearly so severe on us as he used to be at times when he was among us. When the other Altrurians are discussing us he often puts in a reason for us against their logic; and I think he has really forgotten, a good deal, how bad things are with us, or else finds his own memory of them incredible. But his experience of the world outside his own country has taught him how to temper the passion of the Altrurians for justice with a tolerance of the unjust; and when they bring him to book on his own report of us he tries to explain us away, and show how we are not so bad as we ought to be.

For weeks after we came to Altruria I was so unhistorically blest that if I had been disposed to give you a full account of myself I should have had no events to hang the narrative on. Life here is so subjective (if you don't know what that is, you poor dear, you must get Mr. Twelvemough to explain) that there is usually nothing like news in it, and I always feel that the difference between Altruria and America is so immense that it is altogether beyond me to describe it. But now we have had some occurrences recently, quite in the American sense, and these have furnished me with an incentive as well as opportunity to send you a letter. Do you remember how, one evening after dinner, in New York, you and I besieged my husband and tried to make him tell us why Altruria was so isolated from the rest of the world, and why such a great and enlightened continent should keep itself apart? I see still his look of horror when Mr. Makely suggested that the United States should send an expedition and "open" Altruria, as Commodore Perry "opened" Japan in 1850, and try to enter into commercial relations with it. The best he could do was to say what always seemed so incredible, and keep on assuring us that Altruria wished for no sort of public relations with Europe or America, but was very willing to depend for an indefinite time for its communication with those regions on vessels putting into its ports from stress of one kind or other, or castaway on its coasts. They are mostly trading-ships or whalers, and they come a great deal oftener than you suppose; you do not hear of them afterwards, because their crews are poor, ignorant people, whose stories of their adventures are always distrusted, and who know they would be laughed at if they told the stories they could of a country like Altruria. My husband himself took one of their vessels on her home voyage when he came to us, catching the Australasian steamer at New Zealand; and now I am writing you by the same sort of opportunity. I shall have time enough to write you a longer letter than you will care to read; the ship does not sail for a week yet, because it is so hard to get her crew together.

Now that I have actually made a beginning, my mind goes back so strongly to that terrible night when I came to you after Aristides (I always use the English form of his name now) left New York that I seem to be living the tragedy over again, and this happiness of mine here is like a dream which I cannot trust.

It was not all tragedy, though, and I remember how funny Mr. Makely was, trying to keep his face straight when the whole truth had to come out, and I confessed that I had expected, without really knowing it myself, that Aristides would disregard that wicked note I had written him and come and make me marry him, not against my will, but against my word. Of course I didn't put it in just that way, but in a way to let you both guess it. The first glimmering of hope that I had was when Mr. Makely said, "Then, when a woman tells a man that all is over between them forever, she means that she would like to discuss the business with him?" I was old enough to be ashamed, but it seemed to me that you and I had gone back in that awful moment and were two girls together, just as we used to be at school. I was proud of the way you stood up for me, because I thought that if you could tolerate me after what I had confessed I could not be quite a fool. I knew that I deserved at least some pity, and though I laughed with Mr. Makely, I was glad of your indignation with him, and of your faith in Aristides. When it came to the question of what I should do, I don't know which of you I owed the most to. It was a kind of comfort to have Mr. Makely acknowledge that though he regarded Aristides as a myth, still he believed that he was a thoroughly *good* myth, and couldn't tell a lie if he wanted to; and I loved you, and shall love you more than any one else but him, for saying that Aristides was the most real man you had ever met, and that if everything he said was untrue you would trust him to the end of the world.

But, Dolly, it wasn't all comedy, any more than it was all tragedy, and when you and I had laughed and cried ourselves to the point where there was nothing for me to do but to take the next boat for Liverpool, and Mr. Makely had agreed to look after the tickets and cable Aristides that I was coming, there was still my poor, dear mother to deal with. There is no use trying to conceal from you that she was always opposed to my husband. She thought there was something uncanny about him, though she felt as we did that there was nothing uncanny *in* him; but a man who pretended to come from a country where there was no riches and no poverty could not be trusted with any woman's happiness; and though she could not help loving him, she thought I ought to tear him out of my heart, and if I could not do that I ought to have myself shut up in an asylum. We had a dreadful time when I told her what I had decided to do, and I was almost frantic. At last, when she saw that I was determined to follow him, she yielded, not because she was convinced, but because she could not give me up; I wouldn't have let her if she could. I believe that the only thing which reconciled her was that you and Mr. Makely believed in him, and thought I had better do what I wanted to, if nothing could keep me from it. I shall never, never forget Mr. Makely's goodness in coming to talk with her, and how skilfully he managed, without committing himself to Altruria, to declare his faith in my Altrurian. Even then she was troubled about what she thought the indelicacy of my behavior in following him across the sea, and she had all sorts of doubts as to how he would receive me when we met in Liverpool. It wasn't very reasonable of me to say that if he cast me off I should still love him more than any other human being, and his censure would be more precious to me than the praise of the rest of the world.

I suppose I hardly knew what I was saying, but when once I had yielded to my love for him there was nothing else in life. I could not have left my mother behind, but in her opposition to me she seemed like an enemy, and I should somehow have *forced* her to go if she had not yielded. When she did yield, she yielded with her whole heart and soul, and so far from hindering me in my preparations for the voyage, I do not believe I could have got off without her. She thought about everything, and it was her idea to leave my business affairs entirely in Mr. Makely's hands, and to trust the future for the final disposition of my property. I did not care for it myself; I hated it, because it was that which had stood between me and Aristides; but she foresaw that if by any wild impossibility he should reject me when we met, I should need it for the life I must go back to in New York. She behaved like a martyr as well as a heroine, for till we reached Altruria she was a continual sacrifice to me. She stubbornly doubted the whole affair, but now I must do her the justice to say that she has been convinced by the fact. The best she can say of it is that it is like the world of her girlhood; and she has gone back to the simple life here from the artificial life in New York, with the joy of a child. She works the whole day, and she would play if she had ever learned how. She is a better Altrurian than I am; if there could be a bigoted Altrurian my mother would be one.

II

I SENT YOU a short letter from Liverpool, saying that by the unprecedented delays of the *Urania*, which I had taken because it was the swiftest boat of the Neptune line, we had failed to pass the old, ten-day, single-screw Galaxy liner which Aristides had sailed in. I had only time for a word to you; but a million words could not have told the agonies I suffered, and when I overtook him on board the Orient Pacific steamer at Plymouth, where she touched, I could just scribble off the cable sent Mr. Makely before our steamer put off again. I am afraid you did not find my cable very expressive, but I was glad that I did not try to say more, for if I had tried I should simply have gibbered, at a shilling a gibber. I expected to make amends by a whole volume of letters, and I did post a dozen under one cover from Colombo. If they never reached you I am very sorry, for now it is impossible to take up the threads of that time and weave them into any sort of connected pattern. You will have to let me off with saying that Aristides was everything that I believed he would be and was never really afraid he might not be. From the moment we caught sight of each other at Plymouth, he at the rail of the steamer and I on the deck of the tender, we were as completely one as we are now. I never could tell how I got aboard to him; whether he came down and brought me, or whether I was simply rapt through the air to his side. It would have been embarrassing if we had not treated the situation frankly; but such odd things happen among the English going out to their different colonies that our marriage, by a missionary returning to his station, was not even a nine days' wonder with our fellow-passengers.

We were a good deal more than nine days on the steamer before we could get a vessel that would take us on to Altruria; but we overhauled a ship going there for provisions at last, and we were all put off on her, bag and baggage, with three cheers from the friends we were leaving; I think they thought we were going to some of the British islands that the Pacific is full of. I had been thankful from the first that I had not brought a maid, knowing the Altrurian prejudice against hireling service, but I never was so glad as I was when we got aboard that vessel, for when the captain's wife, who was with him, found that I had no one to look after me, she looked after me herself, just for the fun of it, she said; but *I* knew it was the love of it. It was a sort of general trading-ship, stopping at the different islands in the South Seas, and had been a year out from home, where the kind woman had left her little ones; she cried over their photographs to me. Her husband had been in Altruria before, and he and Aristides were old acquaintances and met like brothers; some of the crew knew him, too, and the captain relaxed discipline so far as to let us shake hands with the second-mate as the men's representative.

I needn't dwell on the incidents of our home-coming—for that was what it seemed for my mother and me as well as for my husband—but I must give you one detail of our reception, for I still think it almost the prettiest thing that has happened to us among the millions of pretty things. Aristides had written home of our engagement, and he was expected with his American wife; and before we came to anchor the captain ran up the Emissary's signal, which my husband gave him, and then three boats left the shore and pulled rapidly out to us. As they came nearer I saw the first Altrurian costumes in the lovely colors that the people wear here, and that make a group of them look like a flower-bed; and then I saw that the boats were banked with flowers along the gun-wales from stem to stern, and that they were each not *manned*, but *girled* by six rowers, who pulled as true a stroke as I ever saw in our boat-races. When they caught sight of us, leaning over the side, and Aristides lifted his hat and waved it to them, they all stood their oars upright, and burst into a kind of welcome song: I had been dreading one of those stupid, banging salutes of ten or twenty guns, and you can imagine what a relief it was. They were great, splendid creatures, as tall as our millionaires' tallest daughters, and as strong-looking as any of our college-girl athletes; and when we got down over the ship's side, and Aristides said a few words of introduction for my mother and me, as we stepped into the largest of the boats, I thought they would crush me, catching me in their strong, brown arms, and kissing me on each cheek; they never kiss on the mouth in Altruria. The girls in the other boats kissed their hands to mother and me, and shouted to Aristides, and then, when our boat set out for the shore, they got on each side of us and sang song after song as they pulled even stroke with our crew. Half-way, we met three other boats, really *manned*, these ones, and going out to get our baggage, and then you ought to have heard the shouting and laughing, that ended in more singing, when the young fellows' voices mixed with the girls, till they were lost in the welcome that came off to us from the crowded quay, where I should have thought half Altruria had gathered to receive us.

I was afraid it was going to be too much for my mother, but she stood it bravely; and almost at a glance people began to take her into consideration, and she was delivered over to two young married ladies, who saw that she was made comfortable, the first of any, in the pretty Regionic guest-house where they put us.

I wish I could give you a notion of that guest-house, with its cool, quiet rooms, and its lawned and gardened enclosure, and a little fountain purring away among the flowers! But what astonished me was that there were no sort of carriages, or wheeled conveyances, which, after our escort from the ship, I thought might very well have met the returning Emissary and his wife. They made my mother get into a litter, with soft cushions and with lilac curtains blowing round it, and six girls carried her up to the house; but they seemed not to imagine my not walking, and, in fact, I could hardly have imagined it myself, after the first moment of queerness. That walk was full of such rich experience for every one of the senses that I would not have missed a step of it; but as soon as I could get Aristides alone I asked him about horses, and he said that though horses were still used in farm work, not a horse was allowed in any city or village of Altruria, because of their filthiness. As for public vehicles, they used to have electric trolleys; in the year that he had been absent they had substituted electric motors; but these were not running, because it was a holiday on which we had happened to arrive.

There was another incident of my first day which I think will amuse you, knowing how I have always shrunk from any sort of public appearances. When Aristides went to make his report to the people assembled in a sort of convention, I had to go too, and take part in the proceedings; for women are on an entire equality with the men here, and people would be shocked if husband and wife were separated in their public life. They did not spare me a single thing. Where Aristides was not very clear, or rather not full enough, in describing America, I was called on to supplement, and I had to make several speeches. Of course, as I spoke in English, he had to put it into Altrurian for me, and it made the greatest excitement. The Altrurians are very lively people, and as full of the desire to hear some new things as Paul said the men of Athens were. At times they were in a perfect gale of laughter at what we told them about America. Afterwards some of the women confessed to me that they liked to hear us speaking English together; it sounded like the whistling of birds or the shrilling of locusts. But they were perfectly kind, and though they laughed it was clear that they laughed at what we were saying, and never at us, or at least never at *me*.

Of course there was the greatest curiosity to know what Aristides' wife looked like, as well as sounded like; he had written out about our engagement before I broke it; and my clothes were of as much interest as myself, or more. You know how I had purposely left my latest Paris things behind, so as to come as simply as possible to the simple life of Altruria, but still with my big leg-of-mutton sleeves, and my picture-hat, and my pinched waist, I felt perfectly grotesque, and I have no doubt I looked it. They had never seen a lady from the capitalistic world before, but only now and then a whaling-captain's wife who had come ashore; and I knew they were burning to examine my smart clothes down to the last button and bit of braid. I had on the short skirts of last year, and I could feel ten thousand eyes fastened on my high-heeled boots, which you know *I* never went to extremes in. I confess my face burned a little, to realize what a scarecrow I must look, when I glanced round at those Altrurian women, whose pretty, classic fashions made the whole place like a field of lilacs and irises, and knew that they were as comfortable as they were beautiful. Do you remember some of the descriptions of the undergraduate maidens in the "Princess"—I know you had it at school—where they are sitting in the palace halls together? The effect was something like that.

You may be sure that I got out of my things as soon as I could borrow an Altrurian costume, and now my Paris confections are already hung up for monuments, as Richard III. says, in the Capitalistic Museum, where people from the outlying Regions may come and study them as object-lessons in what not to wear. (You remember what you said Aristides told you, when he spoke that day at the mountains, about the Regions that Altruria is divided into? This is the Maritime Region, and the city where we are living for the present is the capital.) You may think this was rather hard on me, and at first it did seem pretty intimate, having my things in a long glass case, and it gave me a shock to see them, as if it had been my ghost, whenever I passed them. But the fact is I was more ashamed than hurt—they were so ugly and stupid and useless. I could have borne my Paris dress and my picture-hat if it had not been for those ridiculous high-heeled, pointed-toe shoes, which the Curatress had stood at the bottom of the skirts. They looked the most frantic things you can imagine, and the mere sight of them made my poor feet *ache* in the beautiful sandals I am wearing now; when once you have put on sandals you say good-bye and good-riddance to shoes. In a single month my feet have grown almost a tenth as large again as they were, and my friends here encourage me to believe that they will yet measure nearly the classic size, though, as you know, I am not in my first youth and can't expect them to do miracles.

I had to leave off abruptly at the last page because Aristides had come in with a piece of news that took my mind off everything else. I am afraid you are not going to get this letter even at the late date I had set for its reaching you, my dear. It seems that there has been a sort of mutiny among the crew of our trader, which was to sail next week, and now there is no telling when she will sail. Ever since she came the men have been allowed their liberty, as they call it, by watches, but the last watch came ashore this week before another watch had returned to the ship, and now not one of the sailors will go back. They had been exploring the country by turns, at their leisure, it seems, and their excuse is that they like Altruria better than America, which they say they wish never to see again.

You know (though I didn't, till Aristides explained to me) that in any European country the captain in such a case would go to his consul, and the consul would go to the police, and the police would run the men down and send them back to the ship in irons as deserters, or put them in jail till the captain was ready to sail, and then deliver them up to him. But it seems that there is no law in Altruria to do anything of the kind; the only law here that would touch the case is one which obliges any citizen to appear and answer the complaint of any other citizen before the Justiciary Assembly. A citizen cannot be imprisoned for anything but the rarest offence, like killing a person in a fit of passion; and as to seizing upon men who are guilty of nothing worse than wanting to be left to the pursuit of happiness, as all the Altrurians are, there is no statute and no usage for it. Aristides says that the only thing which can be done is to ask the captain and the men to come to the Assembly and each state his case. The Altrurians are not anxious to have the men stay, not merely because they are coarse, rude, or vicious, but because they think they ought to go home and tell the Americans what they have seen and heard here, and try and get them to found an Altrurian Commonwealth of their own. Still they will not compel them to go, and the magistrates do not wish to rouse any sort of sentiment against them. They feel that the men are standing on their natural rights, which they could not abdicate if they would. I know this will appear perfectly ridiculous to Mr. Makely, and I confess myself that there seems something binding in a contract which ought to act on the men's consciences, at least.

III

WELL, my dear Dorothea, the hearing before the Assembly is over, and it has left us just where it found us, as far as the departure of our trader is concerned.

How I wish you could have been there! The hearing lasted three days, and I would not have missed a minute of it. As it was, I did not miss a syllable, and it was so deeply printed on my mind that I believe I could repeat it word for word if I had to. But, in the first place, I must try and realize the scene to you. I was once summoned as a witness in one of our courts, you remember, and I have never forgotten the horror of it: the hot, dirty room, with its foul air, the brutal spectators, the policemen stationed among them to keep them in order, the lawyers with the plaintiff and defendant seated all at one table, the uncouth abruptness of the clerks and janitors, or whatever, the undignified magistrate, who looked as if his lunch had made him drowsy, and who seemed half asleep, as he slouched in his arm-chair behind his desk. Instead of such a setting as this, you must imagine a vast marble amphitheatre, larger than the Metropolitan Opera, by three or four times, all the gradines overflowing (that is the word for the "liquefaction of the clothes" which poured over them), and looking like those Bermudan waters where the colors of the rainbow seem dropped around the coast. On the platform, or stage, sat the Presidents of the Assembly, and on a tier of seats behind and above them, the national Magistrates, who, as this is the capital of the republic for the time being, had decided to be present at the hearing, because they thought the case so very important. In the hollow space, just below (like that where you remember the Chorus stood in that Greek play which we saw at Harvard ages ago), were the captain and the first-mate on one hand, and the seamen on the other; the second-mate, our particular friend, was not there because he never goes ashore anywhere, and had chosen to remain with the black cook in charge of the ship. The captain's wife would rather have stayed with them, but I persuaded her to come to us for the days of the hearing, because the captain had somehow thought we were opposed to him, and because I thought she ought to be there to encourage him by her presence. She sat next to me, in a hat which I wish you could have seen, Dolly, and a dress which would have set your teeth on edge; but inside of them I knew she was one of the best souls in the world, and I loved her the more for being the sight she was among those wonderful Altrurian women.

The weather was perfect, as it nearly always is at this time of year—warm, yet fresh, with a sky of that "bleu impossible" of the Riviera on the clearest day. Some people had parasols, but they put them down as soon as the hearing began, and everybody could see perfectly. You would have thought they could not hear so well, but a sort of immense sounding-plane was curved behind the stage, so that not a word of the testimony on either side was lost to me in English. The Altrurian translation was given the second day of the hearing through a megaphone, as different in tone from the thing that the man in the Grand Central Station bellows the trains through as the *vox-humana* stop of an organ is different from the fog-horn of a light-house. The captain's wife was bashful, in her odd American dress, but we had got seats near the tribune, rather out of sight, and there was nothing to hinder our hearing, like the *frou-frou* of stiff silks or starched skirts (which I am afraid we poor things in America like to make when we move) from the soft, filmy tissues that the Altrurian women wear; but I must confess that there was a good deal of whispering while the captain and the men were telling their stories. But no one except the interpreters, who were taking their testimony down in short-hand, to be translated into Altrurian and read at the subsequent hearing, could understand what they were saying, and so nobody was disturbed by the murmurs. The whispering was mostly near me, where I sat with the captain's wife, for everybody I knew got as close as they could and studied my face when they thought anything important or significant had been said. They are very quick at reading faces here; in fact, a great deal of the conversation is carried on in that way, or with the visible speech; and my Altrurian friends knew almost as well as I did when the speakers came to an interesting point. It was rather embarrassing for me, though, with the poor captain's wife at my side, to tell them, in my broken Altrurian, what the men were accusing the captain of.

I talk of the men, but it was really only one of them who at first, by their common consent, spoke for the rest. He was a middle-aged Yankee, and almost the only born American among them, for you know that our sailors, nowadays, are of every nationality under the sun—Portuguese, Norwegians, Greeks, Italians, Kanucks, and Kanakas, and even Cape Cod Indians. He said he guessed his story was the story of most sailors, and he had followed the sea his whole life. His story was dreadful, and I tried to persuade the captain's wife not to come to the hearing the next day, when it was to be read in Altrurian; but she would come. I was afraid she would be overwhelmed by the public compassion, and would not know what to do; for when something awful that the sailor had said against the captain was translated the women all about us cooed their sympathy with her, and pressed her hand if they could, or patted her on the shoulder, to show how much they pitied her. In Altruria they pity the friends of those who have done wrong, and sometimes even the wrong-doers themselves; and it is quite a luxury, for there is so little wrong-doing here: I tell them that in America they would have as much pitying to do as they could possibly ask. After the hearing that day my friends, who were of a good many different Refectories, as we call them here, wanted her to go and lunch with them; but I got her quietly home with me, and after she had had something to eat I made her lie down awhile.

You won't care to have me go fully into the affair. The sailors' spokesman told how he had been born on a farm, where he had shared the family drudgery and poverty till he grew old enough to run away. He meant to go to sea, but he went first to a factory town and worked three or four years in the mills. He never went back to the farm, but he sent a little money now and then to his mother; and he stayed on till he got into trouble. He did not say just what kind of trouble, but I fancied it was some sort of love-trouble; he blamed himself for it; and when he left that town to get away from the thought of it, as much as anything, and went to work in another town, he took to drink; then, once, in a drunken spree, he found himself in New York without knowing how. But it was in what he called a sailors' boarding-house, and one morning, after he had been drinking overnight "with a very pleasant gentleman," he found himself in the forecastle of a ship bound for Holland, and when the mate came and cursed him up and cursed him out he found himself in the foretop. I give it partly in his own language, because I cannot help it; and I only wish I could give it wholly in his language; it was so graphic and so full of queer Yankee humor. From that time on, he said, he had followed the sea; and at sea he was always a good temperance man, but Altruria was the only place he had ever kept sober ashore. He guessed that was partly because there was nothing to drink but unfermented grape-juice, and partly because there was nobody to drink with; anyhow, he had not had a drop here. Everywhere else, as soon as he left his ship, he made for a sailors' boarding-house, and then he did not know much till he found himself aboard ship and bound for somewhere that he did not know of. He was always, he said, a stolen man, as much as a negro captured on the west coast of Africa and sold to a slaver; and, he said, it was a slave's life he led between drinks, whether it was a long time or short. He said he would ask his mates if it was very different with them, and when he turned to them they all shouted back, in their various kinds of foreign accents, No, it was just the same with them, every one. Then he said that was how he came to ship on our captain's vessel, and though they could not all say the same, they nodded confirmation as far as he was concerned.

The captain looked sheepish enough at this, but he looked sorrowful, too, as if he could have wished it had been different, and he asked the man if he had been abused since he came on board. Well, the man said, not unless you called tainted salt-horse and weevilly biscuit abuse; and then the captain sat down again, and I could feel his poor wife shrinking beside me. The man said that he was comparatively well off on the captain's ship, and the life was not half such a dog's life as he had led on other vessels; but it was such that when he got ashore here in Altruria, and saw how *white* people lived, people that *used* each other white, he made up his mind that he would never go back to any ship alive. He hated a ship so much that if he could go home to America as a first-class passenger on a Cunard liner, John D. Rockefeller would not have money enough to hire him to do it. He was going to stay in Altruria till he died, if they would let him, and he guessed they would, if what he had heard about them was true. He just wanted, he said, while we were about it, to have a few of his mates tell their experience, not so much on board the *Little Sally*, but on shore, and since they could remember; and one after another did get up and tell their miserable stories. They were like the stories you sometimes read in your paper over your coffee, or that you can hear any time you go into the congested districts in New York; but I assure you, my dear, they seemed to me perfectly incredible here, though I had known hundreds of such stories at home. As I realized their facts I forgot where I was; I felt that I was back again in that horror, where it sometimes seemed to me I had no right to be fed or clothed or warm or clean in the midst of the hunger and cold and nakedness and dirt, and where I could only reconcile myself to my comfort because I knew my discomfort would not help others' misery.

I can hardly tell how, but even the first day a sense of something terrible spread through that multitude of people, to whom the words themselves were mere empty sounds. The captain sat through it, with his head drooping, till his face was out of sight, and the tears ran silently down his wife's cheeks; and the women round me were somehow awed into silence. When the men ended, and there seemed to be no one else to say anything on that side, the captain jumped to his feet, with a sort of ferocious energy, and shouted out, "Are you all through, men?" and their spokesman answered, "Ay, ay, sir!" and then the captain flung back his grizzled hair and shook his fist towards the sailors. "And do you think I *wanted* to do it? Do you think I *liked* to do it? Do you think that if I hadn't been *afraid* my whole life long I would have had the *heart* to lead you the dog's life I know I've led you? I've been as poor as the poorest of you, and as low down as the lowest; I was born in the town poor-house, and I've been so afraid of the poor-house all my days that I hain't had, as you may say, a minute's peace. Ask my wife, there, what sort of a man I *am*, and whether I'm the man, *really* the man that's been hard and mean to you the way I know I been. It was because I was *afraid*, and because a coward is always hard and mean. I been afraid, ever since I could remember anything, of coming to want, and I was willing to see other men suffer so I could make sure that me and mine shouldn't suffer. That's the way we do at home, ain't it? That's in the day's work, ain't it? That's playing the game, ain't it, for everybody? You can't say it ain't." He stopped, and the men's spokesman called back, "Ay, ay, sir," as he had done before, and as I had often heard the men do when given an order on the ship.

The captain gave a kind of sobbing laugh, and went on in a lower tone. "Well, I know you ain't going back. I guess I didn't expect it much from the start, and I guess I'm not surprised." Then he lifted his head and shouted, "And do you suppose *I* want to go back? Don't you suppose *I* would like to spend the rest of my days, too, among *white* people, people that *use* each other white, as you say, and where there ain't any want or, what's worse, *fear* of want? Men! There ain't a day, or an hour, or a minute, when I don't think how awful it is over there, where I got to be either some man's slave or some man's master, as much so as if it was down in the ship's articles. My wife ain't so, because she ain't been ashore here. I wouldn't let her; I was afraid to let her see what a white man's country really was, because I felt so weak about it myself, and I didn't want to put the trial on her, too. And do you know *why* we're going back, or want to go? I guess some of you know, but I want to tell these folks here so they'll understand, and I want you, Mr. Homos," he called to my husband, "to get it down straight. It's because we've got two little children over there, that we left with their grandmother when my wife come with me this voyage because she had lung difficulty and wanted to see whether she could get her health back. Nothing else on God's green earth could take me back to America, and I guess it couldn't my wife if she knew what Altruria was as well as I do. But when I went around here and saw how everything was, and remembered how it was at home, I just said, 'She'll stay on the ship.' Now, that's all I got to say, though I thought I had a lot more. I guess it'll be enough for these folks, and they can judge between us." Then the captain sat down, and to make a long story short, the facts of the hearing were repeated in Altrurian the next day by megaphone, and when the translation was finished there was a general rush for the captain. He plainly expected to be lynched, and his wife screamed out, "Oh, don't hurt him! He isn't a bad man!" But it was only the Altrurian way with a guilty person: they wanted to let him know how sorry they were for him, and since his sin had found him out how hopeful they were for his redemption. I had to explain it to the sailors as well as to the captain and his wife, but I don't believe any of them quite accepted the fact.

The third day of the hearing was for the rendering of the decision, first in Altrurian, and then in English. The verdict of the magistrates had to be confirmed by a standing vote of the people, and of course the women voted as well as the men. The decision was that the sailors should be absolutely free to go or stay, but they took into account the fact that it would be cruel to keep the captain and his wife away from their little ones, and the sailors might wish to consider this. If they still remained true to their love of Altruria they could find some means of returning.

When the translator came to this point their spokesman jumped to his feet and called out to the captain, "Will you *do* it?" "Do what?" he asked, getting slowly to his own feet. "Come back with us after you have seen the kids?" The captain shook his fist at the sailors; it seemed to be the only gesture he had with them. "Give me the *chance!* All I want is to see the children and bring them out with me to Altruria, and the old folks with them." "Will you *swear* it? Will you say, 'I hope I may find the kids dead and buried when I get home if I don't do it'?" "I'll take that oath, or any oath you want me to." "Shake hands on it, then."

The two men met in front of the tribunal and clasped hands there, and their reconciliation did not need translation. Such a roar of cheers went up! And then the whole assembly burst out in the national Altrurian anthem, "Brothers All." I wish you could have heard it! But when the terms of the agreement were explained, the cheering that had gone before was a mere whisper to what followed. One orator after another rose and praised the self-sacrifice of the sailors. I was the proudest when the last of them referred to Aristides and the reports which he had sent home from America, and said that without some such study as he had made of the American character they never could have understood such an act as they were now witnessing. Illogical and insensate as their system was, their character sometimes had a beauty, a sublimity which was not possible to Altrurians even, for it was performed in the face of risks and chances which their happy conditions relieved them from. At the same time, the orator wished his hearers to consider the essential immorality of the act. He said that civilized men had no right to take these risks and chances. The sailors were perhaps justified, in so far as they were homeless, wifeless, and childless men; but it must not be forgotten that their heroism was like the reckless generosity of savages.

The men have gone back to the ship, and she sails this afternoon. I have persuaded the captain to let his wife stay to lunch with me at our Refectory, where the ladies wish to bid her good-bye, and I am hurrying forward this letter so that she can take it on board with her this afternoon. She has promised to post it on the first Pacific steamer they meet, or if they do not meet any to send it forward to you with a special-delivery stamp as soon as they reach Boston. She will also forward by express an Altrurian costume, such as I am now wearing, sandals and all! Do put it on, Dolly, dear, for my sake, and realize what it is for once in your life to be a *free* woman.

Heaven knows when I shall have another chance of getting letters to you. But I shall live in hopes, and I shall set down my experiences here for your benefit, not perhaps as I meet them, but as I think of them, and you must not mind having a rather cluttered narrative. To-morrow we are setting off on our round of the capitals, where Aristides is to make a sort of public report to the people of the different Regions on the working of the capitalistic conditions as he observed them among us. But I don't expect to send you a continuous narrative of our adventures. Good-bye, dearest, with my mother's love, and my husband's as well as my own, to both of you; think of me as needing nothing but a glimpse of you to complete my happiness. How I should like to tell you fully about it! You *must* come to Altruria!

I came near letting this go without telling you of one curious incident of the affair between the captain and his men. Before the men returned to the ship they came with their spokesman to say good-bye to Aristides and me, and he remarked casually that it was just as well, maybe, to be going back, because, for one thing, they would know then whether it was real or not. I asked him what he meant, and he said, "Well, you know, some of the mates think it's a dream here, or it's too good to be true. As far forth as I go, I'd be willing to have it a dream that I didn't ever have to wake up from. It ain't any too good to be true for me. Anyway, I'm going to get back somehow, and give it another chance to be a fact." Wasn't that charming? It had a real touch of poetry in it, but it was prose that followed. I couldn't help asking him whether there had been nothing to mar the pleasure of their stay in Altruria, and he answered: "Well, I don't know as you could rightly say *mar*; it hadn't ought to have. You see, it was like this. You see, some of the mates wanted to lay off and have a regular bange, but that don't seem to be the idea here. After we had been ashore a day or two they set us to work at different jobs, or wanted to. The mates didn't take hold very lively, and some of 'em didn't take hold a bit. But after that went on a couple of days, there wa'n't any breakfast one morning, and come noontime there wa'n't any dinner, and as far forth as they could make out they had to go to bed without supper. Then they called a halt, and tackled one of your head men here that could speak some English. He didn't answer them right off the reel, but he got out his English Testament and he read 'em a verse that said, 'For even when we were with you this we commanded you, that if any one would not work neither should he eat.' That kind of fetched 'em, and after that there wa'n't any sojerin', well not to speak of. They saw he meant business. I guess it did more than any one thing to make 'em think they wa'n't dreamin'."

IV

YOU MUST NOT THINK, Dolly, from anything I have been telling you that the Altrurians are ever harsh. Sometimes they cannot realize how things really are with us, and how what seems grotesque and hideous to them seems charming and beautiful, or at least *chic*, to us. But they are wonderfully quick to see when they have hurt you the least, and in the little sacrifices I have made of my wardrobe to the cause of general knowledge there has not been the least urgence from them. When I now look at the things I used to wear, where they have been finally placed in the ethnological department of the Museum, along with the Esquimau kyaks and the Thlinkeet totems, they seem like things I wore in some prehistoric age—

"When wild in woods the noble savage ran."

Now, am *I* being unkind? Well, you mustn't mind me, Dolly. You must just say, "She *has* got it bad," and go on and learn as much about Altruria as you can from me. Some of the things were hard to get used to, and at first seemed quite impossible. For one thing, there was the matter of *service*, which is dishonorable with us, and honorable with the Altrurians: I was a long time getting to understand that, though I knew it perfectly well from hearing my husband talk about it in New York. I believe he once came pretty near offending you by asking why you did not do your own work, or something like that; he has confessed as much, and I could not wonder at you in your conditions. Why, when we first went to the guest-house, and the pretty young girls who brought in lunch sat down at table to eat it with us, I felt the indignation making me hot all over. You know how democratic I am, and I did not mind those great, splendid boat-girls hugging and kissing me, but I instinctively drew the line at cooks and waitresses. In New York, you know, I always tried to be kind to my servants, but as for letting one of them sit down in my presence, much less sit down at table with me, I never dreamed of such a thing in my most democratic moments. Luckily I drew the line subjectively here, and later I found that these young ladies were daughters of some of the most distinguished men and women on the continent, though you must not understand distinction as giving any sort of social primacy; that sort of thing is not allowed in Altruria. They had drawn lots with the girls in the Regionic school here, and were proud of having won the honor of waiting on us. Of course, I needn't say they were what we would have felt to be ladies anywhere, and their manners were exquisite, even to leaving us alone together as soon as we had finished luncheon. The meal itself was something I shall always remember for its delicious cooking of the different kinds of mushrooms which took the place of meat, and the wonderful salads, and the temperate and tropical fruits which we had for dessert.

They had to talk mostly with my husband, of course, and when they did talk to me it was through him. They were very intelligent about our world, much more than we are about Altruria, though, of course, it was by deduction from premises rather than specific information, and they wanted to ask a thousand questions; but they saw the joke of it, and laughed with us when Aristides put them off with a promise that if they would have a public meeting appointed we would appear and answer all the questions anybody could think of; we were not going to waste our answers on them the first day. He wanted them to let us go out and help wash the dishes, but they would not hear of it. I confess I was rather glad of that, for it seemed a lower depth to which I could not descend, even after eating with them. But they invited us out to look at the kitchen, after they had got it in order a little, and when we joined them there, whom should I see but my own dear old mother, with an apron up to her chin, wiping the glass and watching carefully through her dear old spectacles that she got everything bright! You know she was of a simpler day than ours, and when she was young she used to do her own work, and she and my father always washed the dishes together after they had company. I merely said, "*Well*, mother!" and she laughed and colored, and said she guessed she should like it in Altruria, for it took her back to the America she used to know.

I must mention things as they come into my head, and not in any regular order; there are too many of them. One thing is that I did not notice till afterwards that we had had no meat that first day at luncheon—the mushrooms were so delicious, and you know I never was much of a meat-eater. It was not till we began to make our present tour of the Regionic capitals, where Aristides has had to repeat his account of American civilization until I am sick as well as ashamed of America, that I first felt a kind of famine which I kept myself from recognizing as long as I could. Then I had to own to myself, long before I owned it to him, that I was hungry for *meat*—for roast, for broiled, for fried, for hashed. I did not actually tell him, but he found it out, and I could not deny it, though I felt such an ogre in it. He was terribly grieved, and blamed himself for not having thought of it, and wished he had got some canned meats from the trader before she left the port. He was really in despair, for nobody since the old capitalistic times had thought of killing sheep or cattle for food; they have them for wool and milk and butter; and of course when I looked at them in the fields it did seem rather formidable. You are so used to seeing them in the butchers' shops, ready for the range, that you never think of what they have to *go through* before that. But at last I managed to gasp out, one day, "If I could only have a chicken!" and he seemed to think that it could be managed. I don't know how he made interest with the authorities, or how the authorities prevailed on a farmer to part with one of his precious pullets; but the thing was done somehow, and two of the farmer's children brought it to us at one of the guest-houses where we were staying, and then fled howling. That was bad enough, but what followed was worse. I went another day on mushrooms before I had the heart to say chicken again and suggest that Aristides should get it killed and dressed. The poor fellow did try, I believe, but we had to fall back upon ourselves for the murderous deed, and—Did you ever see a chicken have its head cut off, and how hideously it behaves? It made us both wish we were dead; and the sacrifice of that one pullet was quite enough for me. We buried the poor thing under the flowers of the guest-house garden, and I went back to my mushrooms after a visit of contrition to the farmer and many attempts to bring his children to forgiveness. After all, the Altrurian mushrooms are wonderfully nourishing, and they are in such variety that, what with other succulent vegetables and the endless range of fruits and nuts, one does not wish for meat—meat that one has killed one's self!

v

I wish you could be making tour of the Regionic capitals with us, Dolly! There are swift little one-rail electric expresses running daily from one capital to another, but these are used only when speed is required, and we are confessedly in no hurry: Aristides wanted me to see as much of the country as possible, and I am as eager as he. The old steam-roads of the capitalistic epoch have been disused for generations, and their beds are now the country roads, which are everywhere kept in beautiful repair. There are no horse vehicles (the electric motors are employed in the towns), though some people travel on horseback, but the favorite means of conveyance is by electric van, which any citizen may have on proof of his need of it; and it is comfortable beyond compare— mounted on easy springs, and curtained and cushioned like those gypsy vans we see in the country at home. Aristides drives himself, and sometimes we both get out and walk, for there is plenty of time.

I don't know whether I can make you understand how everything has tended to simplification here. They have disused the complicated facilities and conveniences of the capitalistic epoch, which we are so proud of, and have got back as close as possible to nature. People stay at home a great deal more than with us, though if any one likes to make a journey or to visit the capitals he is quite free to do it, and those who have some useful or beautiful object in view make the sacrifice, as they feel it, to leave their villages every day and go to the nearest capital to carry on their studies or experiments. What we consider modern conveniences they would consider a superfluity of naughtiness for the most part. As *work* is the ideal, they do not believe in what we call labor-saving devices.

When we approach a village on our journey, one of the villagers, sometimes a young man, and sometimes a girl, comes out to meet us, and when we pass through they send some one with us on the way a little. The people have a perfect inspiration for hospitality: they not only know when to do and how much to do, but how little and when not at all. I can't remember that we have ever once been bored by those nice young things that welcomed us or speeded us on our way, and when we have stopped in a village they have shown a genius for leaving us alone, after the first welcome, that is beautiful. They are so regardful of our privacy, in fact, that if it had not been for Aristides, who explained their ideal to me, I should have felt neglected sometimes, and should have been shy of letting them know that we would like their company. But he understood it, and I must say that I have never enjoyed people and their ways so much. Their hospitality is a sort of compromise between that of the English houses where you are left free at certain houses to follow your own devices absolutely, and that Spanish splendor which assures you that the host's house is yours without meaning it. In fact, the guest-house, wherever we go, *is* ours, for it belongs to the community, and it is absolutely a home to us for the time being. It is usually the best house in the village, the prettiest and cosiest, where all the houses are so pretty and cosey. There is always another building for public meetings, called the temple, which is the principal edifice, marble and classic and tasteful, which we see almost as much of as the guest-house, for the news of the Emissary's return has preceded him, and everybody is alive with curiosity, and he has to stand and deliver in the village temples everywhere. Of course I am the great attraction, and after being scared by it at first I have rather got to like it; the people are so kind, and unaffected, and really delicate.

You mustn't get the notion that the Altrurians are a solemn people at all; they are rather gay, and they like other people's jokes as well as their own; I am sure Mr. Makely, with his sense of humor, would be at home with them at once. The one thing that more than any other has helped them to conceive of the American situation is its being the gigantic joke which we often feel it to be; I don't know but it appears to them more grotesque than it does to us even. At first, when Aristides would explain some peculiarity of ours, they would receive him with a gale of laughing, but this might change into cries of horror and pity later. One of the things that amused and then revolted them most was our patriotism. They thought it the drollest thing in the world that men should be willing to give their own lives and take the lives of other men for the sake of a country which assured them no safety from want, and did not even assure them work, and in which they had no more logical interest than the country they were going to fight. They could understand how a rich man might volunteer for one of our wars, but when they were told that most of our volunteers were poor men, who left their mothers and sisters, or their wives and children, without any means of support, except their meagre pay, they were quite bewildered and stopped laughing, as if the thing had passed a joke. They asked, "How if one of these citizen soldiers was killed?" and they seemed to suppose that in this case the country would provide for his family and give them work, or if the children were too young would support them at the public expense. It made me creep a little when my husband answered that the family of a crippled or invalided soldier would have a pension of eight or ten or fifteen dollars a month; and when they came back with the question why the citizens of such a country should love it enough to die for it, I could not have said why for the life of me. But Aristides, who is so magnificently generous, tried to give them a notion of the sublimity which is at the bottom of our illogicality and which adjusts so many apparently hopeless points of our anomaly. They asked how this sublimity differed from that of the savage who brings in his game and makes a feast for the whole tribe, and leaves his wife and children without provision against future want; but Aristides told them that there were essential differences between the Americans and savages, which arose from the fact that the savage condition was permanent and the American conditions were unconsciously provisional.

They are quite well informed about our life in some respects, but they wished to hear at first hand whether certain things were really so or not. For instance, they wanted to know whether people were allowed to marry and bring children into the world if they had no hopes of supporting them or educating them, or whether diseased people were allowed to become parents. In Altruria, you know, the families are generally small, only two or three children at the most, so that the parents can devote themselves to them the more fully; and as there is no fear of want here, the state interferes only when the parents are manifestly unfit to bring the little ones up. They imagined that there was something of that kind with us, but when they heard that the state interfered in the family only when the children were unruly, and then it punished the children by sending them to a reform school and disgracing them for life, instead of holding the parents accountable, they seemed to think that it was one of the most anomalous features of our great anomaly. Here, when the father and mother are always quarrelling, the children are taken from them, and the pair are separated, at first for a time, but after several chances for reform they are parted permanently.

But I must not give you the notion that all our conferences are so serious. Many have merely the character of social entertainments, which are not made here for invited guests, but for any who choose to come; all are welcome. At these there are often plays given by amateurs, and improvised from plots which supply the outline, while the performers supply the dialogue and action, as in the old Italian comedies. The Altrurians are so quick and fine, in fact, that they often remind me of the Italians more than any other people. One night there was for my benefit an American play, as the Altrurians imagined it from what they had read about us, and they had costumed it from the pictures of us they had seen in the newspapers Aristides had sent home while he was with us. The effect was a good deal like that American play which the Japanese company of Sada Yacco gave while it was in New York. It was all about a millionaire's daughter, who was loved by a poor young man and escaped with him to Altruria in an open boat from New York. The millionaire could be distinctly recognized by the dollar-marks which covered him all over, as they do in the caricatures of rich men in our yellow journals. It was funny to the last degree. In the last act he was seen giving his millions away to poor people, whose multitude was represented by the continually coming and going of four or five performers in and out of the door, in outrageously ragged clothes. The Altrurians have not yet imagined the nice degrees of poverty which we have achieved, and they could not have understood that a man with a hundred thousand dollars would have seemed poor to that multi-millionaire. In fact, they do not grasp the idea of money at all. I heard afterwards that in the usual version the millionaire commits suicide in despair, but the piece had been given a happy ending out of kindness to me. I must say that in spite of the monstrous misconception the acting was extremely good, especially that of some comic characters.

But dancing is the great national amusement in Altruria, where it has not altogether lost its religious nature. A sort of march in the temples is as much a part of the worship as singing, and so dancing has been preserved from the disgrace which it used to be in with serious people among us. In the lovely afternoons you see young people dancing in the meadows, and hear them shouting in time to the music, while the older men and women watch them from their seats in the shade. Every sort of pleasure here is improvised, and as you pass through a village the first thing you know the young girls and young men start up in a sort of *girandole*, and linking hands in an endless chain stretch the figure along through the street and out over the highway to the next village, and the next and the next. The work has all been done in the forenoon, and every one who chooses is at liberty to join in the fun.

The villages are a good deal alike to a stranger, and we knew what to expect there after a while, but the country is perpetually varied, and the unexpected is always happening in it. The old railroad-beds, on which we travelled, are planted with fruit and nut trees and flowering shrubs, and our progress is through a fragrant bower that is practically endless, except where it takes the shape of a colonnade near the entrance of a village, with vines trained about white pillars, and clusters of grapes (which are ripening just now) hanging down. The change in the climate created by cutting off the southeastern peninsula and letting in the equatorial current, which was begun under the first Altrurian president, with an unexpended war-appropriation, and finished for what one of the old capitalistic wars used to cost, is something perfectly astonishing. Aristides says he told you something about it in his speech at the White Mountains, but you would never believe it without the evidence of your senses. Whole regions to the southward, which were nearest the pole and were sheeted with ice and snow, with the temperature and vegetation of Labrador, now have the climate of Italy; and the mountains, which used to bear nothing but glaciers, are covered with olive orchards and plantations of the delicious coffee which they drink here.

Aristides says you could have the same results at home—no! *in the United States*—by cutting off the western shore of Alaska and letting in the Japanese current; and it could be done at the cost of any average war.

VI

But I MUST NOT get away from my personal experiences in these international statistics. Sometimes, when night overtakes us, we stop and camp beside the road, and set about getting our supper of eggs and bread and butter and cheese, or the fruits that are ripening all round us. Since my experience with that pullet I go meekly mushrooming in the fields and pastures; and when I have set the mushrooms stewing over an open fire, Aristides makes the coffee, and in a little while we have a banquet fit for kings—or for the poor things in every grade below them that serve kings, political or financial or industrial. There is always water, for it is brought down from the snow-fields of the mountains—there is not much rainfall—and carried in little concrete channels along the road-side from village to village, something like those conduits the Italian peasants use to bring down the water from the Maritime Alps to their fields and orchards; and you hear the soft gurgle of it the whole night long, and day long, too, whenever you stop. After supper we can read awhile by our electric lamp (we tap the current in the telephone wires anywhere), or Aristides sacrifices himself to me in a lesson of Altrurian grammar. Then we creep back into our van and fall asleep with the Southern Cross glittering over our heads. It is perfectly safe, though it was a long time before I could imagine the perfect safety of it. In a country where there are no thieves, because a thief here would not know what to do with his booty, we are secure from human molestation, and the land has long been cleared of all sorts of wild beasts, without being unpleasantly tamed. It is like England in that, and yet it has a touch of the sylvan, which you feel nowhere as you do in our dear New England hill country. There was one night, however, when we were lured on and on, and did not stop to camp till fairly in the dusk. Then we went to sleep without supper, for we had had rather a late lunch and were not hungry, and about one o'clock in the morning I was awakened by voices speaking Altrurian together. I recognized my husband's voice, which is always so kind, but which seemed to have a peculiarly tender and compassionate note in it now. The other was lower and of a sadness which wrung my heart, though I did not know in the least what the person was saying. The talk went on a long time, at first about some matter of immediate interest, as I fancied, and then apparently it branched off on some topic which seemed to concern the stranger, whoever he was. Then it seemed to get more indistinct, as if the stranger were leaving us and Aristides were going a little way with him. Presently I heard him coming back, and he put his head in at the van curtains, as if to see whether I was asleep.

"Well?" I said, and he said how sorry he was for having waked me. "Oh, I don't mind," I said. "Whom were you talking with? He had the saddest voice I ever heard. What did he want?"

"Oh, it seems that we are not far from the ruins of one of the old capitalistic cities, which have been left for a sort of warning against the former conditions, and he wished to caution us against the malarial influences from it. I think perhaps we had better push on a little way, if you don't mind."

The moon was shining clearly, and of course I did not mind, and Aristides got his hand on the lever, and we were soon getting out of the dangerous zone. "I think," he said, "they ought to abolish that pest-hole. I doubt if it serves any good purpose, now, though it has been useful in times past as an object-lesson."

"But who was your unknown friend?" I asked, a great deal more curious about him than about the capitalistic ruin.

"Oh, just a poor murderer," he answered easily, and I shuddered back:

"A murderer!"

"Yes. He killed his friend some fifteen years ago in a jealous rage, and he is pursued by remorse that gives him no peace."

"And is the remorse his only punishment?" I asked, rather indignantly.

"Isn't that enough? God seemed to think it was, in the case of the first murderer, who killed his brother. All that he did to Cain was to set a mark on him. But we have not felt sure that we have the right to do this. We let God mark him, and He has done it with this man in the sorrow of his face. I was rather glad you couldn't see him, my dear. It is an awful face."

I confess that this sounded like mere sentimentalism to me, and I said, "Really, Aristides, I can't follow you. How are innocent people to be protected against this wretch, if he wanders about among them at will?"

"They are as safe from him as from any other man in Altruria. His case was carefully looked into by the medical authorities, and it was decided that he was perfectly sane, so that he could be safely left at large, to expiate his misdeed in the only possible way that such a misdeed can be expiated—by doing good to others. What would you have had us do with him?"

The question rather staggered me, but I said, "He ought to have been imprisoned at least a year for manslaughter."

"Cain was not imprisoned an hour."

"That was a very different thing. But suppose you let a man go at large who has killed his friend in a jealous rage, what do you do with other murderers?"

"In Altruria there can be no other murderers. People cannot kill here for money, which prompts every other kind of murder in capitalistic countries, as well as every other kind of crime. I know, my dear, that this seems very strange to you, but you will accustom yourself to the idea, and then you will see the reasonableness of the Altrurian plan. On the whole, I am sorry you could not have seen that hapless man, and heard him. He had a face like death—"

"And a voice like death, too!" I put in.

"You noticed that? He wanted to talk about his crime with me. He wants to talk about it with any one who will listen to him. He is consumed with an undying pity for the man he slew. That is the first thing, the only thing, in his mind. If he could, I believe he would give his life for the life he took at any moment. But you cannot recreate one life by destroying another. There is no human means of ascertaining justice, but we can always do mercy with divine omniscience." As he spoke the sun pierced the edge of the eastern horizon, and lit up the marble walls and roofs of the Regionic capital which we were approaching.

At the meeting we had there in the afternoon, Aristides reported our having been warned against our danger in the night by that murderer, and public record of the fact was made. The Altrurians consider any sort of punishment which is not expiation a far greater sin than the wrong it visits, and altogether barren and useless. After the record in this case had been made, the conference naturally turned upon what Aristides had seen of the treatment of criminals in America, and when he told of our prisons, where people merely arrested and not yet openly accused are kept, I did not know which way to look, for you know I am still an American at heart, Dolly. Did you ever see the inside of one of our police-stations at night? Or smell it? I did, once, when I went to give bail for a wretched girl who had been my servant, and had gone wrong, but had been arrested for theft, and I assure you that the sight and the smell woke me in the night for a month afterwards, and I have never quite ceased to dream about it.

The Altrurians listened in silence, and I hoped they could not realize the facts, though the story was every word true; but what seemed to make them the most indignant was the treatment of the families of the prisoners in what we call our penitentiaries and reformatories. At first they did not conceive of it, apparently, because it was so stupidly barbarous; they have no patience with stupidity; and when Aristides had carefully explained, it seemed as if they could not believe it. They thought it right that the convicts should be made to work, but they could not understand that the state really took away their wages, and left their families to suffer for want of the support which it had deprived them of. They said this was punishing the mothers and sisters, the wives and children of the prisoners, and was like putting out the eyes of an offender's innocent relatives as they had read was done in

Oriental countries. They asked if there was never any sort of protest against such an atrocious perversion of justice, and when the question was put to me I was obliged to own that I had never heard the system even criticised. Perhaps it has been, but I spoke only from my own knowledge.

VII

WELL, to get away from these dismal experiences, and come back to our travels, with their perpetual novelty, and the constantly varying beauty of the country!

The human interest of the landscape, that is always the great interest of it, and I wish I could make you feel it as I have felt it in this wonderful journey of ours. It is like the New England landscape at times, in its kind of gentle wildness, but where it has been taken back into the hand of man, how different the human interest is! Instead of a rheumatic old farmer, in his clumsy clothes, with some of his gaunt girls to help him, or perhaps his ageing wife, getting in the hay of one of those sweet meadows, and looking like so many animated scarecrows at their work; or instead of some young farmer, on the seat of his clattering mower, or mounted high over his tedder, but as much alone as if there were no one else in the neighborhood, silent and dull, or fierce or sullen, as the case might be, the work is always going on with companies of mowers or reapers, or planters, that chatter like birds or sing like them.

It is no use my explaining again and again that in a country like this, where everybody works, nobody *over* works, and that when the few hours of obligatory labor are passed in the mornings, people need not do anything unless they choose. Their working-dresses are very simple, but in all sorts of gay colors, like those you saw in the Greek play at Harvard, with straw hats for the men, and fillets of ribbon for the girls, and sandals for both. I speak of girls, for most of the married women are at home gardening, or about the household work, but men of every age work in the fields. The earth is dear to them because they get their life from it by labor that is not slavery; they come to love it every acre, every foot, because they have known it from childhood; and I have seen old men, very old, pottering about the orchards and meadows during the hours of voluntary work, and trimming them up here and there, simply because they could not keep away from the place, or keep their hands off the trees and bushes. Sometimes in the long, tender afternoons, we see far up on some pasture slope, groups of girls scattered about on the grass, with their sewing, or listening to some one reading. Other times they are giving a little play, usually a comedy, for life is so happy here that tragedy would not be true to it, with the characters coming and going in a grove of small pines, for the *coulisses*, and using a level of grass for the stage. If we stop, one of the audience comes down to us and invites us to come up and see the play, which keeps on in spite of the sensation that I can feel I make among them.

Everywhere the news of us has gone before us, and there is a universal curiosity to get a look at Aristides' capitalistic wife, as they call me. I made him translate it, and he explained that the word was merely descriptive and not characteristic; some people distinguished and called me American. There was one place where they were having a picnic in the woods up a hillside, and they asked us to join them, so we turned our van into the roadside and followed the procession. It was headed by two old men playing on pipes, and after these came children singing, and then all sorts of people, young and old. When we got to an open place in the woods, where there was a spring, and smooth grass, they built fires, and began to get ready for the feast, while some of them did things to amuse the rest. Every one could do something; if you can imagine a party of artists, it was something like that. I should say the Altrurians had artists' manners, free, friendly, and easy, with a dash of humor in everything, and a wonderful willingness to laugh and make laugh. Aristides is always explaining that the artist is their ideal type; that is, some one who works gladly, and plays as gladly as he works; no one here is asked to do work that he hates, unless he seems to hate every kind of work. When this happens, the authorities find out something for him that he had *better* like, by letting him starve till he works. That picnic lasted the whole afternoon and well into the night, and then the pic-nickers went home through the starlight, leading the little ones, or carrying them when they were too little or too tired. But first they came down to our van with us, and sang us a serenade after we had disappeared into it, and then left us, and sent their voices back to us out of the dark.

One morning at dawn, as we came into a village, we saw nearly the whole population mounting the marble steps of the temple, all in the holiday dress of the Voluntaries, which they put on here every afternoon when the work is done. Last of the throng came a procession of children, looking something like a May-Day party, and midway of their line were a young man and a young girl, hand in hand, who parted at the door of the temple, and entered separately. Aristides called out, "Oh, it is a wedding! You are in luck, Eveleth," and then and there I saw my first Altrurian wedding.

Within, the pillars and the altar and the seats of the elders were garlanded with flowers, so fresh and fragrant that they seemed to have blossomed from the marble overnight, and there was a soft murmur of Altrurian voices that might very well have seemed the hum of bees among the blossoms. This subsided, as the young couple, who had paused just inside the temple door, came up the middle side by side, and again separated and took their places, the youth on the extreme right of the elders, and the maiden on the extreme left of the eldresses, and stood facing the congregation, which was also on foot, and joined in the hymn which everybody sang. Then one of the eldresses rose and began a sort of statement which Aristides translated to me afterwards. She said that the young couple whom we saw there had for the third time asked to become man and wife, after having believed for a year that they loved each other, and having statedly come before the marriage authorities and been questioned as to the continuance of their affection. She said that probably every one present knew that they had been friends from childhood, and none would be surprised that they now wished to be united for life. They had been carefully instructed as to the serious nature of the marriage bond, and admonished as to the duties they were entering into, not only to each other, but to the community. At each successive visit to the authorities they had been warned, separately and together, against the danger of trusting to anything like a romantic impulse, and they had faithfully endeavored to act upon this advice, as they testified. In order to prove the reality of their affection, they had been parted every third month, and had lived during that time in different Regions where it was meant they should meet many other young people, so that if they felt any swerving of the heart they might not persist in an intention which could only bring them final unhappiness. It seems this is the rule in the case of young lovers, and people usually marry very young here, but if they wish to marry later in life the rule is not enforced so stringently, or not at all. The bride and groom we saw had both stood these trials, and at each return they had been more and more sure that they loved each other, and loved no one else. Now they were here to unite their hands, and to declare the union of their hearts before the people.

Then the eldress sat down and an elder arose, who bade the young people come forward to the centre of the line, where the elders and eldresses were sitting. He took his place behind them, and once more and for the last time he conjured them not to persist if they felt any doubt of themselves. He warned them that if they entered into the married state, and afterwards repented to the point of seeking divorce, the divorce would indeed be granted them, but on terms, as they must realize, of lasting grief to themselves through the offence they would commit against the commonwealth. They answered that they were sure of themselves, and ready to exchange their troth for life and death. Then they joined hands, and declared that they took each other for husband and wife. The congregation broke into another hymn and slowly dispersed, leaving the bride and groom with their families, who came up to them and embraced them, pressing their cheeks against the cheeks of the young pair.

This ended the solemnity, and then the festivity began, as it ended, with a wedding feast, where people sang and danced and made speeches and drank toasts, and the fun was kept up till the hours of the Obligatories approached; and then, what do you think? The married pair put off their wedding garments with the rest and went to work in the fields! Later, I understood, if they wished to take a wedding journey they could freely do so; but the first thing in their married life they must honor the Altrurian ideal of work, by which every one must live in order that every other may live without overwork. I believe that the marriage ceremonial is something like that of the Quakers, but I never saw a Quaker wedding, and I could only compare this with the crazy romps with which our house-weddings often end, with throwing of rice and old shoes, and tying ribbons to the bridal carriage and baggage, and following the pair to the train with outbreaks of tiresome hilarity, which make them conspicuous before their fellow-travellers; or with some of our ghastly church weddings, in which the religious ceremonial is lost in the social effect, and ends with that everlasting thumping march from "Lohengrin," and the outsiders storming about the bridal pair and the guests with the rude curiosity that the fattest policemen at the canopied and carpeted entrance cannot check.

VIII

WE HAVE since been at other weddings and at christenings and at funerals. The ceremonies are always held in the temples, and are always in the same serious spirit. As the Altrurians are steadfast believers in immortality, there is a kind of solemn elevation in the funeral ceremonies which I cannot give you a real notion of. It is helped, I think, by the custom of not performing the ceremony over the dead; a brief rite is reserved for the cemetery, where it is wished that the kindred shall not be present, lest they think always of the material body and not of the spiritual body which shall be raised in incorruption. Religious service is held in the temples every day at the end of the Obligatories, and whenever we are near a village or in any of the capitals we always go. It is very simple. After a hymn, to which the people sometimes march round the interior of the temple, each lays on the altar an offering from the fields or woods where they have been working, if it is nothing but a head of grain or a wild flower or a leaf. Then any one is at liberty to speak, but any one else may go out without offence. There is no ritual; sometimes they read a chapter from the New Testament, preferably a part of the story of Christ or a passage from His discourses. The idea of coming to the temple at the end of the day's labor is to consecrate that day's work, and they do not call anything work that is not work with the hands. When I explained, or tried to explain, that among us a great many people worked with their brains, to amuse others or to get handwork out of them, they were unable to follow me. I asked if they did not consider composing music or poetry or plays, or painting pictures work, and they said, No, that was pleasure, and must be indulged only during the Voluntaries; it was never to be honored like work with the hands, for it would not equalize the burden of that, but might put an undue share of it on others. They said that lives devoted to such pursuits must be very unwholesome, and they brought me to book about the lives of most artists, literary men, and financiers in the capitalistic world to prove what they said. They held that people must work with their hands willingly, in the artistic spirit, but they could only do that when they knew that others differently gifted were working in like manner with their hands.

I couldn't begin to tell you all our queer experiences. As I have kept saying, I am a great curiosity everywhere, and I could flatter myself that people were more eager to see me than to hear Aristides. Sometimes I couldn't help thinking that they expected to find me an awful warning, a dreadful example of whatever a woman ought not to be, and a woman from capitalistic conditions *must* be logically. But sometimes they were very intelligent, even the simplest villagers, as we should call them, though there is such an equality of education and opportunity here that no simplicity of life has the effect of dulling people as it has with us.

One thing was quite American: they always wanted to know how I liked Altruria, and when I told them, as I sincerely could, that I adored it, they were quite affecting in their pleasure. They generally asked if I would like to go back to America, and when I said No, they were delighted beyond anything. They said I must become a citizen and vote and take part in the government, for that was every woman's duty as well as right; it was wrong to leave the whole responsibility to the men. They asked if American women took no interest in the government, and when I told them there was a very small number who wished to influence politics socially, as the Englishwomen did, but without voting or taking any responsibility, they were shocked. In one of the Regionic capitals they wanted me to speak after Aristides, but I had nothing prepared; at the next I did get off a little speech in English, which he translated after me. Later he put it into Altrurian, and I memorized it, and made myself immensely popular by parroting it.

The pronunciation of Altrurian is not difficult, for it is spelled phonetically, and the sounds are very simple. Where they were once difficult they have been simplified, for here the simplification of life extends to everything; and the grammar has been reduced in its structure till it is as elemental as English grammar or Norwegian. The language is Greek in origin, but the intricate inflections and the declensions have been thrown away, and it has kept only the simplest forms. You must get Mr. Twelvemough to explain this to you, Dolly, for it would take me too long, and I have so much else to tell you. A good many of the women have taken up English, but they learn it as a dead language, and they give it a comical effect by trying to pronounce it as it is spelled.

I suppose you are anxious, if these letters which are piling up and piling up should ever reach you, or even start to do so, to know something about the Altrurian cities, and what they are like. Well, in the first place, you must cast all images of American cities out of your mind, or any European cities, except, perhaps, the prettiest and stateliest parts of Paris, where there is a regular sky-line, and the public buildings and monuments are approached through shaded avenues. There are no private houses here, in our sense—that is, houses which people have built with their own money on their own land, and made as ugly outside and as molestive to their neighbors and the passers-by as they chose. As the buildings belong to the whole people, the first requirement is that they shall be beautiful inside and out. There are a few grand edifices looking like Greek temples, which are used for the government offices, and these are, of course, the most dignified, but the dwellings are quite as attractive and comfortable. They are built round courts, with gardens and flowers in the courts, and wide grassy spaces round them. They are rather tall, but never so tall as our great hotels or apartment-houses, and the floors are brought to one level by elevators, which are used only in the capitals; and, generally speaking, I should say the villages were pleasanter than the cities. In fact, the village is the Altrurian ideal, and there is an effort everywhere to reduce the size of the towns and increase the number of the villages. The outlying farms have been gathered into these, and now there is not one of those lonely places in the country, like those where our farmers toil alone out-doors and their wives alone indoors, and both go mad so often in the solitude. The villages are almost in sight of each other, and the people go to their fields in company, while the women carry on their housekeeping co-operatively, with a large kitchen which they use in common; they have their meals apart or together, as they like. If any one is sick or disabled the neighbors come in and help do her work, as they used with us in the early times, and as they still do in country places. Village life here is preferred, just as country life is in England, and one thing that will amuse you, with your American ideas, and your pride in the overgrowth of our cities: the Altrurian papers solemnly announce from time to time that the population of such or such a capital has been reduced so many hundreds or thousands since the last census. That means that the villages in the neighborhood have been increased in number and population.

Meanwhile, I must say the capitals are delightful: clean, airy, quiet, with the most beautiful architecture, mostly classic and mostly marble, with rivers running through them and round them, and every real convenience, but not a clutter of artificial conveniences, as with us. In the streets there are noiseless trolleys (where they have not been replaced by public automobiles) which the long distances of the ample ground-plan make rather necessary, and the rivers are shot over with swift motor-boats; for the short distances you always expect to walk, or if you don't expect it, you walk anyway. The car-lines and boat-lines are public, and they are free, for the Altrurians think that the community owes transportation to every one who lives beyond easy reach of the points which their work calls them to.

Of course the great government stores are in the capitals, and practically there are no stores in the villages, except for what you might call emergency supplies. But you must not imagine, Dolly, that shopping, here, is like shopping at home—or in America, as I am learning to say, for Altruria is home now. That is, you don't fill your purse with bank-notes, or have things charged. You get everything you want, within reason, and certainly everything you need, for nothing. You have only to provide yourself with a card, something like that you have to show at the Army and Navy Stores in London, when you first go to buy there, which certifies that you belong to this or that working-phalanx, and that you have not failed in the Obligatories for such and such a length of time. If you are not entitled to this card, you had better not go shopping, for there is no possible equivalent for it which will enable you to carry anything away or have it sent to your house. At first I could not help feeling rather indignant when I was asked to show my work-card in the stores; I had usually forgotten to bring it, or sometimes I had brought my husband's card, which would not do at all, unless I could say that I had been ill or disabled, for a woman is expected to work quite the same as a man. Of course her housework counts, and as we are on a sort of public mission, they count our hours of travel as working-hours, especially as Aristides has made it a point of good citizenship for us to stop every now and then and join in the Obligatories when the villagers were getting in the farm crops or quarrying stone or putting up a house. I am never much use in quarrying or building, but I come in strong in the hay-fields or the apple orchards or the orange groves.

The shopping here is not so enslaving as it is with us—I mean, with *you*—because the fashions do not change, and you get things only when you need them, not when you want them, or when other people think you do. The costume was fixed long ago, when the Altrurian era began, by a commission of artists, and it would be considered very bad form as well as bad morals to try changing it in the least. People are allowed to choose their own colors, but if one goes very wrong, or so far wrong as to offend the public taste, she is gently admonished by the local art commission; if she insists, they let her have her own way, but she seldom wants it when she knows that people think her a fright. Of course the costume is modified somewhat for the age and shape of the wearer, but this is not so often as you might think. There are no very lean or very stout people, though there are old and young, just as there are with us. But the Altrurians keep young very much longer than capitalistic peoples do, and the life of work keeps down their weight. You know I used to incline a little to over-plumpness, I really believe because I overate at times simply to keep from thinking of the poor who had to under-eat, but that is quite past now; I have lost at least twenty-five pounds from working out-doors and travelling so much and living very, very simply.

IX

I HAVE to jot things down as they come into my mind, and I am afraid I forget some of the most important. Everybody is so novel on this famous tour of ours that I am continually interested, but one has one's preferences even in Altruria, and I believe I like best the wives of the artists and literary men whom one finds working in the galleries and libraries of the capitals everywhere. They are not more intelligent than other women, perhaps, but they are more sympathetic; and one sees so little of those people in New York, for all they abound there.

The galleries are not only for the exhibition of pictures, but each has numbers of ateliers, where the artists work and teach. The libraries are the most wonderfully imagined things. You do not have to come and study in them, but if you are working up any particular subject, the books relating to it are sent to your dwelling every morning and brought away every noon, so that during the obligatory hours you have them completely at your disposition, and during the Voluntaries you can consult them with the rest of the public in the library; it is not thought best that study should be carried on throughout the day, and the results seem to justify this theory. If you want to read a book merely for pleasure, you are allowed to take it out and live with it as long as you like; the copy you have is immediately replaced with another, so that you do not feel hurried and are not obliged to ramp through it in a week or a fortnight.

The Altrurian books are still rather sealed books to me, but they are delightful to the eye, all in large print on wide margins, with flexible bindings, and such light paper that you can hold them in one hand indefinitely without tiring. I must send you some with this, if I ever get my bundle of letters off to you. You will see by the dates that I am writing you one every day; I had thought of keeping a journal for you, but then I should have had left out a good many things that happened during our first days, when the impressions were so vivid, and I should have got to addressing my records to myself, and I think I had better keep to the form of letters. If they reach you, and you read them at random, why that is very much the way I write them.

I despair of giving you any *real* notion of the capitals, but if you remember the White City at the Columbian Fair at Chicago in 1893, you can have some idea of the general effect of one; only there is nothing heterogeneous in their beauty. There is one classic rule in the architecture, but each of the different architects may characterize an edifice from himself, just as different authors writing the same language characterize it by the diction natural to them. There are suggestions of the capitals in some of our cities, and if you remember Commonwealth Avenue in Boston, you can imagine something like the union of street and garden which every street of them is. The trolleys run under the overarching trees between the lawns, flanked by gravelled footpaths between flower-beds, and you take the cars or not as you like. As there is no hurry, they go about as fast as English trams, and the danger from them is practically reduced to nothing by the crossings dipping under them at the street corners. The centre of the capital is approached by colonnades, which at night bear groups of great bulbous lamps, and by day flutter with the Altrurian and Regionic flags. Around this centre are the stores and restaurants and theatres, and galleries and libraries, with arcades over the sidewalks, like those in Bologna; sometimes the arcades are in two stories, as they are in Chester. People are constantly coming and going in an easy way during the afternoon, though in the morning the streets are rather deserted.

But what is the use? I could go on describing and describing, and never get in half the differences from American cities, with their hideous uproar, and their mud in the wet, and their clouds of swirling dust in the wind. But there is one feature which I must mention, because you can fancy it from the fond dream of a great national highway which some of our architects projected while they were still in the fervor of excitement from the beauty of the Peristyle, and other features of the White City. They really have such a highway here, crossing the whole Altrurian continent, and uniting the circle of the Regionic capitals. As we travelled for a long time by the country roads on the beds of the old railways, I had no idea of this magnificent avenue, till one day my husband suddenly ran our van into the one leading up to the first capital we were to visit. Then I found myself between miles and miles of stately white pillars, rising and sinking as the road found its natural levels, and growing in the perspective before us and dwindling behind us. I could not keep out of my mind a colonnade of palm-trees, only the fronds were lacking, and there were never palms so beautiful. Each pillar was inscribed with the name of some Altrurian who had done something for his country, written some beautiful poem or story, or history, made some scientific discovery, composed an opera, invented a universal convenience, performed a wonderful cure, or been a delightful singer, or orator, or gardener, or farmer. Not one soldier, general or admiral, among them! That seemed very strange to me, and I asked Aristides how it was. Like everything else in Altruria, it was very simple; there had been no war for so long that there were no famous soldiers to commemorate. But he stopped our van when he came to the first of the many arches which spanned the highway, and read out to me in English the Altrurian record that it was erected in honor of the first President of the Altrurian Commonwealth, who managed the negotiations when the capitalistic oligarchies to the north and south were peacefully annexed, and the descendants of the three nations joined in the commemoration of an event that abolished war forever on the Altrurian continent.

Here I can imagine Mr. Makely asking who footed the bills for this beauty and magnificence, and whether these works were constructed at the cost of the nation, or the different Regions, or the abuttors on the different highways. But the fact is, you poor, capitalistic dears, they cost nobody a dollar, for there is not a dollar in Altruria. You must worry into the idea somehow that in Altruria you cannot buy anything except by *working*, and that work is the current coin of the republic: you pay for everything by drops of sweat, and off your own brow, not somebody else's brow. The people built these monuments and colonnades, and aqueducts and highways and byways, and sweet villages and palatial cities with their own hands, after the designs of artists, who also took part in the labor. But it was a labor that they delighted in so much that they chose to perform it during the Voluntaries, when they might have been resting, and not during the Obligatories, when they were required to work. So it was all joy and all glory. They say there never was such happiness in any country since the world began. While the work went on it was like a perpetual Fourth of July or an everlasting picnic.

But I know you hate this sort of economical stuff, Dolly, and I will make haste to get down to business, as Mr. Makely would say, for I am really coming to something that you will think worth while. One morning, when we had made half the circle of the capitals, and were on the homestretch to the one where we had left our dear mother—for Aristides claims her, too—and I was letting that dull nether anxiety for her come to the top, though we had had the fullest telephonic talks with her every day, and knew she was well and happy, we came round the shoulder of a wooded cliff and found ourselves on an open stretch of the northern coast. At first I could only exclaim at the beauty of the sea, lying blue and still beyond a long beach closed by another headland, and I did not realize that a large yacht which I saw close to land had gone ashore. The beach was crowded with Altrurians, who seemed to have come to the rescue, for they were putting off to the yacht in boats and returning with passengers, and jumping out, and pulling their boats with them up on to the sand.

I was quite bewildered, and I don't know what to say I was the next thing, when I saw that the stranded yacht was flying the American flag from her peak. I supposed she must be one of our cruisers, she was so large, and the first thing that flashed into my mind was a kind of amused wonder what those poor Altrurians would do with a ship-of-war and her marines and crew. I couldn't ask any coherent questions, and luckily Aristides was answering my incoherent ones in the best possible way by wheeling our van down on the beach and making for the point nearest the yacht. He had time to say he did not believe she was a government vessel, and, in fact, I remembered that once I had seen a boat in the North River getting up steam to go to Europe which was much larger, and had her decks covered with sailors that I took for bluejackets; but she was only the private yacht of some people I knew.

These stupid things kept going and coming in my mind while my husband was talking with some of the Altrurian girls who were there helping with the men. They said that the yacht had gone ashore the night before last in one of the sudden fogs that come up on that coast, and that some people whom the sailors seemed to obey were camping on the edge of the upland above the beach, under a large tent they had brought from the yacht. They had refused to go to the guest-house in the nearest village, and as nearly as the girls could make out they expected the yacht to get afloat from tide to tide, and then intended to re-embark on her. In the mean time they had provisioned themselves from the ship, and were living in a strange way of their own. Some of them seemed to serve the others, but these appeared to be used with a very ungrateful indifference, as if they were of a different race. There was one who wore a white apron and white cap who directed the cooking for the rest, and had several assistants; and from time to time very disagreeable odors came from the camp, like burning flesh. The Altrurians had carried them fruits and vegetables, but the men-assistants had refused them contemptuously and seemed suspicious of the variety of mushrooms they offered them. They called out, "To-stoo!" and I understood that the strangers were afraid they were bringing toadstools. One of the Altrurian girls had been studying English in the nearest capital, and she had tried to talk with these people, pronouncing it in the Altrurian way, but they could make nothing of one another; then she wrote down what she wanted to say, but as she spelled it phonetically they were not able to read her English. She asked us if I was the American Altrurian she had heard of, and when I said yes she lost no time in showing us to the camp of the castaways.

As soon as we saw their tents we went forward till we were met at the largest by a sort of marine footman, who bowed slightly and said to me, "What name shall I say, ma'am?" and I answered distinctly, so that he might get the name right, "Mr. and Mrs. Homos." Then he held back the flap of the marquee, which seemed to serve these people as a drawing-room, and called out, standing very rigidly upright, to let us pass, in the way that I remembered so well, "Mr. and Mrs. 'Omos!" and a severe-looking, rather elderly lady rose to meet us with an air that was both anxious and forbidding, and before she said anything else she burst out, "You don't mean to say you speak English?"

I said that I spoke English, and had not spoken anything else but rather poor French until six months before, and then she demanded, "Have you been cast away on this outlandish place, too?"

I laughed and said I lived here, and I introduced my husband as well as I could without knowing her name. He explained with his pretty Altrurian accent, which you used to like so much, that we had ventured to come in the hope of being of use to them, and added some regrets for their misfortune so sweetly that I wondered she could help responding in kind. But she merely said, "Oh!" and then she seemed to recollect herself, and frowning to a very gentle-looking old man to come forward, she ignored my husband in presenting me. "Mr. Thrall, Mrs. ——"

She hesitated for my name, and I supplied it, "Homos," and as the old man had put out his hand in a kindly way I took it.

"And this is my husband, Aristides Homos, an Altrurian," I said, and then, as the lady had not asked us to sit down, or shown the least sign of liking our being there, the natural woman flamed up in me as she hadn't in all the time I have been away from New York. "I am glad you are so comfortable here, Mr. Thrall. You won't need us, I see. The people about will do anything in their power for you. Come, my dear," and I was sweeping out of that tent in a manner calculated to give the eminent millionaire's wife a notion of Altrurian hauteur which I must own would have been altogether mistaken.

I knew who they were perfectly. Even if I had not once met them I should have known that they were the ultra-rich Thralls, from the multitudinous pictures of them that I had seen in the papers at home, not long after they came on to New York.

He was beginning, "Oh no, oh no," but I cut in. "My husband and I are on our way to the next Regionic capital, and we are somewhat hurried. You will be quite well looked after by the neighbors here, and I see that we are rather in your housekeeper's way."

It *was* nasty, Dolly, and I won't deny it; it was *vulgar*. But what would *you* have done? I could feel Aristides' mild eye sadly on me, and I was sorry for him, but I assure you I was not sorry for them, till that old man spoke again, so timidly: "It isn't my—

it's my wife, Mrs. Homos. Let me introduce her. But haven't we met before?"

"Perhaps during my first husband's lifetime. I was Mrs. Bellington Strange."

"Mrs. P. Bellington Strange? Your husband was a dear friend of mine when we were both young—a good man, if ever there was one; the best in the world! I am so glad to see you again. Ah—my dear, you remember my speaking of Mrs. Strange?"

He took my hand again and held it in his soft old hands, as if hesitating whether to transfer it to her, and my heart melted towards him. You may think it very odd, Dolly, but it was what he said of my dear, dead husband that softened me. It made him seem very fatherly, and I felt the affection for him that I felt for my husband, when he seemed more like a father. Aristides and I often talk of it, and he has no wish that I should forget him.

Mrs. Thrall made no motion to take my hand from him, but she said, "I think I have met Mr. Strange," and now I saw in the background, sitting on a camp-stool near a long, lank young man stretched in a hammock, a very handsome girl, who hastily ran through a book, and then dropped it at the third mention of my name. I suspected that the book was the Social Register, and that the girl's search for me had been satisfactory, for she rose and came vaguely towards us, while the young man unfolded himself from the hammock, and stood hesitating, but looking as if he rather liked what had happened.

Mr. Thrall bustled about for camp-stools, and said, "Do stop and have some breakfast with us, it's just coming in. May I introduce my daughter, Lady Moors and—and Lord Moors?" The girl took my hand, and the young man bowed from his place; but if that poor old man had known, peace was not to be made so easily between two such bad-tempered women as Mrs. Thrall and myself. We expressed some very stiff sentiments in regard to the weather, and the prospect of the yacht getting off with the next tide, and my husband joined in with that manly gentleness of his, but we did not sit down, much less offer to stay to break-fast. We had got to the door of the tent, the family following us, even to the noble son-in-law, and as she now realized that we were actually going, Mrs. Thrall gasped out, "But you are not *leaving* us? What shall we *do* with all these natives?"

This was again too much, and I flamed out at her. "*Natives!* They are cultivated and refined people, for they are Altrurians, and I assure you you will be in much better hands than mine with them, for I am only Altrurian by marriage!"

She was one of those leathery egotists that nothing will make a dint in, and she came back with, "But we don't speak the language, and they don't speak English, and how are we to manage if the yacht doesn't get afloat?"

"Oh, no doubt you will be looked after from the capital we have just left. But I will venture to make a little suggestion with regard to the natives in the mean time. They are not proud, but they are very sensitive, and if you fail in any point of consideration, they will understand that you do not want their hospitality."

"I imagine our own people will be able to look after us," she answered quite as nastily. "We do not propose to be dependent on them. We can pay our way here as we do elsewhere."

"The experiment will be worth trying," I said. "Come, Aristides!" and I took the poor fellow away with me to our van. Mr. Thrall made some hopeless little movements towards us, but I would not stop or even look back. When we got into the van, I made Aristides put on the full power, and fell back into my seat and cried a while, and then I scolded him because he would not scold me, and went on in a really scandalous way. It must have been a revelation to him, but he only smoothed me on the shoulder and said, "Poor Eveleth, poor Eveleth," till I thought I should scream; but it ended in my falling on his neck, and saying I knew I was horrid, and what did he want me to do?

After I calmed down into something like rationality, he said he thought we had perhaps done the best thing we could for those people in leaving them to themselves, for they could come to no possible harm among the neighbors. He did not believe from what he had seen of the yacht from the shore, and from what the Altrurians had told him, that there was one chance in a thousand of her ever getting afloat. But those people would have to convince themselves of the fact, and of several other facts in their situation. I asked him what he meant, and he said he could tell me, but that as yet it was a public affair, and he would rather not anticipate the private interest I would feel in it. I did not insist; in fact, I wanted to get that odious woman out of my mind as soon as I could, for the thought of her threatened to poison the pleasure of the rest of our tour.

I believe my husband hurried it a little, though he did not shorten it, and we got back to the Maritime Region almost a week sooner than we had first intended. I found my dear mother well, and still serenely happy in her Altrurian surroundings. She had begun to learn the language, and she had a larger acquaintance in the capital, I believe, than any other one person. She said everybody had called on her, and they were the kindest people she had ever dreamed of. She had exchanged cooking-lessons with one lady who, they told her, was a distinguished scientist, and she had taught another, who was a great painter, a peculiar embroidery stitch which she had learned from my grandmother, and which everybody admired. These two ladies had given her most of her grammatical instruction in Altrurian, but there was a bright little girl who had enlarged her vocabulary more than either, in helping her about her housework, the mother having lent her for the purpose. My mother said she was not ashamed to make blunders before a child, and the little witch had taken the greatest delight in telling her the names of things in the house and the streets and the fields outside the town, where they went long walks together.

x

WELL, my dear Dorothea, I had been hoping to go more into detail about my mother and about our life in the Maritime Capital, which is to be our home for a year, but I had hardly got down the last words when Aristides came in with a despatch from the Seventh Regionic, summoning us there on important public business: I haven't got over the feeling yet of being especially distinguished and flattered at sharing in public business; but the Altrurian women are so used to it that they do not think anything of it. The despatch was signed by an old friend of my husband's, Cyril Chrysostom, who had once been Emissary in England, and to whom my husband wrote his letters when he was in America. I hated to leave my mother so soon, but it could not be helped, and we took the first electric express for the Seventh Regionic, where we arrived in about an hour and forty minutes, making the three hundred miles in that time easily. I couldn't help regretting our comfortable van, but there was evidently haste in the summons, and I confess that I was curious to know what the matter was, though I had made a shrewd guess the first instant, and it turned out that I was not mistaken.

The long and the short of it was that there was trouble with the people who had come ashore in that yacht, and were destined never to go to sea in her. She was hopelessly bedded in the sand, and the waves that were breaking over her were burying her deeper and deeper. The owners were living in their tent as we had left them, and her crew were camped in smaller tents and any shelter they could get, along the beach. They had brought her stores away, but many of the provisions had been damaged, and it had become a pressing question what should be done about the people. We had been asked to consult with Cyril and his wife, and the other Regionic chiefs and their wives, and we threshed the question out nearly the whole night.

I am afraid it will appear rather comical in some aspects to you and Mr. Makely, but I can assure you that it was a very serious matter with the Altrurian authorities. If there had been any hope of a vessel from the capitalistic world touching at Altruria within a definite time, they could have managed, for they would have gladly kept the yacht's people and owners till they could embark them for Australia or New Zealand, and would have made as little of the trouble they were giving as they could. But until the trader that brought us should return with the crew, as the captain had promised, there was no ship expected, and any other wreck in the mean time would only add to their difficulty. You may be surprised, though I was not, that the difficulty was mostly with the yacht-owners, and above all with Mrs. Thrall, who had baffled every effort of the authorities to reduce what they considered the disorder of their life.

With the crew it was a different matter. As soon as they had got drunk on the wines and spirits they had brought from the wreck, and then had got sober because they had drunk all the liquors up, they began to be more manageable; when their provisions ran short, and they were made to understand that they would not be allowed to plunder the fields and woods, or loot the villages for something to eat, they became almost exemplarily docile. At first they were disposed to show fight, and the principles of the Altrurians did not allow them to use violence in bringing them to subjection; but the men had counted without their hosts in supposing that they could therefore do as they pleased, unless they pleased to do right. After they had made their first foray they were warned by Cyril, who came from the capital to speak English with them, that another raid would not be suffered. They therefore attempted it by night, but the Altrurians were prepared for them with the flexible steel nets which are their only means of defence, and half a dozen sailors were taken in one. When they attempted to break out, and their shipmates attempted to break in to free them, a light current of electricity was sent through the wires and the thing was done. Those who were rescued—the Altrurians will not say captured— had hoes put into their hands the next morning, and were led into the fields and set to work, after a generous breakfast of coffee, bread, and mushrooms. The chickens they had killed in their midnight expedition were buried, and those which they had not killed lost no time in beginning to lay eggs for the sustenance of the reformed castaways. As an extra precaution with the "rescued," when they were put to work, each of them was fitted with a kind of shirt of mail, worn over his coat, which could easily be electrized by a metallic filament connecting with the communal dynamo, and under these conditions they each did a full day's work during the Obligatories.

As the short commons grew shorter and shorter, both meat and drink, at Camp Famine, and the campers found it was useless to attempt thieving from the Altrurians, they had tried begging from the owners in their large tent, but they were told that the provisions were giving out there, too, and there was nothing for them. When they insisted the servants of the owners had threatened them with revolvers, and the sailors, who had nothing but their knives, preferred to attempt living on the country. Within a week the whole crew had been put to work in the woods and fields and quarries, or wherever they could make themselves useful. They were, on the whole, so well fed and sheltered that they were perfectly satisfied, and went down with the Altrurians on the beach during the Voluntaries and helped secure the yacht's boats and pieces of wreckage that came ashore. Until they became accustomed or resigned to the Altrurian diet, they were allowed to catch shell-fish and the crabs that swarmed along the sand and cook them, but on condition that they built their fires on the beach, and cooked only during an offshore wind, so that the fumes of the roasting should not offend the villagers.

Cyril acknowledged, therefore, that the question of the crew was for the present practically settled, but Mr. and Mrs. Thrall, and their daughter and son-in-law, with their servants, still presented a formidable problem. As yet, their provisions had not run out, and they were living in their marquee as we had seen them three weeks earlier, just after their yacht went ashore. It could not be said that they were molestive in the same sense as the sailors, but they were even more demoralizing in the spectacle they offered the neighborhood of people dependent on hired service, and in their endeavors to supply themselves in perishable provisions, like milk and eggs, by means of money. Cyril had held several interviews with them, in which he had at first delicately intimated, and then explicitly declared, that the situation could not be prolonged. The two men had been able to get the Altrurian point of view in some measure, and so had Lady Moors, but Mrs. Thrall had remained stiffly obtuse and obstinate, and it was in despair of bringing her to terms without resorting to rescue that he had summoned us to help him.

It was not a pleasant job, but of course we could not refuse, and we agreed that as soon as we had caught a nap, and had a bite of breakfast we would go over to their camp with Cyril and his wife, and see what we could do with the obnoxious woman. I confess that I had some little consolation in the hope that I should see her properly humbled.

XI

MR. THRALL and Lord Moors must have seen us coming, for they met us at the door of the tent without the intervention of the footman, and gave us quite as much welcome as we could expect in our mission, so disagreeable all round. Mr. Thrall was as fatherly with me as before, and Lord Moors was as polite to Cyril and Mrs. Chrysostom as could have been wished. In fact he and Cyril were a sort of acquaintances from the time of Cyril's visit to England where he met the late Earl Moors, the father of the present peer, in some of his visits to Toynbee Hall, and the Whitechapel Settlements. The earl was very much interested in the slums, perhaps because he was rather poor himself, if not quite slummy. The son was then at the university, and when he came out and into his title he so far shared his father's tastes that he came to America; it was not slumming, exactly, but a noble-man no doubt feels it to be something like it. After a little while in New York he went out to Colorado, where so many needy noblemen bring up, and there he met the Thralls, and fell in love with the girl. Cyril had understood—or rather Mrs. Cyril,—that it was a love-match on both sides, but on Mrs. Thrall's side it was business. He did not even speak of settlements—the English are *so* romantic when they *are* romantic!—but Mr. Thrall saw to all that, and the young people were married after a very short court-ship. They spent their honeymoon partly in Colorado Springs and partly in San Francisco, where the Thralls' yacht was lying, and then they set out on a voyage round the world, making stops at the interesting places, and bringing up on the beach of the Seventh Region of Altruria, en route for the eastern coast of South

America. From that time on, Cyril said, we knew their history.

After Mr. Thrall had shaken hands tenderly with me, and cordially with Aristides, he said, "Won't you all come inside and have breakfast with us? My wife and daughter"—

"Thank you, Mr. Thrall," Cyril answered for us, "we will sit down here, if you please; and as your ladies are not used to business, we will not ask you to disturb them."

"I'm sure Lady Moors," the young nobleman began, but Cyril waved him silent.

"We shall be glad later, but not now! Gentlemen, I have asked my friends Aristides Homos and Eveleth Homos to accompany my wife and me this morning because Eveleth is an American, and will understand your position, and he has lately been in America and will be able to clarify the situation from both sides. We wish you to believe that we are approaching you in the friendliest spirit, and that nothing could be more painful to us than to seem inhospitable."

"Then why," the old man asked, with business-like promptness, "do you object to our presence here? I don't believe I get your idea."

"Because the spectacle which your life offers is contrary to good morals, and as faithful citizens we cannot countenance it."

"But in what way is our life immoral? I have always thought that I was a good citizen at home; at least I can't remember having been arrested for disorderly conduct."

He smiled at me, as if I should appreciate the joke, and it hurt me to keep grave, but suspecting what a bad time he was going to have, I thought I had better not join him in any levity.

"I quite conceive you," Cyril replied. "But you present to our people, who are offended by it, the spectacle of dependence upon hireling service for your daily comfort and convenience."

"But, my dear sir," Mr. Thrall returned, "don't we *pay* for it? Do our servants object to rendering us this service?"

"That has nothing to do with the case; or, rather, it makes it worse. The fact that your servants do not object shows how completely they are depraved by usage. We should not object if they served you from affection, and if you repaid them in kindness; but the fact that you think you have made them a due return by giving them money shows how far from the right ideal in such a matter the whole capitalistic world is."

Here, to my great delight, Aristides spoke up:

"If the American practice were half as depraving as it ought logically to be in their conditions, their social system would drop to pieces. It was always astonishing to me that a people with their facilities for evil, their difficulties for good, should remain so kind and just and pure."

"That is what I understood from your letters to me, my dear Aristides. I am willing to leave the general argument for the present. But I should like to ask Mr. Thrall a question, and I hope it won't be offensive."

Mr. Thrall smiled. "At any rate I promise not to be offended."

"You are a very rich man?"

"Much richer than I would like to be."

"How rich?"

"Seventy millions; eighty; a hundred; three hundred; I don't just know."

"I don't suppose you've always felt your great wealth a great blessing?"

"A blessing? There have been times when I felt it a millstone hanged about my neck, and could have wished nothing so much as that I were thrown into the sea. Man, you don't *know* what a curse I have felt my money to be at such times. When I have given it away, as I have by millions at a time, I have never been sure that I was not doing more harm than good with it. I have hired men to seek out good objects for me, and I have tried my best to find for myself causes and institutions and persons who might be helped without hindering others as worthy, but sometimes it seems as if every dollar of my money carried a blight with it, and infected whoever touched it with a moral pestilence. It has reached a sum where the wildest profligate couldn't spend it, and it grows and grows. It's as if it were a rising flood that had touched my lips, and would go over my head before I could reach the shore. I believe I got it honestly, and I have tried to share it with those whose labor earned it for me. I have founded schools and hospitals and homes for old men and old women, and asylums for children, and the blind, and deaf, and dumb, and halt, and mad. Wherever I have found one of my old workmen in need, and I have looked personally into the matter, I have provided for him fully, short of pauperization. Where I have heard of some gifted youth, I have had him educated in the line of his gift. I have collected a gallery of works of art, and opened it on Sundays as well as week-days to the public free. If there is a story of famine, far or near, I send food by the shipload. If there is any great public calamity, my agents have instructions to come to the rescue without referring the case to me. But it is all useless! The money grows and grows, and I begin to feel that my efforts to employ it wisely and wholesomely are making me a public laughing-stock as well as an easy mark for every swindler with a job or a scheme." He turned abruptly to me. "But you must often have heard the same from my old friend Strange. We used to talk these things over together, when our money was not the heap that mine is now; and it seems to me I can hear his voice saying the very words I have been using."

I, too, seemed to hear his voice in the words, and it was as if speaking from his grave.

I looked at Aristides, and read compassion in his dear face; but the face of Cyril remained severe and judicial. He said: "Then, if what you say is true, you cannot think it a hardship if we remove your burden for the time you remain with us. I have consulted with the National and Regional as well as the Communal authorities, and we cannot let you continue to live in the manner you are living here. You must pay your way."

"I shall be only too glad to do that," Mr. Thrall returned, more cheerfully. "We have not a great deal of cash in hand, but I can give you my check on London or Paris or New York."

"In Altruria," Cyril returned, "we have no use for money. You must *pay* your way as soon as your present provision from your yacht is exhausted."

Mr. Thrall turned a dazed look on the young lord, who suggested: "I don't think we follow you. How can Mr. Thrall pay his way except with money?"

"He must pay with *work*. As soon as you come upon the neighbors here for the necessities of life you must all work. To-morrow or the next day or next week at the furthest you must go to work, or you must starve." Then he came out with that text of Scripture which had been so efficient with the crew of the *Little Sally*: "For even when we were with you this we commanded you, that if any would not work neither should he eat."

Lord Moors seemed very interested, and not so much surprised as I had expected. "Yes, I have often thought of that passage and of its susceptibility to a simpler interpretation than we usually give it. But—"

"There is but one interpretation of which it is susceptible," Cyril interrupted. "The apostle gives that interpretation when he prefaces the text with the words, 'For yourselves know how you ought to follow us; for we behaved not ourselves disorderly among you. Neither did we eat any man's bread for nought; but *wrought with travail* night and day, that we might not be chargeable to any of you: not because we have not power, but to make ourselves an ensample unto you to follow us.' The whole economy of Altruria is founded on these passages."

"Literally?"

"Literally."

"But, my dear sir," the young lord reasoned, "you surely do not wrench the text from some such meaning as that if a man has money, he may pay his way without working?"

"No, certainly not. But here you have no money, and as we cannot suffer any to 'walk among us disorderly, working not at all,' we must not exempt you from our rule."

XII

AT THIS POINT there came a sound from within the marquee as of skirts sweeping forward sharply, imperiously, followed by a softer *frou-frou*, and Mrs. Thrall put aside the curtain of the tent with one hand, and stood challenging our little Altrurian group, while Lady Moors peered timidly at us from over her mother's shoulder. I felt a lust of battle rising in me at sight of that woman, and it was as much as I could do to control myself; but in view of the bad time I knew she was going to have, I managed to hold in, though I joined very scantly in the polite greetings of the Chrysostoms and Aristides, which she ignored as if they had been the salutations of savages. She glared at her husband for explanation, and he said, gently, "This is a delegation from the Altrurian capital, my dear, and we have been talking over the situation together."

"But what is this," she demanded, "that I have heard about our not paying? Do they accuse us of not paying? You could buy and sell the whole country."

I never imagined so much mildness could be put into such offensive words as Cyril managed to get into his answer. "We accuse you of not paying, and we do not mean that you shall become chargeable to us. The men and women who served you on shipboard have been put to work, and you must go to work, too."

"Mr. Thrall—Lord Moors—have you allowed these people to treat you as if you were part of the ship's crew? Why don't you give them what they want and let them go? Of course it's some sort of blackmailing scheme. But you ought to get rid of them at any cost. Then you can appeal to the authorities, and tell them that you will bring the matter to the notice of the government at Washington. They must be taught that they cannot insult American citizens with impunity." No one spoke, and she added, "What do they really want?"

"Well, my dear," her husband hesitated, "I hardly know how to explain. But it seems that they think our living here in the way we do is disorderly, and—and they want us to go to work, in short."

"To *work!*" she shouted.

"Yes, all of us. That is, so I understand."

"What nonsense!"

She looked at us one after another, and when her eye rested on me, I began to suspect that insolent as she was she was even duller; in fact, that she was so sodden in her conceit of wealth that she was plain stupid. So when she said to me, "You are an American by birth, I believe. Can you tell me the meaning of this?" I answered:

"Cyril Chrysostom represents the authorities. If *he* asks me to speak, I will speak." Cyril nodded at me with a smile, and I went on. "It is a very simple matter. In Altruria everybody works with his hands three hours a day. After that he works or not, as he likes."

"What have we to do with that?" she asked.

"The rule has no exceptions."

"But we are not Altrurians; we are Americans."

"I am an American, too, and I work three hours every day, unless I am passing from one point to another on public business with my husband. Even then we prefer to stop during the work-hours, and help in the fields, or in the shops, or wherever we are needed. I left my own mother at home doing her kitchen work yesterday afternoon, though it was out of hours, and she need not have worked."

"Very well, then, we will do nothing of the kind, neither I, nor my daughter, nor my husband. He has worked hard all his life, and he has come away for a much-needed rest. I am not going to have him breaking himself down."

I could not help suggesting, "I suppose the men at work in his mines, and mills, and on his railroads and steamship lines are taking a much-needed rest, too. I hope you are not going to let them break themselves down, either."

Aristides gave me a pained glance, and Cyril and his wife looked grave, but she not quite so grave as he. Lord Moors said, "We don't seem to be getting on. What Mrs. Thrall fails to see, and I confess I don't quite see it myself, is that if we are not here *in forma pauperis*—"

"But you *are* here *in forma pauperis*," Cyril interposed, smilingly.

"How is that? If we are willing to pay—if Mr. Thrall's credit is undeniably good—"

"Mr. Thrall's credit is not good in Altruria; you can pay here only in one currency, in the sweat of your faces."

"You want us to be Tolstoys, I suppose," Mrs. Thrall said, contemptuously.

Cyril replied, gently, "The endeavor of Tolstoy, in capitalistic conditions, is necessarily dramatic. Your labor here will be for your daily bread, and it will be real." The inner dulness of the woman came into her eyes again, and he addressed himself to Lord Moors in continuing: "If a company of indigent people were cast away on an English coast, after you had rendered them the first aid, what should you do?"

The young man reflected. "I suppose we should put them in the way of earning a living until some ship arrived to take them home."

"That is merely what we propose to do in your case here," Cyril said.

"But we are not indigent—"

"Yes, you are absolutely destitute. You have money and credit, but neither has any value in Altruria. Nothing but work or love has any value in Altruria. You cannot realize too clearly that you stand before us *in forma pauperis*. But we require of you nothing that we do not require of ourselves. In Altruria every one is poor till he pays with work; then, for that time, he is rich; and he cannot otherwise lift himself above charity, which, except in the case of the helpless, we consider immoral. Your life here offers a very corrupting spectacle. You are manifestly living without work, and you are served by people whose hire you are not able to pay."

"My dear sir," Mr. Thrall said at this point, with a gentle smile, "I think they are willing to take the chances of being paid."

"We cannot suffer them to do so. At present we know of no means of your getting away from Altruria. We have disused our custom of annually connecting with the Australasian steamers, and it may be years before a vessel touches on our coast. A ship sailed for Boston some months ago, with the promise of returning in order that the crew may cast in their lot with us permanently. We do not confide in that promise, and you must therefore conform to our rule of life. Understand clearly that the willingness of your servants to serve you has nothing to do with the matter. That is part of the falsity in which the whole capitalistic world lives. As the matter stands with you, here, there is as much reason why you should serve them as they should serve you. If on their side they should elect to serve you from love, they will be allowed to do so. Otherwise, you and they must go to work with the neighbors at the tasks they will assign you."

"Do you mean at once?" Lord Moors asked.

"The hours of the obligatory labors are nearly past for the day. But if you are interested in learning what you will be set to doing to-morrow, the Communal authorities will be pleased to instruct you during the Voluntaries this afternoon. You may be sure that in no case will your weakness or inexperience be overtasked. Your histories will be studied, and appropriate work will be assigned to each of you."

Mrs. Thrall burst out, "If you think I am going into my kitchen—"

Then I burst in, "I left my mother in *her* kitchen!"

"And a very fit place for her, I dare say," she retorted, but Lady Moors caught her mother's arm and murmured, in much the same distress as showed in my husband's mild eyes, "Mother! Mother!" and drew her within.

XIII

WELL, Dolly, I suppose you will think it was pretty hard for those people, and when I got over my temper I confess that I felt sorry for the two men, and for the young girl whom the Altrurians would not call Lady Moors, but addressed by her Christian name, as they did each of the American party in his or her turn; even Mrs. Thrall had to answer to Rebecca. They were all rather bewildered, and so were the butler and the footmen, and the *chef* and his helpers, and the ladies' maids. These were even more shocked than those they considered their betters, and I quite took to my affections Lord Moors' man Robert, who was in an awe-stricken way trying to get some light from me on the situation. He contributed as much as any one to bring about a peaceful submission to the inevitable, for he had been a near witness of what had happened to the crew when they attempted their rebellion to the authorities; but he did not profess to understand the matter, and from time to time he seemed to question the reality of it.

The two masters, as you would call Mr. Thrall and Lord Moors, both took an attitude of amiable curiosity towards their fate, and accepted it with interest when they had partly chosen and partly been chosen by it. Mr. Thrall had been brought up on a farm till his ambition carried him into the world; and he found the light gardening assigned him for his first task by no means a hardship. He was rather critical of the Altrurian style of hoe at first, but after he got the hang of it, as he said, he liked it better, and during the three hours of the first morning's Obligatories, his ardor to cut all the weeds out at once had to be restrained rather than prompted. He could not be persuaded to take five minutes for rest out of every twenty, and he could not get over his life-long habit of working against time. The Altrurians tried to make him understand that here people must not work *against* time, but must always work *with* it, so as to have enough work to do each day; otherwise they must remain idle during the Obligatories and tend to demoralize the workers. It seemed that Lady Moors had a passion for gardening, and she was set to work with her father on the border of flowers surrounding the vegetable patch he was hoeing. She knew about flowers, and from her childhood had amused herself by growing them, and so far from thinking it a hardship or disgrace to dig, she was delighted to get at them. It was easy to see that she and her father were cronies, and when I went round in the morning with Aristides to ask if we could do anything for them, we heard them laughing and talking gayly together before we reached them.

They said they had looked their job (as Mr. Thrall called it) over the afternoon before during the Voluntaries, and had decided how they would manage, and they had set to work that morning as soon as they had breakfast. Lady Moors had helped her mother get the breakfast, and she seemed to regard the whole affair as a picnic, though from the look of Mrs. Thrall's back, as she turned it on me, when I saw her coming to the door of the marquee with a coffee-pot in her hand, I decided that she was not yet resigned to her new lot in life.

Lord Moors was nowhere to be seen, and I felt some little curiosity about him which was not quite anxiety. Later, as we were going back to our quarters in the village, we saw him working on the road with a party of Altrurians who were repairing a washout from an overnight rain. They were having all kinds of a time, except a bad time, trying to understand each other in their want of a common language. It appeared that the Altrurians were impressed with his knowledge of road-making, and were doing something which he had indicated to them by signs. We offered our services as interpreters, and then he modestly owned in defence of his suggestions that when he was at Oxford he had been one of the band of enthusiastic undergraduates who had built a piece of highway under Mr. Ruskin's direction. The Altrurians regarded his suggestions as rather amateurish, but they were glad to act upon them, when they could, out of pure good feeling and liking for him; and from time to time they rushed upon him and shook hands with him; their affection did not go further, and he was able to stand the handshaking, though he told us he hoped they would not feel it necessary to keep it up, for it was really only a very simple matter like putting a culvert in place of a sluice which they had been using to carry the water off. They understood what he was saying, from his gestures, and they crowded round us to ask whether he would like to join them during the Voluntaries that afternoon, in getting the stone out of a neighboring quarry, and putting in the culvert at once. We explained to him, and he said he should be very happy. All the time he was looking at them admirably, and he said, "It's really very good," and we understood that he meant their classic working-dress, and when he added, "I should really fancy trying it myself one day," and we told them, they wanted to go and bring him an Altrurian costume at once. But we persuaded them not to urge him, and in fact he looked very fit for his work in his yachting flannels.

I talked him over a long time with Aristides, and tried to get his point of view. I decided finally that an Englishman of his ancient lineage and high breeding, having voluntarily come down to the level of an American millionaire by marriage, could not feel that he was lowering himself any further by working with his hands. In fact, he probably felt that his merely undertaking a thing dignified the thing; but of course this was only speculation on my part, and he may have been resigned to working for a living because like poor people elsewhere he was obliged to do it. Aristides thought there was a good deal in that idea, but it is hard for an Altrurian to conceive of being ashamed of work, for they regard idleness as pauperism, and they would look upon our leisure classes, so far as we have them, very much as we look upon tramps, only they would make the excuse for our tramps that they often cannot get work.

We had far more trouble with the servants than we had with the masters in making them understand that they were to go to work in the fields and shops, quite as the crew of the yacht had done. Some of them refused outright, and stuck to their refusal until the village electrician rescued them with the sort of net and electric filament which had been employed with the recalcitrant sailors; others were brought to a better mind by withholding food from them till they were willing to pay for it by working. You will be sorry to learn, Dolly, that the worst of the rebels were the ladies' maids, who, for the honor of our sex, ought not to have required the application of the net and filament; but they had not such appetites as the men-servants, and did not mind starving so much. However, in a very short time they were at work, too, and more or less resigned, though they did not profess to understand it.

You will think me rather fickle, I am afraid, but after I made the personal acquaintance of Mr. Thrall's *chef*, Anatole, I found my affections dividing themselves between him and his lordship's man Robert, my first love. But Anatole was magnificent, a gaunt, little, aquiline man, with a branching mustache and gallant goatee, and having held an exalted position at a salary of ten thousand a year from Mr. Thrall, he could easily stoop from it, while poor Robert was tormented with misgivings, not for himself, but for Lord and Lady Moors and Mr. Thrall. It became my pleasing office to explain the situation to Monsieur Anatole, who, when he imagined it, gave a cry of joy, and confessed, what he had never liked to tell Mr. Thrall, knowing the misconceptions of Americans on the subject, that he had belonged in France to a party of which the political and social ideal was almost identical with that of the Altrurians. He asked for an early opportunity of addressing the village Assembly and explaining this delightful circumstance in public, and he profited by the occasion to embrace the first Altrurian we met and kiss him on both cheeks.

His victim was a messenger from the Commune, who had been sent to inquire whether Anatole had a preference as to the employment which should be assigned to him, and I had to reply for him that he was a man of science; that he would be happy to serve the republic in whatever capacity his concitizens chose, but that he thought he could be most useful in studying the comestible vegetation of the neighborhood, and the substitution of the more succulent herbs for the flesh-meats to the use of which, he understood from me, the Altrurians were opposed. In the course of his preparation for the rôle of *chef*, which he had played both in France and America, he had made a specialty of edible fungi; and the result was that Anatole was set to mushrooming, and up to this moment he has discovered no less than six species hitherto unknown to the Altrurian table. This has added to their dietary in several important particulars, the fungi he has discovered being among those highly decorative and extremely poisonous-looking sorts which flourish in the deep woods and offer themselves almost inexhaustibly in places near the ruins of the old capitalistic cities, where hardly any other foods will grow. Anatole is very proud of his success, and at more than one Communal Assembly has lectured upon his discoveries and treated of their preparation for the table, with sketches of them as he found them growing, colored after nature by his own hand. He has himself become a fanatical vegetarian, having, he confesses, always had a secret loathing for the meats he stooped to direct the cooking of among the French and American bourgeoisie in the days which he already looks back upon as among the most benighted of his history.

XIV

THE SCENE has changed again, Dolly, and six months have elapsed without your knowing it. Aristides and I long ago completed the tour of the capitals which the Thrall incident interrupted, and we have been settled for many months in the Maritime Capital, where it has been decided we had better fill out the first two years of my husband's repatriation. I have become more and more thoroughly naturalized, and if I am not yet a perfect Altrurian, it is not for not loving better and better the best Altrurian of them all, and not for not admiring and revering this wonderful civilization.

During the Obligatories of the forenoons I do my housework with my own hands, and as my mother lives with us we have long talks together, and try to make each other believe that the American conditions were a sort of nightmare from which we have happily awakened. You see how terribly frank I am, my dear, but if I were not, I could not make you understand how I feel. My heart aches for you, there, and the more because I know that you do not want to live differently, that you are proud of your economic and social illogicality, and that you think America is the best country under the sun! I can never persuade you, but if you could only come here, once, and see for yourselves! Seeing would be believing, and believing would be the wish never to go away, but to be at home here always.

I can imagine your laughing at me and asking Mr. Makely whether the *Little Sally* has ever returned to Altruria, and how I can account for the captain's failure to keep his word. I confess that is a sore point with me. It is now more than a year since she sailed, and, of course, we have not had a sign or whisper from her. I could almost wish that the crew were willing to stay away, but I am afraid it is the captain who is keeping them. It has become almost a mania with me, and every morning, the first thing when I wake, I go for my before-breakfast walk along the marble terrace that overlooks the sea, and scan the empty rounding for the recreant ship. I do not want to think so badly of human nature, as I must if the *Little Sally* never comes back, and I am sure you will not blame me if I should like her to bring me some word from you. I know that if she ever reached Boston you got my letters and presents, and that you have been writing me as faithfully as I have been writing you, and what a sheaf of letters from you there will be if her masts ever pierce the horizon! To tell the truth, I do long for a little American news! Do you still keep on murdering and divorcing, and drowning, and burning, and mommicking, and maiming people by sea and land? Has there been any war since I left? Is the financial panic as great as ever, and is there as much hunger and cold? I know that whatever your crimes and calamities are, your heroism and martyrdom, your wild generosity and self-devotion, are equal to them.

It is no use to pretend that in little over a year I can have become accustomed to the eventlessness of life in Altruria. I go on for a good many days together and do not miss the exciting incidents you have in America, and then suddenly I am wolfishly hungry for the old sensations, just as now and then I *want meat,* though I know I should loathe the sight and smell of it if I came within reach of it. You would laugh, I dare say, at the Altrurian papers, and what they print for news. Most of the space is taken up with poetry, and character study in the form of fiction, and scientific inquiry of every kind. But now and then there is a report of the production of a new play in one of the capitals; or an account of an open-air pastoral in one of the communes; or the progress of some public work, like the extension of the National Colonnade; or the wonderful liberation of some section from malaria; or the story of some good man or woman's life, ended at the patriarchal age they reach here. They also print selected passages of capitalistic history, from the earliest to the latest times, showing how in war and pestilence and needless disaster the world outside Altruria remains essentially the same that it was at the beginning of civilization, with some slight changes through the changes of human nature for the better in its slow approaches to the Altrurian ideal. In noting these changes the writers get some sad amusement out of the fact that the capitalistic world believes human nature cannot be changed, though cannibalism and slavery and polygamy have all been extirpated in the so-called Christian countries, and these things were once human nature, which is always changing, while brute nature remains the same. Now and then they touch very guardedly on that slavery, worse than war, worse than any sin or shame conceivable to the Altrurians, in which uncounted myriads of women are held and bought and sold, and they have to note that in this the capitalistic world is without the hope of better things. You know what I mean, Dolly; every good woman knows the little she cannot help knowing; but if you had ever inquired into that horror, as I once felt obliged to do, you would think it the blackest horror of the state of things where it must always exist as long as there are riches and poverty. Now, when so many things in America seem bad dreams, I cannot take refuge in thinking that a bad dream; the reality was so deeply burnt into my brain by the words of some of the slaves; and when I think of it I want to grovel on the ground with my mouth in the dust. But I know this can only distress you, for you cannot get away from the fact as I have got away from it; that there it is in the next street, perhaps in the next house, and that any night when you leave your home with your husband, you may meet it at the first step from your door.

You can very well imagine what a godsend the reports of Aristides and the discussions of them have been to our papers.

They were always taken down stenographically, and they were printed like dialogue, so that at a little distance you would take them at first for murder trials or divorce cases, but when you look closer, you find them questions and answers about the state of things in America. There are often humorous passages, for the Altrurians are inextinguishably amused by our illogicality, and what they call the perpetual *non sequiturs* of our lives and laws. In the discussions they frequently burlesque these, but as they present them they seem really beyond the wildest burlesque. Perhaps you will be surprised to know that a nation of working-people like these feel more compassion than admiration for our working-people. They pity them, but they blame them more than they blame the idle rich for the existing condition of things in America. They ask why, if the American workmen are in the immense majority, they do not vote a true and just state, and why they go on striking and starving their families instead; they cannot distinguish in principle between the confederations of labor and the combinations of capital, between the trusts and the trades-unions, and they condemn even more severely the oppressions and abuses of the unions. My husband tries to explain that the unions are merely provisional, and are a temporary means of enabling the employees to stand up against the tyranny of the employers, but they always come back and ask him if the workmen have not most of the votes, and if they have, why they do not protect themselves peacefully instead of organizing themselves in fighting shape, and making a warfare of industry.

There is not often anything so much like news in the Altrurian papers as the grounding of the Thrall yacht on the coast of the Seventh Region, and the incident has been treated and discussed in every possible phase by the editors and their correspondents. They have been very frank about it, as they are about everything in Altruria, and they have not concealed their anxieties about their unwelcome guests. They got on without much trouble in the case of the few sailors of the *Little Sally*, but the crew of the *Saraband* is so large that it is a different matter. In the first place, they do not like the application of force, even in the mild electrical form in which they employ it, and they fear that the effect with themselves will be bad, however good it is for their guests. Besides, they dread the influence which a number of people, invested with the charm of strangeness, may have with the young men and especially the young girls of the neighborhood. The hardest thing the Altrurians have to grapple with is feminine curiosity, and the play of this about the strangers is what they seek the most anxiously to control. Of course, you will think it funny, and I must say that it seemed so to me at first, but I have come to think it is serious. The Altrurian girls are cultivated and refined, but as they have worked all their lives with their hands they cannot imagine the difference that work makes in Americans; that it coarsens and classes them, especially if they have been in immediate contact with rich people, and been degraded or brutalized by the knowledge of the contempt in which labor is held among us by those who are not compelled to it. Some of my Altrurian friends have talked it over with me, and I could take their point of view, though secretly I could not keep my poor American feelings from being hurt when they said that to have a large number of people from the capitalistic world thrown upon their hands was very much as it would be with us if we had the same number of Indians, with all their tribal customs and ideals, thrown upon our hands. They say they will not shirk their duty in the matter, and will study it carefully; but all the same, they wish the incident had not happened.

XV

I AM GLAD that I was called away from the disagreeable point I left in my last, and that I have got back temporarily to the scene of the Altrurianization of Mr. Thrall and his family. So far as it has gone it is perfect, if I may speak from the witness of happiness in those concerned, except perhaps Mrs. Thrall; she is as yet only partially reconstructed, but even she has moments of forgetting her lost grandeur and of really enjoying herself in her work. She is an excellent housekeeper, and she has become so much interested in making the marquee a simple home for her family that she is rather proud of showing it off as the effect of her unaided efforts. She was allowed to cater to them from the canned meats brought ashore from the yacht as long as they would stand it, but the wholesome open-air conditions have worked a wonderful change in them, and neither Mr. Thrall nor Lord and Lady Moors now have any taste for such dishes. Here Mrs. Thrall's old-time skill as an excellent vegetable cook, when she was the wife of a young mechanic, has come into play, and she believes that she sets the best table in the whole neighborhood, with fruits and many sorts of succulents and the everlasting and ever-pervading mushrooms.

As the Altrurians do not wish to annoy their involuntary guests, or to interfere with their way of life where they do not consider it immoral, their control has ended with setting them to work for a living. They have not asked them to the communal refectory, but, as long as they have been content to serve each other, have allowed them their private table. Of course, their adaptation to their new way of life has proceeded more slowly than it otherwise would, but with the exception of Mrs. Thrall they are very intelligent people, and I have been charmed in talking the situation over with them. The trouble has not been so great with the ship's people, as was feared. Such of these as have imagined their stay here permanent, or wished it to be so, have been received into the neighboring communes, and have taken the first steps towards naturalization; those who look forward to getting away some time, or express the wish for it, are allowed to live in a community of their own, where they are not molested as long as they work in the three hours of the Obligatories. Natural-ly, they are kept out of mischief, but after their first instruction in the ideas of public property and the impossibility of enriching themselves at the expense of any one else, they have behaved very well. The greatest trouble they ever gave was in trapping and killing the wild things for food; but when they were told that this must not be done, and taught to recognize the vast range of edible fungi, they took not unwillingly to mushrooms and the ranker tubers and roots, from which, with unlimited eggs, cheese, milk, and shell-fish, they have constructed a diet of which they do not complain.

This brings me rather tangentially to Monsieur Anatole, who has become a fanatical Altrurian, and has even had to be restrained in some of his enthusiastic plans for the compulsory naturalization of his fellow castaways. His value as a scientist has been cordially recognized, and his gifts as an artist in the exquisite water-color studies of edible fungi has won his notice in the capital of the Seventh Regional where they have been shown at the spring water-color exhibition. He has printed several poems in the *Regional Gazette*, villanelles, rondeaux, and triolets, with accompanying versions of the French, translated into Altrurian by one of the first Altrurian poets. This is a widow of about Monsieur Anatole's own age; and the literary friendship between them has ripened into something much more serious. In fact they are engaged to be married. I suppose you will laugh at this, Dolly, and at first I confess that there was enough of the old American in me to be shocked at the idea of a French *chef* marrying an Altrurian lady who could trace her descent to the first Altrurian president of the Commonwealth, and who is universally loved and honored. I could not help letting something of the kind escape me by accident, to a friend, and presently Mrs. Chrysostom was sent to interview me on the subject, and to learn just how the case appeared to me. This put me on my honor, and I was obliged to say how it would appear in America, though every moment I grew more and more ashamed of myself and my native country, where we pretend that labor is honorable, and are always heaping dishonor on it. I told how certain of our girls and matrons had married their coachmen and riding-masters and put themselves at odds with society, and I confessed that marrying a cook would be regarded as worse, if possible.

Mrs. Chrysostom was accompanied by a lady in her second youth, very graceful, very charmingly dressed, and with an expression of winning intelligence, whom she named to me simply as Cecilia, in the Altrurian fashion. She apparently knew no

English, and at first Mrs. Chrysostom translated each of her questions and my answers. When I had got through, this lady began to question me herself in Altrurian, which I owned to understanding a little. She said:

"You know Anatole?"

"Yes, certainly, and I like him, as I think every one must who knows him."

"He is a skilful *chef?*"

"Mr. Thrall would not have paid him ten thousand dollars a year if he had not been."

"You have seen some of his water-colors?"

"Yes. They are exquisite. He is unquestionably an artist of rare talent."

"And it is known to you that he is a man of scientific attainments?"

"That is something I cannot judge of so well as Aristides; but *he* says M. Anatole is learned beyond any man he knows in edible fungi."

"As an adoptive Altrurian, and knowing the American ideas from our point of view, should you respect their ideas of social inequality?"

"Not the least in the world. I understand as well as you do that their ideas must prevail wherever one works for a living and another does not. Those ideas are practically as much accepted in America as they are in Europe, but I have fully renounced them."

You see, Dolly, how far I have gone!

The unknown, who could be pretty easily imagined, rose up and gave me her hand. "If you are in the Region on the third of May you must come to our wedding."

The same afternoon I had a long talk with Mr. Thrall, whom I found at work replanting a strawberry-patch during the Voluntaries. He rose up at the sound of my voice, and after an old man's dim moment for getting me mentally in focus, he brightened into a genial smile, and said, "Oh, Mrs. Homos! I am glad to see you."

I told him to go on with his planting, and I offered to get down on my knees beside him and help, but he gallantly handed me to a seat in the shade beside his daughter's flower-bed, and it was there that we had a long talk about conditions in America and Altruria, and how he felt about the great change in his life.

"Well, I can truly say," he answered much more at length than I shall report, "that I have never been so happy since the first days of my boyhood. All care has dropped from me; I don't feel myself rich, and I don't feel myself poor in this perfect safety from want. The only thing that gives me any regret is that my present state has not been the effect of my own will and deed. If I am now following the greatest and truest of all counsels it has not been because I have sold all and given to the poor, but because my money has been mercifully taken from me, and I have been released from its responsibilities in a state of things where there is no money."

"But, Mr. Thrall," I said, "don't you ever feel that you have a duty to the immense fortune which you have left in America, and which must be disposed of somehow when people are satisfied that you are not going to return and dispose of it yourself?"

"No, none. I was long ago satisfied that I could really do no good with it. Perhaps if I had had more faith in it I might have done some good with it, but I believe that I never did anything but harm, even when I seemed to be helping the most, for I was aiding in the perpetuation of a state of things essentially wrong. Now, if I never go back—and I never wish to go back—let the law dispose of it as seems best to the authorities. I have no kith or kin, and my wife has none, so there is no one to feel aggrieved by its application to public objects."

"And how do you imagine it will be disposed of?"

"Oh, I suppose for charitable and educational purposes. Of course a good deal of it will go in graft; but that cannot be helped."

"But if you could now dispose of it according to your clearest ideas of justice, and if you were forced to make the disposition yourself, what would you do with it?"

"Well, that is something I have been thinking of, and as nearly as I can make out, I ought to go into the records of my prosperity and ascertain just how and when I made my money. Then I ought to seek out as fully as possible the workmen who helped me make it by their labor. Their wages, which were always the highest, were never a fair share, though I forced myself to think differently, and it should be my duty to inquire for them and pay them each a fair share, or, if they are dead, then their children or their next of kin. But even when I had done this I should not be sure that I had not done them more harm than good."

How often I had heard poor Mr. Strange say things like this, and heard of other rich men saying them, after lives of what is called beneficence! Mr. Thrall drew a deep sigh, and cast a longing look at his strawberry-bed. I laughed, and said, "You are anxious to get back to your plants, and I won't keep you. I wonder if Mrs. Thrall could see me if I called; or Lady Moors?"

He said he was sure they would, and I took my way over to the marquee. I was a little surprised to be met at the door by Lord Moors' man Robert. He told me he was very sorry, but her ladyship was helping his lordship at a little job on the roads, which they were doing quite in the Voluntaries, with the hope of having the National Colonnade extended to a given point; the ladies were helping the gentlemen get the place in shape. He was still sorrier, but I not so much, that Mrs. Thrall was lying down and would like to be excused; she was rather tired from putting away the luncheon things.

He asked me if I would not sit down, and he offered me one of the camp-stools at the door of the marquee, and I did sit down for a moment, while he flitted about the interior doing various little things. At last I said, "How is this, Robert? I thought you had been assigned to a place in the communal refectory. You're not here on the old terms?"

He came out and stood respectfully holding a dusting-cloth in his hand. "Thank you, not exactly, ma'am. But the fact is, ma'am, that the communal monitors have allowed me to come back here a few hours in the afternoon, on what I may call terms of my own."

"I don't understand. But won't you sit down, Robert?"

"Thank you, if it is the same to you, ma'am, I would rather stand while I'm here. In the refectory, of course, it's different."

"But about your own terms?"

"Thanks. You see, ma'am, I've thought all along it was a bit awkward for them here, they not being so much used to looking after things, and I asked leave to come and help now and then. Of course, they said that I could not be allowed to serve for hire in Altruria; and one thing led to another, and I said it would really be a favor to me, and I didn't expect money for my work, for I did not suppose I should ever be where I could use it again, but if they would let me come here and do it for—"

Robert stopped and blushed and looked down, and I took the word, "For love?"

"Well, ma'am, that's what they called it."

Dolly, it made the tears come into my eyes, and I said very solemnly, "Robert, do you know, I believe you are the sweetest soul even in this land flowing with milk and honey?"

"Oh, you mustn't say that, ma'am. There's Mr. Thrall and his lordship and her ladyship. I'm sure they would do the like for me if I needed their help. And there are the Altrurians, you know."

"But they are used to it, Robert, and—Robert! Be frank with me! What do you think of Altruria?"

"Quite frank, ma'am, as if you were not connected with it, as you are?"

"Quite frank."

"Well, ma'am, if you are sure you wouldn't mind it, or consider it out of the way for me, I should say it was—rum."

"*Rum?* Don't you think it is beautiful here, to see people living *for* each other instead of living *on* each other, and the whole nation like one family, and the country a paradise?"

"Well, that's just it, ma'am, if you won't mind my saying so. That's what I mean by rum."

"Won't you explain?"

"It doesn't seem *real*. Every night when I go to sleep, and think that there isn't a thief or a policeman on the whole continent, and only a few harmless homicides, as you call them, that wouldn't hurt a fly, and not a person hungry or cold, and no poor and no rich, and no servants and no masters, and no soldiers, and no—disreputable characters, it seems as if I was going to wake up in the morning and find myself on the *Saraband* and it all a dream here."

"Yes, Robert," I had to own, "that was the way with me, too, for a long while. And even now I have dreams about America and the way matters are there, and I wake myself weeping for fear Altruria *isn't* true. Robert! You must be honest with me! When you are awake, and it's broad day, and you see how happy every one is here, either working or playing, and the whole land without an ugly place in it, and the lovely villages and the magnificent towns, and everything, does it still seem—rum?"

"It's like that, ma'am, at times. I don't say at all times."

"And you don't believe that the rest of the world—England and America—will ever be rum, too?"

"I don't see how they can. You see the poor are against it as well as the rich. Everybody wants to have something of his own, and the trouble seems to come from that. I don't suppose it was brought about in a day, Altruria wasn't, ma'am?"

"No, it was whole centuries coming."

"That was what I understood from that Mr. Chrysostom—Cyril, he wants me to call him, but I can't quite make up my mouth to it—who speaks English, and says he has been in England. He was telling me about it, one day when we were drying the dishes at the refectory together. He says they used to have wars and trusts and trades-unions here in the old days, just as we do now in civilized countries."

"And you don't consider Altruria civilized?"

"Well, not in just that sense of the word, ma'am. You wouldn't call heaven civilized?"

"Well, not in just that sense of the word, Robert."

"You see, it's rum here, because, though everything seems to go so right, it's against human nature."

"The Altrurians say it isn't."

"I hope I don't differ from you, ma'am, but what would people—the best people—at home say? They would say it wasn't reasonable; they would say it wasn't even possible. That's what makes me think it's a dream—that it's rum. Begging your pardon, ma'am."

"Oh, I quite understand, Robert. Then you don't believe a camel can ever go through the eye of a needle?"

"I don't quite see how, ma'am."

"But you are proof of as great a miracle, Robert."

"Beg your pardon, ma'am?"

"Some day I will explain. But is there nothing that can make you believe Altruria is true here, and that it can be true anywhere?"

"I have been thinking a good deal about that, ma'am. One doesn't quite like to go about in a dream, or think one is dreaming, and I have got to saying to myself that if some ship was to come here from England or America, or even from Germany, and we could compare our feelings with the feelings of people who were fresh to it, we might somehow get to believe that it was real."

"Yes," I had to own. "We need fresh proofs from time to time. There was a ship that sailed from here something over a year ago, and the captain promised his crew to let them bring her back, but at times I am afraid that was part of the dream, too, and that we're all something I am dreaming about."

"Just so, ma'am," Robert said, and I came away downhearted enough, though he called after me, "Mrs. Thrall will be very sorry, ma'am."

Back in the Maritime Capital, and oh, Dolly, Dolly, Dolly! They have sighted the *Little Sally* from the terrace! How happy I am! There will be letters from you, and I shall hear all that has happened in America, and I shall never again doubt that Altruria is real! I don't know how I shall get these letters of mine back to you, but somehow it can be managed. Perhaps the *Sara-*

band's crew will like to take the *Little Sally* home again; perhaps when Mr. Thrall knows the ship is here he will want to buy it and go back to his money in America and the misery of it! Do you believe he will? Should I like to remind my husband of his promise to take me home on a visit? Oh, my heart misgives me! I wonder if the captain of the *Little Sally* has brought his wife and children with him, and is going to settle among us, or whether he has just let his men have the vessel, and they have come to Altruria without him? I dare not ask anything, I dare not think anything!

THE END

APPENDIX

The first part of "Letter" ix of "Letters of an Altrurian Traveller" (*Cosmopolitan*, xvii, July 1894, 352–356), which follows, was omitted from *Through the Eye of the Needle*. Portions of this material were used in "New York Streets," in *Impressions and Experiences* (BAL 9706).

THE SELLING AND THE GIVING OF DINNERS

New York, December 15, 1893.

MY DEAR CYRIL:

In answer to the inquiry in your last letter concerning the large shops here, I cannot say they are very attractive, and as I have told you, they are not so many as we have been led to suppose. There are, perhaps, fifty, at most, on Broadway and the different avenues. They are vast emporiums, sometimes occupying half a city-block, and multiplying their acreage of floor space by repeated stories, one above another, reached by elevators perpetually lifting and lowering the throngs of shoppers. But I do not find any principle of taste governing the arrangement of their multitudinous wares; and they have always a huddled and confused effect. I miss the precious and human quality of individuality in them. I meet no one who seems to have a personal interest in the goods or the customers; it is a dry and cold exchange of moneys and wares; and the process is made the more tedious by the checks used to keep the salesmen and saleswomen from robbing their employers. They take your money, but it must be sent with their written account and your purchase to a central bureau, where the account is audited and returned with your purchase, after a vexatious delay. But in the system of things here, fully a fifth of the people seem employed in watching that the rest do not steal, and fully a fifth of the time is lost.

You have perhaps imagined these great stores like our Regionic bazaars, where we go with our government orders to supply our needs, or indulge our fancies. But they are not at all like these, except in their vastness and variety. I cannot say that there is no aim at beauty in their display, but the sordid motive of advertising running through it

445

all destroys this. You are not pressed to buy, here, any more than with us, and the salespeople are not allowed to misrepresent the quality of the goods, for that would be bad business; but the affair is a purely business transaction. That friendly hospitality which our bazaars show all comers, and that cordial endeavor to seek out and satisfy their desires are wholly unknown here. What you experience is the working of a vast, very intricate, and rather clumsy money-making machine, with yourself as a part of the mechanism.

For this reason I prefer the smaller shops where I can enter into some human relation with the merchant, if it is only for the moment. I have already tried to give you some notion of the multitude of these; and I must say now that they add much in their infinite number and variety to such effect of gaiety as the city has. They are especially attractive at night, where, under favor of the prevailing dark, the shapeless monster is able to hide something of its deformity. Then the brilliant lamps, with the shadows they cast, unite to an effect of gaiety which the day will not allow.

The great stores contribute nothing to this, however, for they all close at six o'clock in the evening. On the other hand, they do not mar such poor beauty as the place has with the multitude of signs that the minor traffic renders itself so offensive with. One sign, rather simple and unostentatious, suffices for a large store; a little store will want half a dozen, and will have them painted and hung all over its façade, and stood about in front of it as obtrusively as the police will permit. The effect is bizarre and grotesque beyond expression. If one thing in the business streets makes New York more hideous than another it is the signs, with their discordant colors, their infinite variety of tasteless shapes. If by chance there is any architectural beauty in a business edifice, it is spoiled, insulted, outraged by these huckstering appeals; while the prevailing unsightliness is emphasized and heightened by them. A vast, hulking, bare brick wall, rising six or seven stories above the neighboring buildings, you would think bad enough in all conscience: how, then, shall I give you any notion of the horror it becomes when its unlovely space is blocked out in a ground of white with a sign painted on it in black letters ten feet high?

But you could not imagine the least offensive of the signs that deface American cities, where they seem trying to shout and shriek each other down, wherever one turns; they cover the fronts and sides and tops of the edifices; they deface the rocks of the meadows and the cliffs of the rivers; they stretch on long extents of fencing in the vacant suburban lands, and cover the roofs and sides of the barns. The darkness does not shield you from them, and by night the very sky is starred with the electric bulbs that spell out, on the roofs of the lofty city edifices, the frantic announcement of this or that business enterprise.

The strangest part of all this is, no one finds it offensive, or at least no one says that it is offensive. It is, indeed, a necessary phase of the economic warfare in which this people live, for the most as unconsciously as people lived in feudal cities, while the nobles fought out their private quarrels in the midst of them. No one dares relax his vigilance or his activity in the commercial strife, and in the absence of any public opinion, or any public sentiment concerning them, it seems as if the signs might eventually hide the city. That would not be so bad if something could then be done to hide the signs.

Nothing seems so characteristic of this city, after its architectural shapelessness, as the eating and drinking constantly going on in it. I do not mean, now, the eating and drinking in society alone, though from the fact that some sort of repast is made the occasion of nearly every social meeting, you might well suppose that society was altogether devoted to eating and drinking, and that this phase of the feasting might altogether occupy one. But I was thinking of the restaurants and hotels, of every kind and quality, and the innumerable saloons and bars. There may not be really more of them in New York, in proportion to the population than in other great plutocratic cities, but there are apparently more; for in this, as in all her other characteristics, New York is very open; her virtues and her vices, her luxury and her misery, are in plain sight, so that no one can fail of them; and I fancy that a famishing man must suffer peculiarly here from the spectacle of people everywhere visible at sumptuous tables.

Many of the finest hotels, if not most of them, have their diningrooms on the level of the street, and the windows, whether curtained or uncurtained, reveal the continual riot within. I confess that the effect upon some hungry passer is always so present to my imagination that I shun the places near the windows; but the Americans are so used to the perpetual encounter of famine and of surfeit in their civilization, that they do not seem to mind it; and one of them very logically made me observe when he conceived my reluctance, that I was not relieving anybody's want when I chose an uncomfortable place on the dark side of the room. It was, indeed, an instance of the unavailing self-denial so frequent here. Still, I prefer either the restaurants in the basements or on the second floor; and these are without number, too, though I do not think they are so many as the others; at least they do not make as much effect. But of every sort, as I say, there is an immense variety, because New York is so largely a city of strangers, whose pleasures or affairs call them here by whole populations. Every day the trains and boats fetch and carry hundreds of thousands of visitors, who must be somehow housed and fed, and who find shelter in the hotels, and food wherever they happen to be at the moment of lunch or dinner.

But the restaurants have to cater besides to the far vaster custom of the business men who live at such a distance from their shops and offices that they never take the midday meal with their families except on Sunday. So far they are like the workingmen, whom you see seated on piles of rubbish in the street, with their dinner-pails between their knees; but I need not tell you that the business men are not so simple or so sparing in the satisfaction of their hunger. I am not sure that they are always much more comfortable; and in fine weather I think I would rather sit out doors on a heap of brick or lumber than on a bracketed stool-top before a lunch-counter amidst a turmoil of crockery and cookery that I should in vain try to give you a sense of. These lunch-counters abound everywhere, and thousands throng them every day, snatching the meat and drink pushed across the counter to them by the waiters from the semi-circle within, and then making room for others. But of late, a new kind of lunch-room has come into fashion, which I wish you could see, both for the sake of the curious spectacle it affords, and the philosophy it involves. You would find yourself in a long room, if you came with me, where you would see rows of large chairs, each with one arm made wide enough to hold a cup and saucer, and a plate. At a convenient place in the room is a counter or table, with cups for tea and coffee set out on it, and plates of pie, sandwiches, and such viands as need not be cut with a knife, and may be gathered up in the fingers. Each comer goes up to the counter, and takes from it what he likes and carries it off to some chair, where he eats his lunch in peace, and then goes back to the counter and pays for it. His word is implicitly taken as to what he has had; he goes as he came, without question; and the host finds his account in the transaction; for even if he is now and then cheated, he saves the cost of a troop of waiters by letting his guests serve themselves, and he is able for the same reason to afford his provisions at half the price they must pay elsewhere. His experience is that he is almost never cheated, and the Altrurian theory of human nature, that if you will use men fairly and trust them courageously, they will not betray you, finds practical endorsement in it.

Most of the better class of clerks and small business men frequent the chop-houses, which affect the back rooms of old-fashioned dwellings, and the basement restaurants in the cellarways of business buildings, down town. Some of the lofty edifices which deform that quarter of the city have restaurants in them on a grand scale, as to prices and fare, and all the appointments of the table; these are for a still better sort of lunchers, or richer sort (you always say better when you mean richer, in America), and these often have lunch clubs, of difficult membership, and with rooms luxuriously appointed, where, if they choose, people can linger over their claret and cigars as quietly as if they were in their own houses. Sometimes a whole house is fitted up with all the comforts of a club, which is frequented by its members, or the greater part of them, only for luncheon. Others, of the kind which form effectively the home of their members, are resorted to at midday by all who do business within easy reach of them; though the breakfasting and dining goes on there, too, day in and day out, as constantly as at private houses. In fact, the chief use of the clubs is through their excellent kitchens.

There are foreign restaurants in all parts of the town,—French, German, Italian, Spanish,—where you can have your lunch served in courses at a fixed sum for the whole. The Hebrews, who are so large and so prosperous an element of the commercial body of New York, have restaurants of this sort, where they incur no peril of pork, or meat of any kind that is not *kosher*. Signs in Hebrew give them warrant of the fact that nothing unclean, or that has been rendered unlawful by hanging from a nail, is served within; and the Christian, if he sits down at a table, is warned that he can have neither milk nor butter with his meat, since this is against their ancient and most wholesome law.

Far round on the East side, and in all the poorer quarters of the town, there are eating-houses and cook-shops of lower and lower grade, which are resorted to by those workingmen who do not bring their dinners with them in pails, or who would rather take their drink and their food together. But these are seldom the older-fashioned laborers, of Irish or American descent; the frequenters of such places are Germans or Italians, or of the newer immigrations from eastern Europe, who find there some suggestions of their national dishes, and some touch of art in the cookery, no matter how common and vile the material. This, as you see it in the butcher-shops and the green-grocers of those parts, is often revolting and unwholesome enough—pieces of loathsome carnage, and bits of decaying vegetation. It is to be supposed that the poorer restaurants supply themselves from the superfluity of the better sort and of the hotels, but this is not always the case. In many cases, the hotels cast this into the great heap of offal, which the garbage carts of the city dump into the vessels used to carry it out to sea, so that not even the swine may eat of it, much less the thousands of hungering men and women and children, who never know what it is to have quite enough. But this is only one phase of the wilful waste that in manifold ways makes such woeful want in pluto-cratic conditions. Every comfortable family in this city throws away at every meal the sustenance of some other family; or, if not that then, so much at least as would keep it from starvation. The predatory instinct is very subtle, and people who live upon each other, instead of for each other, have shrewdly contrived profit within profit until it is hard to say whether many things you consume have any value in themselves at all. If they could be brought at once to the consumer they would cost infinitely little, almost nothing; but they reach him only after half a dozen sterile agencies have had their usury of them; and then they are most wonderfully, most wickedly wasted in the system of each household having its own black, noisy, unwholesome kitchen, with a cook in it chiefly skilled to spoil God's gifts.

From time to time, there is great talk in the newspapers of abolish-ing the middlemen, as the successive hucksters are called; but there is no way of doing this, short of abolishing the whole plutocratic system, for the middleman is the business man, and the business man is the cornerstone of this civilization; if, indeed, a civilization which seems poised in air by studying the trick of holding itself from the ground by the waistband, can be said to have any foundation whatever.

There is not so much hope of the middleman's going as there is of the individual kitchen's, which really seems threatened, at times, by the different new ways of living which Mrs. Makely, you remember, told me of. It is, in fact, a survival of the simpler time when the housewife prepared the food of her family herself; but that time is long past, with the well-to-do Americans, and what was once the focal center of the home, has no longer any just place in it, and only forms the great rent through which half the husband's earnings escape. Yet, if I tell them of our coöperative housekeeping, they make the answer which they seem to think serves all occasions, and say that such a system will do very well for Altruria, but that it is contrary to human nature, and it can never be made to work in America. They much prefer to go on wasting into the kitchen, and wasting out of it; the housewife either absolutely neglects her duty, or else she maddens herself with the care of it, and harries the poor drudge who slaves her life away in its heat and glare, and fails, with all her toil, of results which we have for a tithe of the cost and suffering.

But whenever I touch one of the points of economic contrast with ourselves, I feel as if I were giving it undue importance, for I think at once of a hundred others which seem to prove as conclusively that, as yet, the life of the Americans, in what most nearly concerns them, is not reasoned. They are where they are because some one else had arrived there before them, and they do most of the things that they do because the English do something like them. In a wholly different climate, a climate which touches both arctic and tropic extremes, they go on living as their ancestors lived in the equable seasons of the British Isles. They have not yet philosophized their food, or dress, or shelter, for their blazing summers, and swelter through them with such means of comfort as the ignorant usage of the mother-country provides.

In fact, the Americans have completed their reductio ad absurdum in pleasure as well as in business. Eating and drinking no longer suffice to bring people together, and the ladies say that if you want any one to come now, you must have something special to entertain your guests. You must have somebody sing, or recite, or play; I believe it has not yet come to a demand for hired dancing, as it presently will, if it does in London. Only very primitive people would now think of giving an afternoon tea without some special feature, though the at-homes still flourish, as a means of paying off the debts ladies owe one another for visits. Luncheons and dinners are given with a frequency that would imply the greatest financial prosperity, and the gayest social feeling as well as unlimited leisure, and unbounded hospitality. But these must always have some raison d'étre, such as we do not dream of offering, who in our simplicity think it reason enough to ask our friends to join us at meat if we wish for their company. Here, apparently, no one wishes for your company personally, the individual is as completely lost in the social as he is in the economic scheme. You are invited as a factor in the problem which your hostess wishes to work out, and you are invited many days in advance, and sometimes several weeks; for every one is supposed to be in great request, and it is thought to be a sort of slight to bid a guest for any entertainment under a week, so that people excuse themselves for doing it.

Notes to the Text

3.13   J. L. F.: George Arms suggests that these initials stand for J. L. Ford. "Howells's Unpublished Prefaces," *NEQ*, XVII (1944), 590, note 22.

4.26   an apartment hotel: at this time Howells was living at the Hotel Regent, New York City. Arms, "Howells's Unpublished Prefaces," p. 590, note 25.

18.9–10   From *Matthew*, XX, 27: "And whosoever will be chief among you, let him be your servant."

28.13–14   From Coleridge's *The Rime of the Ancient Mariner*, ll. 7–8: "The guests are met, the feast is set . . ."

32.7   The tariff has killed our shipbuilding: an allusion to the Tariff Act of 1890.

34.3–4   You have hitched your wagon to a star: from Emerson's essay, "Civilization," *Society and Solitude* (Boston, 1870).

49.30   From *Genesis*, III, 19. The King James Version reads, "In the sweat of thy face . . ."

50.26   From Samuel Johnson, "The Vanity of Human Wishes," l. 160.

51.10–20   Of course, we all recognize . . . . scientific occupation: Howells expanded this thought in "The Man of Letters as a Man of Business," *Scribner's*, XIV (1893), 429–445.

453

63.32–33   It is something that Matthew Arnold urged with great effect in his paper on that crank of a Tolstoi: "Count Leo Tolstoi," *Fortnightly Review*, n.s. XLII (1887), 783–799; reprinted in *Essays in Criticism, Second Series* (London, 1888).

65.17–18   a Remnant, as Matthew Arnold calls them: "Spinoza and the Bible," *Lectures and Essays in Criticism* in *Complete Prose Works of Matthew Arnold*, edited by R. H. Super (Ann Arbor, Michigan, 1962), III, 164.

78.12   a good, old-fashioned love-story: see *Criticism and Fiction*, Section XVIII, for Howells' views on "a good, old-fashioned love-story."

83.11   this new party in the west: the Populist Party.

88.2–3   From *Matthew*, XXVI, 11: "For ye have the poor always with you."

88.14   From I *Corinthians*, XIII, 13.

111.25–29   A man sells his vote . . . . Dr. Johnson told them he didn't see the necessity: we cannot find this remark in the works of Dr. Johnson, but it is well known from Voltaire, "Discours preliminaire," *Alzire, ou les Américains* (1736).

112.3–4   you have cakes and ale, and at times the ginger is hot in the mouth: from *Twelfth Night*, II, iii, 113–116.

116.25ff.   the failure of a business man: Howells here tells the story of *The Rise of Silas Lapham*.

119.15–16   so little ambition for distinction: Arnold finds little "distinction" in the United States; see "Civilization in the United States," *Nineteenth Century*, XXIII (1888), 481–496.

121.21   the public land is gone: the frontier was closed in 1890.

122.12ff.   if the case is so bad with the business men who have made the great fortunes: cf. *The Quality of Mercy* for the development of this idea.

126.23   a Russian revolutionist: the Russian novelist, Sergius Mikhailovich Kravchinski (1852–1895); see *Life in Letters of William Dean Howells*, ed. Mildred Howells (Garden City, N.Y., 1928), II, 12.

126.34–35   'make war with the water of roses': Howells here humorously paraphrases a remark made by the French writer Sebastien Chamfort to Jean François Marmontel during the French Revolution: "Do you think then that revolutions are made with the water of roses?"

127.7   the Battle of Dorking: a fictitious invasion of England; see General G. T. Chesney, "The Battle of Dorking: Reminiscences of a Volunteer," *Blackwood's Edinburgh Magazine*, CIX (1871), 539–572.

128.31ff.   *That* was settled once for all, in Chicago: the Haymarket Riot occurred on 4 May 1886. Several men were killed by a bomb thrown by an unknown hand, and strong public feeling was aroused. In an effort to secure "Clemency for the Anarchists" Howells wrote a letter to the New York *Tribune*, 6 November 1887, p. 5. By "International Groups" Howells is apparently referring to such organizations as the International Working Men's Association (1864), the International Brotherhood of Maintenance of Way Employees (1887), and other labor organizations with the word "International" in their titles.

130.4   *Parole femmine, fatti maschi:* women's words, men's deeds.

130.7   a little tract of William Morris's: *News from Nowhere* (London, 1891).

147.23   'rose like an exhalation': from Milton's *Paradise Lost*, I, 711.

157.20   He has got *that* out of William Morris: William Morris' *News from Nowhere*; see note to 130.7.

164.2   City of the Sun: *City of the Sun*, by Tommaso Campanella (1568–1639). It was translated by Thomas W. Halliday and published by Henry Morley in *Ideal Commonwealths* (New York, 1885).

184.25   The great event at Homestead: a strike against the owners of the Carnegie Steel Company at Homestead, Pennsylvania, occurred in July 1892.

185.7   something like a civic convulsion: during July and August of 1892, many strikes took place all over the country. A notable one was against Coeur d'Alene by Idaho miners; New York *Tribune*, 16 July 1892, p. 6. Another took place in Tennessee; *Public Opinion*, 27 August 1892, p. 489.

185.8–9   a strike of railroad employés at Buffalo: at Buffalo the switchmen went on strike; New York *Tribune*, 14 August–26 August 1892.

187.30   the cyclone: Howells is referring to the Depression of 1893.

187.33–34ff.   the export of gold: the panic of 1893 was brought on in part by the export of gold to foreign countries. The Sherman Act of 1890 revived the coinage of silver dollars.

188.2   touching the tariff: the tariff had long been the subject of controversy, and, as Howells was writing this passage, plans were going forward for a revision in 1894.

188.24–25   a world of chance: cf. Howells' novel, *The World of Chance*.

191.25   quiet opposition: the Populist Party, representing "the Altrurian principles," won twenty-two votes in the Electoral College in 1892. See note to 83.11.

200.17   one mind large enough: Daniel Hudson Burnham (1846–1912), whom Howells visited for five days during the Exposition.

200.21–22   the national part in the work was chiefly obstructive, and finally null: the Fair was unable to meet its obligations, and had to be financed by Congress.

201.28–29ff.   the beautiful Agricultural building: William Rutherford Mead, Howells' brother-in-law, was of the firm of McKim, Mead, and White, which designed the Agricultural Building. Larkin Mead, another brother-in-law, designed the pediment, the Triumph of Ceres.

206.14   the banker: Mr. Bullion in "A Traveller from Altruria."

208.5   the greatest good to the greatest number: the original phrase is attributed to Francis Hutcheson (1694–1746): "the greatest happiness for the greatest numbers."

210.14–15   From Poe's *To Helen*, ll. 9–10:
    "To the glory that was Greece,
    And the grandeur that was Rome."

223.12–13   this hotel where I am now lodged: Howells was staying at the Plaza Hotel in New York when he was writing the "Letters."

225.23   "but as pictures": *Macbeth*, II, ii, 54.

226.1 the right man: Frederick Law Olmsted, the landscape architect of the Exposition, laid the plans for all these parks.

226.23 the bust of a poet: the bust of Thomas Moore (1779–1852) stands at the southeast corner of Central Park, near the Plaza Hotel.

226.33–34ff. one thoroughly good piece of sculpture: this bronze statue by J. Q. A. Ward still stands in Central Park.

232.16 the Egyptian obelisk: the Egyptian obelisk was erected in Central Park in 1881.

234.26–27 Lord Orville and Sir Clement Willoughby are two of the characters in Fanny Burney's novel *Evelina* (1778).

257.3–4 the labor due to all from all: Karl Marx derived this slogan from J. J. Louis Blanc (1811–1882).

272.28–29 Age on a Gold Basis: Howells jokingly refers to the controversy over gold support for United States currency.

304.30ff. And they never gossip . . .: W. S. Gilbert and A. S. Sullivan, *Pinafore*, I.

325.7 more than kin, and less than kind: *Hamlet*, I, ii, 65.

325.21ff. *The Challenge* is a poem of eleven four-line stanzas. Howells has quoted the last twenty-four lines.

330.36ff. a description of a surgical operation: Howells had seen Thomas Eakins' painting, "Dr. Agnew's Clinic," which so shocked the American public at the Philadelphia Centennial, 1876, and he perhaps transferred to literature the current discussion of realism in art.

337.12 and Paul says ——: I *Corinthians*, XIII.

339.5 From *The Merchant of Venice*, IV, i, 197: "It blesseth him that gives, and him that takes."

356.25–26ff. the solemn words of the Bible: *Ruth*, I, 16.

369.23–24 as Paul said the men of Athens were: *Acts*, XVII, 22.

370.14 "Princess": *The Princess* by Tennyson.

370.19 hung up for monuments: *Richard III*, I, i, 6.

370.30–31 my Paris dress and my picture-hat: see the article by Mrs. B. O. Flower, "Eight Months' Experience in the Syrian Costume," *Arena*, IX (1894), 323–326.

372.30 "liquefaction of the clothes": Robert Herrick, "Upon Julia's Clothes," l. 3.

373.4 that Greek play: the play was *Agamemnon*; see *Life in Letters*, II, 225.

381.14ff. 'For even when we were with you . . .': II *Thessalonians*, III, 10. The word "one" is here inserted. At 420.9–10 the verse is correctly quoted.

381.32 John Dryden, *Almanzor and Almahide; or, The Conquest of Granada*, Part First, I, i.

388.18 the Japanese company of Sada Yacco: an illustrated account of this troupe is given in *Harper's Bazar*, XXXIII (1889), 249, 251–252.

402.22 working-phalanx: the idea of the social phalanx was originated by François Marie Charles Fourier (1772–1837).

404.29 the White City: here Howells refers to the account he had given of the Columbian Exposition in the first two "Letters of an Altrurian Traveller."

404.36 Commonwealth Avenue in Boston: Howells lived at 184 Commonwealth Avenue from 1889 to 1891.

416.17 Toynbee Hall: Toynbee Hall, situated in the White-chapel section of London, was founded in 1884 by S. A. Barnett. Other settlement houses were later established in Whitechapel.

420.9–10 "For even when we were with you . . .": see Note to 381.14ff.

426.22 Mr. Ruskin's direction: as a lecturer at Oxford in the early 1880's, John Ruskin (1819–1900) had encouraged the students to work at road building. See *Fors Clavigera* (1871–1884), letters written to the working men of England.

428.14–15 a party of which the political and social ideal was almost identical with that of the Altrurians: Étienne Cabet (1788–1856) taught Christian socialistic ideas and wrote a utopian book, *Voyage et aventures de Lord Villiam Carisdall en Icarie* (1840).

C. K.

R. K.

TEXTUAL APPARATUS

Textual Commentary

Between November 1892 and September 1894 Howells published in the *Cosmopolitan* two romances, different in their points of view but connected in narrative line. The first was "A Traveller from Altruria," deposited for book copyright by Harper on 29 May 1894 (BAL 9685), eight months after its completion in the serial. There were at least two printings of the book in 1894, the first of which comprised 2,500 copies; another impression was made in 1895 as part of the Harper's Franklin Square Library (2,000 copies),[1] another in 1898, and another in 1900. A British edition of the book, deposited in the British Museum on 26 May 1894, was published by David Douglas in Edinburgh. A new American edition was published on 8 October 1908 (G&A 08–09n) and was designed to match *Through the Eye of the Needle* (BAL 9779), which Harper had published in April 1907.[2] This latter book was divided into two narrative parts; Howells wrote the second part in January and February 1907, but for the first he drew upon the last six of the eleven "Letters of an Altrurian

---

1. For these figures see the Harper "Memorandum Book" for 1892–1894, p. 56. The Howells Edition is indebted to Harper and Row, Publishers, for permission to cite this material, which is surveyed in Edwin and Virginia Price Barber, "A Description of Old Harper and Brothers Publishing Records Recently Come to Light," *Bulletin of Bibliography*, XXV (1967), 1–6, 29–34, 39–40.

2. Howells wrote to his brother Joseph A. Howells on 24 February 1907 that *The Eye of the Needle*, which he had set in type for him "twelve years ago," was finally being published (*Life in Letters of William Dean Howells*, ed. Mildred Howells [Garden City, N.Y., 1928], II, 235). The difference in title, which reflects the new ending Howells gave his story in 1907, and the difference in type design between Howells' novels in 1894 and the 1907 volume suggest that the plates Joseph Howells made were not the ones used in 1907. It is likely, however, that a proof taken from these plates was used by Harper in setting the 1907 volume. At 314.1 the *Cosmopolitan* reads "last year," possibly a reference to the flower show described in *Harper's Weekly* (18 November 1893, p. 1099). This reading was altered in the book to "year before last," which suggests that Howells revised the *Cosmopolitan* text in 1895 when he still intended to republish it immediately. The appearance of this variant in the 1907 book is inexplicable except on the assumption that the first part of *Through the Eye of the Needle* was set from a proof taken from the plates Joseph Howells made in 1895.

Traveller," the second of the two original *Cosmopolitan* romances. *Through the Eye of the Needle* was re-impressed in 1916. No manuscripts are known to exist for either original romance or for the 1907 continuation of the second.

If the genealogy of these texts is slightly complicated, the history of their transmission is not. Howells carefully revised "A Traveller from Altruria" for the 1894 Harper book, but there is no evidence that he paid any attention to its accidentals, then or later. Indeed, the fact that a second impression in 1894 was made from plates which had been corrected or altered in more than eighty percent of their pages suggests that initially neither Howells nor Harper paid much attention even to proofreading this book.[3] The 1894 British edition, issued simultaneously with the American edition, was set from a proof of the unaltered plates (designated as A1 in the apparatus)—as is amusingly evident in its readings at 117.22—whereas the altered plates (A2) provided copy for the 1908 Harper edition. There is nothing in the substantive or accidental variants of either the British or the 1908 Harper edition to suggest that they have any authority. The *Cosmopolitan*, therefore, is copy-text.

The facts for the first part of *Through the Eye of the Needle* are even simpler. Again, Howells revised his serial text, but there is nothing about the inordinately large number of variants in accidentals between serial and book to indicate that those of the book are authorial. It is of course possible that the changes in accidentals reflect a change in Howells' idiom between 1894 and 1907, but there is no evidence that they do. Accordingly, the *Cosmopolitan* is copy-text for the first part of *Through the Eye of the Needle*; for the "Introduction" and the second part of this book, published for the first and only time in 1907, the book is of course copy-text. For the "Bibliographical" introduction written for the projected but never-published Library Edition of *A Traveler from Altruria* and *Through the Eye of the Needle*, the page proofs, which are the only surviving text, are copy-text.[4]

---

3. For details on these two printings, and an argument that the accidentals of the second are not authorial, see Scott Bennett, "A Concealed Printing in W. D. Howells," *PBSA*, LXI (1967), 56–60. A copy of *A Traveler from Altruria* in the New York Public Library (call number NBO) contains sheets from both printings; gatherings 15 and 18 in this copy were printed from the altered plates, whereas the other gatherings were printed from the unaltered plates.

4. See George Arms, "Howells's Unpublished Prefaces," *NEQ*, XVII (1944), 580–591.

Almost everything in the present volume, then, appeared either in only one printed form during Howells' lifetime or in both periodical and book form, with only the substantives of the latter reflecting authorial revision. The *Altrurian Romances* thus offer a textual problem of classic simplicity: with a few exceptions duly recorded in the Emendations and Rejected Substantives lists, the accidental readings of the periodical copy-texts have been combined with the authorial substantive revisions of the first editions to produce eclectic texts which approximate as closely as one can infer them the texts which Howells would have most approved.[5]

There is one special circumstance which bears on, but does not finally alter, this description of the editorial problem. The first five of the "Letters of an Altrurian Traveller" were never reprinted, but three of them were extensively rewritten for "Glimpses of Central Park" and "New York Streets" in *Impressions and Experiences* (BAL 9706). Since the original "Letters" are in mode and tone (and sometimes in the order of the material) so radically different from the essays of *Impressions and Experiences*, these later totally rewritten essays are irrelevant to the determination of the text of the original *Cosmopolitan* romance.

The genealogy of the *Altrurian Romances* raises one special editorial problem: the texts of different generations have distinct and sometimes contradictory authority, with the result that a few apparent inconsistencies of form have to be allowed in a volume like the present one, which combines what Howells wrote in the period 1892–1894 with what he wrote in 1907. For instance, Tolstoy's name is spelled in the present text in both the -*i* and -*y* forms. *Tolstoi* was Howells' spelling in 1892–1894 and was the spelling used by the *Cosmopolitan*; by 1907, however, Howells had changed to the *Tolstoy* spelling, a change which is reflected both in his own letters and in the second part of *Through the Eye of the Needle*. Likewise, *New-Yorker* has been accepted in the "Introduction" to *Through the Eye of the Needle*, though the words, frequently used in the earlier *Cosmopolitan* text, are not

---

5. This volume therefore accords with both the intention and the practices outlined in the Center for Editions of American Authors, *Statement of Editorial Principles: A Working Manual for Editing Nineteenth Century American Texts*, July 1967. Fredson Bowers' "The Centenary Texts: Editorial Principles," printed in volumes of the Centenary Edition of Nathaniel Hawthorne, concisely spells out these principles and procedures and illustrates their application.

hyphenated there. In both cases a conservative rationale of emendation has prevailed, as it did generally. There were a few cases, however, where substantive emendation had to be made on Howells Edition authority alone; all but one occur in those parts of "Letters of an Altrurian Traveller" and *Through the Eye of the Needle* for which only one text, the copy-text, exists. In three instances (279.2, 404.35, 411.1) emendation was necessary for obvious grammatical reasons; in two instances (262.24 and 396.11) obviously needed prepositions have been supplied. In three other cases, where the copy-text is manifestly incoherent (196.14, 414.32, and 435.13), emendation seemed desirable even though no claim of unique authenticity can be made for the Howells Edition readings.

No effort has been made to preserve in the present text the merely visual appurtenances of the copy-texts; only obviously needed punctuation has been supplied silently.[6]

S. B.

---

6. The following books, including at least first and last impressions, were collated in the preparation of the present text: copies of the *Cosmopolitan* in the libraries of Indiana University (AP2.C8), the University of Illinois (051.CO), and the University of Texas; copies of *A Traveler from Altruria* (BAL 9685), A1, in the Howells Edition Center (HE9685.1, copies 1, 2, and 3), in the Ohio State University Library (EL140.H859Tr, copies 1 and 2), in the Cincinnati Public Library (copy 4), and in the New York Public Library (NBO); of *A Traveler from Altruria* (BAL 9685), A2, in the Lilly Library (PS2025.T7 and PS2025.T7 1895), in the Bryn Mawr College Library (813.H83tr), in the Cincinnati Public Library (copy 2), and in the McGill University Library (YF.H833tr); copies of the 1894 British edition of *A Traveler from Altruria* in William M. Gibson's collection and in the British Museum (012705. ee.30); copies of the 1908 edition of *A Traveler from Altruria* (G&A 08–09n) in the Howells Edition Center (HE G&A 08–09n.1), in the collection of Donald Pizer, in the Carleton College Library (819.H85Rtr), and in the Middlebury College Library (150s.9Ag.41.F); copies of *Through the Eye of the Needle* (BAL 9779) in the Lilly Library (PS2025.T6), in the Howells Edition Center (HE9779.1, copies 1, 2, and 3, and HE9779.2.1), in the Indiana University Library (PS2025.T5), in the Harvard College Library (AL1783.385A), and in the University of Illinois Library (813. H83thr).

Textual Notes

47.2   Both A1 and A2, though they capitalize the word, spell it incorrectly as "Christain."

130.2   Here and at 158.8–9, S1 is emended to "workingmen" and "workingman," the forms otherwise used consistently throughout the copy-text.

139.8   Here and at 140.16 the copy-text form "talk" has been emended to the capitalized form used in all other instances of the word in its restricted meaning.

145.28–29   Here and at 151.15 and 154.24 the copy-text form "evolution" is capitalized to accord with all the succeeding instances of the word.

196.14 The "that" of the copy-text (which is here the only text) is omitted as the simplest way to restore grammatical order to this sentence. The copy-text reading may be explained by the supposition that Howells first wrote "because they say that" and then revised the phrase to the reading of the present text, failing to strike out the superfluous "that."

262.24 Here and at 396.11 obviously needed prepositions are supplied; the copy-text is the only text in both cases.

290.14 The copy-text has been emended here to accord with its otherwise consistent use of the "oh" form.

396.11 See 262.24 above.

396.26   The copy-text (which is here the only text) is emended to "elders" to parallel the "eldresses" of the next line and to accord with the implication in 397.21 that there was more than one elder.

414.32   The main verb of this sentence, obviously missing in the copy-text (which is here the only text), has been supplied by the editors.

435.13   The verb of this phrase, obviously missing in the copy-text (which is here the only text), has been supplied by the editors. The sentence, thus emended, remains problematic however. Is M. Anatole the author of the villanelles, rondeaux, and triolets? The sentence as it stands suggests this, though grammatically it makes him author of neither the "accompanying versions of the French" nor of the Altrurian translations. If M. Anatole is not the author of these songs, one must assume either that he printed each of them in three languages, which seems unlikely, or that the sentence needs to be revised so that the French versions are made to accompany not the poems M. Anatole printed but the Altrurian translations. To correct an obvious grammatical error with an obvious word seems proper here, but to try to untangle the imperfectly realized intentions of this sentence seems to the editors too speculative to be consistent with a conservative policy of emendation.

Emendations

The following list records all substantive and accidental changes introduced into the copy-text for each part, except for required but missing punctuation, which has been supplied silently. The reading of the present edition appears to the left of the bracket; the authority for that reading, followed by a semicolon, the copy-text reading, and the copy-text symbol appear to the right of the bracket. The curved dash ∼ represents the same word that appears before the bracket and is used in recording punctuation variants. The abbreviation HE indicates emendation made on the authority of the Howells Edition. Occasionally changes in accidentals have been made on Howells Edition authority, with the first book edition which records them cited as their source, though these editions of course have no general authority for accidentals; that is, an edition is cited because it is the first to incorporate a change and not because the change is thought to have resulted from Howells' intervention. An asterisk indicates that the reading is discussed in the Textual Notes. *Om.* means that the reading to the left of the bracket does not appear in the text cited to the right of the semicolon.

The following texts are referred to:

S1   "A Traveller from Altruria," *Cosmopolitan*, XIV–XV (November 1892–October 1893)

S2   "Letters of an Altrurian Traveller," *Cosmopolitan*, XVI–XVII (November 1893–September 1894)

A1   *A Traveler from Altruria*, Harper and Brothers, 1894, first impression

A2   *A Traveler from Altruria*, Harper and Brothers, 1894, second impression

B   *A Traveller from Altruria*, David Douglas, 1894

C   *Through the Eye of the Needle*, Harper and Brothers, 1907

D   *A Traveler from Altruria*, Harper and Brothers, 1908

A Traveller from Altruria

7.1	I] A1; *om.* S1
8.23	saying] A1; saying that S1
9.36	noting] A1; noticing S1
10.32	with] A1; with new S1
11.11	and] A1; *om.* S1
11.12	simply] A1; simply that S1
11.12	and] A1; *om.* S1
11.14	were] A1; are S1
12.28	to send] A1; of sending S1
13.12	our esteem for labor] A1; the esteem in which labor was held S1
13.33	traditions] A1; tradition S1
14.13	I'm] A1; I am S1
14.30	workings] A1; working S1
17.8	now is] A1; is now S1
17.25	work] A1; labor S1
19.28–31	confessed. "I imagine . . . kings' mistresses. Not] A1; confessed. "Not S1
20.10	music] A1; vespers S1
20.12	drip] A1; airy drip S1
20.34	summer-boarders] A1; summer-board S1
21.23	the] A1; a S1
21.35	him." Before] A1; him." ¶ "And do you call that a free country where such an outrage upon private rights as that can be perpetrated?" ¶ "Tell me," said the Altrurian, "do you consider it a free country where such an outrage upon public feelings as this can be perpetrated?" Before S1
21.36	think of anything to say to this] A1; answer S1
22.10–12	paternalism." ¶ It] A1; paternalism. Is that the way you manage in Altruria? To be sure, it's better than confiscation, which I supposed was your method when you spoke of the community taking his property." ¶ "Ah, that would be very unjust. It is a good many centuries since the landscape rights passed entirely into the keeping of the commonwealth in the Altrurian Synthesis, but one of the last cases of state purchase was rather remarkable, and it is remembered perhaps be-

cause it was one of the last. The expropriated owner was a man of very old family and extremely conservative. He was rather cherished among us as a bit of archaic poetry, a relic of former times, a kind of romantic ruin. The savage sense of greed persisted very strongly in him; he thought he had a right to do what he pleased with his own, to do wrong with his own if he pleased; and one night he broke the dam of a beautiful lake on his estate, and destroyed the lovely cataract that the waters flowed into below, and left a bed of ugly ooze and barren sand where the waves had danced and the lilies swayed. He contended that the lake was his and that it covered an area of valuable farmland, which he was entitled to the use of. His act was regarded as a public outrage; nothing like it had happened for generations; and the feeling was very strong against him, but of course he was left to the operation of law. The state took his property, and paid him for it at his own valuation; there was some talk of trying him for *lese communitatis,* but it was finally decided merely to have him instructed in the first simple principles of political economy, such as that regard for others is the primal law of human nature, and that a public wrong can never be a private right. I am not sure, but I think his was the very last case of the kind that we had to deal with." ¶ It S1

22.14 prospect; I said] A1; prospect; and the fact is that what he had said about political economy appeared to me so grotesque that I longed to see him in the grip of an eminent political economist of our own, who was staying in the hotel; I thought he could teach my friend a thing or two about political economy. But I was impatient to give him a foretaste of what he would probably get a surfeit of before our economist was through with him, and I said S1

22.16–18 "You know... personal virtue."] A1; "You Altrurians, then, have actually tried that hazardous experiment of legislating personal virtue?" ¶ He halted me, and even in that vague light, which was rather an obscurity, I

could see the astonishment in his eyes. "Good heavens!"
he said, "haven't you?" ¶ I could not help laughing.
"Well, not yet." S1

22.22	there] A1; for once S1
22.22	your expectation] A1; an expectation of yours S1
23.26	heart.] A1; heart. I can't tell you how proud and glad I am to find it so. It is like getting home again, after the lapse of centuries, to realize this fact. S1
23.31	personally.] A1; personally. I relented a little toward my guest, but all the same I meant to deliver him over to our political economist as soon as we reached the hotel. S1
23.32	the hotel] A1; it S1
24.7	made] A1; made haste S1
25.25	nest] A1; congeries S1
26.20	it] A1; *om.* S1
26.34	they are not] A1; are not they S1
27.27	I suppose] A1; Well, I suppose that S1
28.21	lives] A1; days S1
28.23	days] A1; hours S1
29.33	now,] A1; ∼ S1
31.2	being] A1; *om.* S1
31.11–12	of political economy in one of our colleges] A1; in one of our colleges, the political economist whom I had in view for the enlightenment of my friend S1
31.27	that] A1; *om.* S1
33.5	had] A1; *om.* S1
33.10	will] A1; *om.* S1
33.19	polite] A1; polite or in any wise possible S1
35.28	labor-unions] A1; unions S1
41.4	don't] A1; do not S1
43.1	in] A1; *om.* S1
43.33	is] A1; *om.* S1
44.6	plenitude] A1; sovereign plenitude S1
45.12–13	it is] A1; is it S1
45.19	this] A1; this tremendous S1
45.26	said] A1; said that S1
45.35	do] A1; did S1
45.35–36	best." ¶ We] A1; ∼." ∼ S1

46.3	question, "And] A1; ~ — ¶ " ~ S1
46.19	until] A1; till S1
*47.2	Christian] B; christian S1
48.30	industrial] A1; economical S1
48.35	scruples] A1; scruple S1
49.2	him. The] A2; him—the S1
49.17	"There's] A1; ' ~ S1
52.12	calling] A1; life S1
52.32	passed A1; got S1
52.35–53.2	But wouldn't . . . more for? Doesn't . . . subject?] A1; But doesn't the money consideration influence his choice of subject? Wouldn't he rather do something he would get less for, if he could afford it, than the thing he knows he will get more for? S1
54.6	condition] A1; conditions S1
56.1	a] A1; *om.* S1
56.4	where] A1; *om.* S1
57.8	maybe] A1; may-be S1
57.15	finds] A1; finds it S1
57.36	but] A1; and S1
59.19	are] A1; seem S1
61.15	forgot that] A1; forgot S1
61.16	sempstress] A2; semptress S1
63.4	into] A1; into a S1
63.20	see the] A1; see that S1
63.27	any] A1; any use S1
63.29	time,] A1; ~ S1
63.34	need] A1; needed S1
64.23	the] A1; *om.* S1
64.35	can't] A1; cannot S1
64.36	better] A1; better have S1
65.9	you're] A1; you are S1
66.15	theatre] A1; theatres S1
67.24	of the] A1; of a S1
68.18	cheap] A1; the cheap S1
69.2	any] A1; *om.* S1
73.8	a Saratoga] A1; it S1
73.12–13	It needed] A1; I found that it required S1
73.33	thing] A1; matter S1

74.35	should] A1; would S1
75.1	would] A1; could S1
79.21	of] A1; in S1
79.30–31	sometimes] A1; sometime S1
80.16	fellow,] A1; fellow quietly and S1
82.25	new] A1; *om.* S1
82.32	one] A1; *om.* S1
82.34	took] A1; lifted S1
83.17	these] A1; those S1
84.11	got] A1; got to S1
84.16	up short] A1; short up S1
84.20	least] A1; least there were S1
85.5	little] A1; small S1
85.11	boy. I followed] A1; boy, and following S1
85.12	and] A1; I S1
85.22	threshold] B; threshhold S1
85.23	a] A1; its S1
85.25	to us] A1; *om.* S1
87.2	would] A1; could S1
87.27	tell us just] A1; just tell us S1
87.33	incivism?"] A1; incivism?" asked Mrs. Makely. S1
88.17	lasted] A1; held S1
88.26	in the] A1; in S1
89.15	returned.] A1; ~, S1
89.22	operations] A1; operators S1
89.35	and as] A1; and as uncompromisingly S1
90.14	it] A1; it in S1
91.14	this] A1; the S1
91.33	politely, but vaguely] A1; vaguely, but politely S1
94.16–17	like as] A1; like S1
95.14	inside] A1; inside of S1
96.5	close] A1; end S1
96.29	say] A1; say that S1
97.12	we] A1; the natives S1
100.28	man] A1; man that S1
102.20	of] A1; of the S1
103.24	foreclose] A1; foreclose it S1
109.17	thought so, too] A1; agreed with her S1
109.17	glad] A1; glad that S1

109.28	sha'n't] A1; sha'nt S1
113.5	mill] A1; mills S1
113.22	of] A1; of the S1
113.25	paternalism] A1; parentalism S1
113.25	won't] A2; wont S1
114.4	clergy] A1; clergyman S1
114.5	A very] A1; An S1
114.14	some] A1; some some S1
114.20	into] A1; in a S1
115.10	isn't . . . living, even] A1; isn't even . . . living S1
115.15	not] A1; not to have S1
115.23	incompatibility] A1; incompatability S1
115.33–34	That education] A1; It S1
116.2	gentleman] A1; gentlemen S1
116.13	anything] A1; om. S1
117.3	pity] A1; be pitying S1
117.20	We used to] A1; The time was when we S1
119.28	say that . . . our] A1; say . . . that our S1
120.20	that] A1; om. S1
120.25	that] A1; om. S1
121.2–3	but this may be merely] A1; but I doubt it. If it is so, it is because we are merely in S1
121.5	Perhaps] A1; No doubt S1
121.15	all] A1; om. S1
121.15	changes] A1; changes which have taken place S1
123.25	and] A1; and when he began again he S1
125.28	know] A1; see S1
126.4–5	The banker . . . and the minister] A1; The minister S1
126.16	stopped; . . . there] A1; stopped, and the banker pursued: ¶ "Do you mean that there S1
126.19	forbore] A1; forebore S1
126.25	or sympathy] A1; om. S1
127.14–15	manufacturer,] A1; manufacturer, not anxiously, but S1
127.25	so] A1; so that S1
127.26	short-sighted] A1; short-sighted and illogical S1
127.34	about] A1; about it S1
128.11	quite so] A1; quite as S1
128.11	leaders] A1; leaders should S1

128.14	so] A1; as S1
128.15	be] A1; be always S1
128.23	it] A1; *om.* S1
128.33	up.] A1; up. Oh, no! Their only hope for mischief is to remain in the militia and weaken it by their disaffection in the event of a fight. But they have always managed so badly that I should not be surprised if they threw away this advantage too. S1
129.21	though] A1; although S1
129.27	generally] A1; *om.* S1
129.27	He] A1; He generally S1
129.32	so just that it] A1; that S1
*130.2	workingmen] A1; working men S1
130.13	protested] A1; protested, from a *chauvanism* deeper even than my awe of a financier S1
131.7	many] A1; several S1
131.19	had] A1; *om.* S1
131.21	candor] A1; frankness S1
131.21	too] A1; to S1
133.7	there is] A1; there's S1
133.8	use] A1; one S1
133.12	so] A1; therefore S1
133.16–17	Oh! How does he come in there?" ¶ "Why, get] A1; Oh!" ¶ "Yes. Get S1
134.10	greatest] A1; utmost S1
134.32	afterwards] A1; *om.* S1
135.2	lord,] A1; ~ S1
135.17	only] A1; only resolve to S1
135.18	hope] A1; hope that S1
135.18	I had] A1; At first I S1
135.19	should] A1; should come and S1
135.30	won't] A1; wont S1
136.1	admission] A1; admission to the noblest form of entertainment that they have known S1
136.4	one] A1; a S1
136.11	together] A1; together; but to let him do all the talking S1
136.26	heard] A1; heard something S1
136.27	an] A1; an outward S1

136.32	want] A1; what we want is S1
136.33	outside] A1; outside—it's never had but one— S1
137.1	that] A1; *om.* S1
137.9	educational] A1; devotional S1
137.9	wall] A1; *om.* S1
137.10	and] A1; and the S1
138.28	in] A1; to S1
138.31	me, though] A1; ~ ~, S1
*139.8	Talk] B; talk S1
139.10	evening; she put] A1; evening; and she got S1
139.14	especially] A1; especially in cases S1
139.19	know] A1; know that S1
140.11	upon] A1; on S1
140.16	Talk] A1; talk S1
140.30	as] A1; so S1
140.33	won't] A1; wont S1
141.1	won't] A1; wont S1
142.13	house;] A1; house; and S1
142.19	They] A1; She S1
142.22	time] A1; séance S1
143.1	dinner] A1; lunch S1
143.3	afternoon] A1; after-dinner S1
143.15	white] A1; *om.* S1
143.17	expected] A1; had expected S1
143.24	for now] A1; for S1
143.27	until] A1; till S1
144.11	are always] A1; have always been S1
145.13	and there] A1; and here and there the faded blue of an ancient cotton-blouse on a farmer's back had the distinction and poetry of a bit from Millet. There S1
145.20	yellow] A1; brown S1
145.21	the] A1; their S1
145.24	rose] A1; arose S1
*145.28–29	Evolution] A1; evolution S1
145.30	make] A1; making S1
147.13	annals,] A1; ~ S1
147.18	warp] A1; woof S1
147.19	woof] A1; warp S1
150.2	these] A1; these more enlightened S1

150.30	co'perations, nor] A1; co'perations, and S1
150.35	on] A1; of S1
153.36	called] A1; called out S1
155.12	all] A1; all that S1
155.28	from] A1; in one of S1
156.13	sham shoes] A1; shams S1
156.21	dishonest] A1; *om.* S1
157.5	rigor] A1; vigor S1
159.6	form] A1; forms S1
159.13	them] A1; them, each S1
159.21	parasites] A1; parasites and necessary concomitants, S1
159.35	laugh . . . weep] A1; weep . . . laugh S1
160.9	houses] A1; houses built one upon the bases of another S1
160.35	and] A1; *om.* S1
161.11	it] A1; it on cruciform lines, S1
161.13	literary man] A1; littérateur S1
162.26	a] A2; *om.* S1
162.27	money in your sense] A1; sort of money S1
162.34	like yours] A1; in your sense S1
164.1	rehash] A1; réchauffé S1
164.16	reckonings] A1; reckoning S1
165.4	not a] A1; not S1
165.19	a loaf] A1; *om.* S1
165.28	wished] A1; wish S1
165.31	human] A1; the human S1
166.3	workmen's] D; workman's S1
166.4–7	servants; and . . . individuality] A1; servants S1
166.24	whisper] A1; say S1
167.23	perhaps] A1; ~, S1
167.23	has] A1; has any longer S1
167.23	interest] A1; interest of his own S1
168.3	these] A1; those S1
168.21	our] A1; our own S1
168.23	dominion of the egoistic empire] A1; imperium in the egoistic imperio, S1
168.33	on,] A1; on, at every possible point, S1
169.5	proportion] A1; proportions S1
169.28	love] A1; have S1

171.1	upon] A1; upon the S1
171.2	when] A1; *om.* S1
171.3	again,] A1; again, and S1
172.34	only steal] A1; steal only S1
172.35	was he to] A1; could he S1
173.8	by] A1; with S1
173.10	clad fitly] A1; fitly clad S1
173.17	by] A1; by the S1
174.32	prominence] A1; distinction S1
175.5	approaches,] A1; approaches, and S1
175.22	killed] A1; filled S1
176.4	one] A1; *om.* S1
177.33	no] A1; any S1
178.12	was] A1; was all S1
178.22	was] A1; was all S1

LETTERS OF AN ALTRURIAN TRAVELLER

187.15	sort,] HE; ~ S2
*196.14	say,] HE; say, that S2
196.23	suppose,] HE; ~ S2
196.23	whole] HE; ~, S2
200.11	light,] HE; ~ S2
207.34	companion] HE; companions S2
211.33	'r,'] HE; "r," S2
218.14	ugly] HE; ulgy S2
226.6	puerile] HE; peurile S2
230.6	woman] HE; women S2
*262.24	to] HE; *om.* S2

THROUGH THE EYE OF THE NEEDLE

275.1	*Part First*/I] C; HOW PEOPLE LIVE IN A PLUTO-CRATIC CITY./VI./New York, November 9, 1893./ My dear Cyril: S2
275.3	my dear Cyril,] C; *om.* S2
275.10	here] C; *om.* S2
277.5	somehow] C; *om.* S2
277.6	others] C; others somehow S2

277.14	illogically, blindly,] C; however illogically, however blindly S2
277.18	a] C; *om.* S2
277.19	II] C; *om.* S2
278.7	rears] C; areas S2
278.22	changed] C; changed into them S2
279.2	rent] HE; rents S2
279.18	reputation] C; repute S2
279.25	III] C; *om.* S2
279.34	and] C; and it S2
280.30	the] C; these S2
281.6	rush] C; vivid rush S2
281.10	season] C; the season S2
281.30	endure] C; bear S2
281.34	a] C; a Harlem S2
282.1	IV] C; *om.* S2
282.12	now] C; before I get back S2
282.14	type from the account of her I gave you] C; type S2
282.20	with them] C; here S2
282.21	is] C; *om.* S2
283.2–3	They . . . as] C; As S2
284.19	houses in the poor quarters of the city] C; houses, S2
284.23	V] C; *om.* S2
285.23	much] C; any S2
285.26	Sometimes] C; Generally, S2
285.33	housekeeping] C; the housekeeping S2
286.23	sufficed] C; sufficed for S2
287.20	VI] C; *om.* S2
288.17	naïveté] C; naïvetè S2
288.22	lady—"aren't] C; lady. "Aren't S2
288.23	*every*] C; every S2
289.9	their] C; their own S2
289.24	thought] C; thought that S2
289.25	office] C; offices S2
289.28	half so] C; half as S2
290.9	Europe; then] C; Europe, and S2
290.13	in] C; *om.* S2
*290.14	oh] C; O S2
290.20	house!"] C; house!"/A. Homos. S2

290.21	VII] C; PLUTOCRATIC HOUSEKEEPING./VII./ New York, November 25, 1893. S2
291.7	I have] C; have I S2
292.8	talk about reading] C; talking about their reading, S2
292.24	give] C; gives S2
293.11	only] C; *om.* S2
293.18	should] C; would S2
293.23	fences] C; ~ , S2
293.31	should] C; would S2
293.32	Street] C; *om.* S2
294.10	Put] C; Put you S2
294.32	the] C; a S2
295.16	VIII] C; *om.* S2
295.28	year—fifteen,"] C; year," S2
296.13	$2000] C; $2500 S2
296.28	the] C; *om.* S2
297.30	conditions] C; stations S2
298.20	with] C; *om.* S2
298.21–22	subject,] C; ~ S2
298.22	hours] C; hours, from six in the morning till any time of night S2
298.23	Every] C; In fine, every S2
298.23	to] C; to their pride, to S2
298.29	most] C; most business S2
298.29	trust] C; trust in the plutocracy S2
298.32	IX] C; *om.* S2
299.7	honored . . . like] C; as honored . . . as S2
299.8	I said] C; *om.* S2
299.19–20	that I was not, as her husband said,] C; that, as her husband said, I was not S2
299.28	storage warehouses] C; storehouses S2
301.16	servants] C; servants, even when you can get them S2
301.36	her husband said] C; said her husband S2
302.1	friend] C; Cyril S2
303.1	X] C; *om.* S2
303.6	association] C; associations S2
303.23	and] C; and the S2
303.28	club] C; clubs S2
303.29	Often] C; Usually, S2

304.14	her.] C; her. I suppose it's as broad as it's long. S2
304.27	stories] C; stories, either S2
305.6	confess] C; must confess S2
306.2	and] C; than S2
306.29	XI] C; *om.* S2
307.12	are] C; are in these days of adversity, S2
307.14	degrees] C; degree S2
307.25	reality;] C; ~, S2
307.25	that —] C; ~ ; S2
308.26	Catholic] C; catholic S2
309.2–3	on. ¶ Meantime] C; ~. ~ S2
309.4	avenues. The] C; ~. ¶ ~ S2
309.4	colors] C; color S2
309.30	forget.] C; forget./A. Homos. S2
309.31–34	XII . . . Thanksgiving.] C; DINNER, VERY IN-FORMALLY./VIII./New York, December 1, 1893./ My dear Cyril: ¶ I did not suppose that I should be writing you so soon again, but I was out for my first dinner of the season, last night, and I must try to give you my impressions of it while they are still fresh. Only the day after I posted my last letter, I received the note which I enclose: S2
310.14	tell] C; explain to S2
310.18	this] C; her S2
310.19	and] C; and I S2
310.25	founded on more] C; more founded in S2
311.2	begged] C; begged to S2
311.5	their customs] C; theirs S2
311.7	in] C; at S2
311.15	dinner] C; *om.* S2
311.21	token] C; token, after her letter, S2
311.21	be] C; be in the last degree S2
312.5	XIII] C; *om.* S2
312.28–29	of fashion, which affects me] C; to fashion, S2
313.25	stage-setting] C; mise en scène S2
313.32	appointments] C; appointment S2
313.34	tint] C; dye S2
314.1	year before last] C; last year S2
314.9	they] C; we S2

314.13	XIV] C; *om.* S2
315.34	taste] C; taste that S2
316.7	Makely] C; ~, S2
316.32	XV] C; *om.* S2
316.33	The sally of the hostess] C; This S2
317.24	canvasback?] C; ~. S2
319.7	'at home'] C; "~ ~" S2
320.13	March.] C; ~, S2
320.34	the] C; the generous S2
320.35	I . . . functions only] C; I only . . . functions S2
321.5	known] C; opened S2
321.8	on to] C; onto S2
321.10	hand] HE; hands S2
321.10	By-the-by] C; By the way S2
321.26	smaller] C; small S2
321.36	my] C; *om.* S2
322.32	XVI] C; *om.* S2
323.1	not] C; not often S2
323.2	sometimes] C; *om.* S2
323.29	or] C; and S2
324.13	dining, a great deal,] C; dining so much, S2
324.16	consommé] C; consommé soup S2
324.24	that] C; *om.* S2
324.29	glance] C; glance round S2
324.29	cigars] C; different cigars S2
324.35	a] C; the S2
326.8	pity."] C; pity."/A. Homos. S2
326.9	XVII] C; *om.* S2
326.9	[SEE APPENDIX, PAGES 443–452.]
326.21	impersonal and selfish] C; as impersonal and as selfish S2
326.25	think our] C; think your S2
327.3	When] C; Where S2
327.20	benefactors] C; benefactor S2
327.21	their tables] C; his table S2
328.24	say] C; said S2
328.28	dislike] C; disliked S2
328.30	had] C; had simply got sick of being a teacher in a girls' school, and had S2

328.34	and] C; and as S2
329.19	XVIII] C; *om.* S2
329.20	the guests] C; her guests S2
330.30–31	the first lady triumphed] C; triumphed the first lady S2
330.31	and] C; and then S2
330.32	anything] C; any question S2
330.32	but] C; but the S2
331.32	impostors] C; imposters S2
332.12	night] C; ~, S2
332.17	the artist suggested] C; suggested the artist S2
333.27	ourselves."] C; ourselves."/A. Homos. S2
333.28	XIX] C; AN ALTRUISTIC PLUTOCRAT./X./ New York, December 16, 1893./My dear Cyril: S2
333.33	society; out] C; society. Out S2
333.35	lectors] C; the lectors S2
335.3	usually] C; often S2
335.27	don't] C; didn't S2
336.28	up] C; *om.* S2
336.31	shoe-tops] C; shoe-top S2
336.33	that] C; and that S2
337.1	XX] C; *om.* S2
337.12	says] C; said S2
339.5	'It . . . takes.'] HE; "~ . . . ~." S2
340.27	XXI] C; *om.* S2
340.28	of] C; to S2
340.32	quiet] C; retrusive quiet S2
342.25	were] C; were taken S2
342.33	in] C; in all S2
342.33	seeing how estimable plutocratic people] C; meeting plutocratic people, and seeing how estimable they S2
342.35	said] C; said that S2
342.35	was] C; was so logical, S2
342.36	economic] C; economic and political S2
343.3	premises] C; premises for myself S2
343.9	A slight sigh escaped] C; I heard a slight sigh escape S2
343.10	of fatigue;] C; of the fatigue she might well feel, for S2
343.10	o'clock,] C; ~ ; S2
343.11	for] C; for an instant S2
343.17	inculpation.] C; inculpation./A. Homos. S2

343.18	XXII] C; A PLUTOCRATIC TRIUMPH./XI./New York, April 20, 1894./My dear Cyril: S2
344.4	forbade] C; forbade any S2
344.4	any] C; a S2
344.5	of] C; of new and S2
345.3–4	had as] C; had S2
345.13	an] C; any S2
345.26	a] C; *om.* S2
346.16	XXIII] C; *om.* S2
347.11	my] C; *om.* S2
348.3	it.] C; it. As far as I could see, Australia and New Zealand occupied the place that Altruria ought to have had on the map." ¶ "Australia and New Zealand are more like Altruria than any other countries of the plutocratic world, in their constitution," I said, "and perhaps that was what made them seem to occupy our place." ¶ "No, it wasn't that; it couldn't have been, for I didn't know that they were like Altruria. I can't explain it — I never could. S2
348.3–4	but . . . it] C; but it S2
348.14	"She] C; Mrs. Gray shook her head vaguely. "She S2
349.7	I hold] C; that is S2
349.11	her] C; her, something S2
349.12	won't] C; will not S2
349.28–29	that that] C; that S2
350.6	which] C; that S2
350.23	might] C; should S2
350.27	XXIV] C; *om.* S2
351.19	surprising] C; surpassing S2
351.34	opinion] C; opinions S2
352.19	found,] C; ∼ S2
352.19	to refer tentatively] C; tentatively to refer S2
352.32	XXV] C; *om.* S2
354.19–20	questions] C; questions which S2
354.23	sympathy] C; sympathy in all things S2
354.24	XXVI] C; *om.* S2
355.14	for] C; to S2
355.18	polity] C; polity and economy S2
355.36	seen] C; seen all S2

356.11	wilful] C; wilful, hopeless S2
357.7	we'll] C; will S2
358.7	work] C; toil S2
358.29	money] C; money all S2
358.33	have a] have the S2
359.3	go and] C; go to S2
359.17	XXVII] C; *om.* S2
359.29	and] C; and his S2
359.30	be as] C; be S2
360.21	told him] C; said S2
360.23	yet,] C; yet, either, S2
361.12	myself.] C; myself. After all, S2
361.30	END OF PART I] C; A. Homos. S2
*396.11	in] HE; *om.* C
*396.26	elders] HE; elder C
404.35	them] HE; him C
409.35	you] HE; him C
411.1	were] HE; are C
414.6	spirits] HE; spirts C
*414.32	was fitted] HE; *om.* C
*435.13	translated] HE; *om.* C

Rejected Substantives

The following list records all substantive variants in editions published after copy-text for each part and rejected as non-authorial in the present text. The reading of the present edition appears to the left of the bracket; the authority for that reading, followed by a semicolon, the variant reading, and the source of that reading appear to the right of the bracket. The curved dash ∼ represents the same word that appears before the bracket and is used in recording punctuation and paragraphing variants. *Om.* means that the reading to the left of the bracket does not appear in the text cited to the right of the semicolon. The reading of any unlisted edition, other than copy-text, may be presumed to agree with the reading to the left of the bracket. If the authority of the present reading is other than the copy-text, the copy-text reading is recorded in Emendations.

The following texts are referred to:

S1   "A Traveller from Altruria," *Cosmopolitan*, XIV–XV (November 1892–October 1893)

S2   "Letters of an Altrurian Traveller," *Cosmopolitan*, XVI–XVII (November 1893–September 1894)

A1   *A Traveler from Altruria*, Harper and Brothers, 1894, first impression

A2   *A Traveler from Altruria*, Harper and Brothers, 1894, second impression

B   *A Traveller from Altruria*, David Douglas, 1894

C   *Through the Eye of the Needle*, Harper and Brothers, 1907

D   *A Traveler from Altruria*, Harper and Brothers, 1908

A TRAVELLER FROM ALTRURIA

7.9   amidst] S1; amid D
7.16   he] S1; for he D
7.26   sunburnt] S1; sunburned D
7.26–27   seaburnt] S1; seaburned D

9.29	is] S1; is is A1
12.36	of the] S1; of D
13.7	it." I] S1; ~." ¶ ~ D
13.13	on." I] S1; ~." ¶ ~ D
13.29	he] S1; he he A1
15.33	willingly] S1; willing D
16.5	oneself] S1; one's self A2, D
16.14	do] S1; did D
17.14	each other's] S1; one another's D
31.31	obscure] S1; obscured A1–B
36.17	workingman] S1; workman A1–B, D
36.20	said the] S1; said the the A1
37.6	some] S1; some some A1
38.8	been a] S1; been B
39.19	silent. Perhaps] S1; ~. ¶ ~ D
41.7	than] S1; that D
41.13	he] S; *om.* D
41.15	joke. The] S1; ~. ¶ ~ D
43.10	workingmen's] S1; workingman's A1–B, D
43.18	believed] S1; believe B
44.11	workingman] S1; workingmen A1–B, D
44.12	workingman] S1; workingmen A1–B
45.2	and] S1; but B
45.12–13	it is] A1; is it D
46.5	principle] S1; principal A1
46.16–17	workingmen] S1; working-man D
53.5	embraces] S1; embrace A2
53.6	possible. I] S1 ~. ¶ ~ D
54.2	have] S1; have have A1
59.33	polity] S1; policy D
60.27	I'm] S1; I am B
62.2	past] S1; passed A1, B
63.17	the] S1; the the A1–A2
66.6	that] S1; it A2, D
66.6	you're] S1; your A1
71.11	could] S1; would D
73.36	realized] S1; realize A2, D
74.28	each other] S1; one another D
84.4	farmer] S1; former D

85.18	banked] S1; backed B
86.35	had] S1; has D
88.25	side to] S1; side of D
91.5	bubbled] S1; babbled B
92.1	collusion] S1; collision B
93.1	error. Does] S1 ~. ¶ "~ D
97.22	differently." I] S1; ~." ¶ ~ D
97.29	said. "Suppose] S1; ~. ¶ "~ D
98.10	each other] S1; one another D
99.30	each other] S1; one another D
102.8	tramp. "Ah] S1 ~. ¶ "~ A1–B, D
102.12	round the] S1; round a A2, D
107.22	each other] S1; one another D
107.25	each other] S1; one another D
107.32	each other] S1; one another D
108.31	long." I] S1; ~." ¶ ~ D
109.1	The men] S1; Then men D
111.4	know that] S1; know, A2, D
111.5	yeomen] S1; yeoman A1
113.4–5	machinery, every now and then, in the mill,] A1; machinery in the mill, every now and then, A2, D
117.1–2	Altrurian, and the] S1; Altrurian, the A1; Altrurian; the A2, D; Altrurian. The B
117.22	American spreadeaglers] S1; Americans preadeaglers A1; American preadeaglers B
119.28	had] S1; has D
119.36	dominated] S1; denominated A1
123.24	question farther] S1; further question A2, D
124.19	This] S1; That D
128.9	as] S1; so B
128.22–23	proceeded: ¶ "I] S1 ~. "~ A1–B, D
132.33	explosive] S1; explosion D
134.30	afternoon. I] S1; ~. ¶ ~ D
140.3	desk. One] S1; ~. ¶ ~ D
140.25	amongst] S1; among D
142.2	aisles] S1; isles A1
142.15–16	twenty-five. ¶ "I] S1; ~-~. "~ A1–B, D
145.17	dreamed] S1; streamed A2, D
147.15	rapt] S1; wrapped A1–B, D

149.32   recuperation. There] S1; ~. ¶ ~ D
150.10   git] S1; get B
154.8   for] S1; for the D
156.6   shoe] S1; shoes D
156.9   done. Then] S1; ~. ¶ ~ D
157.16   employments] S1; employment D
157.31–32   thing. Once] S1; ~. ¶ ~ D
158.12   swarth] S1; swath A1–D
158.29   pleasure] S1; ~, B
160.12   amidst] S1; amid D
160.33   inspirations] S1; inspiration D
164.35   America] S1; American A1
165.28   wished] A1; wish B
169.25   theologic] S1; theological A1–B, D
171.4   they] S1; theirs D
171.33   Oh,] S; Oh, I D
174.34   overdrinking. Anything] S1; ~. ¶ ~ D
176.30   you] S1; your D

THROUGH THE EYE OF THE NEEDLE

277.5   million] S2; millions C
286.33   air's] S2; air is C
302.9   oneself] S2; one's self C
311.22   unceremonious. She] S2; ~. ¶ ~ C
321.4   kept] S2; kept it C
321.15–16   inalienably] S2; inalienable C

Word-Division

List A records compounds or possible compounds hyphenated at the end of the line in copy-text (or in later readings if authoritative) and resolved as hyphenated or one word as listed below. If Howells' manuscripts of this period fairly consistently followed one practice respecting the particular compound or possible compound, the resolution was made on that basis. Otherwise his *Harper's* or other periodical texts of this period were used as guides. List B is a guide to transcription of compounds or possible compounds hyphenated at the end of the line in the present text: compounds recorded here should be transcribed as given; words divided at the end of the line and not listed should be transcribed as one word.

	LIST A		
		57.7	dining-room
		60.11	outlined
7.26–27	seaburnt	61.11	outgrown
10.33	white-washed	67.30	working-classes
16.8	outlive	68.16	workingman's
22.16	joy-haunted	77.28	rye-and-
26.1	household	78.35	boarding-houses
29.14–15	overworking	84.16	barefooted
33.34	little-finger	88.24	flat-arched
35.1	labor-union	89.33	farmhouse
35.28	labor-unions	90.5	high-hung
36.24	working-classes	90.25	southeast
37.21	manhood-suffrage	91.3	nobly-moulded
38.8	wood-chopper	94.34	home-made
40.27	high-spirited	100.19	railroad
40.32	story-paper	102.2	fortnight's
47.11	outlaw	104.10	spike-tail
52.14	workingman	104.17	week-days
54.10	fellowmen	105.27–28	well-dressed

108.31	black-listed	207.28	noble-willed
112.29	railroad	211.18	fellow-
113.12	poorhouse		countrymen
114.17	supernumerary	211.27	southwestern
114.30	unbusinesslike	212.16	windmill
120.8	cake-walk	221.2	disease-germs
125.11–12	workingman	225.12	workman
127.32	workingman	225.28	pathways
127.36–128.1	workingmen	226.18	well-kept
128.18–19	bookkeepers	226.28	free-stone
128.34	good-humored	227.22	old-fashioned
129.4	overwhelming	230.9	threadbare
139.5	hand-bills	232.1	coachman
142.27	forenoon	232.1–2	bright-buttoned
144.9	over-looking	234.2	driveways
144.29	hotel-cries	235.8	coachman
144.30	tennis-court	236.17	Ninety-nine
150.16	First-rate	238.16	fruit-peel
153.32	overwhelming	239.27	cross-streets
154.1	post-office	240.7	Fifty-seventh
156.22	shoemaking	240.24	cross-streets
156.24	shoemakers	241.14	sky-scraping
159.22	misgoverning	241.16–17	outcast
172.28	overwork	241.32	foster-child
174.31	semi-barbaric	243.24	waterway
175.30–31	work-people	243.26–27	tenement-houses
177.5	oversight	243.33	waterfronts
185.8	railroad	244.17	canal-wives
187.23	outbreak	247.12	short-sighted
187.32–33	weather-wiseacres	248.12	roadways
190.4	workingman	252.6	overhead
191.27	overthrow	252.18	railroads
193.18	brotherhood	254.19	sky-line
196.31–32	masterpieces	255.3	drinking-shop
201.13	care-worn	255.10	sandstone
201.17	overflowed	255.36	drinking-saloon
204.8	mail-carts	257.5	overworked
205.9	Midway	267.4	well-known
206.5	money-making	270.26	tenement-houses

272.17	heaping-up	405.24	highway
273.8	wrong-doers	408.13	men-assistants
283.15	-a-brac	408.16	toadstools
285.33	housekeeping	408.26	footman
292.20	brownstone	410.18	camp-stool
293.7	dining-room	419.11	shipload
293.16	overhangs	424.17	overtasked
293.19	bay-window	432.19	trades-unions
294.26	basement-house	445.7	city-block
294.29	basement-house	449.8	chop-houses
296.28	-of-the-	450.1	older-fashioned
298.24	self-respect	450.33	cornerstone
302.8	outcasts	451.9	housewife
304.33–34	catch-phrase		
307.25	lifelike		LIST B
311.26	highways		
313.25	stage-setting	10.29	well-dressed
315.26	side-dishes	12.24	bird-bath
319.31	to-day	20.10	hermit-thrushes
338.21	madman	26.5	lawn-tennis
338.30	money-earning	38.8	bobbin-boy
342.11	hereafter	40.30	story-papers
350.24	interchange	65.16	nineteen-
352.3	well-meaning		twentieths
366.13	single-screw	71.18	self-evident
368.2	upright	71.20	self-seeking
380.4	special-delivery	74.19	fellow-being
384.29	one-rail	78.20	two-seated
386.4	guest-house	83.27	every-day
388.31	multi-millionaire	83.36	money-lender
388.35	misconception	89.3	thirty-five
389.12	highway	92.23	un-American
395.22	hillside	93.15	un-American
398.15	outbreaks	100.34	black-listed
401.12	apartment-houses	105.27	well-dressed
401.20	out-doors	138.23	dining-room
401.23	housekeeping	142.14	twenty-five
402.5	ground-plan	145.20	newly-fallen
405.12	sidewalks	151.6	bread-troughs